I heal thee
I heal thee
I heal thee
I heal thee
I heal thee
I heal thee
I heal thee

# CRITICAL FAILURES VIII

## GALLEONS OF SEA MEN

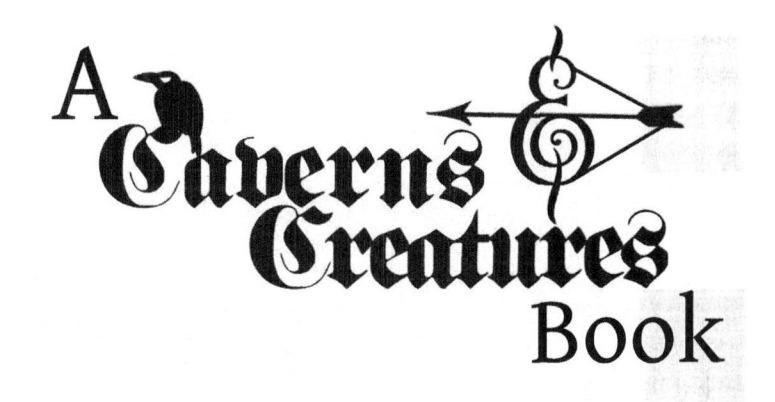

A Caverns & Creatures Book

by

# ROBERT BEVAN

Caverns & Creatures logo by EM Kaplan. Used with permission by the creator. All rights reserved.

"I Heal Thee" Illustration by John Luther Davis.

Used with permission by the creator. All rights reserved.

20-Sided Die icon provided by Shutterstock.com and used and adapted in conjunction with its licensing agreement. For more information regarding Shutterstock licensing, visit www.shutterstock.com/license

All content edited by Joan Reginaldo.
Layout design by Christopher Dowell.

Copyright 2020 Robert Bevan
All rights reserved.

ISBN: 9798663478076

## SPECIAL THANKS TO:

My editor, Joan Reginaldo.

My wife No Young Sook.

My cover designer, No Hyun Jun.

And Crystal Wood for helping me through some tight narrative spots

# SPECIAL THANKS TO:

My editor, Joan Reginaldo.

My wife No Young Sook.

My cover designer, No Hyun Jun.

And Crystal Wood for helping me through some tight narrative spots

# CHAPTER 1

𝒯ensions were high on the beach while everyone waited for Katherine to shit a precious magical artifact out of her shark ass.

Julian would have liked to spend this otherwise idle time preparing his spells or doing something else useful. But like everyone else on the beach, he couldn't concentrate on anything but the dorsal fin cutting slowly back and forth through the surface of the shallow blue water.

Chaz strummed on his lute strings. He wasn't playing a song or casting a spell. It sounded more like the nervous drumming of fingers on a desk, but more melodic. "What's taking her so long?"

"Give her a break," said Julian. "I'd like to see you take a dump while everyone you knew was watching you. Maybe she didn't eat enough, and she doesn't have to go yet."

Frank sat down hard on the sand. "She ate half of Mordred. Between her and her brother, that's two Mordreds down."

"What she did isn't anything like what Tim did," said Tony the Elf. "Tim was deliberately trying to sabotage our chance to go home. Katherine was trying to save all our asses, and she did." He sighed. "At least for the time being."

"I know, I know." Frank's gaze followed Katherine's dorsal fin as it made another turn. "I just hope it's still in there."

"Why wouldn't it be?" asked Julian.

Frank shrugged. "Who knows how this stuff works? You've

seen how wonky this game can be. If something is irregular in a way the rules haven't anticipated, the game tends to get creative with its interpretations."

"Fuckin' tell me about it," said Denise. She was the only one on the beach not looking at Katherine. Instead, she sat glumly on a log watching her newborn baby scorpion person, Fatty, as he and Ravenus nibbled at what was left of Mordred's corpse.

There was only so much of that Julian could stomach watching. He turned back to Frank. "You sound like you have something in particular you're worried about."

Frank nodded. "Think about when a wererat changes forms. When Dave turned back at the Whore's Head, he was still wearing his armor."

Julian hadn't actually seen Dave turn, but he'd seen enough werewolf movies to form a pretty good image in his head of what it might have looked like. "Okay. So?"

"He grew some hair and claws, and his insides probably morphed a bit, but it was fundamentally a relatively straightforward change."

"How far have you been sucked into this game to call that straightforward?"

Frank shot Julian an annoyed look. "I said *relatively*."

"Relatively to what?" asked Julian.

"To Katherine. When she changes, all her clothes, whatever she's carrying, it all changes with her. It kind of ceases to exist as it's absorbed into her chosen form. It's more magical, more mysterious, less straightforward."

Julian had considered a similar distinction when he first started playing around with his Invisibility spell and was grateful that he didn't have to strip down completely naked for it to be effective.

"I see what you're saying," he said. "But when she changes back, she's got all of her stuff back with her."

"When she changes back into her standard half-elven

form, she does. Does that work the same way when she takes an animal form? If Katherine is wearing a sweater, then turns into a monkey, the monkey won't be wearing a sweater. But what if she turns into a monkey and then puts on a sweater? I guess what I'm asking is, when she changes into a monkey, is she changing back into the same monkey every time? Or just *a* monkey? If she turns into a half-elf, then back into a monkey, will the monkey still be wearing the sweater?"

Julian shrugged. "I think so. I mean, probably, right?"

"With all that's at stake, is *probably* and *I think so* enough to put your mind at ease?"

"I just think it's premature to get all mopey over problems you're only speculating about. If she comes back empty-handed, we can have her do a monkey sweater test... or some kind of equivalent. If the hypothetical monkey is wearing the sweater, will you feel better?"

"A little," Frank grumbled. "But there's also the fact that she ate it. What if the game auto-digests whatever you've eaten when you change forms? Katherine might have literally absorbed the die into her body when she turned back into a half-elf."

Julian laughed. "Listen to yourself, Frank. You're getting way too far ahead of yourself with problems that don't yet exist. Even if this wild auto-digestion theory that you completely pulled out of your ass turns out to be true, I'd rather Katherine auto-digest the die than for Mordred to use it to get back to Earth and rule over us."

"But what if we need the same die that brought us here to get us back?" asked Rhonda, repeating a theory she'd brought up back at the Whore's Head. "If Katherine digested one, that would mean that one sixth of us are stuck here permanently."

"Again," said Julian. "We don't know that that's even a thing, so there's no point in worrying about it yet. Also, would that really be such a travesty? I mean, we've already established that we can go back to the real world if we want to, but as elves and orcs and whatever. Or we could make lives for ourselves here. Maybe it's not what we want, but it's hardly the end of the world."

Julian felt he'd made a good Diplomacy roll, but noticed that several pairs of eyes on the beach had turned their attention from Katherine to him, and they didn't look very *diplomafied*.

"Tell that to my family," snarled a dwarf who's name Julian didn't know. "No amount of hard personal questions I answer correctly will convince my wife and kids that this bearded circus freak I'm inhabiting is who I say I am. My choices amount to never seeing them again, or getting arrested for stalking them and locked up in an asylum."

Several others grumbled their agreement. Julian felt like such a dickhead for forgetting that a lot of these people had more important things in their lives to get back to than the group he'd come here with.

"I'm really sorry," he said. "I didn't mean to –"

"Where'd she go?" asked Frank, scrambling to his feet as he peered out at the vast open ocean. "She's disappeared."

Everyone stared out at the water, but all Julian could see was vast glittering stillness reaching all the way out to the flat horizon.

He didn't even realize he'd been holding his breath until he, along with everyone else on the beach, let out a long collective sigh when she broke the surface.

In her half-elven form, Katherine swam toward them until she could wade.

"Sorry it took me so long," she said when she stepped out of the water, her thick black cloak dripping what seemed like half the ocean, darkening the sand beneath her. She tossed the die to Frank. "I had a little trouble finding it in the cloud of Mordred I shat out."

# Critical Failures VIII

Frank, who had been staring in awe at his long lost prize, now grimaced.

"Grow up, Frank," said Chaz. "She rinsed it off. Besides, she took it in her mouth after Julian had been keeping it next to his sweaty nuts for God only knows how long."

Neither Frank nor Katherine looked any more comforted for Chaz's efforts. Despite the part he'd played in acquiring another die, he had clearly not earned his way back into their good graces.

"Listen, everyone," said Katherine after she broke her disgusted scowl away from Chaz. "While I was swimming out there, it occurred to me that some of you might be pissed that I killed another Mordred. I'm sorry about that. All I can say is that sharks have strong cravings and poor impulse control. And when you turn into one, those things are also part of you. Also, I just lost a friend and ate half a guy, so that's pretty traumatic too. Maybe cut me a little slack?"

Frank pocketed the die and looked up at her. "Being a leader means making hard decisions," he said. "We all had a similar discussion while you were out there and came to the conclusion that you made the right one. I'll admit that I was a little grouchy about your family's growing pattern of murdering our only ticket home. But what you did kept Mordred from retaking control of this world, and kept us all alive to fight another day."

Katherine smiled at him. "Thank you, Frank."

"We have one of the dice in our possession again. Now we just have to find ourselves another Mordred." Frank narrowed his eyes at Katherine. "And *not* kill him."

"We got a lead on one," said Randy. He stood straighter and cleared his throat as all eyes turned his way. "That's what we was coming here to tell you. There's this city called Hollin up north of here. Some guy calling himself Jordan Knight is building himself an army of followers."

Tony the Elf laughed. "Jordan Knight? Isn't that –"

"Yes," said Randy. "That's why we strongly suspect him of being one of Mordred's avatars."

Frank looked Chaz up and down. "At least as a bard, he should be easy enough to capture and keep control of."

Chaz scowled but kept his mouth shut.

"He knows where we are," said Tony the Elf. "He'll be coming for the die. If we get to work now, it shouldn't take us long to make this island defensible against a bard and a boatload of groupies and backup dancers."

Katherine laughed. "I'm picturing a confrontation like the music video for *Beat It*."

"Even better," said Denise. "We could have Mordred and Chaz go at it *Deliverance* style."

Every hint of murmur on the beach was silenced as if through a spell as all eyes turned to Denise.

"What the fuck is wrong with you, man?" said Chaz. The suggestion that he participate in competitive butt-raping was apparently his threshold for his ability to keep quiet.

"What the hell's gotten into everyone?" Denise asked defensively. "I only meant that he and Mordred could settle the matter with a fiddle-playing contest like the Devil and Johnny."

"That's *The Devil Went Down to Georgia*! *Deliverance* was a movie about banjos and ass-rape."

Denise chuckled. "Oh, right. I always get those two confused."

"Yeah, laugh it up. Let's all have another big laugh at how much bards suck. It'll be fucking hilarious when dragons start raining fire down on us."

Frank grinned smugly at him. "Is that one of the higher-level bard spells? I don't seem to recall it."

"Chaz might be on to something," said Julian, trying to think a couple steps ahead as to what Chaz was referring to.

# Critical Failures VIII

Frank's smug grin turned to Julian. "Now who's getting ahead of themselves with speculation? What makes you think a bard has dragons at his beck and call?"

"I don't know. Mordred knows where to get stuff, right? Maybe he has dragon-summoning crystals or something. I'm just saying that he might not be as much of a pushover as you think."

"I wasn't suggesting he'd be a pushover," said Frank. "But I like our chances better against a bard Mordred than whatever his other avatars might be."

"And I'm talking about his other avatars!" said Chaz. "What makes any of you think he''ll come here as a bard? *All of the Mordreds know where we are.* Sure, Cooper and I got lucky nabbing one of the more powerful ones while he was in hibernation mode or whatever, but Mordred won't want to risk capture again. He'll come at us with the most powerful Mordred he's got. Or worse, he'll come at us with all of them."

Julian had to hand it to Chaz. He was making a lot of sense. Julian's own thoughts continued down that track.

He nodded down at the remains of Mordred's dwarf avatar. "He'll probably be pissed that we killed this one. If not pissed, then at least threatened. Keeping us alive to rule over might not be as high a priority now. After all, it's not like he can't lure some other schmucks into the game after he retakes full control."

The beach was silent except for the lapping waves and sounds of dwarf meat being picked apart by Ravenus and Fatty.

"Maybe we could reason with Mordred," said the dwarf who had brought up his family a few minutes ago. "If, like Julian suggests, Mordred doesn't care about ruling over us, then we could convince him to send us all home in exchange for the die. If we put forth a big enough show of strength, or bluffed it well enough at least, he might find that preferable to risking another death."

Julian didn't want to rub salt in this guy's wound again, but felt compelled to point out a huge flaw in his proposal.

"But the reason I said he might not care about ruling over us is because he could lure other schmucks in. Would you be okay knowing that other innocent people were taking your place here?"

The dwarf glared at him. "Considering the alternative, yes. Absolutely."

"Well, I'm not."

"Then you can stay. But if you think I'm going to go one more day than I have to without seeing my kids so you can sleep a little better at night, then you can go –"

"Enough!" said Katherine. She was wearing her captain's hat and standing on a large rock. When she had everyone's attention, she continued. "He won't make a deal like that anyway."

"You don't know that!" said the dwarf.

"Yes, I do. Think about it for a second. He can't risk having us running around free on Earth. He'll be his normal fat tub of shit self, and some of us would almost certainly be hunting him down. You can bet your ass I would be. Besides, like Julian said, he could lure in other schmucks to take our places. But that's never not been the case."

"That's right," said Julian. "There are only two possible reasons he hasn't killed us already. He either hates us so much that he's deeply invested in keeping us alive so that we know we've been defeated and he can rub it in our faces by making the rest of our lives as miserable as possible, or…" He shivered at the ramifications implied by what he was about to say.

"Or what?" asked Frank.

"Or the luring in other schmucks thing hasn't occurred to him yet, and that's infinitely more frightening."

Denise shrugged. "I don't know about *infinitely*. The way you was bein' all dramatic about it, I was expecting something a little more profound."

"If he hasn't thought of that," said Tony the Elf. "Then it could be the only thing keeping him from having slaughtered us already."

"He *did*," snapped Rhonda. "Or did you forget about that little incident with the *Phantom Pinas*?"

"He wasn't in control of that situation. He may have been cocky and gotten in over his head with that one. But if Julian's right, and we offer him that bargain, all we'd be doing is tipping him off that he doesn't actually need us alive. We'd be fucking over ourselves as well as the schmucks that inevitably replace us." Tony the Elf looked sharply at the dwarf. "*And you'll never see your kids again, Victor.*"

Julian made a mental note to remember Victor's name.

Victor balled his fists tightly in frustration. "Fine. So what do we do?"

"We get the fuck out of here for one," said Katherine. "We're sitting ducks on this island."

"And go where?" demanded Victor. "I thought we decided we were going to stop all the running and cowering. Be more proactive. All that bullshit."

Katherine smiled. "We're only running *from* the Mordreds that are likely already on their way here. We're running *to* the shittiest one of them all."

Julian, Frank, Tony the Elf, and Rhonda all spoke at once. "The bard!"

Chaz sighed. "Fuck all of you."

# CHAPTER 2

"This desert sucks," said Cooper. He'd already made his feelings on the matter known several times, but he had to say something to break the monotony.

Tim poured cool water from the Decanter of Endless Water on Cooper's head. "It's not all that bad."

"That's easy for you to say, riding on my shoulders."

"Believe me, I'd much prefer to be walking on my own."

Cooper glanced down at Tim's severed half foot, for which he felt at least partially responsible. The skin that had grown over the wound was noticeably cleaner than the rest of him, which made the little nub look even weirder. "I'm sorry, man. I should have ditched that axe the second that bitch got into my head."

"Don't sweat it. I can have my foot regrown easily enough when we get back to civilization. I'm more bummed about the Boots of Teleportation. I hope we can get those repaired. It'll be a pain in the ass to try and hunt down a new pair. In the meantime, look on the bright side. At least we're together again, right?"

Cooper sighed. "Yeah, that's nice. It doesn't feel quite the same though."

"We both said some not-so-nice things to each other, but we've said worse before. Let's see how we feel after we get good and shitfaced together. There's no greater glue with which to mend a fractured friendship than hard liquor, after all."

# Critical Failures VIII

"What was that? Confucius or some shit?"

Tim laughed. "No. That one was all me."

"That's what I missed about you," said Cooper. "You're smart. Way smarter than me. Not just here, but back home, too. I should have listened to you when we had that argument on the road."

"Rein it in there, buddy," said Tim. "Let's have that drink before you start jerking me off too hard."

Cooper let out a shallow chuckle. "I just feel so fucking stupid, and it makes me want to beat the shit out of something."

"You want to try the geyser again?"

"Yeah, if you don't mind."

Tim rolled back off Cooper's shoulders, landing on his feet in the sand. He was still pretty nimble for a guy missing half a foot. He held the Decanter of Endless Water up for Cooper.

Cooper took it and pointed the mouth down at the sand. Water flowed out gently, bringing forth a few heads of cabbage from the Fertile Desert sand. A nice giant cabbage might be fun to punch. The huge watermelons they'd grown earlier that day seemed like the perfect target for channeling Cooper's aggression, but his fists went through the rind way too easily, and they only lasted a few punches before collapsing in on themselves. A cabbage might offer more resistance and a satisfying explosion of leaves.

"You mind if we hurry this up?" said Tim. "I haven't been sober this long in a while. I'm starting to remember high school again."

Bracing himself for the kickback from the decanter, Cooper spoke the incantation that triggered its highest setting. "Geyser."

Water gushed out of it, carving a small crater in the sand. A tree sprouted up, swiftly growing branches, then leaves, then small white flowers which swelled into oranges. Cooper let the water continue to flow so the lower branches could reach a thickness he was satisfied with.

"Save some of those oranges," said Tim.

"Huh?" Cooper was still getting used to not having Nabi in his head.

"They keep well. Throw some in your bag for when we get hungry."

"Yeah, okay. First I'm going to – Shit!" His interjection was punctuated with actual shit squirting out of his ass as he saw that the tree had grown too thick. He hurriedly deactivated the Decanter of Endless Water.

"Jesus, Cooper," said Tim, turning away from the rapidly drying shit-puddle Cooper had sprayed the sand with. "I appreciate the warning, but maybe tell me a second or two in advance next time. You know, so I have time to look away."

Cooper grabbed the end of a branch weighted down by a bunch of oranges and snapped it off where it was about two inches thick. He tried to whack it against the trunk, but all he managed to do was fling oranges all over the place. It wasn't satisfying at all. He'd meant to stop the tree's growth when the branch was still small enough to break off near the trunk, and when the trunk was still skinny enough so that he could damage it with the branch. Both branch and trunk were too thick for that now... unless...

*What the hell? It's not like they would need any tremendous feats of Strength out here in the desert before tomorrow anyway.*

"I'm really angry!"

As his heart raced to feed blood into his rapidly expanding muscles, Cooper felt a strange sense of comfort in his Barbarian Rage. It was like taking off his tie at the end of a long day at the office. Or at least that was what he imagined it would feel like if he ever had a job that required him to wear a tie. He was letting his true self out, and his true self wanted nothing more than to tear apart this orange tree limb from limb.

He gripped the lowest branch close to the trunk with both of his massive Rage-imbued hands and pulled down as hard as he could. Even with the bonus to his Strength score, he still wasn't quite able to break it off.

With a roar that shook the tree's leaves, he started climbing.

"Cooper!" cried a faint but shrill voice below him. "What the fuck do you think you're doing?"

*First kill tree! Then kill whining bitch!*

When he got as high up as the tree could support him, Cooper looked back down at the branch that had dared to defy him. He'd torn away several smaller branches on the way up, and would no doubt take several more with him on the way down, but that wasn't good enough. That branch at the bottom had to learn not to fuck with him. He let go of the trunk and cannonballed down on top of the offending branch. The sweet sound of snapping wood provided a bit of comfort against the intense pain he now felt in his ass bone.

He picked himself up from the sand and looked for his branch. He found it still hanging onto the trunk by a tendril of bark, then ripped it free.

"You like that?" he shouted as he slammed the branch repeatedly against the trunk. "Do you like that, you fucking branch? Fuck you!"

The branch finally snapped in half, only having done cosmetic damage to the bark on the tree trunk. This pissed off Cooper even more. He backed up and prepared to ram it.

"Knock it off, Cooper!" shrieked that little bitch voice in the periphery of Cooper's attention. "You're going to hurt yourself!"

Cooper kept his focus on the enemy before him. He charged the tree at full speed and tackled it like it had just mugged his mother. The trunk didn't snap like he'd hoped, but the roots broke loose from the sand, allowing him to take the tree down. He reveled in the sound of dozens of branches smashing and cracking in unison.

Satisfied with his victory, he farted out his Barbarian Rage until his body deflated back down to its normal size.

"Fuck," he said with a sigh. "I needed that."

Tim threw an orange at him. It bounced off his head.

"Are you out of your goddamn mind?" He sounded just like that little bitch voice that was...

"Dude, were you talking to me while I was fighting this tree?"

"Yes, dumbass," said Tim.

"Sorry. I guess I was really in the zone. What did you want?"

Tim rolled his eyes. "I wanted you to not kill yourself fighting a fucking tree."

Cooper sat up and leaned against the upturned tree roots. "I got you some oranges." He was surrounded by a perimeter of oranges that had fallen during his altercation.

"I filled my bag with as many as it can hold. Can we get moving again now?"

"Give me a few minutes. I get fatigued when I come out of my Rage. You know that."

"I didn't ask you to go into a fucking Rage. You've blown both of yours for the day now, and for what?"

Cooper scratched his balls in thought. "I'll admit it was kind of wasted on the giant watermelons, but I don't think I could have taken down that tree with my normal Strength."

Tim shook his head, then sat on the sand and started peeling an orange. "This must have something to do with your alignment shift."

"You think I'm gay?" Cooper didn't know what signals he was unintentionally putting out, but Tim was surely reading them wrong.

"You're Evil."

Cooper lay back down on the sand and farted in despair. "Fucking hell. Did you go all born again after we split? I'm not gay. And even if I was, there's nothing evil about it. You sound like your fucking dad."

"I didn't say you were –"

"Don't forget it was *you* who asked *me* to jerk you off."

"Cooper! Shut up! Nobody's jerking anybody off, so cool it with the gay. You're Evil now, in game terms. Your alignment changed when you became a wererat."

"We have alignments here?"

Tim shrugged. "Apparently so."

"I don't want to be Evil."

"It's not such a big deal. Just game mechanics. You're still the same person you were before, at least pretty much so. Maybe with an added quirk or two. For example, Dave is still shitty and useless, but now he's got some fucked-up sexual fetishes he feels compelled to act on."

Cooper sat up. "Again, I feel I should point out that it was *you* who –"

"And *you*," Tim interrupted in a forceful tone. "You appear to have some severely violent impulses."

"That sounds like it could be dangerous."

Tim grinned. "For anyone that fucks with us, sure. But we'll figure out ways to manage it. We'll get you a punching bag or something. Maybe we can put you in a pit with a wild boar or something and let you two fight it out. That would be fucking hilarious."

Cooper thought back on the boar he had punched in Glittersprinkles Grove and agreed that there was potential entertainment value in that.

"How did turning Evil affect you?" he asked Tim.

Tim shrugged. "I don't know. It may be harder to see the

differences in myself than it is to see them in other people. Do you notice anything different about me?"

The obvious answer was staring Cooper right in the face. "Half your foot is missing!" He felt so much less guilty about it now.

Tim laughed. "That was an accident. Turning Evil doesn't make your feet fall off."

"Oh." Cooper's feeling of guilt returned. "Shit."

"Shit is right," said Tim, looking past Cooper into the distance. "Cooper, get up."

"Dude. I'm fatigued."

"Get your fat fatigued ass up. Somebody's coming."

With the support of the fallen orange tree, Cooper pulled himself up to his feet and turned around. A cloud of pale yellow dust billowed menacingly on the otherwise featureless horizon. At its center, two dark figures rode hard and fast on horseback toward them.

"Do you think they're coming for us?" asked Cooper. "Maybe they were just headed this way already."

Without taking his annoyed eyes off the approaching riders, Tim pointed straight up. "I don't think so."

Cooper looked up and spotted a falcon circling high above them. "Shit."

Tim pulled out his crossbow and loaded a bolt. "Do you have any weapons?"

"All I had was Nabi." Cooper looked down at the tree, wishing he hadn't broken that branch on the trunk. In his current state, and with both of his Barbarian Rages for the day used up, there was no way he would be able to rip off another branch substantial enough to use as a weapon. He picked up a couple of oranges instead.

"Let me do the talking," said Tim. "And hide the Decanter of Endless Water." He squinted at the riders. "There only appears to be two of them. If we play our cards right, we might be able to get ourselves a couple of horses."

Cooper's stomach rumbled at the thought of meat. "I say we eat one and ride the other."

"There shouldn't be any need for that. These guys had to come from somewhere, which means that they've got plenty of food on them or we're close to the edge of the desert. We'll be eating well soon enough."

Cooper looked up. "Can we at least eat the bird?"

"Too fucking right we're going to eat that bird." Tim set his crossbow down behind the orange tree roots. "Here's the plan. We look weak, defenseless, and lost in the desert."

"I'm with you so far."

"When they get close enough, or dismount their horses, I'll say a code word. Then you jump the closest one. I'll pull my crossbow on the other one. If he resists, we'll kill him. If he surrenders, we'll beat directions out of him before we kill him."

Simple and straightforward. Cooper nodded. "What's the code word?"

"We want to catch them by surprise, so it needs to be something I can work into the conversation, but something I don't need to say."

"Fuckbiscuit."

"How am I supposed to work fuckbiscuit into a conversation?"

"Oh, right. I was more focused on the last part of what you said."

"I've got one," said Tim. "Ally."

Cooper thought about it. "I don't know, man. That's a pretty common word."

"That's the point."

"But what if it comes up in the conversation and you need to say it?"

"Then I'll say something else."

"What if they say it?"

Tim scowled at him. "This isn't the goddamn secret word on *Pee-wee's Playhouse*. It's a code between you and me. You don't do shit until *I* say the code word. Got it?"

"Yeah." That put Cooper's mind at ease.

"Jesus Christ, Cooper. I'm glad you got all your stupid questions out of the way."

"Fuck your mother."

Tim grinned. "It's good to have you back, man."

Cooper grinned back. "You too."

"Okay. Now shut the fuck up and look weak and defenseless."

"Uuuunnnnngggggghhhh," Cooper groaned as he limped forward.

"What the fuck is that supposed to be?"

Cooper stopped his act and turned back to Tim. "Weak and defenseless."

"Stop it. You look like a fucking zombie. Just stand here and don't do or say anything."

As the riders got closer, Cooper identified them as orcs. One of them was bigger than Cooper, shirtless, and covered in scars. The other wore a brown turban and thin flowing robe. Only his face was visible. They were riding two of the biggest and blackest horses Cooper had ever seen.

They slowed down as they got closer, their horses trotting to a halt twenty feet away from them.

"Greetings, travelers," said the one in the turban with a wide smile. He was friendlier than Cooper was accustomed to orcs being, though his companion's stone-faced don't-fuck-with-me expression more than made up for it. "Have you lost your way?"

"Please," pleaded Tim. "We have traveled for many days. We are weary from the relentless desert heat."

"Then it is fortunate that you have stumbled upon this

bountiful orange tree."

Cooper thought he noticed a flicker of doubt and panic in Tim's eyes as he glanced down at the piles of oranges surrounding them, but he quickly recovered.

"Most fortunate indeed," Tim responded. "Truly have the gods shown us mercy. I pray you do the same. Take as much of this fruit as you can carry, but I beg you spare our lives."

When the orc wearing the turban reached into a saddlebag, Cooper looked to Tim for a sign. Tim had clearly been expecting that and gave him an almost imperceptible shake of the head.

Desperate squeals came from the bag as the orc lifted a fat white rat by the tail. He swung it around once, then flung it skyward. The falcon that had been circling above them swooped down and snatched it out of the air. The squeals grew more intense right up until the bird landed on one of the orange tree's thicker branches and began tearing into its meal.

After admiring his pet for a few seconds more, the turbaned orc turned his attention back to Cooper and Tim. "A person might walk for weeks or even months in the Fertile Desert without being so fortunate. What have you done to so please the gods?" He narrowed his eyes at Tim. "Or perhaps there's a less divine explanation."

Tim dropped to his knees. "Please, friends. I beg you to –"

"FUCK YOU!" shouted Cooper as he ran toward the bigger of the two orcs. He'd expected Tim to try and reel them in a little closer before they sprang their trap, but he was confident that Tim knew what he was doing.

The big orc grabbed a coiled bullwhip at his side and flicked it, wrapping the end of it around Cooper's leg. The next thing Cooper knew, he was lying on the ground, gasping to replace the air that had just been knocked out of his lungs, staring up at the sky, and rubbing sand burns on his ass.

"Cooper!" snapped Tim from back near the tree. "What the fuck was that for?"

Cooper sat up and turned around as he caught his breath. "You said the word."

Tim glared at him over the tree trunk, on which he had his crossbow leveled at the riders. "I said *friends*."

"It means the same fucking thing!"

"Fucking... fuck!" Tim responded, obviously frustrated by his blunder.

"I told you we should have used fuckbiscuit," said Cooper. "That's not a thing you ever accidentally say."

"Just shut the fuck up for a minute, would you?" Tim's glare shifted to the riders. "Let my friend go, and don't make any sudden moves."

The orc in the turban turned to his companion. "You'd better do as he says, Oslof. He has a *crossbow*."

Cooper couldn't be sure, but his tone didn't seem to match his words. It was more like how an adult might react to a child pointing a Nerf gun at him. Still, Oslof jiggled his whip, loosening its hold on Cooper's ankle.

"Please, halfling," the orc continued as he raised his hands slowly. "Tell us your demands."

"All I want is for –"

"SUCK MY DICK!" said Cooper as he sprang to his feet and lunged at the big rider. He was too close to be whipped again, and was received instead with a hard leather boot to the jaw.

The world spun backwards before Cooper found himself on his back and out of breath, only this time with severe jaw pain.

"What the fuck, man?" cried Tim.

Cooper raised a hand to give him the finger.

"Seriously! What the fuck is wrong with you?"

There didn't seem to be much point in trying to hide their intentions anymore. Cooper rolled away from the horse onto

# Critical Failures VIII

his belly and glared up at Tim, still taking cover behind the tree without even having fired a shot.

"If you don't want me to attack, then stop saying the fucking code word!"

"I didn't say anything remotely close to the fucking code word. I said... Jesus Christ, Cooper. *All I.* That was two words."

"I thought you were hiding it in the conversation. That's what you said you were going to do."

"Not that deeply. You're a fucking moron, for crying out loud."

"Fuck you!" said Cooper. "I was smart enough to catch your stupid code word, wasn't I?"

"Is this a bad time?" asked the orc in the turban. "Should we come back later?"

Thankful that the big guy with the whip wasn't keeping him from doing so, Cooper crab-walked slowly in Tim's direction.

"You probably shouldn't come back at all," said Tim in a more threatening tone than Cooper felt was justified given the circumstances. "We may look like nice easy prey for a couple of guys like yourselves, but there's more to us than meets the eye."

Cooper looked back to visually confirm that Tim's threat was a giant load of shit, and found him unbuttoning the front of his shirt while sucking on the business end of one of his crossbow bolts like it was Pinocchio's dick. If nothing else, the element of surprise was on their side.

"Dude," he said to Tim. "I appreciate that you're willing to take one for the team. But these guys are orcs. Unless you're prepared to take something the size of a kielbasa all the way down to your stomach, maybe you should offer a handjob instead."

Tim ignored Cooper, keeping his steely-eyed stare focused on the riders as he pulled the heavily-slobbered-on bolt of his mouth. "We're wererats, you see." He looked at Cooper. "Show them, Cooper. Try to take your hybrid form." He demonstrated, becoming even hairier as his body changed into a horrifying combination of rat and halfling.

The two riders sat silently on their horses. The one in the turban looked mildly impressed.

Tim stared expectantly at Cooper.

"Oh, right." Cooper supposed his own rat-man form would be a little more intimidating than Tim's. He only had Tim's word and the aftermath of an unrestful sleep as evidence that he'd actually turned into a rat monster during the night, and he wasn't exactly sure how to change voluntarily.

He squatted, grunted, and tried to will his body to shift. He felt like he was getting close, as if a slight change of mindset was all he needed to do it right, some kind of fine-tuning finesse.

"I think I've got it," he said, closing his eyes and concentrating harder. "Al...most... there..."

SSSPPPPPBBBBBBTTT!

A massive shart sprayed the sand beneath his loincloth. He looked down. It was a grisly shade of dark green. All that fucking fruit was wreaking havoc on his insides. Even grislier, something was writhing around in the puddle, like a snake or something. He bent over to look farther between his legs and found that the writhing snake-like thing rose out of the shit puddle and up toward his ass.

"Holy fucking shit! I just shat out the mother of all tapeworms!"

"That's not a tapeworm," said Tim, having changed back to his halfling form. "That's your tail. You fucked up the transformation, but it was a good first try." He turned back to the riders, who both appeared a little ill. "If this bolt breaks your skin, you'll be cursed with the same horrible disease that we have." He stood fully upright. "I see I have your full undivided attention. That's great. Now, tell us the nearest way out of this goddamn desert."

The orc in the turban pointed his thumb back in the direction they'd come from. "Meb' Garshur is only a few hours' journey that way."

Tim grinned smugly at Cooper. Cooper had to hand it to him, he had them on the ropes. He nodded for Tim to wrap this up.

"Fantastic," said Tim, limping out from behind the tree. "Now, get down off your horses, drop your weapons, money, food, and whatever other valuables you've got on you, and back away."

Cooper would have preferred to get this over with sooner rather than later, but he appreciated Tim's dedication to milking their advantage for all it was worth. He'd feel better when he had a weapon again, even if it was just a whip. He wondered if Tim would shoot them anyway once they were safely mounted on those big-ass horses. It seemed like a Tim thing to do. Maybe these fuckers would think twice about mugging people in deserts from now on.

The orc in the turban turned to his stoic companion. "What do you think, Oslof?"

The big one nodded. "You were right to trust the Oracle, Luglo. There is indeed gold in the desert. Zimbra will pay handsomely for a half-orc lycanthrope to fight in the arena, even if it is just a rat."

"I was thinking the same thing. The timing couldn't be more perfect. He shall have plenty of time to break him for the next Full Moon Brawl."

"Excuse me," said Tim. "Oslof? Luglo? I don't think you understand the gravity of your situation. I really will shoot you."

Oslof frowned at Tim. "There is little value in a crippled halfling."

"We can throw it in for free as a token of goodwill. Zimbra will find a use for it. It is a feisty one, after all. Perhaps it could serve as a jester."

"Fuck this," said Tim. "I warned you motherfuckers." He fired his slobbery bolt at Luglo, who caught it in his gloved hand without even looking.

"Or he could use it to infect fighters he deems worthy," Luglo continued. "The half-orc won't last forever, after all."

Oslof laughed. "The way it fights, it will be lucky to survive training."

Luglo joined him with a chuckle. "Zimbra can feed them both to the chimeras for all I care, so long as we get paid."

Cooper looked back, hoping that Tim had another trick up his sleeve. He was disheartened to find that the trick was turning into a dire rat and running away. Even having ditched his clothes and weapons, he wasn't much faster on three of four functional feet than he was on one of two. Certainly not fast enough to outrun horses. It was kind of sad to watch.

If he couldn't outrun them, Cooper thought he might be able to fight them from a position of higher ground. If he could grow another orange tree, or even something larger, he could force them to chase him up. With a few lucky rolls, gravity could do the fighting for him. It was a long shot, but better than running up and getting kicked in the jaw again.

He pulled the Decanter of Endless Water out of his bag and pointed it directly down at his feet, hoping to catch a ride up as the tree grew. "Geyser!"

Lush, green vines erupted out of the sand, radiating outward instead of upward. They sprouted thick, waxy leaves and basketball-sized lime green melons which Cooper didn't recognize. The horses, on the other hand, seemed to recognize them immediately as one of their favorite treats as they excitedly bit into them.

"Fuck," said Cooper as he deactivated the decanter.

# Critical Failures VIII

"A Decanter of Endless Water," said Oslof, his eyebrows raised as he stared greedily at the valuable magic item in Cooper's hands. "We should visit the Oracle more often."

Cooper bolted after Tim, trying to figure out his next move as he ran.

"Geyser!" he said again, keeping the decanter pointed behind him and tucked tightly under his arm. Maybe if he produced enough foliage, the horses would have a difficult time pursuing them. Or maybe they'd keep getting distracted by tasty fruits? Or maybe they'd accidentally eat something poisonous and shit themselves to death. It was an even shittier plan than the tree thing, but it was all he currently had to work with.

He paused only briefly to grab Tim by the fur on the back of his neck, then dared not look back as he continued running.

Looking back, as it turned out, wasn't necessary. He could hear the horses' hooves pounding the sand behind him, then feel them as they quickly drew closer, like a second pulse running up through his legs. The stench of melon-infused horse breath grew stronger and stronger.

Something leathery coiled around his neck and yanked him off his feet. He crashed down on the sand once again. The Decanter of Endless Water shot out from under his arm and sailed through the air in a high arc before hitting the ground fifty feet away where it then skittered erratically across the sand as it continued to spew water.

Tim yanked himself out of Cooper's grip and turned back into his normal form, except that he was naked.

"Nice move, asshole," he snapped at Cooper.

Unable to speak through the whip constricting his neck, Cooper settled again for giving him the finger.

"Run and fetch the decanter," Luglo said to Oslof as his horse trotted casually onto the scene. "I will mind these two."

When Oslof went after the decanter, Luglo smiled down at Tim. "I picked up your clothes for you. If you promise to behave, I will not make you march into Olan Meb naked. Where you are going is not the kind of place you want to call that sort of attention to yourself."

# CHAPTER 3

*The* nights were getting cooler now. It must be getting into autumn. This particularly breezy night was not a great one to be homeless and effectively naked on the streets of Cardinia. The shredded remains of Dave's clothes were barely enough to keep him from being arrested for public indecency, and they did little to keep the night wind from slithering against his skin.

He was tempted to take his dire rat form. That layer of fur might not keep him toasty warm, but it would make for a nice barrier against the wind. But as a rat, he wouldn't be able to carry all the shit he'd just swiped from that sadistic bitch Stacy.

Knowing he'd outsmarted her provided him a little bit of warmth. It would have been extra nice to spend her money on a nicer room than the one he'd just ditched her in, but that was out of the question. In his current state, barely covered in shreds of blood-stained rags and missing a finger, he'd be lucky if an innkeeper didn't shout for the Kingsguard while throwing him out the door.

Even if he managed to find some sleazebag slumlord who would rent him a room, no questions asked, Stacy would be hunting him down as soon as she realized he was missing. If she started asking around at inns, Dave was nothing if not very easily identifiable.

But most importantly, his current resources were extremely limited. He couldn't afford to blow what little coin he'd stolen on luxuries that wouldn't last more than a couple of days. If the bitter autumn wind told him anything, it was that the approaching Cardinian winter would be far worse. That was just one more problem on the heap of shit Dave had to deal with in his life, but it was a problem for tomorrow. Right now, he had to focus on finding some place to hide and sleep before he passed out here in the middle of the street.

An alley seemed like his best bet. He trudged down the street until he felt he'd put enough distance between himself and Stacy, then started looking for a suitable one.

The first one he passed was too clean. Just a wide, empty space between two buildings. He'd be way too easy to spot.

The second one had a couple of piles of bricks and lumber he could hide behind. But if Stacy was looking for him, there was nothing here to deter her from peeking behind them.

A clearer picture of his ideal criteria formed in his mind. He wanted an alley with heaps of festering garbage. In his rat form, he could deal with the smell, but Stacy would likely decide it was far more trouble than it was worth to look for him. It would also keep him warm.

Dave sighed. This is what his life had come to now. It wasn't fair. He'd always tried to do the things he was supposed to do. He wasn't like Tim and Cooper. He'd put in the work to finish college, and he'd been putting in the time at Home-Tec to move up to a management position. Tim and Cooper had always been destined to fail. They were lead weights pulling him down, and he should have cut them loose a long time ago. He'd been right on the cusp of going places in life, and now he was actively seeking the most filth-ridden alley in a strange city to sleep in.

He slowed as he approached the next alley because of the sounds coming from it. Some kind of grunting and moaning. It might have been a large animal dying, or two hobos fucking. A glance as he passed didn't reveal what was causing the noise, but the alley itself seemed to be a great contender for filthiest in the city. Piles of festering garbage acted like connective tissue between a leather boiler and an apartment building for people who couldn't afford to not live right next to a leather boiler. The pungent stench of decaying animal scraps mingled with that of piss, vomit, and whatever garbage the residents of the apartments on this side of the building chucked out of their windows. Aside from whoever – or whatever – was occupying the alley already, it was as perfect as he could hope for.

He thought about waiting around for the occupants to finish fucking or dying so he could have the place to himself. But just in case that took too long, he decided to check a few more alleys up the street and come back to this one later if he couldn't find any other suitable options.

The clopping of hooves on cobblestones alerted him to someone approaching on horseback, probably a Kingsguard on patrol.

*Shit!*

Dave had no plausible explanation for his ragged, bloody appearance, or what he was doing on the street at this hour, so he crouched down in the alley to wait for the guard to pass.

The grunting and moaning from deeper within the alley intensified. It had to be sex. Nothing died with that kind of fervor. Dave wanted to tell them to shut up, but that would only call attention to himself from both parties he didn't want alerted to his presence.

The hoofbeats slowed to a stop right outside the alley as a half-elf in a Kingsguard uniform came into view on a slender brown horse. He shined the light from his lantern right on Dave.

*Shit.*

"You there!" the guard demanded. The grunting and moaning from further in immediately came to a halt.

"Hello," was all Dave could think to say in response.

"What are you doing in there? What was all that noise?" The half-elven guard sniffed the air, then scowled at Dave. "Were you defecating in the alley?"

That was as good an explanation as Dave could have possibly hoped for. "Yes."

The guard scowled at him. "Disgusting."

Dave wasn't about to try to argue that point, but he had a more pressing concern. "Is that a crime?"

"The king spares no expense to keep the streets of this great city as beautiful as they are. When a filthy lowlife such as yourself shits upon these streets, it is the same as shitting upon the king's very face!" What an unnecessarily long-winded way to not answer his question.

"So..."

"Do you know what it costs the city every time a vagrant shits in an alley?"

"No."

"Five silver pieces."

Dave nodded. He was impressed that this guy could pull that sort of statistic off the top of his head.

"Did you hear what I said?"

"Yes," said Dave to the guard who was still staring expectantly at him. "I did."

"It costs the city *five silver pieces* every time a vagrant shits in an alley."

He clearly meant for Dave to be impressed by that figure. Maybe there was some wastefulness in the bureaucracy somewhere? Street cleaners unions, perhaps? Whatever it was, the guy was still waiting for Dave to respond.

Dave thought up the most non-specific agreement he could come up with. "That does seem excessive."

The guard let out a shallow laugh. "Oh, does it?"

The sarcastic tone really wasn't necessary. What the hell

did this guy want from him? He decided to try again, a little more specific this time.

"Smells like corruption to me."

The guard's eyes widened, then narrowed as he sneered down at Dave. He rested his hand on the hilt of the sword on his belt. "Are you quite sure this is the path you want to travel down, dwarf?"

What the fuck did that mean?

Dave shook his head. "No," he answered very honestly. He had no idea what he'd done to make this guy accelerate from boring to violent so quickly.

"Good," said the guard. "As I was saying, it costs the city *seven* silver pieces every time a vagrant shits in an alley."

Jesus Christ. This guy was a fucking broken record. Not only had he gone back to square one with his boring rant about city finances, but he wasn't even keeping his statistics consistent.

"That's really something," said Dave. He wanted to say that it might be better spent on education or providing shelter for the homeless or something, but talking to this guy was like walking through a minefield.

The guard looked even more frustrated. He opened his mouth to speak again but was interrupted by a crash of broken glass from further up the street. He glanced that way, then glared down at Dave.

"Do not go anywhere, dwarf. This conversation is not yet concluded." He flicked his horse's reins, and it carried him up the street toward the disturbance.

"Fucking hell," Dave muttered to himself. With conversation skills like that, it was no wonder this guy was resigned to chatting up vagrants.

Dave considered making a break for it now that the guard was distracted. There were bound to be other filthy alleys in the vicinity. But he was slow, and he didn't know how long the guard would be gone.

Then again, as far as the guard knew, Dave had only stopped in the alley to take a shit. If Dave hid deep enough inside the filth, he'd probably assume Dave had concluded his business, putting the city between five and seven silver pieces in debt, and moved on. Surely, he couldn't be so desperate to hear Dave's views on the city maintenance budget that he would dig through piles of refuse in order to continue their conversation. Feeling confident with his decision, he turned back into the alley. He found himself face-to-face with a beastly human man. He was close to seven feet tall and covered from head to toe in filth and grime. It was impossible to tell what his natural skin color was. He had an open robe and a raging erection. In spite of the latter, he did not look at all pleased to see Dave.

"Have you been watching me, dwarf?"

"No! Of course not. I was just –"

"Is that how you get your jollies?"

"I was just passing by," said Dave. "I didn't even know –"

"Is there nowhere in this city that a man can pleasure himself without being spied upon by roaming degenerates?"

"Degenerates? Dude, you were the one jerking off in an alley full of garbage."

"Do you know why I come to this alley?"

Dave was growing weary of people's fucking riddles tonight. "To jerk off?"

The grimy man grew enraged. "Because it is so full of garbage that I thought I might have some privacy! But I see that even this is not enough to keep the lowest of the lowly deviants away."

Dave was feeling pretty goddamn lowly right about now, but it had nothing to do with this giant man whacking his schlong in an alley.

"I just saved your ass, buddy. That Kingsguard was

## Critical Failures VIII

following the sounds you were making. If I wasn't here to run interference, you'd be having the most boring fucking conversation of your life right now."

"Well, well, well. My fucking hero, you are. How shall I ever repay you?"

"Just leave me the fuck alone," said Dave.

"Maybe you'd like to do more than just watch. What do you say, dwarf?" The man stroked his grimy, hard penis. "Would you like to finish me off?"

Dave grimaced. "Fuck, no."

The man took a step toward Dave and narrowed his eyes. "That wasn't a question."

Dave narrowed his eyes back at him. "Yes, it was."

After taking a moment to consider Dave's point, the man growled as his fist flew straight into Dave's face.

Dave felt the crunch of his nose breaking as his Darkvision went totally black. Before he could open his eyes or orientate himself, he felt the huge man's strong hands grab his beard and pull him further into the alley. Was he about to be raped?

Several kicks and punches later, Dave felt relieved that the Back Alley Boner seemed content to merely beat the shit out of him. But there was only so much even of that he could take.

Knowing he couldn't take this guy in a straight-up fist fight, but not knowing where in the alley he'd dropped the weapons he'd stolen from Stacy, he defended himself the only way he knew how. He changed into his hybrid wererat form.

The beating ceased immediately. Dave opened his rat eyes to find the robed man backing away from him in terror, his wang having deflated like a popped balloon snake.

Dave snarled and bared his teeth, but didn't attack. This disgusting beast wasn't worthy of his gift. It was better to let him run and live with his cowardice.

And run he did. Dave smiled to himself as the huge man fled. There was power in lycanthropy. Tonight he would sleep in this putrid garbage-filled alley. But some day soon, he would turn the tables. Like he'd always said, it was just a matter of hard work, ambition, and focusing on defined goals.

He'd start his own wererat gang. He had the same inside scoop that Tim had, plus the Wisdom to not let it get out of his control. Before long, the name David Scott Ferguson would be synonymous with power in this city. Men would fear him, women would beg for his seed, and his so-called friends would –

*CLANG!*

The sudden sharp pain in the back of his skull was too much to bear. Darkness engulfed him. He was out like a light before he even hit the ground.

# CHAPTER 4

Stacy had suffered her share of catcalls, unwanted advances, and even an unsolicited dick pic or two during her time on Earth. But to the best of her knowledge, no man had ever masturbated over her and called her a cunt while she slept.

Fortunately, Dave only thought he was doing the first part of that, but she still had half a mind to ditch him and let him see how he did without her. Why should she lose a wink of sleep as he got himself arrested or killed after the terrible things he'd called her?

Yet here she was walking the streets in the middle of a brisk autumn night with only a Cloak of Elvenkind to keep her warm and mostly invisible. As cool as her Goggles of the Night were, the grainy night vision they provided put even more strain on her already weary eyes.

There were several reasons she couldn't just ditch him. As much of an asshole as he was being right now, he was still her friend. They didn't have a lot of history together, but she'd been around him long enough to suspect that the Dave she witnessed a few minutes ago was acting out of character. At least, she had to hope so.

Also, there was the possibility he'd harm other people if left to his own devices. She had assumed responsibility for him, which would put any misdeeds he committed on her shoulders.

Finally, but not the least of her concerns, he had all her shit.

## Robert Bevan

One thing that hadn't changed about Dave, thankfully, was his walking speed. Tailing him was like tailing an old lady with a walker. More than once, as she followed him down the empty street, she felt like she might fall asleep on her feet, and that she probably still wouldn't have much trouble catching up to him again when she woke up. Not only was he slow, but he kept stopping to examine every alley he passed. What the hell was he looking for? A stray cat to eat? A tarp to cover himself with? A cheap hooker?

Hoping to get some clue as to what he was after, she stopped to better examine one alley that had piqued his interest. The only difference between this one and the other ones they'd passed was that there were some stacks of building materials. Bricks, wooden planks, some metal pipes. Maybe he was going to build himself a tree house in the woods or something. Or maybe he'd just toyed with the idea, then reconsidered.

As long as she was there, she picked up a pipe. It was heavier than she'd expected. Lead, most likely. She gave it a couple of test swings and jabs and deemed it an acceptable substitute weapon until she got hers back.

When she came out of the alley, she expected to find Dave staring into the next one, but he wasn't there. Had he finally found whatever he was looking for? Had he continued past that alley and turned the corner? Stacy's heart sank as the worst-case scenario occurred to her. Had he ditched her?

Was that even possible? Could he have known this whole time that she was following him, then played her like a fool, tempting her to go investigate that alley, then taking off while she was distracted? The jerking off, the name calling, had that all been part of a larger master plan?

Stacy shook the thought out of her head. Dave wasn't smart enough to think of a plan that intricate, or talented enough to pull it off. He was just... Dave.

# Critical Failures VIII

"You there!" said a half-elven kingsguard on horseback.

Instinctively, Stacy brandished her lead pipe, ready to defend herself. Fortunately, she was still mostly invisible. It wouldn't have been ideal to be seen threatening a cop with an improvised weapon when he wasn't even talking to her.

"What are you doing in there?" he demanded of someone in the alley. Stacy had a pretty good hunch who that might be. "What was all that noise?" After giving the air a sniff, he scowled. "Were you defecating in the alley?"

Stacy shook her head. *Oh, Dave.*

The guard lectured Dave about how serious an offense shitting in public was. Maybe this was as good a scenario as Stacy could hope for. Let Dave do some time. While he was incarcerated, she could focus on finding Cooper, Tim, the dice, and maybe bag herself another Mordred.

On the other hand, they might just kill him when they discovered he was a wererat.

Stacy sighed. Dave was her responsibility, and she had to get this guard off his back.

"Do you know what it costs the city every time a vagrant shits in an alley?" the guard asked Dave. After a short pause, he said, "Five silver pieces."

Finally, a spot of luck. A cheap bribe, easily affordable with the money Dave had stolen from her.

"Did you hear what I said?" he continued more impatiently. "It costs the city *five silver pieces* every time a vagrant shits in an alley."

What the hell was Dave waiting for? Was he really that dense? Or was he just being cheap? Stacy moved in closer to hear Dave's part of the conversation.

"That does seem excessive," said Dave.

The guard looked as shocked as Stacy felt. "Oh, does it?"

*Come on, Dave! You don't haggle over petty change when a cop shakes you down for a bribe. What are you thinking?*

"Smells like corruption to me."

*DAVE!*

He was trying to get arrested. That was the only possible explanation. Maybe he had gotten sick and tired of being homeless and on the run, and was willing to sacrifice his freedom for four walls and a bowl of cold gruel every day.

Stacy thought about the way Dave's own friends talked to him, and how he just took it. He wouldn't make it on the inside. He'd be some hobgoblin's bitch within a week. They'd paint his face, put his hair in pigtails, and pass him around the yard.

Could lycanthropy be transmitted through butt sex? There would be riots during the next full moon. The inmates would take over and break loose, putting the whole city at risk.

Stacy couldn't let that happen. She didn't want to club the guard if she didn't have to. That would only compound their troubles when he came to again. Instead, she sneaked back to the alley full of construction materials, found a loose cobblestone off the street, and hoped that destruction of private property was a grave enough offense to distract the Kingsguard from Dave's dump in the alley. After scanning the street for a good target, she hurled the stone at a window across the street about seventy yards away.

*SMASH!*

She became instantly visible as she threw the stone, as if she was materializing like one of Julian's horses. Satisfied with her handiwork, Stacy re-donned her cloak and hoped the guard would take the bait. She breathed a sigh of relief when his horse galloped past her alley, then hurried back to grab Dave before the guard came back.

"Is there nowhere in this city that a man can pleasure himself without being spied upon by roaming degenerates?" asked a gruff voice from the garbage alley.

# Critical Failures VIII

Was it possible for Dave to go two minutes without attracting more trouble? Was he peeping at masturbating hobos now? Was that why he took such a fancy to this alley in the first place? Geez Louise, was he letting his perv flag fly.

Stacy crept closer while Dave bickered with the man in the alley. She peeked around the corner just in time to see him get his face caved in by a huge man's fist. Good for him. If anyone needed some sense beat into him right now, it was Dave.

She kept a wary eye up the street for the guard while the filthy Colossus of a hobo kicked the snot out of Dave.

When Dave finally decided he'd had enough of a beating, he changed into his hybrid rat-dwarf form and sprang to his feet. He snarled, drooled, and clawed at the air, but stopped short of attacking the giant hobo, who backed away from him out of the alley.

Stacy flattened herself against the wall, fearful of being spotted. Fortunately, the big man was too terrified of Dave for his attention to stray. When he fled down the street, Stacy sneaked around the corner to find Dave still in his hybrid form, catching his breath and seemingly lost in thought as he stared further into the alley.

He'd caused more than enough trouble for one night. Stacy didn't know what their next move would be, but it was going to have to involve Dave being unconscious.

*Sorry, Dave.*

She lifted her lead pipe with both hands, then brought it down hard against the back of Dave's rat head.

*CLANG!*

He went down like a sack of potatoes.

After feeling under his neck fur to confirm he still had a pulse, Stacy wasn't as burdened with guilt as she thought she'd be for clubbing someone in the back of the head with a lead pipe. In fact, she felt pretty good about it. It was like they were even now.

She thought again about the awful things he'd called her while he was whacking his noodle. No, they weren't even. Not even close. She clobbered him on the head to save him from himself. If anything, he was *more* in debt to her now.

"Help!" cried the big man from down the street, near where Stacy had smashed the window.

*Shit.*

She peeked out of the alley, thankful for a breath of not-so-rancid air, to find the hobo and the guard in a heated exchange.

The guard seemed to be berating him for his cock swinging around freely between the sides of his open robe. When he finally managed to get a word in, he pointed back toward Stacy. She ducked back, hopefully before the guard spotted her.

*Shit.*

He was ratting out Dave for being a rat. How wonderfully ironic. She could muse on that later, after she figured out what the hell she was going to do. Sure, she had gone into this without a game plan, but she thought she'd at least have a little time to come up with something.

Hiding Dave was the top priority. That giant hobo had probably embellished his story a bit, and if that guard came back to discover an actual wererat, that would be plenty enough evidence to corroborate whatever he'd been told.

Stacy spread her Cloak of Elvenkind over Dave's unconscious body, then kicked some rotting cabbage leaves over him until he looked like just more garbage. She mentally added a cleaning bill to the list of things he now owed her.

Horse hooves tapped cobblestones approaching at a slow trot, as if the guard dreaded confronting a wererat alone.

"Ho there!" he called out from the other side of the street. He was trying to sound strong and confident, but Stacy picked up a slight tremor in his voice. "Show yourself!"

He was afraid, but he didn't run off. Was it because he was bound by a sacred sense of honor? That didn't jive too well with him soliciting a bribe from Dave. Was it a matter of pride then? Did he not want to lose face in front of some filthy hobo? How much less face would he want to lose in front of a stunningly attractive woman such as herself?

She got into the character of a victim, removed her goggles and put down her pipe, then staggered out into the street. "Thank the gods!" she cried. "If you hadn't shown up, I dare not think of what might have become of me!"

*Yikes. Tone it down a bit, Scarlet O'Hara.*

"What happened?" asked the guard, his gaze darting up and down the street, and past her into the alley.

"The most horrible creature. A hideous combination of dwarf and rat." She wasn't ratting out Dave, she told herself. She was just further corroborating the information this guard had already been given.

"Did he bite or scratch you?"

Stacy shook her head. "He snarled and wagged his naked rat genitalia at me." Now to give his ego a little stroke. "Then he spotted you and ran off that way." She pointed further down the street.

As she'd hoped, he looked very pleased with himself. Not as she'd hoped, he didn't ride away.

"Fear not, good lady. You are safe now."

"Thank you, kind sir. May the gods bless you." Was he waiting for an invitation?

"May I ask what you are doing out here alone at this hour?"

Stacy concentrated on not rolling her eyes. "I was on my way to work," she said. "I'm a..." She tried to think of something plausible to follow that up with, taking into account the time and what she was wearing. "...hooker."

*Why did I say that? And to a cop, of all people!* She was losing her edge. She needed sleep.

"Is that right?" The guard's tone sounded more interested than scornful. "Forgive me, as I don't know the preferred parlance. But what are your rates?"

*What a slimeball!*

"Please, sir. I have just been through a traumatic experience, and my attacker is getting away."

The guard glanced casually up the street, then down to Stacy's breasts. "Yeah, he's probably long gone by now."

Stacy resisted the urge to pick up her lead pipe. "Perhaps not. He appeared to be injured."

"Oh? How so?"

"He had a limp." With another little nudge, she might convince him that he could actually take this made up wererat. "And one of his hands was missing."

"Is that right?" The guard rubbed the stubble on his chin.

"But it might be best if you just leave him be," said Stacy, seeking to push his pride button. "Those things are dangerous. Or maybe you could call for backup?" If the pride thing didn't work, there was no harm in extending one more invitation for him to go away.

He chuckled condescendingly. "Rest assured, good lady. I fear no crippled rodent. He shall be apprehended within the hour. I suggest you find a safe place indoors."

"I'll get right on that. Thanks."

"And perhaps I shall see you again at some point?"

Stacy faked a smile. "I certainly hope so."

When the guard finally trotted off, Stacy felt as dirty as the alley she was standing in. It was one thing to proposition her. That was really on her, for telling him she was a hooker. But to think that he could afford *her* rates when he was shaking down hobos for five-silver-piece bribes? That was just insulting.

# Critical Failures VIII

She looked down at Dave, barely visible under her Cloak of Elvenkind even though she knew exactly where he was. What was she going to do with him? Even if she thought up a more effective way to bind him, she couldn't risk carrying him back to the room while he was in his hybrid form. And she certainly couldn't leave him here and hope that he didn't run off as soon as he woke up... or could she?

Was the situation here any worse than it had been in the room? It might actually be even better. First, she'd knocked him on the noggin pretty hard. He would probably be asleep for a couple hours. Second, he didn't know it was her who knocked him out. Sure, she was probably on his list of suspects. But given how much commotion he'd already experienced in this alley, it could have been a territorial hobo for all he knew.

And if he didn't know it was her, he'd have no reason to expect there to be caltrops hidden among the garbage on either side of him. Meanwhile, she could get some sleep on the roof of one of the adjacent buildings.

It wasn't a foolproof plan, but it was the best her sleep-deprived mind could come up with right now. She'd think of something less shitty in the morning.

She took back her cloak, then dragged Dave deeper into the alley and covered him in enough garbage to completely hide him, but not enough to suffocate him. After spreading the caltrops around and making sure they were sufficiently concealed, she gathered up her goggles, the things that Dave had stolen from her, and even her lead pipe. It felt good to wield and might come in handy again.

With the rope she'd used to tie up Dave in their room, she caught an exposed beam sticking out from the top of the shorter building, then scaled the wall.

The roof appeared to be someone's private hideaway. A small wooden table and chair stood in the corner overlooking the street. Stacy imagined a weary old shopkeeper winding down with a book and a glass of whiskey after a hard day's work, watching the people walk by on the street below him.

She lay close to the wall where she'd buried Dave so she'd be able to hear his screams if he stepped on a caltrop. Her cloak provided little warmth, and her bag made for a lumpy pillow, but she was grateful for a chance to lie down and close her eyes. She was out within seconds.

# CHAPTER 5

"Take it," Katherine said to Randy, holding out the sword she'd taken from Captain Logan when she'd single-handedly crippled his ship at sea, stopping him and his crew from taking her ship, *Nightwind*.

Randy stepped back. "I couldn't. It's too much."

"What's too much is you rowing that little boat back and forth to *Nightwind* so many times. I don't know why you didn't just let Basil ferry everyone across."

"It don't feel right using his Jesus powers when they ain't totally necessary," said Randy. "Besides, I reckon I row faster than he walks anyway."

Katherine held the sword by the scabbard and offered Randy the pommel. "I want you to have it." She could tell by the look in his eyes that he wanted to take it.

"You're drunk," he said.

"That's true, but that's not why I'm giving this to you. You're a paladin. I'm a druid. I like swinging scythes. A sword like this is much better suited to someone like you. I only kept it as long as I did because it felt good knowing that Captain Logan knew I had it. Now that he's dead, it's kind of lost its luster for me." Sensing he was nearly convinced, she added, "If I decide I want it back after I sober up, you can give it to me then."

Randy nodded. "Alright. That sounds fair. He accepted the sword and pulled it halfway out of the scabbard, admiring the mirror-like polish of the blade. After gently resheathing it, he grinned at Katherine. "Either way, it means a whole lot that you was thinking of me."

"You're a good man, Randy."

"I should probably get moving now. I'll be right back for you."

"Don't sweat it," said Katherine. "I'll just turn into a shark and swim."

"Are you sure? It ain't no trouble."

"I'm good." Katherine held up the bottle she'd been drinking from, a prize she'd taken from Captain Logan that she wasn't about to hand over to Randy. "I'm going to hang back and talk to Butterbean. I'll catch up with you in a minute."

When Randy started rowing the last of the Whore's Head gang over to *Nightwind*, Katherine sat on the sand next to Butterbean and wrapped an arm around him to pull him in close. His fur was a shade or two darker than normal and reeked of salt and dead fish, but the same was probably true for her as well. She supposed they were both long overdue for a bath in water that wasn't contaminated by rotting fish carcasses.

There was something special about having an Animal Companion, and Katherine would call bullshit on anyone who said that was just a matter of game mechanics. Almost every person she'd counted on here had let her down in one way or another, but not Butterbean. Sure, he may have wanted to kill her when she was a vampire, but those were extenuating circumstances. She had no doubt that he would gladly lay down his life in her defense, and he never had an agenda or asked for anything in return. The cherry on top of all of that was that they could occasionally talk.

Katherine cast her Speak With Animals spell.

"What did you think about your first experience with alcohol?"

"It was very pleasant while I was drinking it," Butterbean responded. "But it doesn't feel so good now."

Katherine smiled at him. "That's called a hangover. You'll learn to endure them eventually."

"May I ask you a question?"

"Is it about licking your balls?"

"No," said Butterbean. "I was curious as to why everyone is leaving us."

"They aren't leaving us. We're just last in line because there are still hostile pirates on the island, and I'm the only one who can turn into a shark and swim away if they attack us." She looked back at the treeline. There was no sign of any pirates.

Butterbean sniffed the air. "I don't smell them nearby."

That was even more reassuring than her own visual check.

"They probably fled to the other side when all the shit went down and they saw what a badass they were fucking with. Did you see me fly out of that hole and bite Mordred in half?"

"I did see that. I was very relieved that you didn't die."

Katherine sighed. "It's a bummer that he died, but that must have looked so fucking epic."

Butterbean responded, but it came out as a bark. The spell had timed out.

Randy had just about reached *Nightwind*, so it was probably time to start swimming anyway.

Katherine gulped down what was left in the bottle, then stood up with wobbly knees. She'd perhaps overdone it on the booze, but she felt she deserved it after what she'd been through.

As she waded into the water, a problem occurred to her. How the hell was Butterbean supposed to get to the ship?

*Shit.*

The ship was a ways off. Butterbean could swim, but he

wasn't very fast, and the ocean was full of dangerous creatures, all of which were seeking their next meal.

Then she had an idea.

"Come on, Butterbean," she said, running clumsily out into the water. Butterbean followed.

Katherine kept going until she was submerged up to her armpits so she would have plenty of swimming room and Butterbean would be easier to hold.

When he paddled up next to her, she wrapped her arms around him and hugged him tightly.

"This might feel a little weird," she said.

She turned into a shark, absorbing Butterbean as part of her form just like her clothes and equipment. It was a good thing, too. With her shark-brain-compromised mind, she would have found it hard not to eat him. In the future, she would try to change into less primitively violent animals when she was around friends.

Even though she knew she was supposed to be swimming to *Nightwind*, she couldn't resist chasing down some fat meaty fish when she caught their scent. She'd chased down a few fish while she was waiting to shit out the magic die, but what the hell else was she going to do? She hadn't realized until now how much of a compulsion it was.

She allowed herself to gobble down one last fish before she fought her shark instincts and swam for the ship. When she got there, she turned back into her normal form and was startled to find Butterbean paddling next to her.

Sobered up a bit by the swim and shapeshifting, she was relieved that plan had actually worked, but regretted not having tested it first with a bug or something.

She looked up, annoyed that nobody was lowering a rope or ladder for her, and was about to shout to her crew, when she heard voices that gave her pause.

"That's the last of them, Captain," said a voice that

# Critical Failures VIII

Katherine didn't recognize as anyone from the Whore's Head. Who the hell did he think he was calling *Captain* aboard her ship? "The big fella who was doing all the rowing had this on him."

"My father's sword!" The responding voice was weaker and raspier than it had been last time she heard it, but Katherine recognized it as Captain Logan's. "Was the girl with this group?"

"She was not, I'm afraid. The big one claims he left her on the island talking to her pet wolf."

Captain Logan let out a wheezing laugh. He sounded like he was in pretty bad shape. But considering that he'd been fried with lightning bolts before falling forty feet into the mud, as the others had claimed, Katherine supposed that being alive at all was actually pretty good shape.

"Shall we send a landing party to hunt her down?"

"No," said Logan. "I have what I came for, plus two additional ships and a cargo hold full of slaves to sell. Let us not get greedy, Ponston." Katherine held her breath and Butterbean's mouth shut as Logan leaned over *Nightwind*'s rear bulwark. His face was dark with soot and blood, making his blue eyes brighter than she remembered them. Not a friendly blue, like the sky or Cookie Monster, but a pale cold blue, like the Ice Queen's frozen palace, full of hate and smugness. "Let her remain there and reap the rewards of stealing from Captain Logan. If she's already mad enough to converse with her wolf now, it won't be long before the hunger sets in. When we return here in a month's time, one of them will have eaten the other."

Three ships? How did he have three ships? Had he taken over the *Maiden's Voyage*, too?

Katherine had a pretty clear picture of how he'd taken *Nightwind*. She'd only left a couple of people aboard to look after it. Hopefully, they surrendered peacefully. With Randy only rowing in a small boatload of people at a time, it must have been easy to capture and subdue the rest of the unsuspecting crew. But how had they taken Captain Longfellow's ship?

The answer was sailing around from the other side of the island. Two ships approached, sailing side by side on the horizon. She recognized the *Maiden's Voyage* immediately by the tiered stack of cabins, and the other ship fell in line with her vague memory of what Logan's ship looked like.

"The rest of your fleet approaches, Captain," said Ponston cheerily.

"Excellent. Divide the prisoners among all three ships. Keep the strongest ones here and sail for Meb' Garshur."

"Does that mean…"

"Yes, Ponston," said Logan with a hint of annoyance in his voice. "I'm naming you Captain of *Nightwind*."

*The fuck you are.*

"Oh, thank you, Captain!"

"Yes, yes. Just remember you are still sailing under my command."

"Of course. Who will be captaining the *Maiden's Voyage*?"

Logan sighed. "I had Faldor in mind, but Marcus has a better rapport with the Khalzharis. They will pay handsomely for spellcasters."

"Faldor has served loyally and is popular among the crew. He may take this as a slight."

"His loyalty shall be rewarded with a ship worthy of it. We have the beginning of a small navy here. With three ships working as one force, a fourth ship shan't be difficult to acquire."

"You are very wise, Captain," said Ponston. Katherine didn't know how he could still talk with his nose shoved so far up Logan's ass. "Where will you take the rest of the prisoners?"

"I haven't decided yet. Normally, I would dump them in Hollin, but those damned cultists have taken over the port and disrupted the slave trade."

"Speaking of the cultists, are we planning to recapture the prisoners we set loose on Longfellow's crew?"

"Our own crew is spread too thin as it is. We'll drop them off at the next port we come to and leave them to their silly quest."

"I may have a solution that may not only get them to work for us, but also allow you safe passage in and out of Hollin."

"Oh?" said Logan. After a pause, he continued. "What is this? Some child's bauble?"

*Shit. He wasn't talking about...*

"I know not what it is. We took it from a gnome in the cargo hold. Aside from a vile dwarf woman, he was the only one to put up any resistance. Whatever this thing is, he did *not* want to let it go."

*Shit. He was.*

"Intriguing."

Katherine forced herself to remain calm. This didn't make their situation any worse. Logan had no idea what he had possession of. She was going to have to get her ship back from him anyway. She'd get the die back as well.

"Even more intriguing," said Ponston. "It matches the description of what the cultists seek."

"Does it now?"

"If you offer them what they want in exchange for safe passage, they can appease their bard master. You can use the disruption to your advantage. The Barovian slavers will pay twice what these prisoners are worth since so few are being delivered."

*SHIT!* This was the worst possible scenario. Not only would her friends be sold into slavery, but Logan was going to deliver the die right into Mordred's hands.

Katherine couldn't hang around and eavesdrop any longer. The other two ships were getting too close, and someone aboard one of them was bound to spot her. She needed a place to hide.

There weren't a lot of great places to hide on the outside of a ship, she discovered. Imagining Nightwind's layout, she couldn't think of many good places to hide on deck either. At least, not good enough to risk climbing aboard. The only thing she could think to do was hang on to the anchor chain. Hopefully, everyone would be gathered at the rear of the ship, waiting for the other two. Maybe she'd have better luck finding a place to hide on Logan's ship. All three ships were about to sail off in different directions. And unless she could pull a miracle out of her ass really soon, she would have to abandon *Nightwind* for the time being in order to keep Logan from delivering the die to Mordred.

"Sorry, Butterbean. You'll need to ride in the bag for a few minutes."

Butterbean groaned softly, but didn't resist when Katherine brought the Bag of Holding over him.

She rolled up the bag and shoved it down the back of her jeans, then pressed her hand against *Nightwind*'s hull. "Spiderbitch." Now able to climb freely along the side of the ship, she stayed close to the water as she made her way as fast as she could to the anchor chain.

Once she had her arm locked around the slippery iron chain, she let Butterbean out of the bag and held him close with her other arm. She couldn't see anyone on the ship, which meant that they couldn't see her either. She was safe for now.

Her relief was short-lived, though, when she saw that the *Maiden's Voyage* and Logan's ship were both approaching on her side of *Nightwind*. If they were going to swap prisoners and crew from ship to ship, they'd be pulling up as close as possible to one another, which meant that they'd be carefully watching the exact area where she was hiding.

Katherine sighed. "Can't I catch a goddamn break for once?"

She could climb around to the other side of the ship and hang on the hull for as long as her Spider Climb spell lasted, but what would be the point? She needed to get to Logan's ship.

The ships were moving in fast, and Katherine had very little time to think of something before she'd be spotted.

*Think! Think! Think!*

Nothing.

There was nowhere to go but down and hope that an additional minute underwater would yield better results.

"Sorry, Butterbean." She swallowed him up in the Bag of Holding again and shimmied down the anchor chain.

Why hadn't she just let Randy ferry her back? If she hadn't used up her one shapeshift for the day to swim here, she could use it to swim to Logan's ship.

No, that would have been even worse. She would have been caught unawares just like everyone else and been captured. Captain Logan might have even decided that killing her was more satisfying than whatever gold he could get by selling her into slavery. At least here she was clinging on to life a little longer... as long as she could hold her breath, anyway. That time was quickly coming to an end.

She wished she could think of some clever way out of this, but her mind kept nagging her to turn back into a shark.

*Come on, Katherine. Change the fucking record. You haven't got much time left.*

Maybe if she gave it a try, her mind would allow her to move on to other ideas. She pulled Butterbean out of the Bag of Holding, wrapped her arms around him, and willed herself into shark form. Much to her surprise, it actually worked.

*Holy shit! How did I – Ooooh, a fish!*

She swam after the fish, then deliberately changed course.

*No, Katherine! You have to be stronger than the shark.* She dived further down, fearing the pirates might enjoy taking some pot shots at a shark just to pass the time while they waited for the ships' captains to finish divvying up their prisoners.

When she came back up, she recognized Logan's ship as the biggest of the three. She swam up close to the bottom of the hull and tried to think of how she could board the ship without being seen and where she could hide once she got on deck. Her brief memory of her time aboard the ship didn't bring back much of a recollection of its layout, and it wasn't helping that her shark brain was still preoccupied with food.

One of her pectoral fins brushed up against the barnacle-studded hull, and something felt off about the way it made contact. It was clingy, like she'd be able to stick to it if she stopped. Curious, she brushed her belly against the hull, and discovered that she was stuck to it. Not like shoes on a movie theater floor, but more like shoes on a clean floor. It was like gravity holding her onto the bottom of the ship. Or even like...

She urinated through her skin as she realized what was happening. Her Spider Climb spell was still in effect. The question of how she was going to climb aboard the ship had been answered.

The rear of the ship felt like the best place to make her move. Since the crew was spread as thin as it was, most of their attention would be focused on not banging into the *Maiden's Voyage* and preparing prisoners for transport to one of the other ships. Also, there was a little alcove halfway up the ship's rear, a mid-level platform probably used for fishing or easier access to the rudder. If it wasn't a heavily frequented place, it might serve well as the nook Katherine needed to catch her breath and plan her next move.

# Critical Failures VIII

Climbing the hull proved easy until she surfaced. Once she was out of the water, continuing to drag herself forward with only her pectoral fins was a lot more challenging. Sweeping her tail back and forth moved her, but not in a very targeted direction. The obvious solution was changing back into a half-elf. But then she'd have to carry Butterbean, which would likely be even more difficult than trying to climb up the hull of a boat as a giant fish.

Inch by inch, she crept closer to the alcove. The fact that she was able to take an animal form twice a day now, as opposed to only once, must have meant that she'd increased her druid level. Hopefully, that also meant that the duration of her Spider Climb spell had extended. She was glad no one was watching her. Not only would that be dangerous, but also embarrassing. She must look ridiculous.

The inability to breathe with gills was a different sensation than not being able to breathe with lungs, but no less urgent and terrifying... especially while she was exerting so much energy trying to flap and flop her way upward. She wasn't sure that she could make it to the alcove, and the temptation to drop back down into the water mounted with every inch she struggled to progress.

If the spell timed out before she could get Butterbean in the Bag of Holding and climb up there again, they'd be fucked. Then again, they'd be just as fucked if it timed out before she could flap her way up there as a shark, but at least then she could hide out underwater for a little while and try to think of something else.

Another thing she noticed while she slowly climbed to the alcove was that her sense of hearing outside of the water was greatly diminished. In the water, she could hear prey she estimated to be about two hundred yards away. Up here above the surface, everything was mostly wind and white noise. But there was one distinct sound she could make out as she dragged herself closer to the alcove. Someone up there wasn't having any trouble breathing at all. Someone was up there, and his lungs were working overtime. While that was alarming, it had nothing on her state of panic at not having seawater flowing through her gills.

*Come on, Katherine. Don't give up. We're almost there.*

Getting more of a feel for the rhythm of movement that would propel her further up the hull, Katherine swung her tail harder and flexed her fins for all they were worth. She was going to make it.

"Wha... what the fuck?" said a voice that seemed distantly familiar, even through the filter of her compromised shark sense of hearing.

Flapping herself so that her left eye was facing upward, she saw Bosley, the creep whose life she'd been on the fence about sparing last time she was aboard this ship. Unsurprisingly, he was holding a fistful of his own junk, still stroking even as he gawked down in disbelief at a shark climbing up toward him.

Katherine redoubled her efforts, flopping herself upward as fast as she could.

Bosley snapped out of his shock and tucked his dick back in his pants.

*Flop.*

*Flip.*

*Flop.*

She was over the railing and had Bosley's leg in her mouth just as he was reaching for the handle of the door that led into the ship's interior. She so longed to breathe, but she could quiet his screaming more quickly as a shark than she would a half-elf.

The next bite accomplished that. She got a mouthful of his crotch all the way up past his navel and bit down hard. He wasn't quite dead yet, but he'd definitely lost the will to be so vocal in his objections.

The shark had taken over now, and Katherine let it finish its meal. She couldn't very well dump the body in the water while they were anchored, after all, and this would be less mess to put in her Bag of Holding.

When nothing remained of Bosley but a puddle of blood on the alcove floor, Katherine changed back into her half-elf form and relished in the sensation of oxygen entering her lungs.

Butterbean loped shakily out of the bag, but he soon got distracted lapping up tiny pieces of Bosley viscera.

Katherine was a little freaked out about that, but then considered that she'd just eaten most of two separate people within the past twenty-four hours. She mentally declared to herself that it's not cannibalism if you're not a person when you eat someone.

Now that she had her breathing under control and her moral ambiguities sorted out, Katherine took stock of her current situation. Finding Bosley spanking the monkey here might actually have been a good thing. He was a scumbag whom Katherine wouldn't lose any much-needed sleep over having killed, especially now that he'd taken part in imprisoning her friends. But on a practical note, the fact that he was pulling his pork back here meant that he'd had a reasonable expectation of privacy. She wasn't completely free of worry, but she had a little time to think rationally about her next move.

The obvious one was to clean up all the blood on the floor. It wouldn't make a whole lot of difference if someone spotted it now, seeing as how they'd see her sitting there as well. But if she was sneaking around somewhere else on the ship, this big puddle of fresh blood might indicate that something amiss was going on.

The Bag of Holding had enough seawater in it from when

she'd scooped up Butterbean to wash most of the blood off the side. There was still a little left, but Katherine deemed it less than what would arouse suspicion aboard a pirate ship.

She sat back against the door and stared at Nazere in the morning sunlight, wondering how tall the trees would be if she ever returned.

# CHAPTER 6

$\mathcal{J}$ulian woke up feeling like shit. Every part of him ached, his vision was blurry, and his dark surroundings smelled like pee and BO. It was like a really bad night at the Whore's Head, except without the silver lining of being too drunk to care. His wrists were shackled together, as were his ankles, with rusty iron bands so tightly that he was surprised his fingers weren't purple from loss of blood circulation. The rest of the Whore's Head crew was there with him, every one of them in shackles.

Memories of the ambush came back to him. When Randy had ferried his group to the ship, a sailor whom Julian didn't recognize welcomed them with a rope ladder. He'd assumed it was one of the sailors from the ship that Randy and Denise had arrived on, and nobody thought anything of it until he and a bunch of other sailors, as well as some half-starved wild-eyed men, jumped them. Between the element of surprise and how vastly they were outnumbered, Julian and the five others who'd ridden in with him hadn't stood a chance.

Judging by all the split lips, black eyes, and bleeding crooked noses around him, the other boarding parties had gotten the same treatment.

After the beating they'd all endured, Julian was grateful to see that everyone appeared to have survived the attack. That is, all the *people* appeared to have survived.

"Ravenus!" he said, realizing suddenly that his familiar wasn't with him.

"They took all the familiars and animal companions up onto the deck," said Frank, who was sitting next to him. "They're being held hostage so we don't step out of line."

Denise sobbed across the aisle and shook her chains. "They took my baby!"

Julian calmed himself. He could sense through their Empathic Link that Ravenus was frightened, but otherwise okay.

"Who took them hostage?" he asked. "Who are these people?" One of them stood out in Julian's memory as the person overseeing the attack, as well as the only person who'd looked worse than Julian currently felt. "Who was that guy with all the burns all over his body?"

"I guess you slept through the part where he showed up on the island."

"Most of what happened after Mordred started casting spells on me is a blur. I remember getting shot with arrows."

"The man with the burns is Logan, captain of *Seastalker*. We had a run in with him on the way here. He pegged us for an easy target at sea, but Katherine got the better of him, at least temporarily. She took him for everything they had and left his ship on the verge of sinking."

"*She* did all that? As in, all by herself?"

Frank nodded. "She's not someone you want to underestimate. I only wish she had let the damned ship sink. Captain Logan didn't appreciate her stealing his sword."

"He's taking us all prisoner because she took his sword?"

"Of course not," said Frank. "He's taking us all prisoner because he's a pirate and we were easy to catch. Since he hasn't killed us already, I'm guessing he'll probably sell us into slavery. He hunted us down because of the sword. Apparently, it was a family heirloom or something."

Julian scanned the rest of the ship's cargo hold by the dim light of a small Light stone hanging near the front by a length of twine. He saw no sign of Katherine.

"Where is Katherine?"

Frank shrugged. "Who knows? Probably passed out drunk on the island."

"Then this Logan guy still doesn't have his sword?"

"I reckon he's got it by now," said Randy, who was chained across from Julian, between Tony the Elf and Denise. "Katherine gave it to me before my last trip on account of me being a paladin. She said it was better suited to me."

"That's not all he's got," said Frank. "His men frisked us all good. They took the die."

Julian's heart beat faster as pieces started to fall into place. "Did it not occur to any of you that maybe he wasn't after the sword at all? Maybe he was after the die. Maybe he's one of the other Mordreds!"

"I don't think so," said Frank, uncharacteristically calm for someone who had a track record for losing his shit whenever his dice got stolen.

"Why not?"

"Because Mordred's the one who gave him those burns."

"Oh."

"Right after you checked out, this Logan guy arrives on the scene carried by a huge-ass water elemental. I had no idea who he was, but was grateful that someone showed up who might be able to go head-to-head with Mordred."

"Did he?"

Frank laughed. "Fuck no. Mordred blasted him and his elemental with lightning bolts until the elemental exploded and he fell a good thirty feet to the ground. We all assumed he was dead, but it turns out he's a tough bastard. Mordred probably assumed he was dead as well, though. So as long as Captain Logan doesn't know what he's got, the die might be safer with him than it is with us, at least until we bag ourselves another Mordred."

There was one thing that still didn't make sense to Julian.

"How did he manage to get to the ship?"

"While we were all licking our wounds on the beach, his men must have fed him a healing potion or something. That water elemental had to have come from somewhere, so he might have a magic item that summons them. That big bastard could have easily ferried him and all his men to the ship."

"But if he –"

Light poured into the cargo hold as the hatch leading out to the deck creaked open. Six hulking men who looked like they'd seen their share of sea battles stomped down the stairs. They took positions three by three on either side of the stairs, making way for a seventh man, or rather a one-eyed half-orc. He wasn't quite as big as the others, but he carried himself with a confidence that made him seem much less like someone Julian wanted to fuck with.

"Good morning," said the half-orc. "You are now the property of Captain Logan."

"I ain't no man's property!" cried Denise. "I'm an independent fuckin' –"

CRACK!

The half-orc gave her a controlled, but very hard, punch in the face, knocking her out. He sighed with satisfaction, as if he'd been hoping someone would give him the opportunity to do that.

"My name is Faldor," he continued now that he had everyone but Denise's undivided attention. "Those of you who remain aboard this ship will be under my charge as we sail to my homeland of Meb'Garshur."

Julian remembered that name. That was the place where all those orcs had come from to attack Cardinia when Mordred set loose the Phantom Pinas.

"Excuse me," said Randy, like he was dissatisfied with his

current facial bone structure.

Faldor, surprisingly, did not immediately punch him in the face. Instead, he responded very cordially. "Yes?"

"You said *those of us who remain aboard this ship*. Does that mean that some of us ain't staying aboard?"

"Excellent question," said Faldor, – CRACK! – just before punching Randy in the face.

Randy, like Denise before him, slumped forward unconscious.

Faldor licked a bit of blood from his knuckles. "Does anyone else have a question?"

Those who weren't dumbstruck with fear shook their heads.

"Very good. To answer this gentleman's question, some of you will board one of the captain's two other ships, on which you will be taken to different destinations in accordance to your talents." He glanced dismissively at Chaz. "Or lack thereof. First, I would like all the spellcasters to make themselves known."

Was this a trick? Speaking thus far had proven to be an invitation to get punched in the face. Of course, not answering his question might yield similar results, but nobody wanted to volunteer to be the first to find out.

"I pray you do not test my patience," said Faldor as he scanned the cargo hold. His gaze met Chaz's once again.

"Okay!" cried Chaz. "I'm a spellcaster! Please don't hit me!"

"Wizard or sorcerer?"

"What?"

Faldor's eyes smoldered like he was making a herculean effort not to punch Chaz in the face. "What manner of spellcaster are you?" He said slowly and deliberately. "A wizard or a sorcerer?"

Chaz gulped. "Neither. I'm a bard."

The other six sailors broke into hearty laughter. Even Faldor's eyes lightened as he smiled at Chaz, whose eyes were shut tight in anticipation of a punch in the face.

Instead, Faldor patted his cheek lightly. "That is good to know. Perhaps Captain Logan will have you dance for his men aboard *Seastalker*." He turned to the rest of the prisoners. "For the rest of you, I am seeking *real* spellcasters, specifically wizards and sorcerers."

"I'm a wizard," said Frank.

Julian turned to him. "Are you?" he asked before he could stop himself. It only occurred to him now that he'd never known what Frank's class was. He'd never seen Frank do any magic, or much of anything at all. As far as Julian knew, he was just... Frank.

"I'm an illusionist."

"How about that." Julian looked forward again to find Faldor approaching and glaring at him. "And I'm a sorcerer!" he said quickly, hoping that it would save him a punch in the face.

Faldor paused, as if still considering it, then other spellcasters started making themselves known. They were escorted individually out of the cargo hold, with three of Captain Logan's men accompanying each prisoner outside. It was a slow process, and Julian guessed it must have been close to noon by the time they took him.

The sun felt good on Julian's face when he stepped out onto the deck. Also comforting was the visual confirmation that Ravenus was alive and unharmed. Julian spotted him flapping angrily in a cage sitting on top of other cages which held the larger familiars and animal companions. The cages were roomier than Julian expected kennels on a ship to be. But they would be uncomfortably small for human-sized people, which he suspected was their actual purpose. Between all the shackles and cages Captain Logan had at the

# Critical Failures VIII

ready, Julian suspected this was not his first slaving rodeo.

"Julian!" Ravenus cried. "Where are you going?"

"Stay calm, Ravenus! Everything will be okay."

"Quiet!" shouted one of the three sailors accompanying Julian to the plank leading from Katherine's ship to the larger but shabbier-looking one anchored next to it.

"Will our familiars be coming with us?" Julian asked him.

"I said *quiet!*" He punched Julian hard in the gut. While Julian was doubled over in pain and trying not to throw up, he leaned over with him and whispered, "Your familiar will be on board with you to be used as a hostage to keep you in line."

"Thank you," Julian groaned.

The sailor pulled him upright, then pushed him toward the plank. "Go on. We haven't got all day."

The other two sailors caught him. One of them picked up an enormous set of black pliers that looked like they could easily crush Julian's knees. Is that what they were going to do? Cripple him so he couldn't get away?

"Hold this," said the other sailor, who Julian had forgotten was there until he felt a heavy metal ball being thrust into his gut. It was the size of a softball but felt heavier than a bowling ball. Attached to it was a length of chain.

The sailor who'd handed him the ball took the free end of the chain and hooked the last link on one of the links between Julian's wrist manacles.

The sailor with the pliers pinched the hook-link so that it couldn't come unhooked. "In case you get any funny ideas about trying to swim to freedom," he explained.

Julian was just grateful that the pliers weren't meant for him. He looked ahead at the one-foot-wide plank, slick with ocean spray.

"What if I accidentally slip and fall in?"

The man with the pliers shrugged. "Then I suppose Captain Logan won't make as much money. Please try to be careful."

Julian stepped onto the plank. The gentle sway of the boats on the water felt a lot less gentle with only a rickety old plank standing between him and certain death. He inched out sideways, sliding his feet rather than stepping properly, keeping as much surface area on the board as possible.

*Just imagine you're on a deserted eight-lane highway, walking along the centerline. Either side of you is perfectly solid asphalt, but it doesn't matter because the only part that's actually supporting you is this thin painted line.*

He was at the halfway point, the point of no return. Going the rest of the way would now be easier than going back, and significantly less likely to get him stabbed.

*You've got this, Julian. Inch by inch. You're doing great. Just a little bit –*

"Hurry it up!" shouted one of the sailors on the other ship waiting to receive him.

Julian's legs went wobbly, and his foot slipped. The massive highway in his imagination turned into this tightrope of a board he was standing on. Holding this stupid ball with both hands, he couldn't put his arms out to steady himself. He was going to fall. There was only one thing left to do. With the last of his balance, he turned to the sailors on the receiving end.

"Catch!" He hurled the ball toward them as hard as he could, but the chain connecting it to the chain between his wrists wasn't as long as he thought. The ball jerked him forward. It, as well as his own balls, came down hard on the plank.

Just as he was considering that a crushing underwater death might be preferable to the pain in his nuts, the laughing sailors grabbed the iron ball and dragged him the rest of the way aboard the ship that would be his prison for the remainder of this voyage.

The sailors yanked him to his feet, then shoved him

## Critical Failures VIII

toward the cargo hold of the larger ship, where they seated him among the other Whore's Head spellcasters. The space was larger than *Nightwind*'s cargo hold, but it was just as crowded, and a lot smellier.

Most of the other prisoners were indistinguishable from their captors, except that the evidence of the fights they'd been in was a lot fresher. Julian guessed that they were the former crew of this very ship. He might have asked, but they looked just as ready to punch him in the face as any of Logan's men.

"Which one of ye cock scabbards is in charge here?" asked an older pirate. "Me bladder's fit to burst."

One of Logan's sailors took a step toward the mouthy prisoner, but another one put his hand on his shoulder.

"Captain Longfellow is not to be harmed. Captain's orders."

The sailor shrugged at who Julian assumed was the former captain of this ship. "Then I suppose you'll just have to piss yourself."

His two friends chuckled.

"'Tis a shame," said Captain Longfellow. "I had rather hoped that yer sister could pull me cock out and let me hose her down." This elicited a frustrated scowl from the sailor, but the captain wasn't quite finished. "Again."

"Come on, Rashad," said one of the sailor's companions. "Ignore him. We have to get the next prisoner."

Rashad spat in Captain Longfellow's direction. "Fuck you, sea trash." He turned to follow the other two out of the cargo hold.

Captain Longfellow feigned shock. "Gods have mercy, lads! Did ye hear what he said to me?" He shouted after Rashad. "Tell me, son. Be that the same tongue ye lick yer mother's arse with?"

Rashad stopped. Julian knew a successful reverse-Diplomacy roll when he saw one, and Rashad was playing right into the captain's hand. Did this salty old sea dog actually have a plan to escape?

"Go on ahead," Rashad said to his two companions. "I'll be right up."

"Ignore him," the more reasonable one insisted again. "Captain Logan said –"

"You saw nothing. You heard nothing. I'll be right up."

The other two reluctantly continued up the stairs and let the hatch close behind them.

Rashad turned to Captain Longfelow. "My mother and sister are dead."

"Ye have me condolences. It be too bad they lived not long enough to see what a fine captain's bitch ye've become."

His men enjoyed a chuckle at that.

"Captain's bitch?" said Rashad, squatting down to stare Captain Longfellow in the eye. "You think I'm afraid of what Captain Logan will do to me if I hurt you? Do you know how my mother and sister died?"

"Me gut tells me they drowned in semen."

*CRACK!*

It was a swift but powerful jab to the face.

Rashad took a step back, looking satisfied with himself as he watched blood pour out of Captain Longfellow's nose. He jabbed himself in his bare chest. "*I killed them.*"

Captain Longfellow bowed his head. "I be most impressed."

Rashad shrugged and grinned. "I warned you, did I not. I told you I was not afraid of Captain Logan."

"No," said Longfellow. "I meant I was impressed that ye could produce enough semen to drown yer mother and sister. Me hat goes off to –"

*CRACK!*

Even as their captain spat out gobs of his own blood, his imprisoned crewmen laughed like they were patrons at a comedy club rather than prisoners in their own ship.

"You think this is funny?" said Rashad, getting visibly more agitated. "Keep laughing. You'll see! I'll kill him!" His loss of self-control was exactly what Longfellow was going for. Rashad was doing exactly as the captain wished. But as far as Julian could make out, those wishes involved little more than having Rashad beat the shit out of him.

"Did ye hear that, lads?" said Captain Longfellow. "Kill me, he says. With those dainty little hands."

His crew laughed louder.

CRACK!

Captain Longfellow spat out a tooth. "Yer sister could throw a better punch."

CRACK! Every punch was wilder and harder than the last, and Longfellow's face was starting to look like ground beef, but his crew kept laughing.

"And yes, I mean the dead one."

Rashad roared with anger and madness as he drove his fist forward with a punch that was sure to take the captain's head clean off.

WOOSH!

Captain Longfellow tilted his head sideways. Rashad's fist went straight past it, throwing him off balance. Longfellow wrapped the chain connecting his wrist manacles around Rashad's neck and pulled tightly, bringing Rashad's head to his own bleeding pulpy face.

Julian could only see Rashad's face, but he could tell by the look on it that Captain Longfellow had a mouthful of his right ear.

Rashad's screaming barely rose above the raucous laughter still coming from Longfellow's crew, but his companions still heard it from up on the deck. The hatch opened quickly, and they ran down the stairs and grabbed Rashad's legs. They tried to pull him away, but it was no use with Longfellow's chain around his neck. One of the sailors moved in closer to wrest the chain away but only got a punch in the nose for his trouble.

After a little more struggling and screaming, the confrontation was ended by Captain Longfellow. He yanked his head back as he removed the chain from Rashad's neck and shoved him away.

Rashad lay panting on the floor, blood gushing out of the hole in the side of his head where his ear used to be.

Captain Longfellow pulled the ear out of his mouth and grinned. His face was already covered in his own blood, but now his shirt was wet and sticky with Rashad's.

Julian stared at the ear as Longfellow wagged it playfully at its former owner. He couldn't believe how much ear Longfellow had bitten off. It was practically the whole thing. Not that he'd ever want to try, but Julian didn't think he could remove that much ear at once using a sharp knife, let alone his teeth.

"Hello?" said Captain Longfellow, holding Rashad's ear up to his mouth. "Can ye hear me? Why don't ye come back here and put yer cock in me mouth? Ask any of the lads here. I'll get it as stiff as yer late mother."

"You're dead, Longfellow!" cried Rashad as his companions dragged him up the stairs. "I'll cut you to pieces and make you watch while I feed them to dogs!"

"What's that ye say? Speak up, lad. I've only got three ears."

Longfellow's men continued laughing after the hatch closed again, but the Whore's Head crew sat in stunned silence.

"What be the matter with you lot? Ye look like ye just seen yer parents fucking."

Julian didn't know how much time they had before Logan's men returned, and he figured he should take this

# Critical Failures VIII

opportunity to talk with this tough-as-nails and batshit insane sea captain.

"That was very impressive," he said, using his Diplomacy skill to open the dialogue with a compliment. "The way you took that beating while you riled him up more and more. It was an amazing display of both toughness and manipulation. You were in complete control of that situation."

The captain gave Julian a bloody grin. "Yer pretty impressive yerself, elf."

Julian didn't know what prompted him to say that. He must have made a hell of a Diplomacy roll.

"Thank you. That's very kind of you."

"Not many a man can suck me cock from all the way across the room like that."

Longfellow's men laughed, and even Frank joined in with a small chuckle.

Julian ignored him. He needed more out of Captain Longfellow than playful banter.

"If you don't mind me asking, what's the next phase of your plan?"

"Plan?"

*Come on, Captain. Now's not the time to be coy. We don't know when Logan's men will come back.*

"Your escape plan. I thought maybe we could help."

Captain Longfellow shrugged. "There don't be much point in thinking up an escape plan until I get settled in whichever ship I'll be sailing in."

"You think they're going to move you?"

"Certainly. They moved you, did they not?"

"Yes, but –"

"Ye lot look like wizardly types. If I had three ships at me disposal and were of a mind to sell slaves, I'd be taking ye to Khalzhar. The tougher folks like ourselves I'd take to Meb'Garshur where they'd fetch more coin in the fighting pits."

"Then why wait?" said Julian. "Don't you want to reclaim your own ship?"

"Wipe the cocksnot out of yer eyes, lad. Did ye not just tell me how impressed ye was by me toughness and manipulation? This be no different. Ye take yer beatings and wait for the most opportune time to strike back. Even if we weren't locked in manacles, why would we try to take on three ships' worth of sailors when we can rest up a bit and fight only one undermanned crew?"

Julian's hopefulness started to fade.

"So that thing with the ear wasn't part of any larger plan?"

Captain Longfellow chuckled. "Ye cannot pick a lock with an ear, lad."

"Then why did you do it?"

"For a laugh. A long sea voyage stuck in a cargo hold can get a touch dull."

This guy was certifiably insane. Julian was torn between whether he was distressed or relieved that Longfellow would likely be moved to another ship. He was definitely someone he'd want to be on the same side of in a fight, but Julian couldn't be sure that the captain wouldn't spontaneously switch sides to whichever was losing just for the sheer pleasure of biting people's ears off.

Before Julian could think of any way to steer the conversation toward something useful, the hatch opened again. The footsteps that came down were heavy and slow. A pair of scorched leather boots were the first things Julian saw, followed by charred and tattered remains of pants. He figured it was probably a prisoner who had unwisely tried to put up a fight until he saw a scabbard hanging on the man's belt. His clothes looked like they might have been nice before he raked them over hot coals. When Julian saw his cold blue eyes peering out from his burned and blackened face, he realized who it was.

# Critical Failures VIII

*Captain Logan.*

Julian had caught a slight glimpse of him when he was brought aboard, but he was absolutely terrifying up close. Not only his disfigurement, which Julian felt bad for thinking was scary. That wasn't his fault, after all. But the icy stare with which he scanned the cargo hold. He was clearly still bitter about his brush with a horrible death.

"Top of the morning to ye, Captain," said Captain Longfellow. If he was fishing for another ear, he was out of luck. Most of Logan's had burned away. "To what do we owe the honor?"

Captain Logan limped toward him. "I understand you had a confrontation with one of my men."

"Ye needn't fret about that. 'Twas nothing I couldn't handle. Boys being boys, ye know."

"As a courtesy, captain to captain, I gave my men strict orders not to harm you."

"I expect he gets the message now," said Longfellow. "I gave him an earful."

A few of his crewmen laughed in solidarity with their captain, but most seemed apprehensive.

"So I saw," said Captain Logan. "As I'm sure you are aware, administering discipline aboard a ship is the captain's responsibility."

"As captain of the *Maiden's Voyage*, I accept that responsibility."

"You are captain of shit, Longfellow. You are a slave now, and you would do well to remember that. I have tried to be courteous, but an attack on one of my men cannot go unpunished."

"Yer going in dry, then? I'll try to relax."

"Rashad! Sinclair! Vizzo!"

Rashad's two companions ushered him down the stairs. The hatch closed behind them.

"Yes, Captain!" said the one who had warned Rashad not to hit Longfellow.

"Did you bring the knife?"

Rashad held up a small, unexceptional blade that looked like it had been left out in the sun after gutting fish. "Yes, Captain."

"Take what is yours," said Logan. "You two hold him down."

Captain Longfellow grinned with wild Charles Manson eyes and pink teeth as Sinclair and Vizzo cautiously approached him. He jerked his head forward and bit the air, causing them both to flinch.

"Be quick about it!" demanded Logan.

The two sailors nodded to each other, then jumped Longfellow, pinning him down by the arms but keeping their faces away while he snarled and spat blood at them.

Rashad straddled Longfellow's chest and held his head down by the hair.

As tough as he was, Captain Longfellow couldn't hold back his howls and screams as Rashad dug into the side of his head with that dull, rusty blade.

His crewmen lowered their heads. The Whore's Head crew shut their eyes and grimaced. Julian felt like he was on the verge of throwing up.

The screams seemed to go on forever. Rashad was clearly taking more time than was necessary in order to inflict as much pain as possible.

"That is enough," Captain Logan finally said. "Finish it and get back to work."

With a couple of hard thrusts, Rashad successfully separated Longfellow's ear from his head. Julian didn't know how he did it, but he managed to get even more of the captain's ear than the captain had gotten of his.

*Oh. There it is.*

# Critical Failures VIII

Julian had discovered his tipping point. He bent over and threw up between his feet.

# CHAPTER 7

$\mathcal{T}$im had spent four excruciatingly sober hours trying to figure out a means of escape. The simplicity of their situation was what made it so difficult. They were surrounded by miles and miles of sweet fuck all, and their captors were better-equipped and mounted on horses.

Most frustrating of all was the fact that they weren't even shackled or tied up or anything. They were simply instructed to walk ahead of the horses and had no choice but to obey or be whipped.

Every half hour or so, Luglo would hose them down with the Decanter of Endless Water, more for his own amusement and to rub it in their faces than for their benefit. Still, Tim looked forward to those brief respites from the relentless desert sun.

"Welcome to your new home," said Luglo when the sand gave way to barren dirt. Wherever the hell they were didn't seem all that different from the desert. There were a couple of scraggly trees barely eking their existence out of the parched earth, but it still looked pretty fucking grim.

"What is this shithole?" asked Cooper.

"The land of our forefathers, half-orc. Our orcish blood has returned to Meb'Garshur."

Tim wasn't exactly sure how he wanted to play it, but that felt like fertile ground to at least plant a seed.

"Finally," he said. "I can't wait for your uncle to hear how we've been treated."

Cooper looked at him. "You know this guy's uncle?"

Tim sighed. "Goddammit."

Luglo laughed. "I admire your tenacity, halfling. Truly, I hope it will serve you well when we reach Olan Meb."

"What the fuck is Olan Meb?" Rather than wait for an answer, he followed with a question he gave much more of a shit about. "And how much farther is it?"

"You have never been to Meb'Garshur before, I take it?"

Tim surveyed the barren landscape around them. "Hardly seems believable that I've been depriving myself of all this beauty my whole life."

"There is more beauty than you know. Garshuri culture is rich and colorful. Olan Meb, the capital city to which we are headed, is a tapestry of the nation's long history."

"My dick is hard just thinking about it."

"Sadly, you will not see much from the dungeons beneath the fighting pits. But I expect your half-orc friend will get to experience one of their most exciting traditions firsthand... at least a few times."

Cooper farted nervously, agitating the horses. "Will I have to sing in front of people?"

"Jesus, Cooper," said Tim. "He means you're going to be fighting in the arena, like in *Gladiator*."

"Sweet!"

Oslof chuckled.

"You have a healthy attitude, half-orc," said Luglo. "Mayhap you will survive training after all."

Tim glared back at him as he continued limping deeper into the non-fertile desert. "You didn't answer my other question."

"At this pace, we should be there by morning."

That wasn't so bad. The sun was setting, and Tim's mind was exhausted from trying to figure out how to escape these two assholes. Even if he and Cooper were being sold into slavery, they'd at least be done with this part of the journey. The sooner they got settled into their new routine, the sooner he could start seeking out patterns, spotting weaknesses to exploit, Gathering Information, and developing a plan to escape.

Morning was the best possible time to arrive. There would be details he'd want to note on his way into the city, outside the arena, and just outside the cells that he might only get one shot at observing before they were incarcerated. A well-rested mind was imperative for spotting the finer details that would later aid him in his escape.

"Great," he said. "So when do we set up camp?"

"I beg your pardon? *Set up camp?*"

Was that not a common turn of phrase in this world, or was this guy just retarded?

"Yeah, set up camp," Tim repeated. "You know, rest. Get some shuteye. Turn in for the night. Hit the hay."

"Your sleeping arrangements are a matter you may discuss with Zimbra after Oslof and I get paid."

"I call bottom bunk," said Cooper. "Just as a matter of courtesy. My farts tend to be denser than air, so you'd be better off if –"

"Wait just a goddamn minute," said Tim, stopping in his tracks and turning around. "Do you mean to say that you're planning to march us through the entire fucking night?"

Luglo shrugged. "How else shall we reach Olan Meb by morning?"

"We've been walking for hours through the desert." Tim kicked dirt with his disfigured foot. "I'm missing half of my fucking foot! We can't keep this pace up all night."

"You have my deepest sympathies," said Luglo. "But we have not the resources to look after prisoners and sleep at the same time."

"Well, maybe you should have thought about that before

you took on the responsibility. We didn't ask to be taken prisoner."

Luglo removed a thick wool cloak from one of his saddlebags and wrapped it around himself. "Fear not, little friend, for the desert grows cold in the night. You would not rest easily in such meager clothing anyway. I expect your pace will only increase as the temperature drops and your desire for warmth outweighs your desire for rest."

"I can carry you if you want," said Cooper. "No offense, but you're slow as shit."

"Fuck you. Maybe I'd have a little more pep in my step if you hadn't cut my goddamn foot off."

"I am afraid I cannot allow that," said Luglo. "These horses were bred for long journeys, but I do not wish to make them suffer unnecessarily by pushing them too hard."

Tim shook his head in disbelief. "How fucking humane of you."

Luglo smiled. "Your mind is sharp, halfling. Sharp things can be dangerous if used impulsively. It would do you well to dull it before entering the city, lest you hurt yourself."

So that was it. The evil son of a bitch was marching them to the brink of exhaustion on purpose. Out here in the desert, there was nowhere to run or hide. But once they reached the city, they could make a break for it.

Tim had been out-assholed, and he knew it. He turned around and continued limping forward. The only hope he had now was that he might have more resolve in him than Luglo estimated, hope for a lucky series of Fortitude saves against exhaustion. That hope would diminish with every second he wasted arguing about it.

*Luglo. Oslof. Luglo. Oslof.* Tim repeated their names to himself over and over again. When he broke out of whatever shithole dungeon these two were bringing him to, he would hunt their asses down and march them across the entire

Fertile fucking Desert until they died of exposure.

He could already feel the temperature dropping, or was it his blood turning cold as he fantasized about what other horrors he could put these motherfuckers through?

Nope. Definitely the temperature. It was dropping faster than Hans Gruber from Nakatomi Plaza. After an hour, Tim was considering walking behind Cooper to warm his hands in fart.

*No, Tim. Use this time. Embrace the suffering. Remember it. Just like everyone else, these two assholes want to break you. You've been eating shit all your life, but that's not who you are anymore.*

Unfortunately, there wasn't a whole lot of specific planning he could do without knowing the finer details of what their situation would be, so he whiled away most of the night with more revenge fantasies.

The faster he forced himself to walk, the warmer he felt. But as soon as he slowed down just a little bit, his sweat chilled him down to his bones. On the bright side, he was wide awake when the worst of the cold had come and gone, but that was only because he was still freezing his ass off. This wasn't going to last. When the temperature started to get bearable again, that's when the real exhaustion would set in.

*Fucking assholes.* Tim trembled with further frustration as he admitted to himself that he admired how truly and utterly they'd fucked him and Cooper over.

With every degree the temperature rose, Tim's vision grew blurrier as his eyelids grew heavier. That exhaustion he'd predicted wasn't fucking around. He finally decided he couldn't take anymore. Fuck these guys. If they wanted him to keep going, they could carry him, or drag him, or whatever. He didn't give a shit. Dropping to his knees, he relished the thought of his face hitting the dirt and the long deep sleep that would follow.

*SNAP!*

## Critical Failures VIII

His throat constricted as a leather cord coiled tightly around his neck. Oslof's horse whinnied loudly as it reared up, and his whip lifted Tim off the ground. He instinctively landed back on his feet.

"Do not give up now, halfling," said Luglo. "We are nearly there. Look." He pointed at the horizon ahead of them.

Tim's eyes were once again wide open thanks to the not-often-celebrated benefits of being strangled. There was an unrecognizable smudge of something in the distance, but he couldn't make out any distinct shape in the morning haze.

"What am I looking at?" he croaked.

"That is where you shall spend the remainder of your life, my friend. That is Olan Meb."

# CHAPTER 8

Stacy woke up suddenly in complete darkness, stifled by the warm, stuffy air. A rough thick fabric was pressing against her face. She must have been captured and stuffed in a bag. It was a testament to how tired she was that she could have slept through something like that.

Doing her best to stay calm, she prodded different parts of her body to see if she'd sustained any injuries. As far as she could tell, she was completely unharmed. What's more, she still had her weapons, none of which had even been hidden in her boots. What kind of incompetent kidnapper would bag her without even bothering to take her weapons away.

*Dolazar!*

Stacy didn't know how she'd found her, but it fit her MO. She was more of a constant pest than the criminal mastermind she liked to think she was. This time it would cost her. Stacy wasn't sure how yet, but she had to put her foot down. Dave would probably be gone by the time she made her way back to that alley. It was going to be a major pain in the ass to track him down again. She hated to have to resort to violence, but this needed to stop. It would be best for both of them in the long run. Stacy wouldn't keep getting captured and inconvenienced, and Dolazar would learn to stop harassing people who were clearly smarter than she was.

The first thing Stacy needed to do was get out of this bag. Her dagger punched through the fabric easily. When she'd sawed open a hole big enough to fit her hands through, she tore it wide enough to escape.

Wherever she was, it was pouring down rain. Though it smelled of rotting animal carcasses and garbage, the cool morning air felt good in her lungs, at least compared to the recycled air she'd been breathing inside that...

She was still on the roof. She hadn't been stuffed in a bag at all. The fabric she'd just cut a hole through was a hemp blanket. Where the hell had that come from?

Looking around, she spotted an elderly dwarven woman sitting at the little wooden table on the other side of the roof, staring at her stoically over a steaming cup.

"Hello," was all Stacy could think to say.

"My late husband weaved that blanket forty years ago."

Stacy already felt embarrassed enough for cutting her way out of a blanket after mentally calling Dolazar stupid. This only heaped guilt on top of that.

"I'm so sorry," she said. "I thought I was trapped in a bag."

The old woman nodded. "I shan't pretend to fathom what horrors you've suffered for you to immediately jump to such a conclusion. You whores have a rough life, so I am led to understand."

"I'm not..." Stacy reconsidered correcting her. It would save her from having to explain what she was doing on this roof. "...going to argue with that."

"Come out of the rain. Have some coffee." The old woman poured hot brown liquid into a second cup.

"Thank you," said Stacy. "That's very kind of you." She walked under the tarp and sat down in the chair opposite the dwarf woman. "My name's Stacy."

"Ingrid," said the old woman.

Stacy opened her coin purse. "Let me pay you for the damage I did to your blanket."

"Save your whore money. I shudder to think of what unspeakable acts you performed to earn it. The blanket will stitch up easily enough."

"Thanks." Stacy choked back the urge to set this woman straight. She sipped her coffee and was surprised to find that it tasted like... well, coffee. It didn't live up to the café au lait she used to enjoy at the Mockingbird Cafe during her lunch breaks in Bay St. Louis, but it could hold its own against a higher end gas station coffee. "Are you by any chance from... *somewhere else?*"

Ingrid grinned, showing off what remained of her five teeth. "Most folks wouldn't pick up on a Greystone accent, especially since I've lived here in Cardinia for over two hundred years. But I suppose you meet a lot of sailors from different parts of the world in your line of work."

Stacy sighed. "Sure do."

"I don't suppose you know where your kin hail from."

Stacy shrugged. "Nope. I can only assume I come from a big ol' line of whores."

The wrinkles in Ingrid's face realigned as she frowned. "Such a shame."

That was enough of that. Time to change the subject.

"So," said Stacy. "Coffee is a normal thing in this world, I take it?"

Ingrid placed her ancient hand on top of Stacy's. "Our worlds are not as different as they seem, dear. I was not born into this life of luxury and privilege, you know. I've raised twenty-three children, and I had to work hard to keep them all fed. Mind you, I never sucked cock for coin, but –"

Stacy jerked her hand away to keep from breaking Ingrid's. "Sorry. I have, um... personal space issues."

*No! Why did I say that? She's totally going to –*

"Been slapped around a few times, have you?" Ingrid scowled and shook her head. "These animals drop a couple of copper pieces in your purse, and they think that gives them the right to shove their whole fist up your –"

# Critical Failures VIII

"YEP!" said Stacy. "That's right. Disgusting animals." *Segue! Segue! Segue!* "Speaking of animals, did you happen to hear any strange noises coming from the alley over there before I woke up?"

"Can't say that I did. Of course, my hearing isn't what it used to be. You worried about some other girl moving in on your alley?"

*Goddammit, lady! Is there anything I can say that doesn't come back around to me being a whore? Also, a couple of copper pieces? At least the cop had me pegged in the silver piece range.*

"No." Stacy faked a laugh. "I just thought I heard something. I must have been dreaming." There was no point in trying to salvage any of her reputation with this lady now. She might as well get some useful information out of her if she could. "Do you know anything about..." She paused, barely able to believe what she was about to say. "...*lycanthropy*?"

Ingrid gasped predictably. "Dear child! You must have at least a little self-respect. A pretty young whore like you can surely be more selective about who she lets pump their wicked seed inside her."

*Pump their wicked seed inside me? Really?*

"Yeah well, let's just assume that ship has sailed. Where would one go to get that... *sorted out?*"

Ingrid gave her a stern look as she refilled both their cups. "The life or death of a child is a matter for the gods to determine. A mother's place is to raise it as well as she can so it won't make the same mistakes she made."

*Wow! Just... wow.* That was a whole can of worms Stacy had not meant to step in.

"I'm not pregnant," she said curtly. "I was referring to the lycanthropy."

"Oh." Ingrid took a sip from her coffee cup. "The curse can only be lifted by a cleric of great faith and favor with the gods."

"So, what? I need to go to a church or something?"

"The Temple of Life is home to clerics of sufficient faith. I pray there every Seventh Day."

"How very pious of you." Stacy looked down into her coffee as she sipped, hoping that avoiding eye contact might dampen the sarcastic tone she'd let slip out, but she knew the damage was done.

"It will require a rather sizable donation to the temple." Ingrid's tone was cold and flat. "More sizable, I'm afraid, than a woman of *modest means* is likely to be able to afford."

"I'll see what I can scrape together."

"They will expect to be paid in coin. Not..." Ingrid finished her thought with a jerking off gesture.

Stacy gasped. That was all she could take.

"Listen to me, you gross old bitch. You think you're so pious and holy. Have you ever heard of, *Judge not, lest ye be judged?*"

Ingrid's eyes widened in terror, then narrowed in confusion. "No."

"Well, I've got news for you. I'm *not* a whore, I *don't* have lycanthropy, and I know well enough not to waltz into a temple and try to suck dicks for divine favors."

Ingrid gave her a smoldering glare. "I covered you in the rain. I shared my coffee with you. I tried to set you on the right path. And you dare speak to me in such a way?"

"You called me a whore, like, eighty-seven times."

"I think you should leave now." Tears were welling up in the old woman's eyes. She genuinely believed Stacy was treating her unfairly.

Maybe she had been. She couldn't believe she actually felt guilty. She'd lost her temper a bit, but had she really said anything hurtful enough to warrant... The *gross old bitch* thing might have crossed the line a little.

Suck it up, Stacy. Apologize and be on your way.

# Critical Failures VIII

"I'm really so–"

"YEEEEEEOOOOOOOOOOW!" cried Dave from down in the alley.

"Game on!" said Stacy as she ran to the wall and climbed over the side, then pulled herself back up. "Thanks for the coffee!" She braced herself for a hard landing in a garbage pile, then let go.

# CHAPTER 9

*Oh God! What's that smell?*

Dave had woken up in some godawful places before, including the Chicken Hut bathroom. At least twice he'd drifted off to sleep while sitting on the toilet and once while kneeling in front of it. Thankfully, Cooper only had photographic evidence of the latter. But he'd never woken up completely buried in... Jesus, he didn't even know. Was it rotting meat? Spoiled eggs?

He waved his arms above him and swam out of the pile of filth. Sitting up, he breathed in air that was merely really disgusting. He breathed deeply as he scanned his surroundings.

*Where... the fuck... am –*

"Ungghhh," he said aloud. The smell was no longer distracting him from the pain in the back of his head. "My fucking head."

He crawled out of the trash pile he'd been buried under, then turned around to look back at it. There was no way that garbage had accidentally fallen on him. He'd been deliberately buried alive.

Who would have done that? His first thought was Frank, Tony the Elf, and Rhonda when he remembered them making him dig his own grave. But they meant to kill him. If they had buried him under this trash pile, they would have made sure he was dead first. Besides, how would they know to find him in this alley?

# Critical Failures VIII

He could also rule out that masturbating hobo. He'd been beating the shit out of Dave, but he was talking to that Kingsguard when Dave got clobbered in the back of the head. Maybe it was a different giant hobo taking advantage of Dave's distraction. Looking around, Dave discovered that all of his possessions were missing. This had all the signs of a straight-up mugging. Not too far-fetched, really. Hanging out in alleys at that time of night, he was pretty much asking for it.

The mugger notices him watching the commotion down the street and strikes him in the back of the head. He steals all his shit, but sees that there's a cop not too far away. He quickly buries Dave's unconscious body under a pile of trash so it won't be discovered, then fucks off. Pretty cut and dried, unless...

Was it possible that Stacy had followed him? No way. The stupid bitch had high stats, sure. But she wasn't a gamer. She didn't know the ins and outs of how to use those stats and skills effectively. Dave smiled to himself in spite of the throbbing pain in his head. She was probably just waking up to find the splooge stain he'd left for her on the wall.

What would she do then? Would she lick it with that sassy tongue of hers? Would she scoop it up in her hands and rub it all over those perfect tits?

"I've got more where that came from," Dave whispered as his dwarf dick quickly stiffened. He pulled down the tattered remains of his pants and started priming the pump. "You won't be so chatty with a mouthful of Dave, you dirty cunt. When I'm done with you, you'll look like Peter Venkman after he got slimed."

Dave stopped tugging his wang.

*Okay, that was fucked up. Not the imagery that we want to... Jesus, Dave! What the hell is wrong with you? You're, like, twenty feet away from a street in broad daylight. And you've got to get your* shit together and figure out your next move. Then again, nothing clears a head like a couple of empty balls. Go further back in the alley, fire off a quick one, then get to thinking.

He resumed tugging as he waddled deeper into the –

"YEEEEEEOOOOOOOOOOW!"

Something long and pointy had penetrated deep into the sole of his right foot. He fell over and felt another in his left ass cheek and one more just below the shoulder.

He willed himself not to cry out anymore as he extracted whatever the fuck he'd just stepped on from his foot.

A goddamn caltrop? What the hell was this doing in an alley? Were these hobos really that territorial about their jerk-off spots?

And why did it hurt so bad? Sure, it should have stung a little, but – Dave noticed the caltrop's unbloodied tips glinting in the sliver of sunlight that dared venture this deep into the alley.

"Silver?"

*CRASH!*

Something behind him sounded like a body falling into a garbage pile. He didn't even have to turn around.

"Shit."

"Good morning, Dave," said Stacy. "You bailed on me last night, just when I thought we were starting to – Oh my God. Why aren't you wearing any pants?"

Dave sat up and covered his junk with both hands. He was still erect, and Stacy was glaring daggers at him.

"Really, Dave?" she said. "*Again?*"

*Again? What did again mean? Had she... Oh my God, no!*

"Again?" said Dave, feigning ignorance to see if maybe she was talking about something else.

Stacy looked away. "I mean, I assume you've done... *that* before. Everybody does it, right?"

She'd totally seen him last night, but she was willing to let it go and pretend she hadn't. That was the best he could hope for at this point.

"I didn't think anyone else was around."

"Well, tie a knot in it or whatever, and get your pants on. I've had a rough fucking start to the day."

Dave realized she had him over a barrel here, but he had to draw a line somewhere for how long she got to play the victim card.

"*You've* had a rough start to the day?" he said. "I just woke up buried under a pile of festering garbage, and I've got a hole in my foot the size of a fucking subway tunnel!"

"You brought that all on yourself. None of that would be the case if you hadn't tried to escape last night. I, on the other hand, through no provocation of my own, have been called a whore to my face more times than most whores are called that in a lifetime."

*So she's not letting me off the hook after all.*

Dave sighed. "I thought you were sleeping."

Stacy made a face like she might throw up. "Oh God, Dave! Can we just not? Let's pretend last night never happened and never speak of it again."

"But I thought –"

"I was talking about something else. Now, shut your mouth and put on your fucking pants."

Dave started to pull up his pants again, but then something happened. A switch flipped. Here in this filthy alley, half naked in the presence of someone who was better than him in every conceivable way in this world or their own, with his wilting dick in his hands, Dave suddenly came to terms with just how far he'd fallen and started to cry.

It was a whimper at first, like the initial cracks in a dam, But the dam burst wide open, and he was full on ugly crying. Great gulping sobs like the Cowardly Lion as tears streamed down his grimy face and snot ran freely into his thick mustache.

Stacy sighed. "Why are you crying, Dave?"

"AH... DNN'T... KNMMM!" He knew it was incomprehensible, but she was just going to have to give him some time.

Something soft landed in his lap. Tears blurred his vision, but he recognized it as the pouch the caltrops had come in.

"I don't have a tissue," said Stacy. "That's the cleanest thing I've got on me."

"I'm... so... sorry," Dave finally blurted out when he could control himself enough to form the words. "I don't know what's wrong with me."

Stacy squatted down in front of him. "What do you mean?"

"Last night. I don't know why I did that, why I said those things. That isn't me." He thought about how he was just about to jerk off in this alley. "I mean, it didn't use to be."

Stacy smiled at him. "I know that."

"You *don't* know," said Dave. "I only stopped where I did last night because I knew you could kick my ass. If you weren't so strong, you don't want to know what I would have done to you. *I* don't even want to know what I would have done to you."

Her smile faltered. "I've got something of an idea."

"You should have killed me. I feel like shit about all that because I was caught. But I can still feel the urges inside me. I'm not going to stop."

"That's why I'm here, Dave. We'll get you through this."

"You don't fucking get it, Stacy! You think you can solve everyone's problems with your southern girl charm and sass, but there are some things you can't solve with fucking sweet tea and cornbread."

"What the fuck are you even talking about now? I've literally, never in my life, offered anyone sweet tea and cornbread."

"It's a figure of speech."

"No, it really isn't."

"My wiring is fried," said Dave, jabbing his finger into his temple. "I'm talking some seriously fucked-up Ted Bundy level shit. It's not going to go away. You need to kill me right now." He turned away from her, sat down on a moldy crate, and closed his eyes. "Just bash my head in with a brick or something. Make it quick. Oh, and make sure you stab me a bunch of times to make sure I'm really dead."

"I'm not going to kill you, Dave. We're going to go to the Temple of Life and get your curse removed."

That sounded an awful lot like gay conversion therapy.

Dave turned around and opened his eyes. "You want to pray the rat out of me?"

Stacy put her hands on her hips and gave him a don't-start-that-shit look. "You're more familiar with this game than I am. You know that a high enough level cleric can remove your curse just as easily as you can heal someone's wounds."

"Stop calling it a curse," said Dave. "And I don't *want* it removed."

"You were just ready to let me kill you! Doesn't getting cured seem like the better option?"

"Leaving me the fuck alone seems like the better option."

"That's not on the table." Stacy pulled a heavy steel pipe out of her bag. "I'm not going to kill you, but I will take you up on that offer to let me bash your head in again if I have to. I felt a little bad about it last night. But the longer you keep arguing with me in this alley, the more I'll enjoy it this time. Now, are you going to come with me to the temple voluntarily, or do I have to carry you there?"

Dave didn't believe for a second that Stacy felt bad

about clobbering him over the head last night, but he believed her with every fiber of his being that she would enjoy doing it again.

"Fine," he said. "Let's go pray my gay away."

# CHAPTER 10

*K*atherine woke to the sound of rushing water.
*Did I fall asleep in the bath? It's cold. Fucking Tim used up all the hot water again. Oh no! Is the bathtub overflowing? Water damage! My security deposit!*

Panicked, she opened her eyes. A wolf was staring at her. Her grasp on reality shifted back into place, and she breathed out a sigh of relief.

"Hey, Butterbean. Looks like I dozed off."

She turned to look at Nazere, but it wasn't there. Nothing but open ocean stretched out in every direction. Looking down, she saw the water flowing past the ship's rear. They were sailing.

"Shit! How long was I out?" She thought about asking Butterbean, but she'd already blown most of her spells for the day. Besides, she didn't know if Butterbean would even be familiar with standard time measurements.

It didn't matter. She was awake now, and obviously hadn't been discovered. What she needed to focus on was how to keep this ship from reaching its destination.

The most obvious solution was to slap her Portable Hole on the hull like she did last time. But the circumstances were different now. She could cripple the ship, but then what? She didn't have another ship to escape to.

Still, slowing down the ship might buy her time to think of something better. She played back the events in her head, trying to pinpoint the moment this plan would cease to be effective.

Step 1: Use the Portable Hole to flood the ship. Wait for panic to ensue.

Step 2: Show up on deck and issue demands. There was the chance that they would call her bluff, given that they were all on the same ship, but maybe she could convince them she was willing to face death if she explained the significance of the magic die. Hell, maybe she could even convince herself of that. Or maybe not. It's a brainstorm. Keep going with it.

Step 3: Remove the Portable Hole from the hull.

Step 4: This is where she might gain some leverage. Now that the ship was no longer taking on water, they'd double cross her again and jump in the water after her. But this time, instead of turning into a giant bat, she'd turn into a shark and kill them all. Even if they didn't all jump in after her, she might take out enough so that she and her friends could handle the –

*Oh shit. My friends are probably down in the cargo hold. I drowned them all in Step 1.*

She hoped Captain Logan hadn't been transporting any slaves last time she was aboard.

Next idea.

She could try to *Die Hard* her way through the ship, staying out of sight and taking out the crew one by one. No, that would count on way too many things going exactly how she needed them to. Even if she could catch them all individually – which she couldn't – she'd have to be able to take them in a fight without suffering too much damage – which she also couldn't. And how many could she hope to kill before the others started noticing that the crew was starting to thin out? They'd implement a buddy system, and then her plan would be fucked.

Next.

It was so frustrating that she had so many allies on board the ship with her, but she wasn't able to free them – or even

# Critical Failures VIII

communicate with them – without revealing herself to the crew. Her *Die Hard* plan seemed even stupider now. *Seastalker* was a decent-sized ship, but she had every confidence that she'd be spotted immediately if she dared open this alcove door.

But what was the alternative? Sit here on her ass until another pirate needed a private place to rub one out? No. Sooner or later, she would have to go through that door. Unless...

Katherine looked down at the alcove floor and wondered what was directly below her. She reached into her Bag of Holding.

"Portable Hole." When she felt the silky square of cloth in her hand, she pulled it out of the bag and spread it flat on the wooden floorboards.

"Aaaauuuuuggghhh!" said someone below her.

"What is that?"

"My fucking eyes!"

Katherine crouched down like a cat and peered into the hole at different angles until she could make out a face.

"Who are you?" asked the face squinting up at her. His voice sounded familiar. Was it someone from the Whore's Head? No! The face and voice clicked in her head. It was Captain Longfellow's first mate.

"Alexei!" said Katherine. "It's me, Katherine."

"Katherine?" said a handful of much more familiar voices. They quickly shushed each other.

"How did you get here?" asked another familiar voice from outside Katherine's extremely limited line of sight. She recognized it as Fritz, the little guy who'd been so gung-ho about digging trenches on the beach. "We thought you were still on the island."

Katherine laughed. "While my crew ditched me? Fat chance."

"Did you take over the ship?" asked Tony the Elf.

"No, but I killed one of the crew."

"Oh." He actually sounded disappointed.

"Give me a fucking break. It's just me and Butterbean up here."

"Do you have a plan to rescue us?" asked Fritz.

"I'm working on it. Can any of you get out of those chains?"

"We've tried. Not even any of the rogues could get out. They've got us locked down pretty good."

"Would I be able to set you free if I came down there?"

"I don't know how, but we might be able to figure something out."

Katherine thought about it for a moment. She was bound to have something useful in her Bag of Holding. At any rate, hiding down in the hold felt a lot safer than hiding up here. Well, perhaps not *safer*, necessarily. But there was comfort in being among friends. If there was a way out of this, she definitely liked her odds of discovering it with help over any of the shitty ideas she'd already come up with on her own. "Good enough. I'm coming down."

Alexei shook his head. "The cargo door is up at the bow. You'll never get to it without being seen."

Katherine smiled. "I'm not planning to go through the door." She twisted her Bag of Holding and squeezed the bottom through the Portable Hole. "Can you reach this?"

"No," said Alexei, his voice muffled by the bag. "I can't stand up. They have us chained to our seats."

That would be a problem. Katherine could only stuff the bag about halfway through the hole and still be able to open the mouth wide enough to get into. If the bottom of the bag wasn't heavy enough to pull the rest of it through, she'd suffocate while hanging like a ceiling scrotum.

She pulled the bag out of the hole and put her hand inside.

# Critical Failures VIII

"Scythe."

After pulling the weapon out, she peered back down into the hole. "I'm going to lower my scythe down to you," she said to Alexei. "And then I'll shove the Bag of Holding halfway in and get inside it. If it gets stuck, I'll need you to whack it until it comes loose." She paused until the stifled giggles stopped. "Make sure you hit it with the handle so you don't tear the bag. Can you do that?"

Alexei nodded.

Katherine got the scythe in down to the blade, but couldn't get it all the way through. No matter how she angled it or tried to force it, it stubbornly refused to go through the hole.

"Shit," she said, pulling the scythe back out. "This isn't working." She put the scythe back in the bag and tried to think of what else she had in there that she could use instead. The only thing she could think of was Tanner's dead body. If she cut his arm off at the shoulder, it might be able to –

*No, Katherine. You're not cutting Tanner's fucking arm off. Focus your thoughts on something more useful.*

"Cloak." When she felt the thick wool in her hand, she pulled out her big black Grim Reaper cloak. It was a tight squeeze through the Portable Hole, but she managed to shove it through.

"What am I supposed to do with this?" asked Alexei, spreading the cloak over his knees.

"Twist it around and see if you can swat up to the ceiling with it."

Alexei tried a few swats with the limited range of motion his manacles allowed for. Some were closer to the ceiling than others. None gave her a whole lot of confidence about Alexei's ability to dislodge a stuck Bag of Holding, but it was either this or the *Die Hard* plan.

She stuffed the bag back into the hole as low as she could, then spread the mouth wide enough for her to squeeze into.

"You first," she said to Butterbean.

Butterbean obediently stepped into the bag without so much as a whimper.

Katherine considered jumping in, thinking that might force the bag all the way through, but quickly reconsidered. The inside of the bag had no bottom for her to hit, and she'd probably only end up hurting herself.

Instead, she eased herself in feet first and tried to pull the rim of the bag closed as she slipped inside.

The familiar weightlessness reminded her that she'd probably spent more time in this goddamn bag since she vowed never to get in it again than before she'd made the vow. The only light came from a single enchanted stone, faintly illuminating her floating possessions like a tiny sun in a fucked-up solar system.

"You okay, Butterbean?"

Butterbean responded with a sharp bark as he somersaulted twenty yards to her left.

Poor Tanner floated lifelessly at the center of the void. His black skin would have been nearly invisible against the surrounding darkness if it wasn't covered in mud.

She was going to bring him back, and this time they'd both know she was doing it for him.

Staring at a dead body suspended in darkness wasn't an ideal set of circumstances to be in when she suddenly felt a hand grab her ankle. Before she knew what she was doing, she'd kicked Alexei in the face.

"Shit. Sorry about that," said Katherine as she picked herself up off the wet cargo hold floor. She reached into the Bag of Holding. "Butterbean."

Butterbean spilled out of the bag and sniffed the putrid air.

It stunk something fierce down here. Most of these poor bastards had probably pissed themselves.

# Critical Failures VIII

"It's good to see you again," said Tony the Elf. "I didn't think I ever would."

He looked like shit. Everyone did. They were all looking at her with hope in their eyes, as if she was some miracle-working goddess come down to save them. The light shining down on her from the Portable Hole probably fed that effect.

She thought back to the indoctrinated slaves she and her landing party had slaughtered on the beach of Nazere, and how rotten leadership felt then. It felt even worse now with everyone looking to her for an answer and her not having shit to give them.

"They divided us up," said Fritz. "All the warrior types on one ship, spellcasters on another. We're the leftovers."

Katherine nodded. "Where's Chaz?" There was nobody she could think of who was more of a leftover than him.

"They took him up on deck to entertain the crew."

That seemed like something she should be able to leverage, but she had no idea how. She didn't know what to do at all. The thing with the Bag of Holding and Portable Hole had seemed pretty cool, but it only led to another brick wall.

"Listen, guys," she said. "I don't know what to –"

A loud grinding of gears cut her off as a sliver of light appeared in the ceiling at the front of the cargo hold.

"Somebody's coming!" whispered Alexei. "Get back in the bag, and I'll shove it back under my seat."

Katherine shook her head. "We don't know how long they'll be down here, and I've only got ten minutes' worth of air in there."

"That's ten more minutes than you'll have if they find you down here."

"Then they better not find me." Katherine took her cloak back from him and wrapped it around herself. "This should keep me and Butterbean concealed well enough if nobody knows to look for us." She lay on the floor and rolled under the seats on the starboard side of the ship, then opened her cloak for Butterbean to join her. It was hard to believe the stench of piss could be any more overpowering than it was when she first emerged from the Bag of Holding into the cargo hold a moment ago. But now that the source of the smell was sloshing around right in front of her nose, it was like being trapped in a turned over Porta Potty at the end of a concert in the middle of summer.

When everyone put their feet back down, she opened the hood just enough to peek out from it. She didn't feel as well-hidden as she'd expected.

"Put your cocks away," growled a voice from above. "It's feeding time. I hope you animals like raw shark meat. It's a few days past its prime, but it smells a lot better than you sorry lot of pissbags. Take a chunk and pass it down the – What in the Seven Hells?"

*Shit!*

She and Butterbean had already been discovered. The *Die Hard* plan seemed infinitely stupider now that it was the only option she had left, especially while she was lying in a piss puddle.

"Where is that light coming from?" His heavy footsteps went past Katherine to the rear of the cargo hold. "How did that hole get there?"

"It was always there," said Alexei.

*SMACK!*

The sound was unmistakable. Poor Alexei got another blow to the face.

"Don't you lie to me, you cockswallowing son of a sea whore!" This pirate may have sailed under Captain Longfellow in the past.

"He's not lying," said Tony the Elf. "That hole has been there since we were brought down here. Look at it. It's perfectly square. It's obviously a deliberate design. Maybe it was a secret peep hole or something. There's probably a square chunk of wood sitting up there next to it."

"We shall see about that." The footsteps returned to the front of the cargo hold. "Enjoy your supper."

*SPLAT!*

Chunks of shark meat splattered on the floor right next to Katherine's face. It smelled even worse than she remembered, as if all those rotting fish on the beach were soaked in cat piss.

*Don't throw up. Don't throw up. Don't throw up.*

She held her breath until she heard the cargo door cranking back down. Then she threw up.

When she'd heaved out as much as she was going to, she let go of Butterbean, then rolled out after him.

"We need to get the fuck out of here."

"No argument here," said Tony the Elf. "Do you have any ideas as to how we might do that?"

Katherine thought about it. "I guess Butterbean and I could just jump the next person who comes down here. Did you see if that guy was carrying a key?"

"No."

"No, he wasn't carrying a key? Or no, you didn't look to see if he was?"

"He wasn't carrying a key. There would be no point for him to. I guarantee you the keys to these manacles are either on the captain or in his cabin."

"Maybe I could sneak up to the cabin at night."

Tony the Elf shrugged. "Yeah, maybe." He didn't sound very optimistic. She kept her *Die Hard* idea to herself while she tried to think of something else.

"There it is," said the pirate who had brought down the shark meat. His voice came from up on the alcove at the ship's rear. "Do you remember that being there before?"

"Can't say that I have," said a second voice. "And where did all this blood come from? It looks fresh."

The cargo hold darkened as someone's face leaned close to the hole.

Katherine knew that she was well out of visual range, but she took a step back anyway and crouched down to keep Butterbean calm.

"You know what this looks like to me?" said the second pirate with his face right up next to the hole.

"What's that?" asked the first.

"It looks like someone's been peeping in on the folks down in the hold whilst he tickles his tackle."

"Bosley?"

"Of course it's fucking Bosley. Who else?"

Finally, a little bit of a break. If these guys assumed Bosley was perving at captives, the hole wasn't any real cause for alarm.

"Where is Bosley, anyway?" asked the first pirate. "I ain't seen him since we set sail."

"Don't question the gods when your sails are full of wind."

The first pirate laughed. "He ain't that bad. He's good for a laugh, anyway."

"Not so much since the captain served him up in a bag to that bat whore."

*Bat whore?*

"She didn't leave him any choice. We'd all have drowned if he hadn't given that cunt of a flying rat what she wanted."

*Cunt of a flying rat?*

"Rationalize it all you like. If he'd sell out one of us, he'd sell out any other. I, for one, will be seeking a new ship to sail on once we reach a proper – Moser, take a look at this."

"What is it now?" asked Moser, the pirate who'd brought down the shark meat, as he joined his shipmate down closer to the Portable Hole. "Is one of them slapping his mackerel?"

"No. Feel the edge of this hole."

Fingers poked down into the cargo hold, caressing the

edge of the hole.

"Feels like your sister's cunt," said Moser. "What of it?"

"It's perfectly smooth. What kind of blade cuts a hole like this?"

*Who gives a shit about the hole? Go swab the fucking deck or something.*

"Mercy of the gods!" said the second pirate. "Do you know what this is?"

*No! No! No! No! No!*

"It's a Po–"

The darkness and silence were sudden and absolute. Katherine spoke just to make sure she could still hear.

"Shit."

# CHAPTER 11

"How long was I out?" asked Rhonda, lying on the bed opposite his Her wrists and ankles bound with rope, she looked like a trussed Thanksgiving turkey. She and Julian had been paired as bunkmates in one of the *Maiden Voyage*'s lower cabins.

Julian peered at the small porthole on the door, looking for some indication of how much time had passed. All he could see was rain.

"I don't know. A couple hours maybe."

Rhonda looked like she'd be punching through the walls if her wrists weren't tied together. "How can people treat other people this way?"

"Just be happy that you're able to sleep."

As far as being held prisoner was concerned, Julian didn't feel like they were being treated that badly. It would have been nice to be able to move his arms and legs, but at least they got a cot to lie down on and they were out of the rain. From the shouting and swearing he could hear outside, it sounded like the crew was having a much worse time. Now that they were away from the other ships, Julian found comfort in feeling the mild annoyance coming through his Empathic Link with Ravenus, letting him know that his familiar was indeed aboard the ship with him.

The cabin door swung open. Cold rain pelted Julian's face as one of their captors stood in the doorway wielding a weapon in each hand. He was short and lean for a half-orc, but

## Critical Failures VIII

not someone that Julian would ever want to get in a fight with.

Julian made an attempt to use his Diplomacy skill. "Hello, sir."

"Shut up!" said the half-orc, then slammed the door shut behind him. "Supper time."

Now that he wasn't being blasted in the face with rain, Julian could get a clearer look at their visitor. What he'd initially mistaken for weapons were actually a pot of steamy liquid and a ladle. Under their present circumstances, those could still be very effectively weapons, so Julian did as he was instructed and shut up.

Rhonda, however, did not.

"You have no right to treat us like this!"

The half-orc stood silently for a moment, as if he was truly taking her words into consideration. Finally, he shook his head.

"No. *You* slave. *You* have no right."

Julian shrugged at Rhonda. The man had a valid point.

"You don't have to do this," said Rhonda. "Please let us go."

"Supper time. I have soup."

Now that the steam from the pot was filling the small room, it didn't smell half bad.

Rhonda kicked her bound feet. "I don't want your fucking soup!"

The half-orc nodded. "No soup." He turned around and opened the door.

"Wait!" cried Julian, but it was drowned out by another blast of wind and rain from outside. Then the door closed again. He scowled at Rhonda. "I would have liked some soup."

"Sorry for freaking out," she said. "But we need to get the hell out of here."

"Even if we could get out of these ropes, where would we

go? We're on the ocean. There's nowhere to escape to."

"We can take over the ship. Think about it. They didn't plan on sailing three ships last time they left port. They got greedy and spread themselves out thin. And if that guy was anything to go by, they're not the brightest bunch of knives in the shed."

"They don't have to be. They *have* all the knives."

"And we have all the brains. We're all wizards. We're the smart ones."

Julian sucked up his pride. "I'm actually more of a sorcerer now. I didn't have a high enough Intelligence score to cut it as a wizard."

"But you've been out there having adventures, right? I'll bet you have way better spells than me."

Julian nodded. "I've got some cool stuff."

"Of course you do. Imagine all of us with our magic against their tiny crew with their swords. It wouldn't even be a contest."

"Maybe not," said Julian. He held his bound wrists up. "But I'm guessing that's why they've got us tied up. We can't use magic if we can't move freely."

Rhonda shrugged. "We can get out of a little rope if we set our minds to it. Think about the three ships Captain Logan had at his disposal."

That wasn't the direction Julian thought she was heading toward. It intrigued him.

"What about them?" he asked.

"Why would he put the wizards on this junker?"

"This was Captain Longfellow's ship. I've seen him in action, and he's not a man you want to yield home field advantage to."

"The little black ship looked a lot faster," said Rhonda. "Why wouldn't they put us on that one? If I was transporting a bunch of spellcasters against their will, I'd want to get rid of them as soon as possible."

She was making arguably decent observations, but Julian didn't see them leading up to any kind of conclusion.

"What are you getting at?"

"Logan knows he's spread too thin. He's hedging his bets. Think about it like this. You've got a Ferrari, a Lamborghini, and a Ford Fiesta, and you've got to transport a shipment of gold, a shipment of diamonds, and a shipment of hand grenades. What do you put in each?"

Now he had a clearer idea of where she was going. "I guess I'd put the grenades in the Fiesta."

"Of course you would. Don't you see? *We're* the grenades! That's why we're in this piece of shit tugboat, with the most useless members of Logan's crew."

Now Julian thought she was jumping the gun a bit. "So maybe the soup guy wasn't firing on all cylinders. We can't count on the rest of the crew being as dumb as him. Besides, they're holding the familiars hostage. If we step out of line, they could kill Ravenus. I say we just ride it out and keep our eyes open for an opportunity when we get to wherever we're going."

"They're taking us there because we're spellcasters," said Rhonda. "That means that wherever we're going is well-equipped to deal with the challenges involved with keeping spellcasters captive, and you can bet your ass that will involve holding your bird hostage. If we get there, we're fucked."

Rhonda was making more sense than Julian wanted to admit.

"So how do we get out of these ropes?"

Rhonda smiled. "That's a good question."

"There are some spells that don't require you to be able to move, right?"

"Sure. Anything that doesn't require a somatic component."

That was more of a technical answer than Julian was looking for. "Do you know any that would be useful for getting us untied?"

"I can't think of any."

Julian sighed. "It's frustrating to not be able to cast a Mount spell."

"How would that help?" asked Rhonda. "We're on a ship."

"It's a more versatile spell than you might think. Maybe the horse could gnaw through the ropes or something."

Rhonda's eyes widened. "*We* could gnaw through the ropes."

Julian looked at her doubtfully. His own legs weren't flexible enough for him to pull his wrists to his mouth. He very much doubted her legs – nearly as thick as his waist – were any more flexible.

Rather than mention any of that, he opted instead to demonstrate. He pulled his wrists up as far as the rope attaching them to his ankles would allow, and stretched his neck down as far as it would go, but his teeth were still a good three or four inches away from being able to bite the rope.

"I meant we could bite each other's ropes," said Rhonda. "You roll off your cot, and I'll roll off mine facing the opposite way."

Julian wasn't sure he liked the imagery that brought to mind. "Why do we have to face opposite ways?"

"Because we won't be able to reach each other's wrists at the same time. If we each cut the other's ankle ropes, we could both get to work on our own wrist ropes."

It wasn't a bad idea. The only issue Julian took with it, aside from the possibility of being caught in a 69 position with Rhonda, was the chronology of the steps she'd laid out. What was the most Diplomatic way to ask her to roll off her cot first so that she didn't crush him?

*Just throw it out there casually without giving a reason.*

# Critical Failures VIII

"You go first."

*Shit! Why didn't I feign chivalry and say, 'After you?' Natural 1 for Diplomacy.*

Rhonda looked at him suspiciously. "Why?"

*Don't say, 'Because you're fat.' Don't say, 'Because you're fat.' Don't say, 'Because you're fat.'*

"In case there are spiders," Julian blurted out. It was as good a save as he could have hoped for on such short notice. "I'm really afraid of spiders. Would you mind checking under the cots for me?"

"Whatever." Rhonda rolled off her cot.

Julian cringed at the thud when she hit the floor, imagining all that weight coming down on his delicate elf bones. He scooted and shimmied until his head was on the opposite side of the cot, then rolled off. It wasn't a far fall before his face smashed into Rhonda's ass.

"Oomph," said Rhonda. "I wasn't expecting you so soon. I hadn't finished checking for spiders."

*Shit.*

They squirmed and struggled, groaned and grunted, until finally Julian felt some rope with his face. He got some between his teeth and bit down. It tasted like the rest of the ship smelled, like salt and fish, only more so. He could feel individual filaments breaking as he gnawed, but at the rate he was going, he wasn't confident that he'd be able to make any noticeable difference in however little time they had.

Rhonda, however, was going at his ankle ropes like a starved badger. She should have had some soup.

After feeling them yanked back and forth like they were stuck in a paint shaker, Julian's ankles were finally free.

He relaxed his exhausted jaw and lifted his head to look. Rhonda was breathing heavily.

"You did it!" said Julian.

Rhonda looked up at him, then her weary gaze shifted to

the rope binding her own ankles. "And you didn't do shit."

"I'm sorry. I was doing my best. My jaw isn't as strong as –" Julian heard footsteps approaching from outside. "Shit!" he whispered. "Somebody's coming."

"What do we do?" asked Rhonda.

"I don't know!" Julian had neither the time nor the Strength to lift Rhonda back onto her cot. Instead, he stood up on wobbly legs and pressed his back against the wall next to the door just before it creaked open.

"Last chance for soup," said the half-orc as he stepped into the cabin. "Still hot, if you feeling hung– Hey! Why you no in –"

Julian rushed shoulder-first into the door with everything he had. Unfortunately, the half-orc jumped out of the way in time, and Julian fell to his knees.

The half-orc's confused expression turned into a glare, then he raised his ladle to swat Julian. Julian swung his bound wrists up against the bottom of the soup pot, splashing hot soup into the half-orc's face.

"Aaaauuuggghhh!" he cried as he dropped the ladle and pot and covered his face with both hands, leaving his crotch wide open.

Julian felt bad about it, but he had to do what needed to be done. He drove his foot straight up into the half-orc's balls as hard as he could.

The half-orc doubled over and cradled his balls. Julian picked up the soup pot and brought it down hard on the back of his head, knocking him out cold.

"Hit him again!" said Rhonda. "Hurry!"

Julian looked at the half-orc knocked out at his feet, then at the pot in his hands. "He's unconscious."

"He's not going to stay that way forever, and he's going to be really pissed off when he wakes up."

"I can't just kill a defenseless guy in cold blood," said Julian. "He was nice. I mean, who gives prisoners a second chance at soup?"

The soup smelled really good. Too bad it was splattered all over the room.

"Julian," said Rhonda. "We've got a whole ship's worth of pirates to deal with. We have to take advantage of every opportunity we get."

"We can tie him up."

"*We're* still tied up!"

Julian grinned at her. "Not for long." He knelt next to the half-orc to relieve him of his weapon. A cursory scan, then a more thorough pat down revealed that he was unarmed. "What kind of pirate doesn't carry a sword? Or at least a dagger in his boot or something?"

He settled for the next best thing, shoving his right hand into the half-orc's open mouth and really hoping he didn't choose now to regain consciousness.

Rhonda sighed. "What are you doing?"

"Taking advantage of every opportunity," said Julian as he scraped his wrist rope back and forth against the half-orc's jagged teeth. Their natural sharpness and the half-orc's personal lack of dental hygiene made for a nice abrasive surface, and he was able to saw through his own ropes much more quickly than he'd been able to chew through Rhonda's. Finally, he was completely free. He held his hands up and apart to show Rhonda.

"That's great," she said. "But what about me?"

"Got it covered. You might want to scoot back a bit." When Rhonda scooted against the back wall, Julian pointed at the floor between them. "Horse!"

"Julian!" cried Rhonda when the cabin suddenly became a lot more crowded. "What the hell?"

While keeping one hand on the horse's brown fur to keep it calm, Julian climbed onto his cot to get a better look at Rhonda. "This was the plan, remember?"

"It was an idea for a plan," said Rhonda. "Not a good one."
"Just try to get your ropes in her mouth."
"I can barely move! She's not chewing them."
"Hang on. I've got an idea."
"Oh great. I hope it's another fucking horse."

Julian crawled under the horse and scooped up some soup off the floor. Squeezing past his cot and the horse's front leg, he rubbed his soupy hands on the rope that held Rhonda's ankles and wrists together.

"There you go, Penelope," he said soothingly. "Yummy soup rope."

"You named her?"

Julian put his hands gently on the horse's face and guided her mouth down to the rope. She gave it a couple of sniffs, then a lick, then started gnawing on it. Her teeth weren't sharp, but they were strong and good at grinding. Even at his awkward angle, Julian could see the rope starting to fray.

"I can't believe this is actually working," said Rhonda. "This is literally one of the dumbest ideas I've ever heard of."

Julian shrugged. "People don't give horses enough credit."

When the rope finally snapped, Rhonda stretched her arms and legs out. "Oh, my back! That feels so much better." She smiled up at the horse and cradled her muzzle with her hands as she gently guided her wrist rope into her mouth. "Thank you, Penelope."

Even with no soup on the rope, Penelope started gnawing again. She must have liked the feel of it.

"Good girl!" said Julian when Rhonda's wrist rope snapped. He stroked Penelope's mane, then frowned down at Rhonda's ankles. "How are we going to do your feet?"

Rhonda sat down, then pulled her feet up about six inches off the floor. "Bring her head down here so –"

"Hey!" barked the half-orc, standing up and rubbing the back of his head. "Where horse come –"

## Critical Failures VIII

"NEEEEEIIIIIGGGHHHH!"

*CRASH!*

"WHAAAA!"

Before Julian had time to process what was happening, Penelope had kicked the half-orc through the door. He screamed as he flipped backwards over the ship's railing and splashed down into the water.

Julian didn't know whether to scold Penelope or thank her. He felt bad for that half-orc, but there wasn't anything he could –

"Julian!" snapped Rhonda. "My feet! Hurry up. Someone will have heard that." She lay on her back, pulled her feet up, and held the bottom of her robes tightly to her legs to keep her unmentionables covered.

Julian looked out at the pouring rain beyond the smashed open doorway. "Maybe they didn't. It's raining pretty –"

"Gully!" cried one of the crew. "Man overboard!"

"Shit!" Julian guided Rhonda's ankle rope into Penelope's mouth. "Hurry up, girl. Chew! Chew like the wind!"

Penelope could obviously sense something was wrong. She whinnied nervously and pulled away from the rope.

"What's going on in here?" demanded a bronze-skinned slightly overweight human man. "How did this horse get in –" He took a hoof hard in the face but managed to keep from flipping over the railing.

"Sorry!" said Julian. "They spook easily."

Half blind from his hoof wound, the man glared furiously with his good eye at Penelope and drew a scimitar.

"No!" cried Julian. "That was a natural reaction to a perceived threat. It's your responsibility to respect the –"

"NEEEEEIIIIIIIGG–" Penelope's equine shriek of agony was cut off with her sudden disappearance.

The crewman stood in the doorway, horse blood dripping from his blade, looking more confused by the sudden absence of horse than he'd been by its presence.

Julian felt an anger smoldering inside him but held on to enough presence of mind to keep himself from rushing unarmed at a pissed-off sword-wielding pirate. Instead, he pointed at the floor near the pirate's feet. "Grease!"

A thick coating of translucent white grease coated two thirds of the cabin floor as well as the walkway outside. The pirate slid backwards as the ship swayed in the storm. The vicious glare in his functional eye turned suddenly to panic. He dropped his scimitar as he made a desperate grab for the door frame but only ripped away a loosened chunk of wood before flipping over the railing.

"Get the sword!" cried Rhonda.

Julian held on to his cot with both hands, not wanting to suffer the same fate as the two people he'd just accidentally murdered, and stretched his leg out into the grease to try to pull the sword closer with his foot.

That grease was some slippery stuff. He slipped almost immediately, bumping the sword with his foot. It slid smoothly through the doorway and under the railing.

"Damn it!"

For what little consolation it was worth, he did manage to retrieve the soup pot and ladle. When he was safely out of the grease, he leaned against the wall next to Rhonda and held them up for her to see.

"What do you prefer? Pot or ladle?"

"Julian, my feet are still tied together!"

"Then it makes sense for you to have the more formidable weapon." He offered her the pot.

Rhonda snatched it out of his hand and gave him a look like she wanted to test it out on his face. "I can't cut a rope with a soup pot."

Julian glanced at his ladle. It wouldn't do much good

## Critical Failures VIII

either... Or would it?

"Maybe you don't need to," he said, then feverishly went to work scraping up grease with his ladle.

"I can't fight effectively hopping around with my feet tied together," said Rhonda. "Not even with this amazing weapon you've provided for –"

"What's all this noise?" shouted another approaching crewman. "Why is this door – OOOOOHHHHH!" He was little more than a swift blur as he slid past the doorway toward the front of the ship.

Rhonda banged her pot against the floor. "Julian! What are you doing? That grease isn't going to keep them out forever."

"I know. It doesn't have a very long spell duration, so we need to act fast." He took his ladle full of grease and dumped it carefully on Rhonda's left ankle. "Spread it around. Work it in there. Hurry, before it disappears."

She massaged the grease onto her leg and under the rope.

Julian grabbed the slippery rope as tightly as he could with one hand and pushed on the bottom of her bare foot with the other. "Come on, Rhonda! Pull!"

"Stop it!" she said as she tried to squirm away. "That tickles. Julian, seriously. I can't –"

SMACK!

When Julian shook off the kick in the face and opened his eyes again, he felt heavy rain pouring down on him and soaking through his clothes. He was looking at Rhonda through the busted door frame. She'd kicked him all the way out of the room. He was out on the walkway, his back against the railing.

"It worked!" said Rhonda, shaking her freed leg.

Julian gave her a thumbs up. "Awesome."

"A prisoner has escaped!" shouted one of the crew from near the front of the ship. It sounded like the same voice as the guy who'd slid past while Julian was greasing Rhonda's leg, but he hadn't gotten a good enough look at him to confirm it visually.

It didn't much matter. He was with four other guys, and they were all armed with swords in their right hands as they walked carefully toward him with their left hands on the railing.

Julian considered blocking their way with another horse, but he knew that wouldn't halt their progress long and couldn't bring himself to throw another one to the slaughter so soon anyway. A Grease spell would be equally ineffective, as they were already taking precautions against slipping. He hated to blow a Level 2 spell so early when he didn't know how many total pirates they were up against, but he thought it unlikely that he'd get another chance to net five at a time.

"WEB!"

The five approaching pirates were practically swimming in sticky white strands of magical goop, as if the entire male population of Japan had unloaded on them at once.

"Jesus," said Rhonda, joining him outside. She glanced down at his crotch, then back to the men struggling to free themselves from his Web. "What did you do to them?"

Julian grabbed the top rail and pulled himself up. "It's a Web spell."

"It looks like –"

"I know what it looks like. Come on. We've got to free the others while we have the chance. That Web won't hold them for long."

As if to demonstrate, the sword of the pirate closest to them burst out of the sticky mess.

Julian backed away, holding onto the rail as he moved toward the next cabin. But Rhonda charged toward the Webbed pirates.

"Rhonda!" cried Julian. "What are you doing? They're already busting loose!"

# Critical Failures VIII

"We can't free anyone if we can't cut their ropes."

The lead pirate poked his face out from the Web and sneered at Rhonda. "You'll look like this when we're done with –" A soup pot to the face shut him up.

Rhonda dropped the pot, grabbed his exposed sword arm with both hands, then bit down on his wrist.

Remembering what she'd done to his ankle rope, Julian did not envy that poor bastard one little bit.

He held out for a few seconds as he screamed in agony, but eventually dropped his sword. It landed with a loud clang on the deck and slid precariously close to the edge, but Rhonda stopped it with her foot.

She picked it up, as well as her soup pot, and scurried back toward Julian.

"Nicely done," said Julian.

Rhonda smiled. "Thanks."

By the time they got to the next cabin, four more pirates were approaching from the rear of the ship.

"Hold them off," said Rhonda, thrusting the pot handle into his hand.

"What the hell am I supposed to do with this?"

"The best you can. I need the sword to cut the ropes." She shouldered her way through the door.

Julian felt about as confident with a Diplomacy check as he did with a soup pot, which wasn't confident at all. But at least he could try it from a distance.

"Hello," he started.

The men's angry growls provided little evidence of the effectiveness of his Diplomacy roll.

Like the men struggling in the Web behind him, these men were approaching with swords in one hand and holding onto the railing with the other. The direction they were coming at him meant they had to hold their swords in their left hands. If they were right-handed, then maybe...

Julian tried to use Diplomacy on himself to believe that would make any difference. It didn't work.

"Listen, guys," he said, brandishing his pot as intimidatingly as he could while stepping cautiously backwards and trying to calculate how close they needed to get before he summoned a horse at them. "We don't need anymore bloodshed. Let's put down our weapons and talk this –"

"MAGIC MISSILE!"

A golden bolt of magical energy flew out of the cabin's open door, putting a scorching hole in the lead pirate's upper arm.

"OW!" he cried, then pulled the door shut. "Keep this closed until we deal with the elf." He and two of the others kept moving toward Julian while one stayed behind to keep his friends contained inside the cabin. Julian glanced back. The other five pirates were almost free from the Web spell. A horse just wasn't going to cut it.

Julian didn't want to use the nuclear option, especially aboard a wooden ship, and more especially when he was at the center of it, but he didn't see any other choice. It was raining pretty hard, so hopefully that would keep the whole ship from catching fire.

He closed his eyes, braced himself, and held up a single finger. "Fireball!"

"What?" said the unarmed pirate coming out of the Web. "NOOO–"

*WOOOOOOOOOSH!*

Having been Fireballed once before hadn't prepared him for it as well as he'd hoped. Getting caught at the epicenter of an exploding ball of flames still hurt like a son of a bitch.

It wasn't as bad as last time, though. He was still conscious, and his clothes weren't on fire.

The poor bastards who were still caught in the Web weren't so lucky. Magical jizz, as it turns out, is extremely flammable. Two of them jumped screaming into the water, while two others wrestled each other's flames out on the wet deck. The one who had been leading the group had troubles of his own, rolling around in the apparently also very flammable residue of Julian's Grease spell.

Julian had been correct in predicting the rain would keep the boat from catching fire. At least, it would have under normal circumstances. He and Rhonda were going to need different accommodations, because their former cabin was up in flames.

On his other side, none of the pirates had died or jumped overboard, but they were all severely burned. They still brandished their weapons but were no longer advancing. Julian could tell by the look in their eyes that most of the fight had been taken out of them.

"What the hell just happened?" asked Rhonda, peeking out from the now unattended cabin door.

"I cast Fireball," Julian said proudly.

"We're on a wooden ship in the middle of the ocean!" Her tone was more critical than Julian appreciated under the circumstances.

"That had occurred to me," Julian replied curtly over the sound of the man behind him still screaming in the Grease fire. He narrowed his eyes at the pirate closest to him. "I hope I won't be forced to use it again." It wasn't an empty threat. He had three more Level 3 spells at his disposal for the day, but he preferred not to have to blow up any more of the ship.

"Please," said the pirate in the lead, lowering his sword slowly and deliberately to the deck. "Accept our surrender." The others followed his lead.

Julian nodded. "Very well. Rhonda and whoever's in there with you, gather their weapons."

"NO!" shrieked a voice from above. "It is one elf! Can you cowards not handle a single elf?"

After pausing to make sure the crew wasn't going to have a sudden change of heart, Julian glanced upward and saw who he assumed to be the acting captain of the *Maiden's Voyage*. He was glaring down at Julian from the top cabin tier.

With most of the crew having surrendered, Julian felt that now was as good a time as any to issue demands, hoping they could proceed with no further violence. He hoped the flickering light from the flames would give him a bonus to his Diplomacy roll.

"I am no mere elf, sir!" Julian bellowed as forcefully as he could. "I am Julian, Sorcerer of..." *Come on, Julian. Something big and powerful sounding.* "...the Cosmos!" *Is that laying it on a little thick?*

The captain squinted down at him. "Sorcerer of the Cosmos? What is that? A title? A stage name?"

"It is how I am known far and wide, a name that stirs fear within the hearts of kings." *Definitely laying it on too thick.* Even Rhonda and one of the surrendered crewmen stifled a snort. Julian shot them a disapproving glance.

"I've never heard of you," said the captain.

*Change course. Just move on with the demands.*

"I shall offer you one chance to avoid witnessing the full power of my wrath. If you surrender this ship to me and immediately set a course back to Nazere, I shall be merciful. You and your men need not spill another drop of your –"

*SNAP!*

*CRACK!*

*SNAP! SNAP! SNAP!*

*CRAAAAACK!*

*CRASH!*

"AAAUUUUUGGGGHHHH–"

The fire had burned through one of the ropes tied to the railing which was holding up the hastily repaired mainmast, which Captain Logan's giant water elemental had smashed.

## Critical Failures VIII

That led to a series of other shoddy repairs not holding up, until finally the entire network of mast, sails, and rigging came crashing down on the captain.

"Shit," said Julian. He turned to the surrendered crewmen. "Can you guys fix that?"

# CHAPTER 12

"Maybe if you stopped antagonizing them, they'd stop beatin' the snot out of you," Randy suggested to Captain Longfellow, who looked like he'd been run over by a caravan of eighteen wheelers.

Captain Longfellow's bleeding lips turned up at the corners as he stared back at Randy with the eye that was only half swollen shut. "Save yer cowardly advice for the land folk. This be the sea." He nodded toward the cargo hold door. "That big feller looked like he was about to crack, did he not?"

Randy shrugged. "That ain't the way I interpreted it. I reckon he was just getting exhausted from punching you so many times."

"Ye never know a man's breaking point 'til ye push him to it. Sooner or later one of those scabby-cocked sea-whores is bound to make a mistake, and I'll be ready. Now can ye heal me wounds, or do ye plan to talk me to death."

"Of course." Randy touched his shackled hand to Captain Longfellow's. "In the name of our Lord Jesus Christ, I heal you."

It wasn't a full heal, but at least Captain Longfellow could open both eyes again. "Aye, that be better. Many thanks."

"It's all I've got until tomorrow," said Randy. "Maybe you should take it easy until then."

"I can't say I agree with Randy all that often," said Denise, chained between two of Captain Longfellow's bigger men across from Randy and Longfellow. "And don't get me wrong.

# Critical Failures VIII

You getting the shit repeatedly kicked out of you has made the past three days fly by. I could watch that shit all day. But these folks got my baby up there, and I can't help but feel that we might be better off focusing on trying to think of a way to get out of these chains."

Captain Longfellow sneered at her. "We've all seen how well yer plans have worked, flashing yer hairy tits out and trying to swallow every cock that passes within ten feet of yer semen-craving lips."

"It ain't my fault the crew's all faggots." Denise looked up at the sailor chained to her right. "No offense, Gort."

Gort grimaced and pulled as far away from her as his chains would allow. "I love women. Just not *you*."

"That's a hurtful thing to say, man. I got feelings."

Randy needed to interject before Denise had a chance to further piss off their fellow captives. "I think what Denise was trying to say is –" He thought he heard a caw from outside. Listening closer, he was sure of it. "Birds?"

Denise squinted at Randy. "How the fuck did you get 'birds' out of what I just said?"

"No!" said Randy. "Listen!" He leaned back and concentrated. The caws were getting louder and more frequent. "You hear that?"

"Garshurian buzzards," said Captain Longfellow. "We be entering the Devil's Cunt."

"Oh." Randy frowned. "That sounds unpleasant."

"They feast upon the flesh of the dead whales and porpoises that wash up on the blood-stained beaches."

"Who's killing all them whales?"

"The stupid bastards do themselves in."

Randy felt like he had missed an important part of the story. "Are they part of some kind of religious cult? Or..."

"They swim into Tagrok Bay during the high tide," explained Captain Longfellow. "But when the tide falls, she falls fast. The whales get into a panic, all trying to leave at the same time. The less fortunate ones get their bellies sliced open on the jagged rocks at the mouth of the bay.

Randy caught a whiff of something in the air even fouler than the cocktail of body odor, pee, bad breath, and fart that he'd been smelling for three days.

"Is that what that smell is? Rotting whale corpses?"

Captain Longfellow nodded. "Aye. That and bird shite."

"That don't make no sense," said Denise. "Whales are fuckin' valuable, and hard as shit to catch. What was that book, Randy? The one about Captain Arab and his big dick?"

Captain Longfellow raised his eyebrows in interest.

"You mean *Moby Dick*?" asked Randy.

"That's the one."

"I ain't read it, but I don't think it was about the captain's dick."

"Jesus, Randy. Read between the fuckin' lines. It was written, like, three hundred years ago, at a time when you couldn't be so explicit about these things, so they used metaphors and symbolism and shit. Ask anyone today. They'll tell you straight up it was about a man trying to fuck a fat bitch, but she wouldn't give it up on account of him being an Arab."

"Did you read *Moby Dick*?"

"Fuck you, Randy! You're missing the goddamn point."

"I'm sorry," said Randy. "What was the point you was getting at?"

"Whales are valuable and hard to catch. If this place is a natural whale trap, it should be thriving. How do these fat fucks have time to rot? Why ain't folks picking their bones clean and exporting the meat?"

"The orcs of Meb' Garshur don't care for the taste of whale," said Captain Longfellow. "They much prefer the taste of buzzard. It be more practical as well. The meat from one whale carcass be but a drop in the sea compared to the meat of the thousands of buzzards it attracts. And the buzzards be easier to transport."

Randy thought of the big black buzzards on the side of the highway back home digging into some poor armadillo baking in the Mississippi summer heat. Imagining being hungry enough to eat one of those made his stomach turn.

"I suppose that's what we got to look forward to now. Maybe it ain't so bad if they cook it right."

Captain Longfellow grinned. "No self-respecting orc of Meb' Garshur will cook his buzzard."

"They eat it raw?"

"More times than not, they don't do it the mercy of killing it before tearing in. They say the bird's terror enhances the flavor."

"That's barbaric!"

The captain's men all shared a laugh.

"Did ye think this be some luxury cruise, pally?" said Captain Longfellow. "We're being sold to fight in the gladiator pits of Olan Meb. After a week of what they'll feed us, ye'll be begging for a taste of raw buzzard meat."

Randy wasn't sure why he'd been so excited to be nearing land, but Captain Longfellow had just taken the wind out of his sails.

He thought again, as he had many times over the course of this voyage, about summoning Basil. It felt like such an obvious solution, but there simply wasn't enough room in this already-cramped cargo hold for a basilisk. Basil would almost certainly tear the limbs off a few of the shackled crewmen he hadn't already crushed to death before Randy could calm him down.

The better part of an hour had passed when the cargo door creaked open, letting sunlight flood into the dim hold. Randy recognized Rashad and Unger, the two crewmen who'd been beating on Captain Longfellow most frequently over the past three days, by the sound of their boots on the steps. It seemed they wanted to get in one last beating before unloading their cargo.

"Welcome home, gentlemen," said Unger, the more talkative of the two, as he stepped down into view. While Rashad seemed to have a personal beef with the captain, Randy got the sense that Unger simply enjoyed making other people suffer. "Can you smell all that orc cock? Pretty soon, you'll be tasting it."

Randy instinctively turned to Captain Longfellow, but it was Denise who responded.

"Why don't you come over here and wet my whistle first?"

Unger's grimace matched the groans coming from the crewmen shackled to either side of Denise. Then he turned his attention back to Captain Longfellow.

"The winds blow at our backside. We should be unloading in Olan Meb by nightfall."

There was enough innuendo there for Randy to have to concentrate to avoid giggling, but Captain Longfellow didn't take the bait. He just sat there poker-faced, taking the announcement at face value.

Rashad cleared his throat. "The sails are nice and full." When this elicited no reaction, he continued. "Like a big pair of titties."

Still nothing from Captain Longfellow, but Unger gave him a disapproving shake of the head.

"Get a gander at these titties, sailor boy!" said Denise, opening her shirt to expose her milk-engorged breasts. "Squirt them with something warm and white, and I can return the favor."

"Mercy of the gods," said Rashad. "I feel I may be sick."

Unger sneered at Captain Longfellow. "Let us return to the deck, then. It reeks of cowardice and broken spirit down here." He spat on the captain, then led Rashad back up the steps to the deck.

When the cargo door closed behind them, Randy turned to Captain Longfellow. "You alright?"

"Aye, pally. Right as a ramrod up yer puckered arsehole, I am."

His crewmen shared an uneasy chuckle.

Randy wasn't sure exactly what that meant, but it sounded like the captain was back to his old self.

"I couldn't help but notice you was not as talkative as usual."

"There be another reason the orcs of Meb' Garshur like to keep their beaches littered with bird shit and rotting whale carcasses. It tends to keep most ships from sailing into the bay. The time for escaping has passed. Now it be wiser to conserve our strength. Once ye pass through the Devil's Cunt, there be no turning back."

# CHAPTER 13

"No, no, no," said the director, or choreographer, or whoever the fuck this guy running the show was. "More feeling! If you're going to sell this as an underdog victory, I need the terror to look genuine." He had a lot more swagger in his walk than Cooper would expect from a full-blooded orc. His spindly arms stretching out from his orange linen toga suggested that he'd gone heavy on Charisma and light on Strength.

Cooper and Tim stood at the edge of the pit in an open air arena. The tiered seating which circled above them was brown with streaks and stains from decades of rowdy audiences. The pristine pit floor, however, gleamed with a layer of powdery white desert sand.

About a quarter of the way around the arena, orcish foremen oversaw the construction of two towers that would stand over the arena's entrance. The laborers themselves, doing all the hammering and masonry, were a smaller race. They were too far away to identify from where Cooper was standing, but he guessed they were goblins.

Cooper and Tim's desert captors, Oslof and Luglo, stood on either side of them as they waited patiently for the orc to finish instructing the two gladiators at the center of the pit.

"Show me your best terrified look."

The smaller of the two gladiators made a face that struck Cooper more as wacky than terrified.

The director shook his head, then turned to the larger

man. "Let us try again. Only this time, I want you to actually stab him."

"WHAT?" cried the little guy.

"There it is!" said the director, backing away and clapping giddily. "That's the expression I'm looking for. Ready?"

The big guy shrugged.

"No!" said the little guy. "I thought *I* was supposed to be the winner."

"You *are*! It would be a poor fight indeed if you didn't try to defend yourself." The director snapped his fingers. "On my signal... Fight!"

Cooper had to hand it to the little guy. He'd really mastered that terrified look. At least until the big guy ran a sword through his belly.

"Stop!" said the director. "Good job with the expression. We shall have to work on the fighting. Take him away, will you?"

The big guy picked the little guy up and slung his bleeding, possibly dead, body over his shoulder, then carried him through a gate guarded by two goblins armed with spears.

The director turned around and strutted toward Cooper and Tim.

"Greetings, Zimbra," said Luglo, offering the director a low bow.

"Have you ever in your life seen a more droll performance? Mercy of the gods, some people cannot emote to save their own lives."

"The big one is strong. He wields a sword competently enough."

"I have stabbed day-old potatoes more passionately with a fork. What fine new talent have you brought me?" He looked disdainfully at Tim, then disgustedly at Cooper, waving his hand in front of his nose. "From what godsforsaken sewer did you dredge up these two specimens?"

"They were wandering in the Fertile Desert."

"You should have put an end to their misery. I'll give you a gold piece for the pair of them. The chimeras need to eat, after all." He grimaced at Cooper again. "Though I won't feel good about it. What have my sweet chimeras done to deserve such punishment?"

"Please," said Luglo. "If you would humor us, there is more to these two cretins than there appears."

Standing there listening to these guys insult him and Tim while they casually discussed feeding them to monsters was making Cooper gassy. He tried to let a small fart squeak out, but it erupted as loud as a trumpet signaling the next fight.

"Mercy of the gods!" cried Zimbra, his eyes watering. "More to them, indeed! Get these disgusting creatures out of my sight at once!"

"Shall we escort them to a cell?" asked Oslof, apparently still hoping to salvage that one gold piece offer.

Zimbra scowled at him. "I require fighters worthy of keeping the common folk distracted from the fruitless misery of their lives. Instead, you bring me a flatulent sack of bugbear shit and a crippled halfling. You can toss them in the tar pits on your way out of the city. And if you ever bring me fighters of such low quality again, it will be *you* I feed to my chimeras." He spun around and strutted away.

"We're lycanthropes!" Tim blurted out, not inspiring confidence in Cooper that he knew what he was doing.

Luglo slapped Tim hard in the back of the head.

"OW!" said Tim. "What the fuck, man?"

Zimbra stopped and turned to face them. "Lycanthropes, you say?"

Luglo smiled apologetically at him. "The little one speaks out of turn, but it is a habit I am sure your men can beat out of him."

"What sort of lycanthropes are you?" Zimbra asked Tim.

# Critical Failures VIII

Tim glanced nervously at Luglo.

Luglo slapped him in the head again. "Your new master asked you a question."

Tim raised his bound hands to give Luglo the finger. "Make up your fucking mind." He turned to Zimbra. "We're wererats."

The interest disappeared from Zimbra's face. "Oh."

"What's wrong with wererats?" Tim persisted, flinching in expectation of getting slapped in the head again, but Luglo evidently felt like Tim was doing a better job of selling himself than he'd been doing. "Wererats are cool."

Zimbra scoffed. "If the citizens of Olan Meb wish to see two rats fight to the death, they need only to look down any alley. Werewolves are fierce. Werebears are powerful. Weretigers are exotic. Wererats require as much extra security as any other lycanthrope, but are weak, sniveling cowards. Not very entertaining, I'm afraid. You have my condolences, but you are simply not worth the added effort and expense it would take to keep you."

"We're entertaining as fuck!" said Tim. "Go on, Coop. Make a crack about Luglo's mother."

"What?" Cooper wasn't sure these guys were in the market for a stand-up routine, nor was he sure that talking shit about Luglo's mother was in his own best interest.

"Come on," Tim pleaded. "They're going to kill us anyway. Might as well get in one last jab, right?"

Hopeless as it was, that made sense.

Cooper turned to Luglo, who was staring back at him, confused but not threatening.

"Uh..." Cooper didn't like being put on the spot like this. His mind was totally blank. "Your mother's so fat, um..." He farted again.

"I think I've seen enough," said Zimbra. "I've certainly smelled enough. Throw them in the tar pits."

Luglo bowed. "Very well, Zimbra. We apologize for wasting your time."

Cooper scanned the arena for somewhere to run to. The gate the last two gladiators exited through looked thick and solid. That made sense, considering it was made specifically for the purpose of keeping gladiators from running out of the arena.

"Wait!" shrieked Tim, pulling his shoulder out of Luglo's grip. "Don't you even want to see us fight? I mean, we're already here."

Cooper felt Tim might have a chance against a throwaway rookie gladiator, but it seemed like a pretty desperate request for him to make. Maybe he had some devastating new rogue skill up his sleeve. A Sneak Attack seemed unlikely to work well in a direct fight, and there wasn't anywhere Cooper could see for him to hide. Maybe Tim didn't have a plan at all, and a quick death by sword was simply preferable to suffocating in molten tar.

Zimbra grinned at Luglo. "The little one has spirit. I'll give him that." He sneered down at Tim. "You really want to fight?"

Tim nodded.

"Very well." Zimbra gestured to the center of the arena. "Fight."

Luglo and Oslof laughed as they cut the ropes binding Tim's and Cooper's fists, then shoved them forward.

Cooper and Tim exchanged a glance, then Tim turned to Zimbra.

"Each other?"

Zimbra smiled. "Entertain me, and whichever of you remains alive may stay and be trained. Bore me, and you shall both be thrown in the tar pits."

"What the fuck are we going to do?" Cooper whispered as he baby-stepped toward the center of the arena to match

Tim's hobbling pace.

Tim shrugged. "I guess we're going to fight."

"He was pretty clear about this being to the death, right?"

"Shut up," said Tim. "I'm trying to think."

As slowly as they were walking, the center of the arena was getting nearer at an alarming rate. Cooper didn't want to kill Tim. Hell, it wasn't long ago that he would have taken a bullet for him. But he wasn't about to die for him now. He was surprised at his own readiness to snap Tim's neck to save his own ass, and how little guilt he anticipated having for it after the fact. Probably best to keep those thoughts to himself.

"I've got it," Tim said when they were just a few paces away from the center. "He values entertainment over straight-up violence, right?"

"I kinda feel like he wants both of those things."

"Then that's what we'll give him. We'll talk some trash and pull some WWE moves. Piece of cake."

"We don't know how to do any WWE moves," said Cooper. "Those guys practice for fucking weeks."

They had reached the center.

Tim glared up at Cooper. "We don't have fucking weeks. We have right now. And besides, it's not like we've got a hell of a lot to lose."

Cooper shrugged. "*I* might." Judging by the angry look in Tim's eyes, he didn't need to elaborate.

"This is not very entertaining," shouted Zimbra. "Do you intend to fight, or continue staring longingly into each other's eyes all day?"

Cooper and Tim started circling each other slowly.

"So that's how it is," said Tim, his hair and face drenched with sweat. It was hot outside, so they were both sweating. But Tim was sweating like he was on trial at Nuremberg. "After all I've done for you, you're ready to just murder your best friend to save your own ass?"

"I don't *want* to, but..."

"Is that what you think I'd do if the tables were turned?"

Cooper considered Tim's recent history of abandoning his friends to save his own ass, some instances of which involving murder. "Well, I..."

Tim hopped on his good foot and weaved, throwing some quick practice jabs toward Cooper. "I've got news for you, fucko. Killing me isn't going to cut it. You've got to be entertaining, and you've got the Charisma of a dead hooker under a Motel 6 mattress."

"Enough stalling!" demanded Zimbra, drawing Cooper's attention away from Tim. "If you do not start fighting immediately, I shall –"

Cooper didn't catch the rest of that, but he did catch a fist in the balls. He doubled over in pain as his anxiety sprayed out of his ass.

"Goddammit, Cooper!" said Tim while Zimbra, Luglo, and Oslof quietly applauded.

Cooper turned back to see that Tim had rolled under his legs, and that his hair had caught the worst of his greenish-brown shart. "What the fuck did you expect? You punched me in the fucking nuts!"

Tim wiped shit and sweat from his face. "They were entertained. Let's keep going with that. Throw a punch at me."

Happy to oblige, Cooper stood up, then lunged fist-first at Tim.

"Take it easy, man!" said Tim after barely dodging the blow. "David and Goliath is what we're going for here, just like Zimbra wanted from those two guys before us. Westley and Fezzik. You telegraph your punches so I can easily dodge them, I do some fancy rolls out of the way, sucker punching you when I get the chance, then I hop on your back and put you in a choke hold until you pass out."

# Critical Failures VIII

Cooper took a couple more slow swings at Tim while he thought about what bugged him about that plan. "Zimbra said only one of us can go on to be a gladiator. If you're the winner, then I get thrown in the tar pits."

Tim shrugged. "Maybe. Or maybe we're both not entertaining enough and we both get thrown in the tar pits." He rolled away from Cooper's fist and drove an elbow into his hamstring.

"Fuck!" said Cooper as he dropped to one knee.

"Or *maybe*..." Tim whispered while Cooper was down low enough to hear him. "Maybe we put on such a good show that they decide to keep us both."

While Cooper considered that, Tim punched him hard in the snout.

"Motherfucker!" said Cooper, then grabbed Tim with both hands and lifted him above his head.

"Cooper! What are you doing?"

"I'm being entertaining. WWE style, just like you suggested. Power bomb, baby!"

"Wait! No! You don't know how to –"

THUD!

Cooper had thrown Tim down harder than he'd meant to. He also hadn't meant to slam him on the ground face-down. Their audience of three was clapping slightly more enthusiastically now, which provided at least a little consolation for having just killed Tim.

"Is he dead?" asked Zimbra.

Cooper looked down at Tim. "Dude, are you dead?"

Tim raised a shaky middle finger at him, then turned over. His face was completely white from the sand sticking to his sweat, except for the crimson smudge of blood on his nose.

Cooper snorted.

"What the fuck are you laughing at?" Tim honked.

"Sorry, man," said Cooper. "You look like a clown."

"Fuck you! That could have killed me."

Cooper stopped laughing as an idea occurred to him. "We could use that." He knelt over Tim, whose anger turned to terror.

"Cooper! What are you doing?"

"Hold still." Cooper ran a finger under Tim's bleeding nose and smeared the blood until it covered the rest of his nose. Then he made a little red blood circle on each of his cheeks. "They've clapped twice so far. Once when I shat on your head, and then when I power bombed you into the dirt."

"What does that have to do with you smearing blood all over my face?"

"I may have the low Charisma, but you're a mouthy little asshole." Before Tim could tell him to go fuck himself, Cooper continued. "I'm only saying this because our lives are on the line. It's a cruel world, and these are cruel times. People like to see midgets get thrown around. Especially if that midget is you."

"What are you doing?" demanded Zimbra. "Is the fight over or not?"

"Just a second," Cooper shouted back at him. "We're just getting started."

"Started with what?" whispered Tim. "I still don't understand what the fuck you're doing on top of me."

"We're playing up the clown thing." Cooper caressed Tim's shit-caked hair until it formed a nice Ed Grimley horn at the front. "Perfect."

"Perfect my ass!" said Tim. "What the hell are we going to do?"

Cooper stood up. "Just come at me. I'll take care of the rest."

"Mercy of the gods!" said Zimbra as Tim struggled to his feet. "What have you done to him?"

Oslof laughed. "He looks like a Tamuni whore."

# Critical Failures VIII

Cooper didn't know what a Tamuni whore was, or at least how that differed from a regular run-of-the-mill whore, but Luglo and Zimbra appeared to have picked up on the reference as they laughed at Tim.

Tim hopped at Cooper with his Tamuni whore eyes full of fury and his fist cocked back and ready to swing. He was doing a terrific job, as if this was the role he was born to play.

Waiting until the very last moment, Cooper stepped out of his path and swept Tim's good leg out from under him, planting him hard in the dirt again.

Zimbra laughed and clapped giddily. Luglo and Oslof followed his lead.

"You son of a bitch," said Tim as he pushed himself back up. "That fucking hurt."

"Dude. You're messing up your makeup. Try not to rub your face in the sand any more than you have to."

With a primal scream, Tim hopped at him before he was ready. With no time to think up a flashier move, Cooper settled for a quick jab in the face. To his credit, Tim made up for Cooper's lack of showmanship with a backflip before slamming face-down onto the ground.

"Bravo!" shouted Zimbra. "Absolutely marvelous!"

"Come on!" Cooper whispered to Tim. "Get up, man. They're eating this shit up."

Tim raised his bleeding face with a very convincing look of hate in his eyes. "Fuck... you."

For a moment, Cooper thought Tim had taken as much punishment as he was capable of. That was a shame, because Cooper was really starting to enjoy this. But when Tim took his hybrid rat-man form, Cooper understood. With the Damage Resistance that provided him, it was an open invitation for Cooper to take things up a notch.

Cooper gave him a wink and a thumbs up.

Tim snarled and screeched as he ran at Cooper with teeth

and claws bared. It wasn't the same effect without the makeup, but Cooper was confident they could compensate for that with an escalation in violence.

He let Tim come at him and caught him by the throat while Tim dug his claws into Cooper's upper arms.

"Hey, man," whispered Cooper as he throttled Tim's furry neck. "Take it easy with the claws. We're going to do a pile driver, all right?"

Tim's rat eyes widened with panic. He tried to say something, but all that came out were squeaks.

"Just follow my lead." Cooper swept an arm under Tim's legs and swung him around so that his tail was in Cooper's face. "Fantastic. Here we go."

Tim squealed as Cooper hopped and lifted his feet up to Tim's shoulders.

THUD!

The sandy ground hurt Cooper's ass more than he'd expected. That would probably get easier with time and practice.

Tim collapsed like a big limp dick.

"Spectacular!" cried Zimbra. He and the other two were clapping wildly.

Cooper got up and did half a victory lap around the far side of the arena, pumping his fists in the air triumphantly. He ended with a bow, then waved to the non-existent audience in the seats above.

When he looked back at Tim, Tim was still in his hybrid form, staring lividly back at him.

"Dude," said Cooper. "I think we're in. They fucking loved us."

Tim charged at him.

While Cooper had been satisfied to end on that high note, Tim clearly thought it wasn't quite enough. They would need to work on their communication for future performances. The

# Critical Failures VIII

pile driver had been really good, and he didn't know how they were going to top it.

The way Tim was running at him reminded Cooper of *Dirty Dancing*, if Jennifer Grey was a snarling rat monster. The climactic lift was a fine move for a movie about dancing, but not so much for a gladiator fight. It needed a little something more, and Cooper needed an extra Strength boost to pull it off.

"I'm really angry!" he said. His Barbarian Rage immediately started bubbling inside him.

Tim got cold feet at the very last second and turned to run away, but Cooper caught him by the tail.

He spun around and around, swinging Tim faster and faster, until everything but Tim was a pink blur.

"I'VE... HAD... THE TIME... OF... MY LIFE!" he shouted, then released Tim straight up in the air.

His mission complete, he shat his Rage out into a large greenish-brown puddle on the sand, then prepared to catch Tim.

But was that really how he wanted to end this performance? What if Jennifer Grey had been a snarling rat monster? Would it not make more sense for Patrick Swayze to –

*SPLAT!*

Tim hit Cooper's shit puddle like a runaway dump truck. That was the ending *Dirty Dancing* needed. Nobody would have seen that shit coming. Judging by the sound of his applause, Zimbra agreed.

# CHAPTER 14

"Greetings, Children of Rasha," said a portly man in white robes as Stacy followed Dave through the curtain of vines that served as the entrance to the Temple of Life. "My name is Brother Mayfair." He held out his hand, revealing a smooth brown sphere about the size of a golf ball. "Would you care to plant a Life Tree?"

"Not really," said Dave.

Not a great first impression. Stacy nudged Dave and smiled at Brother Mayfair. "Of course we would." She took the seed from the cleric's hand. "Where would you like us to plant it?"

"You walk on hallowed ground. You may plant the seed wherever Rasha's Spirit guides you."

Stacy scanned the temple grounds. Young trees with pale green almond-shaped leaves were growing at seemingly random spots among the long grass and wildflowers. Breathing in the fresh, nectar-scented air, she became suddenly self-aware of what she and Dave must have smelled like coming here from an alley full of garbage. They needed to hurry this along. One place looked as good as another as far as she was concerned.

After taking a moment to appear as though she was giving it proper consideration, she pointed to a patch of grass twenty feet away. "How about there? That looks nice."

Brother Mayfair smiled. "A fine choice." He and Dave followed her to the spot she'd picked.

## Critical Failures VIII

She looked for someone else planting a tree to see if there was some kind of protocol to follow, but it was a slow day at the Temple of Life.

"So, I just dig a hole and bury the seed?"

"You may say a prayer to Rasha if you like."

"That sounds like a fine idea," said Dave. "I mean, since you're such a devout follower."

Stacy shot him a slight scowl. He wasn't supposed to be enjoying this. She should have just buried the seed and been done with it. Now she had no choice but to say a prayer. Not doing so would make her look like a jerk.

She knelt in the grass and dug into the ground with her fingertips. It yielded easily, releasing a rich earthy aroma that reminded her of walking through the forest the day after a hard rain. While she tried to think up a nice prayer, she dug a larger hole than was probably necessary. When she felt she had something passable, she placed the seed at the bottom of the hole.

"Bless this seed, dear Rasha. Nurture it with the wholesomeness of this hallowed soil and the warmth of your holy light." Not sure if an Amen was appropriate, she left it at that and scooped the unearthed dirt back into the hole.

"That was truly lovely," said Brother Mayfair, holding out his hand again. This time, it was empty.

Stacy didn't want to get his hands or clerical robes dirty after she'd just been digging in the dirt, but neither did she want to be rude. She grabbed his hand and gave it a hearty shake.

"Thank you, sir."

His arm flopped in her grasp like a wet noodle as his eyes flickered with panic. When she let go, he relaxed, then smiled uncomfortably as he brushed the soil from his hand.

"A donation to the temple of ten gold pieces is customary when planting a Life Tree."

Dave snorted.

Stacy shot him a warning glare, then tried not to look as harsh when she turned to Brother Mayfair. "I was unaware of this custom." She pulled out her coin purse. It smelled like the alley she'd stashed Dave in and barely jingled with what little money she had left. "I think there might be six or seven gold pieces' worth of coins in here. I can give you that?" She could only read disappointment in his expression. "Or should I dig the seed up and give it back?"

That got a stronger reaction, but not one that she was going for.

Brother Mayfair's eyes were wide with shock. "Dare you not disturb the holy seed! Life begins when the seed is planted!"

That differed from Stacy's understanding of germination, but it wasn't a can of worms she wanted to open.

"I'm sorry. You might have told me up front about the donation. Not everybody walks around with that kind of money on them." She jingled her purse. "This is what I've got."

"You've got some goggles you could donate," said Dave. "Those are probably worth at least ten gold pieces."

"And you've got some teeth I might be donating if you don't keep your mouth shut."

"Please!" said Brother Mayfair. "Just give what you can afford and be on your way."

Stacy handed him the purse. He caught a whiff of it and gagged. She though he might yack for a second, but he quickly composed himself.

"We didn't actually come here to plant trees," Stacy said when he was over his initial revulsion. She nodded at Dave. "We're here for him."

Brother Mayfair looked down his nose at Dave. "Do you wish to be flagellated for your sins?"

# Critical Failures VIII

"Um... no."

"He's a wererat," said Stacy, figuring it was best to just cut to the chase.

Brother Mayfair looked even more disgusted. "I might have known as much by your foul stench! How dare you desecrate this holy ground with your foulness? Leave this place at once!"

"I didn't even want to come! *She* made me."

Brother Mayfair glared accusingly at Stacy.

"I hoped there was something you could do for him," said Stacy. "Isn't there a spell that can cure him of the disease?"

"Lycanthropy is no mere ailment of the flesh. It is a curse which corrupts the victim's very soul!"

Stacy appreciated the sense of gravity he was trying to instill in her with his dramatic inflections, but he hadn't answered her question.

"Okay," she said. "Do you have a spell for that?"

Brother Mayfair sighed. "A Remove Curse spell will require a donation of one thousand gold pieces."

"A thousand gold pieces?" cried Stacy. "That's outrageous. Where the..." She paused to run her question through a church-appropriate filter. "...*heck* are we supposed to get that kind of money?"

"That is between you and the gods."

"No, that's extortion, plain and simple. You said yourself he's a victim. If you can remove the curse but choose not to, that's on you. So don't give me any of that *the gods work in mysterious ways* mumbo jumbo."

"I give you no such *mumbo jumbo*," said Brother Mayfair. "The gods work in very straightforward ways. You donate one thousand gold pieces to the temple, and we remove the curse through their divine power."

Stacy tried sad puppy eyes. "But it's just a spell. It doesn't cost you anything. Isn't it part of your mission to remove evil from the world when you can?"

Brother Mayfair smiled. "While the gods' ways may not be mysterious, they sometimes require a bit beyond surface-level thought to understand. Tell me, child. How might you obtain such a large sum of money?"

Stacy shrugged. "I don't know. Get a job?"

"That seems inefficient. The fewer full moons that pass over your friend, the more likely the spell will rid him of his curse."

"Then what am I supposed to do?" asked Stacy. "Rob a bank?"

"The gods would surely frown upon coin obtained by such despicable means."

"Kill monsters," Dave said matter-of-factly.

Stacy glared at him. "Shut up, Dave. I'm doing this for you."

"The disgusting black-souled abomination has it right," said Brother Mayfair.

Dave sighed. "Thanks."

"Wait a second," said Stacy. "You're telling me you want us to go out and murder innocent creatures for money?"

Brother Mayfair shook his head. "Of course not. I want you to go forth and destroy *evil* creatures for the Goodness and Glory of Rasha."

'You can sugarcoat it any way you like. That's still murder for hire."

"If I were to cast the spell upon your friend now, I would be removing a tiny speck of evil from the world. How much more evil will be banished when you destroy enough of it to raise the requisite money, which will then of course be used in further pursuits of Good?"

Religion in this world was every bit as fucked up as it was back home. Stacy had one last card to play.

"We were sent here by Katherine. She's the one who

## Critical Failures VIII

retrieved some sort of lost artifact for the temple."

Brother Mayfair smiled. "They Eye of Rasha!" He gestured to a large golden statue behind a stone altar at the other side of the temple. "You are friends of Katherine?"

"Sure," said Stacy, then felt a little uncomfortable lying to a holy man. "Friends of friends. We travel in the same circles."

"We appreciate her efforts. She has done much to restore the balance of Light in the world."

Apparently her relationship with Katherine wasn't enough to sway him. That was a long shot, but it had been worth testing. She took one more step down that road.

"I was hoping you could give us some sort of quest like that. Maybe not so extreme or dangerous, considering we're not asking you to bring anyone back from the dead. But maybe... I don't know... A *toe* of Rasha or something?"

Brother Mayfair frowned. "You want a quest? Very well. There is something lesser than the Eye of Rasha that the temple is in need of."

Stacy sighed with relief. She hadn't actually thought that was going to work. "What is it?"

"One thousand gold pieces."

"Goddammit."

# CHAPTER 15

𝒯he darkness heightened Katherine's other senses, which relayed little to her brain but the overwhelming presence of panic and piss surrounding her.

She reached into her Bag of Holding. "Light stone."

When she pulled out the enchanted rock, bathing the inside of the cargo hold with light, everyone breathed a sigh of relief.

"They'll be curious about that hole," said Tony the Elf, as if he would explode if people around him felt any sense of reprieve for even a second. Unfortunately, he was right.

"Maybe their greed will get the better of them," said Fritz, the elf who had been so gung-ho about digging trenches in the beach on Nazere. Katherine wasn't sure, but he might have also been the one responsible for that weird dick weapon back at the Whore's Head Inn. "That's a valuable magic item. They might decide to keep it to themselves until they can sell it."

"That depends on their loyalty to Logan, and on how much of a security threat they determine it is that a Portable Hole suddenly appeared above the cargo hold where they've got all their prisoners chained."

Fritz shrugged. "Greed will usually win out over common sense."

"I'm not willing to bet my life on that," said Tony the Elf. "It's not like it changes our situation anyway. Whether they keep it to themselves or report it to Logan, we still need to get

# Critical Failures VIII

out of these chains and take over the ship. The farther from Hollin we are when we do, the better. If we make it to Hollin, and Logan gives Mordred that die –"

"Yeah, yeah," said Katherine. "We know the stakes. I don't think anyone here needs convincing to want to get out of these chains. What we need are ideas on how to go about doing that."

Tony the Elf's gaze dropped to the Bag of Holding. "Do you have anything in your bag we could use?"

Katherine shook her head. "I had a look while I was in there just now, hoping to see something I'd forgotten. There was this Light stone, a few pairs of jeans, a couple of weapons, dead Tanner, and a few other odds and ends. Nothing useful that I could see."

"What were the odds and ends? Maybe there's something in there that's useful in a way you didn't think of. We need *Apollo 13*-Ground-Control-specific inventory here. Empty the bag and let's see what you've got."

That seemed like such a waste of time, and Katherine didn't expect that spilling Tanner's corpse on the floor was likely to brighten anyone's day. Also, it was a little insulting to suggest that she'd somehow failed to identify all the practical applications for a black turtleneck with regard to unlocking manacles. If Tony the Elf wanted to get in the bag and have a look around, he was more than welcome to. But he wasn't exactly in a position to –

There it was. The solution had been right there in her hand this whole time.

"The Bag of Holding!" she said more loudly than she wanted to. She clapped her hand over her mouth.

Tony the Elf sighed. "Yes. That is the bag I was referring to. Do you have anything in your *Bag of Holding* that can help?"

"No!" said Katherine. "We can just use the bag itself." She held it open in front of him. "Put your hands inside."

Tony the Elf humored her, shoving his shackled arms into the bag up to his elbows.

Katherine reached in after him. "Manacles." She pulled out the manacles, which were still chained to the ones on either side of Tony the Elf, but they were empty.

Tony the Elf pulled his unchained hands out of the bag and gawked up at Katherine. "You're a goddamn genius."

Katherine smiled at him. "How is it you keep forgetting that?"

Everyone rattled their chains excitedly, wanting Katherine to release them next.

"Calm down," she said. "I'll get to all of you. But you need to keep quiet until I can –"

The loud grinding of rusty gears shut everyone up. The cargo door was opening. Katherine shoved her Light stone back into her bag as its light was replaced by the sunlight flooding in.

"Hurry!" whispered Tony the Elf. "Get under my legs."

Katherine looked down at his free hands. "What about your manacles?"

"Shit." He slid his hands under the chains. "If I don't call attention to myself, maybe they won't notice."

Following the same game plan that worked last time, Katherine rolled under Tony the Elf's seat to absorb piss from the other side of the ship into her cloak. After Butterbean crawled in with her, she pulled a dagger out of her Bag of Holding in case shit went down.

The elf at the back groaned and turned away, feigning a reaction to the sudden increase of light in the hold. Others followed his lead. Katherine nodded her approval. It was a nice touch.

"Stay here and keep an eye out," said Moser, presumably to the shipmate who was with him when he discovered the Portable Hole. "Close the hatch behind me."

# Critical Failures VIII

The hatch cranked shut again as he came down the steps, but the hold didn't go completely dark. He was carrying a small hooded lantern. It gave off about as much light as Katherine's stone, but the flicker of the flame caused shadows to dance all along the hold's inner walls. He waited for the hatch to close completely before he spoke. When he did finally speak, it was in a soft but menacing tone.

"You think you are clever, do you?" he said as he crept along the center aisle. Katherine couldn't see if he was talking to anyone in particular, but she got the sense he was speaking in the plural you. "Too bad for you, I am cleverer." His throaty laugh made Katherine want to throw up again. "What was the big idea? One of you smuggled a familiar down here? A little bird, mayhap? You got it to slap a Portable Hole in the ceiling and fly away to find help?"

He paused in case anyone wanted to answer, then laughed smugly at the utter silence. Katherine had to use every last bit of her Willpower to not point out the flaw in his "clever" theory. The Portable Hole was applied on the other side of the ceiling.

"That is what I thought," he continued. "You are pathetic. Nobody is coming to rescue you. We shall be in Hollin long before anyone can catch us. Now you've lost not only your pet, but your Portable Hole as well. You should have held on to a prize like that. You might have found a more opportune time to use it after we reach Hollin." He was getting closer now, and Katherine noticed Tony the Elf's calves tightening. "But I did not come down here to gloat. I came to give you sorry sacks a word of advice. As clever as you think you are, and as pathetic as you actually are, it occurs to me that you might try to curry favor with the captain by telling him I took the hole, hoping he might spare you. Let me tell you this. There is nothing Captain Logan despises more than a rat. You would be wise to keep your muzzles shut, lest you find yourselves longing for a sweet life of slavery."

Katherine smiled to herself. She'd spread enough of that same kind of covering-her-own-ass bullshit in life to know it when she smelled it.

*It only happened that one time, Deborah. If you tell Lisa I was making out with Spike, she'll blame you for their breakup every bit as much as she'll blame me.*

*You were drinking that vodka, too, Lisa. You think your parents will believe that I swiped it out of your house without you knowing about it?*

*We were both throwing rocks, Tim. I'm the one who broke the window, but Mom will be pissed at both of us. If we keep our mouths shut, she'll assume it was the black kids up the street.*

Now that she thought back on it, Katherine felt bad for how shitty she'd been to Lisa, and even more so for using her mom's racism to throw those poor kids under the bus.

"As it turns out," Moser continued, "I've been put in charge of auctioning you off. If you keep nice and quiet, I can see to it that you are sold to the least cruel owners."

Katherine snorted. That was confirmation of bullshit if she'd ever heard it.

Moser stopped, his feet turning toward her. "Who was that?"

*Shit.* That snort was louder than she thought.

"You there! What happened to your shack–"

CRASH!

Moser's lantern smashed on the floor, and the hold lit up with a puddle of flaming oil.

No point in hiding now. Katherine released Butterbean, then rolled out over the oil, counting on the thickness of her cloak and its piss saturation to put out the fire.

Moser shrieked as Butterbean lunged at him. Katherine barely had time to see the attack before the cargo hold was completely engulfed in darkness again. The piss cloak had worked even better than expected.

Catching him blind, off his guard, and engaged with a wolf, Katherine easily got Moser in a choke hold with her dagger poking into his throat.

"Ease off, Butterbean," she said. "I've got him."

"Katherine?" said Tony the Elf. "What the hell was that? You totally gave me away."

"Sorry. It just slipped out." She pressed the dagger more firmly into Moser's neck. "Fucking amateur with his bullshit threats."

"How do you know it was bullshit?" said Moser, still acting as though he had the upper hand.

"If your stick is big enough, you don't need to dangle a carrot."

"I beg your pardon?"

"They might not use that expression in this world," said Fritz. "And out of context, it sounds... well..."

"Okay, okay," said Katherine. "I get it. Poor choice of words." She tightened her hold on Moser's throat. "Also, that's not how auctions work."

The cargo door started cranking open.

"Get rid of him," Katherine whispered to Moser. She loosened her arm around his throat and released pressure with the dagger.

"Garron!" he shouted. "Close the hatch!" The sliver of light shining in showed an acceptable level of terror in his eyes.

"I thought I heard a noise down there. Are you all right?"

Katherine pressed the flat side of her dagger against Moser's cheek, just to remind him it was there.

"I'm interrogating one of them."

The dark-skinned elf at the back of the ship punched his open palm and let out a small shriek of fake pain. Katherine smiled at him. The dude was nailing it.

"Close the hatch now!" demanded Moser.

The light dimmed as the door started closing again, then went out completely.

"Tony the Elf," said Katherine. "Take my Light stone out of the bag."

After some chain-rattling, bumps, and clumsy fumbling, Tony the Elf finally said, "Light stone." The cargo hold was dimly lit once again.

"Good. Now, take his dagger."

Tony the Elf carefully removed Moser's dagger from the sheath on his belt.

Now that Moser was unarmed and outnumbered three to one, Katherine felt comfortable enough loosening her hold around his throat so she could get a better look at him. An initial scan didn't reveal any conspicuously perfect square holes in his clothes, but he was wearing multiple layers. She looked him in the eye.

"Where is my hole?" She regretted it as soon as she said it.

Moser gave her a cocky grin. "Have you checked between your legs?"

Katherine rolled her eyes. "Yes, yes, that's hilarious. Now, where is my *Portable* Hole?"

"I don't have it."

"Then who does?"

He nodded up toward the cargo door. "My friend there on the other side of that door. You want I should ask him to bring it down here?"

*Nice try, Moser.* There was no good reason that Katherine could think of for him to trust his partner in treachery with such a valuable prize. There was, however, an easy way to fast-track getting the truth out of him.

She turned to Tony the Elf. "Help me put him in the bag."

"What?" said Moser, panicking like he was only now understanding that he didn't have the upper hand in this situation.

Katherine secured her arm around his neck again and made sure he was well aware of the dagger blade against his cheek as Tony the Elf began feeding his legs into the bag.

"Nice and easy," said Katherine. "I'll pull you back out once I get the truth."

Though his body was tense, Moser offered no resistance as Katherine and Tony the Elf fed the rest of him into the Bag of Holding.

"Now what?" said Tony the Elf, standing up and offering the bag to Katherine.

Instead of accepting it, she reached inside. "Portable Hole." She allowed herself a smug grin when she felt the silky magical cloth in her hand. "I knew it."

Tony the Elf returned her smile with a perfunctory smile of his own. "Very impressive. I meant, what are we going to do about him?"

"Let him sweat it out in the bag for a few minutes while you free more people."

"Are we even sure we want to free more people yet?"

The dark-skinned elf at the rear of the boat rattled his chains. "*I'm* sure!"

"Just a second," said Tony the Elf. "What I mean is that we won't be able to conceal the fact that we're all free. Once we take all these shackles off, there's no turning back."

"That's right," said Katherine. "It's go time."

"I know you're eager to get out of this hold, but shouldn't we wait until you've had time to get all your powers back? I don't know how many weapons you've got stashed away in your bag, but most of us are going to be charging up there unarmed."

"We'll have the element of surprise. We'll stick together, catch at least a few of them unaware, and take their weapons. Think about it like *Die Hard*, but with a dozen John McClanes."

Tony the Elf eyed his miserable-looking chained-up friends. "That's very reassuring. And what about our friend in the bag. Are we just going to let him die in here?"

"Of course not," said Katherine. "He's our ticket out of here. That hatch only opens from the outside. We'll need him to get his friend up there to open the hatch for us."

"Again, I think you're being too hasty. They'll eventually open the hatch again to feed us. We could all be ready and waiting when they do."

Katherine shook her head. "No more waiting. And believe me, for what I've got in mind, we'll want to get the timing right on this." She reached into the Bag of Holding. "Moser."

Moser spilled out of the bag, gasping and trembling. "Who... Who was that?"

"What?" Then she remembered Tanner. She hadn't even thought about him when she put Moser in there. Might as well make some use of him. "He's the last man who dared double cross me. Do you get what I'm saying?"

"I have the Portable Hole," Moser confessed. "It's rolled up and stuffed down my pants."

Katherine grimaced at the black square of cloth in her hand, then waved it at Moser. "I know you had it, dumbass. I would have preferred you'd kept it somewhere else, though." She held the Portable Hole with her fingertips and wished even more for a shower. "When I give you the signal, I need you to get your friend to open that hatch. And then I need you to stay the fuck out of our way. Got it?"

Moser nodded.

"Katherine, wait!" said Tony the Elf. His expression was turning more and more frustrated. "Most of these people have never been in a combat situation before. You're asking them to go out unarmed and fight pirates."

*And there we have it.*

Moser chuckled unhelpfully. "*This* bunch? Good luck with that."

Katherine turned away from Tony the Elf and Moser to address the rest of her captive audience. It was time to captain up again.

"Let's make something clear. I'm not *asking* any of you for shit. I know a lot of you don't exactly relish the idea of storming the deck and fighting pirates. I can't say I relish it much myself. The odds might not be in our favor, but they get exponentially worse for every one of you doesn't do their part. All our lives are on the line, not to mention the lives of our friends around this world if Captain Logan delivers that die to Mordred. I know you all realize this, but I also understand that fear can be a strong demotivator, and that some of you may get cold feet at the last second and opt to stay behind when the rest of us make our move. That's not because you're cowards. It's because you're not trained for this and genuinely paralyzed with fear. So for the sake of the mission, and all our lives, I'm not going to give you any choice."

Holding the orc-taint-stained Portable Hole in front of her, she marched to the front of the hold, where it would be most accessible when she came back for it.

"No, Katherine!" cried Tony the Elf. "Don't!"

Katherine didn't like the idea any more than he did, but a captain has to do what a captain has to do.

"You should probably start freeing people. It's about to get wet in here." She slapped the Portable Hole on the bottom of the hull. The gush of water that flowed out from it nearly dislocated her shoulder, then blasted the hatch above them. "Shit."

"Mercy of the gods, woman!" cried Moser. "You've

doomed us all!"

Katherine pointed threateningly at him. "Shut up, and stay out of the way."

"So much for the element of surprise," said Tony the Elf.

Katherine admired the column of water that was already starting to wilt as the cargo hold flooded. It wasn't what she'd been going for, but it would have to do. "I don't know," she said. "I'd be willing to bet they're pretty fucking surprised right now. Hurry up and get these people out of their chains."

# CHAPTER 16

*C*haz was tired of playing Neil Diamond songs, but he dared not deliver anything but his most practiced and crowd-tested work in Captain Logan's presence. Absurd as it seemed, he was even more intimidated by the captain than he'd been by Millard.

Sure, Millard was a vampire, but he was also kind of a lonely old loser who wanted to be loved. Captain Logan was tough as nails and needed to be respected by his men. It didn't help matters at all that Katherine had recently compromised their respect by forcing him to all but surrender his ship. He needed fear to reinforce what respect remained. Chaz had personally witnessed him hurl one of his own crewmen off the upper deck for reporting that he couldn't find some guy named Bosley.

Also unhelpful for Chaz was that he had been among those, at least as far as Captain Logan was concerned, who had been fighting him when he got electrocuted and dropped fifty feet down into the mud.

As long as it kept the captain soothed, Chaz would play *Sweet Caroline* as many times as it was requested.

"This song pleases me," said Captain Logan after Chaz strummed the last note of his eighth performance.

Chaz didn't know whether speaking out of turn or failing to respond was more likely to earn him a flogging. He opted for politeness. "Thank you, Captain."

"It would please me more if you could replace the name

*Caroline* with the name of a former lover of mine."

"What was her name?" asked Chaz.

Captain Logan stared at him with an expression that Chaz couldn't read beyond its intensity.

His heart started pounding harder as he realized he'd just assumed the captain's sexuality. One more reason to fear him over Millard. Captain Logan had a functional dick.

"Svetladellania," he finally responded.

It was a more favorable response than stabbing him would have been, but how the hell was he supposed to even remember how to pronounce that, much less cram it into a three-syllable slot?

"Svetlania?" he whispered to himself. No, he was sure there had been a D in there somewhere. "Svetladonna?" That was closer, but he didn't think it was right.

"Svetladellania," Captain Logan repeated, just a little bit irritably.

Chaz took it one syllable at a time. "Svet... la..." He paused with the tip of his tongue touching the roof of his mouth just behind his front teeth.

"...dellania," said Captain Logan. "Is your tongue weary from too much singing? This is a common name in the Sularian Valley."

That was as close to a safe out as Chaz was going to get. "My tongue is *a bit* weary. And I've never been to the Sularian Valley. The name is kind of a mouthful."

Captain Logan sighed in fond recollection. "So were her tits."

"I'll need some time to weave it into the rest of the lyrics in such a way that does justice to both the beauty of the music and such a beautiful name."

The captain drummed his fingers on the arm of his chair as he considered Chaz's hastily thought up bullshit. "Very well. You have one hour."

## Critical Failures VIII

"I may require some additional time to rehearse, to make sure I pronounce her name correctly."

"I can help you with that." Captain Logan rose from his chair, took a large hourglass from a shelf, and placed it upside-down on the table. "Every time you mispronounce it, I shall remove one of your toes."

Chaz gulped. "Svetladellania." He may not have liked the captain's methods, but he couldn't argue their effectiveness.

"See you in an hour, bard." Captain Logan sat back down in his chair and stared at the sands pouring down from the top of the glass to the bottom. "Roderick, escort our guest to the hold."

"Right away, Captain," said a man Chaz hadn't even realized was standing guard right outside the cabin door. He nodded for Chaz to follow him.

Chaz couldn't believe how relieved he felt to be returning to that putrid-smelling cargo hold and locked in manacles again. Performing under the constant threat of being murdered was mentally exhausting. He'd spend this hour sleeping, then shoehorn that bitch's name into the song as best he could when they dragged him back up to the captain's cabin again.

There were a lot more people on board the ship than Chaz expected, and most of them didn't look like pirates, or even sailors. They didn't have the right build. Some were too fat, others too slender.

Some of them wore the sorts of finery that might have come straight off one of the racks at Hippogriff Hall on the Crescent Shadow, though they were now soiled with who knew how many days' worth of sweat and filth. Chaz imagined them having once been bankers, tailors, or perhaps even politicians. Others wore more sturdy and practical clothing, though not necessarily ideal for a life at sea. Thick, mended coveralls which might be better suited to a farmer or blacksmith.

At least, that was the vibe Chaz got from them. He didn't stare too hard at any of them, because they were all staring at him. It was unnerving.

When they got to the hatch, a crewman was sitting on it. He bit his dirty fingernails as he avoided eye contact with the men escorting Chaz.

"What are you doing, Garron?" asked Roderick. "Is there no more productive task to which you might attend than sitting idly on your ass? We are shorthanded enough as it is."

That corroborated Chaz's theory that the strange people standing around all over the deck weren't sailors. Where did they come from? He was pretty sure they weren't from Nazere, and this ship didn't look the type to be ferrying a bunch of passengers.

"I had a splinter in my foot," said Garron, neither getting up nor removing his boot.

"Do you know what Captain Logan will do if he catches you lazing about on your backside like this?"

"Please. I need only a little bit of rest." Garron's pleading eyes didn't look very restful. "Please come back in a moment."

"Come back?" said Roderick. "I am escorting a prisoner. Go find someplace else to rest your foot."

Garron didn't move. Chaz could see in his face that he was scrambling for something to justify his refusal. "But I don't want to."

Roderick glared curiously at Chaz, as if he had something to do with his shipmate's confusing behavior. Chaz shrugged.

"Stand aside this instant," Roderick said to Garron. "Or else the only foot you'll have to worry about is mine up your ass."

Garron stood up. "Fine."

"Now open the hatch!" demanded Roderick as he pushed

# Critical Failures VIII

Chaz forward.

As soon as Garron started turning the crank, the hatch flew open, and Chaz was punched in the face.

Except, it wasn't a punch. When he sat up, he found himself five feet away from the hatch, out of which was gushing a fifteen foot plume of water. That's what had hit him. It was as though Poseidon himself had pissed directly in his face after holding in a case and a half of beer while he waited for the end of the Super Bowl.

Chaz hugged his lute and glanced behind him. Another five feet would have thrown him clear off the front of the ship.

"The hull has been breached!" cried Roderick.

Crewmen and passengers alike peered over the sides of the ship, searching for what they might have hit. But there hadn't been a jolt or anything. They were out on the open sea.

Garron tried to slink away in the ensuing chaos, but Roderick caught him with a tractor beam glare. "*You* know something about this. What happened?"

"I know nothing!" said Garron. "I swear it!"

Roderick drew his sword, pinning Garron to the bulwark in fear. "He was guarding the hatch," he said without taking his eyes off Garron. "Take him to the captain for questioning."

Four of the strange passengers immediately seized Garron.

"He does the bidding of those who oppose Jordan Knight!"

"He covets the master's prize!"

"Throw him overboard!"

"No!" demanded Roderick. "Take him to the captain, I said. Captain Logan will determine how best to deal with - AAAAUUUUUUGGGGGHHH!"

Tony the Elf emerged from the hatch, bolstered by the weakening gush of water, and drove two daggers deep into the small of Rodericks' back.

Roderick dropped his sword as his body went limp. It fell into the hatch, and Tony the Elf dropped one of his two daggers in after it.

Neither weapon remained below deck for long as more of Chaz's imprisoned companions emerged.

The four men holding Garron hesitated for a second, like they were unsure of which side of this fight they were supposed to be on. They shoved Garron at Tony the Elf, then followed behind him.

Tony the Elf elbowed a bewildered Garron in the nose while simultaneously stabbing one of the other men in the throat.

Fritz wrapped his arms around Garron's legs as one of the Whore's Head elves relieved him of his sword.

Then a woman in a thick hooded black cloak climbed out of the hatch wielding an awkwardly large scythe. She looked like the Angel of Death, except she was jabbing at people with the scythe's handle because she didn't have room to swing it properly.

More of the passengers and crew were splashing out onto the flooding bow as more of Chaz's friends emerged from below. The passengers weren't too good in a fight, but did a fine job of getting in the crewmen's way, making them easier to single out and target. Each fallen crew member meant one more weapon for the escaped prisoners.

When he saw the tide of battle changing, Chaz felt safe enough to do his part. He strummed his lute to Inspire Competence in his allies, singing the first suitable song he could think of.

*O say, can you see, by the dawn's early light,*

"What does he sing of?" asked one of the passengers as they all stopped to listen, further hampering the crew's fighting efforts.

## Critical Failures VIII

"It is late in the afternoon," said another. Others shushed him to allow Chaz to continue.

*What so proudly... da da da... when we Twilight were last reading?*

"What nonsense is this?"
"Quiet! I'm trying to listen!"
Chaz wished he'd picked a song he knew all the words to.

*And some stripes and some stars. Bombs bursting in air!*
*Do di do, in the night, and our flag was still there.*

He wasn't sure if he was helping or not at this point. Both sides were just pushing unarmed music-loving passengers out of the way so they could get close enough to stab each other. Only Stuart, the monk who had joined the guys when they'd raided Millard's castle, and that black elf dude who Chaz had never met before being manacled across from him in the hold, were doing any significant amount of fighting. Stuart was punching out passengers left and right, while the other guy was kicking them. He wasn't as effective as Stuart, but he sure did seem to enjoy using his legs.

Helpful or not, Chaz continued with his song, confident that he could at least nail the end.

*O say do you see that la la la la wave,*

*Maybe not.*
"Star Spangled Banner," snapped Tony the Elf. "For Christ's sake, it's the name of the fucking song."

*O'er the land of the free and the home of the brave!*

He'd nailed that part, at least. He was sure of it.

"ENOUGH!" Captain Logan shouted over the passengers' applause. He stood in his cabin doorway, his sword drawn but high above the actual fighting. "Who is responsible for this?"

"I am!" said the Grim Reaper in a voice that, while very familiar, wasn't very reapery. She pulled down her hood.

"Katherine?" said Chaz. "How did you get here?"

Katherine ignored him. "We meet again, Logan."

Captain Logan, clearly not accustomed to being addressed so informally aboard his own ship, narrowed his eyes at her. "It seems we do."

"Have you memorized my demands by now, or should I repeat them?"

While they were heaps better off than they had been chained in the hold, Chaz didn't feel like they had enough of an advantage to warrant that kind of trash talk. Also, since when did these two have a history?

Captain Logan grinned down at Katherine. "You should not use the same trick every time, druid. Your threats are meaningless when you have nowhere to escape to. If this ship sinks, you and your friends will drown right along with us."

"That's a risk I'm willing to take," said Katherine, though not with a convincing degree of fervor. She didn't sound like someone who was really psyched to die for a cause. She didn't even sound as enthusiastic as these crazy...

*Jordan Knight.*

*Prize.*

*Master.*

The pieces were coming together to form a grim picture in Chaz's mind.

Captain Logan laughed. "You should have stayed in the forest where you belong, druid. The sea is no place for such a pretty little lass. You may sway the minds of squirrels and owls with your empty threats, but I don't believe you've got it in you."

# Critical Failures VIII

"Listen to me, Logan!" said Katherine. "If this ship reaches Hollin –"

"*When* this ship reaches Hollin," Chaz corrected her, pleading with his eyes for Katherine to shut up when she turned to glare at him. "It shall not do so with a cargo of slaves, for we are born free!" Katherine was staring at him like he had two seconds to follow that up with something less stupid before he got his head scythed off. "Also, Katherine can turn into a shark. We'll cling to whatever debris is still floating, and she'll tow us to shore."

"Feed me none of your wild fish tales, bard," said Captain Logan. "Who ever heard of a druid turning into a shark?"

"She's already done it. Ask your crew. Many of them witnessed it with their own eyes."

Captain Logan frowned as several of his crew nodded and murmured their corroboration.

"It's over, Logan," said Katherine. "There's no point in letting your crew drown. We aren't interested in selling you as slaves, and I'd prefer not to kill anyone else if I don't have to. We can part ways peacefully at the next port we come to."

"Which will, of course, be Hollin," said Chaz when he saw hints of alarm and confusion on the passengers' faces.

Captain Logan seemed to be scrutinizing their faces too as he continued to hesitate. Meanwhile, the water level was getting dangerously high. Once it started flowing inside over the bulwark, a lot of options would be off the table.

"Refresh my memory," the captain finally said. "What are your *demands*?"

Katherine held up her Bag of Holding. "First, you surrender all your weapons."

"And my ship?"

"You took mine. I'll need this one to go rescue my friends." After a moment of silence and rising water, she spoke up again. "There's nothing to think about. You're not getting this ship either way. I'm the only one who knows how to stop it from sinking."

"She's using a Portable Hole!" cried the member of Captain Logan's crew who had climbed out of the hold along with the prisoners. "It's on the front of the hull. It should be easy enough to – UGH!"

Fritz punched him in the nuts.

The captain's grin sent shivers up Chaz's spine. He'd finally found the leverage he'd been groping for, and they were all fucked.

"Crew of Seastalker," bellowed Captain Logan. "Stand down."

Chaz sighed. That was an unexpected relief.

"Hollinites, hear my words!" he continued. "These treacherous fools seek to keep you from your homeland. They covet your master's prize for their own nefarious purposes."

*Shit.* That sigh may have been premature.

"No!" said Katherine as the passengers narrowed their eyes at her. "There's nothing nefarious about it. Just the opposite, actually. We –"

"Seize the druid's hole!" cried Captain Logan.

"WHAT?"

"And we shall reach Hollin in three short days."

The passengers crept forward with hungry looks in their eyes. The Whore's Head gang backed away from them, forming a tight perimeter around the hatch.

Not a bad move by Captain Logan. He didn't want to waste any more of his already scant crew, but this was a great way to get his ship back while also thinning out this herd of useless passengers. Acting as a unified mob, they had the numbers to overpower Katherine and the others, even with the few weapons they had to defend themselves.

Still, Chaz thought it strange that the captain hadn't held up the die to add an extra bit of theatrics to his speech. That's

# Critical Failures VIII

what Chaz would have done. That is, unless he didn't have it on him.

*The cabin!*

Before he'd been summoned to sing for Captain Logan, Chaz had spent his time chained down in the hold meditating on his new spell options. There was one spell that could have easily freed him from his chains if it hadn't required freedom of movement to cast. With only a single Level 3 spell available for him to learn, he wanted to think carefully before choosing one. Now he was ready to make that choice.

"Hold them off as long as you can," he said to Katherine. "Good luck." With that, he hopped over the bulwark and into the ocean.

"What the..." Katherine shouted after him. "Fuck you!"

Now that he was out of everyone's field of vision, Chaz strummed Deep Purple's *Smoke on the Water* as quietly as he could. He only got a few strums in before his fingers went through the strings; they were both turning into mist.

Turning into a big blob of fog was slightly nauseating. He felt like he might throw up until he realized he didn't have a stomach. Also lacking eyes, his "vision" was more of a fluid sense of himself and his surroundings. After a moment of concentration, he orientated himself and controlled his movement along the side of the hull. He was as slow as a constipated snail's turd coming out, but he was moving.

He stayed close to the water until he reached the ship's rear, then started to climb. It was still slow-going, but he was pleased to discover that he was able to move up as effortlessly as he moved sideways. Keeping himself as mist-like as he could to avoid being spotted, he snaked his way up the back of Captain Logan's cabin and onto the roof. Here he was at his most vulnerable, but the captain and his crew had their attention on the struggle at the bow, which didn't seem to be turning out so well for Katherine and the others.

Chaz flattened himself and slipped inside through the cabin door over Captain Logan's head. Once inside, he found the chest behind the captain's chair where Logan kept his most valuable possessions.

Unfortunately, there was no way to tell if the chest was locked or not, or even if the die was inside, without breaking the spell. It also now occurred to him how much trouble he would be in if he got caught sneaking around in the captain's cabin with nothing but a lute and his dick in his hands.

Searching as frantically as his vaporous form would allow, he couldn't see any keys hanging conspicuously about. The only option that left was only marginally less terrifying than stealing Captain Logan's shit from right under his nose. He'd never thought of himself as claustrophobic, but he'd never seriously considered being locked inside a midget coffin.

*Come on, Chaz. It's not that bad. At worst, you'll be stuck in a fetal position until the captain comes and murders you. Hey, you'll probably welcome being murdered at that point.*

As long as the locking mechanism was exposed on the inside and his fingers materialized near it, he shouldn't have a problem. Now that he thought about it, those were two pretty dubious contingencies to rely on. Wishing he hadn't thought about it, he oozed himself into the chest's keyhole.

He'd hoped that his unconventional vision might allow him to see in the dark, but that wasn't the case. It was pitch black inside the chest, and he couldn't feel anything his misty form was surrounding. The denser he became, the harder it was to squeeze the rest of himself inside. But finally, the only light he could sense was coming through a tiny hole outside the chest. He was fully inside.

*Here goes nothing.*

Before he could reconsider how stupid an idea this was, he canceled his Gaseous Form spell. For a second, the pain was even more excruciating than he imagined, then –

# Critical Failures VIII

*SMASH!*

The chest was utterly destroyed as Chaz exploded out of it like a chick that had stubbornly waited until its teen years to break out of its shell. Gold and silver coins spilled out onto the cabin floor, along with a few precious stones that had been digging into his back as he materialized, a dagger that might have very well killed him if it hadn't been in a sheath, and a black twenty-sided die with a glowing red light at its core.

"Son of a sea whore!" cried Captain Logan, standing in the doorway between Chaz and the next phase of his ill-thought-out plan.

Chaz grabbed the die, sprang to his feet, and smashed a window with the back of his lute.

"What in the Seven Hells?" Captain Logan's expression showed more annoyance than anger. "What is the point of breaking my window? Do you honestly believe you can squeeze through there before I get to you?" He laughed. "I welcome you to try. You'll gut yourself like a fish on the broken glass."

"I have the hole!" cried a passenger from the ship's bow.

Captain Logan grinned at Chaz, then stepped out of his cabin and to the side so that Chaz could see the futility of his situation.

All of his friends were restrained, each held by two or three of the fanatic passengers. Even Katherine's wolf was subdued by three people with more balls than brains.

Time to shit or get off the pot.

"I have the die!" Chaz shouted back, holding the magic d20 before him. He was still hidden in shadow at the back of the cabin, so he doubted anyone could visually confirm his claim, but it got them murmuring.

Captain Logan chuckled. "Settle down, settle down. I assure you, he shan't have it for long."

Pants-shittingly nervous as he was, Chaz smiled to

himself. That was exactly what he'd needed the captain to say.

"Too fucking right, I shan't!" he said. "Because if you assholes don't let my friends go right now, I'm going to chuck this stupid piece of shit out the goddamn window!"

"NO!" cried the passenger who'd retrieved the Portable Hole. "That belongs to the Master!"

"I don't give a corn-studded fuck about your master."

Captain Logan once again darkened the doorway of his cabin. "You're playing a dangerous game, bard. I can disembowel you in less than five seconds."

"And I can chuck this die out the window in less than one." Honestly, it was kind of sad to hear the captain resorting to that kind of threat, considering that Chaz was essentially as good as dead anyway. "How do you think they'll react when they find out they have to tell their master that his precious prize is at the bottom of the ocean?"

"They'll kill you, of course."

"And I'll die with a smile on my face knowing your sorry ass will be headed to Hell right behind me."

One of Logan's men cleared his throat right outside the cabin door. "Captain?"

"WHAT?" snapped Captain Logan, whirling around like he was itching for something to stab. Facing outside, his shoulders dropped. He turned back around, his eyes heavy with defeat, and laid his sword gently on the table. "Forgive me, Father. I am not worthy to carry your sword."

When he slumped down into one of the lesser chairs, Chaz could see beyond the doorway. The Hollinites had released Katherine and the others and had captured and disarmed a few of Logan's men. United against what few men remained of Logan's crew, the battle was won.

They'd snatched victory from the jaws of defeat. Tony the Elf had even reunited with his dog. Why, then, was there no

# Critical Failures VIII

cheering? No joy in anyone's eyes?

The Hollinites advanced, distributing weapons among themselves as Logan's men surrendered them. Chaz dared not step away from the window, still holding the die up and none too thrilled about the captain and his sword still being in there with him.

Finally, Katherine and one of the Hollinites entered the cabin. Katherine took Captain Logan's sword off the table and slipped it into her Bag of Holding. She didn't gloat or even so much as look at him as she did it. The act was more akin to discreetly alerting someone that their fly was down.

"Chaz, this is Gileon," she said, gesturing to the scrawny bearded human man accompanying her. "Gileon, Chaz."

Chaz nodded. "'Sup."

Gileon said nothing, his weary eyes focused on the die.

"You can lower your hand," said Katherine.

When Chaz lowered his arm, Gileon put his hand out to him. "Hand over the Master's prize, and we shall sail peacefully to Hollin."

"We're not handing over shit," said Katherine. "Chaz, put your arm back up."

Captain Logan laughed sullenly as Chaz raised the die threateningly to the broken window again.

Gileon glared at Katherine. "What treachery is this? We had an agreement!"

"I agreed to sail you to Hollin. You killed two of our men."

That explained all the doom and gloom outside.

"How many of ours did you kill?" asked Gileon.

"We were fighting for our lives. You and your stupid cult just backed the wrong horse. That's on you."

"Do not forget, Miss Katherine. We outnumber you greatly, and we are now armed."

Katherine smiled menacingly at him. "I haven't forgotten. That's exactly why we need this little bit of insurance that you'll keep your part of the bargain." She turned to Captain Logan. "Where's the nearest port?"

Captain Logan shrugged. "Roumont, the Isle of Drow should be about half a day to the east."

"Are you fucking kidding me?"

Chaz was confused by the harshness of her response. "Do you know that place?"

"I know it's got the word *Drow* in it."

Captain Logan smiled. "Don't care much for drow?"

"Back off, man," said Katherine. "Some of my best friends are drow. Well, one. Half drow. He's dead. I have him in my bag."

Chaz, Gileon, and Captain Logan exchanged uncomfortable glances, then Gileon turned to Katherine.

"We must sail to Hollin at once. The Master awaits his prize."

"We're not going to get there without a crew," said Katherine. "None of your people or my people are sailors, and I'm certainly not putting my faith in Logan's crew." She turned to the captain. "Are there any other nearby ports?"

"You need not worry about the drow," said Captain Logan. "They are a small ruling class on the island, interested only in fleecing ship captains with their outrageous taxes and fees. You are unlikely to even see a drow on the island."

"I don't mind seeing a drow. I've just had a couple of bad run-ins with some in the past."

"They have minions of other races to collect their gold. The drow wouldn't be caught dead associating with fish-scented commoners such as ourselves."

"That's fine," said Katherine. "Good for them. I'm just saying that even if we did have to interact with drow, I'd be totally cool with it."

"No," said Gileon. "My people can keep this crew in line. I must insist we sail directly to Hollin."

# Critical Failures VIII

"Don't overplay your hand, Gileon. You aren't in a position to insist shit. You're a crazy cultist." She pointed at the doorway. "You could have fucking legions of trained soldiers out there, and we'll still have more power than you as long as we have the means to send your master's precious piece of junk to the bottom of the ocean. None of us are going anywhere until you get your people to bail out the cargo hold, so I suggest you get them on that."

"Why does it have to be my people? Why not yours as well?"

"Because fuck you! Now get the fuck out of my cabin and start bailing."

Gileon's pale face turned pink with frustration, but he exited the cabin.

Katherine shut the door behind him. "He won't leave us alone in here for long. We need to think of a plan fast."

"Great job, Chaz," said Chaz. "You really saved our asses, Chaz."

"We're still in deep shit, and not all of our asses were saved."

Chaz felt like a dick for choosing that moment to be petty. "Who did we lose?"

"Fritz and Stuart."

"That's the monk, right?"

Katherine turned away from Chaz and nodded. Chaz spotted a small dark spot suddenly appear on her Bag of Holding.

"I'm sorry," he said. "I didn't mean –"

Katherine stopped him with a loud sniffle and a deep breath. "I've got them in my bag." She walked around the table and started shoveling gold and gems into her Bag of Holding. "We'll get them resurrected with Tanner."

"How the hell are we going to do that?"

"We just need to get to a temple. Hopefully, this gold will

cover some of the expense. We've got more immediate shit to worry about right now, though. Like, how are we going to lose these fucking Hollinites? Logan, you can feel free to weigh in on this, too."

Captain Logan sat back with his scorched boots on the table and laughed. "You might do better to ask a man's cooperation at a time when you're not robbing him blind."

"You got us into this shit, and you have no idea what kind of power you're fucking with. If we let you hand that die over to those idiots' master, you'd be as fucked as we were."

"Katherine," said Chaz. "Should we really be telling him about –"

"The balance of power has shifted. Logan has more to gain by siding with us against the Hollinites."

"Is that so?" said Captain Logan. "Please enlighten me. What, precisely, have I to gain by helping you?"

"Well, there's your freedom," said Katherine. "If you and your men help us shake off the Hollinites at the next port, I'll let you go."

"As you sail away on my ship. I am a man of the sea, druid. Being bound to a tiny spit of land is no better than being locked in a dungeon cell."

"You sure do whine a lot for a pirate."

This negotiation was crawling along, and they hadn't made any headway in figuring out what they would do about the Hollinites. Chaz prodded it along the only way he could think of.

"What if we give you your ship back?"

"Excuse me?" said Katherine.

"You need to offer him something."

"What good will that do us? Then *we'll* be the ones stuck on fucking Drow Island with all the fucking Hollinites."

Captain Logan laughed. "Such a set of circumstances sounded so tempting but a moment ago."

# Critical Failures VIII

Katherine glared at Chaz as if he'd betrayed her, then sighed. "Fine. You can have your ship back after you help me retake mine."

"What of my crew? I cannot abandon my men."

"You can come back and get them later."

Captain Logan didn't look any happier about this arrangement than Katherine, but such was the nature of negotiation.

"I want my father's sword."

"Fuck no," said Katherine, clearly not bothering with a Diplomacy check. "You've attacked me three times now. Your actions have consequences. I'm keeping the sword, the gold, and all this other shit. You can have the boat, or you can go fuck yourself."

Captain Logan pulled a dagger from the back of his boot and jumped to his feet.

Chaz raised his lute and brandished it as menacingly as he could.

In the time it took him to do that, Captain Logan could have stabbed him eight times. Instead, he grinned at Katherine, who wasn't even flinching as she stared back into his icy blue eyes.

"I may have to reconsider my preconceptions of druids," he said, setting his dagger on the table before her. "You have yourself a deal."

# CHAPTER 17

*T*he captain's quarters at the top tier of the *Maiden's Voyage* smelled like a combination of an antique store and a petting zoo. The former was due to all the dusty old junk that filled the shelves lining the walls, and the latter due to this being where all the seized familiars were being held.

Despite the painful burns all over his body, and the fact that they were stranded at sea in a ship that was damaged beyond repair, Julian felt good to be back together with Ravenus. Likewise, the other recently freed wizards and sorcerers from the Whore's Head were thankful to be reunited with their own familiars. They whistled and laughed as they put out what remained of Julian's Grease fire and secured their former captors in ropes from the collapsed rigging, despite having to do so in the pouring rain. Only Frank, who had never bothered to cast a Find Familiar spell, wore a sullen expression on his face as he sat in Captain Longfellow's chair, his eyes locked with those of a small monkey that was looking similarly sullen. It had every reason to be, considering it was the only unaccounted for animal on the ship, and nobody had bothered to let it out of its cage yet.

"Do you know who that is?" Julian asked Ravenus.

"I'm afraid not, sir. I am unable to communicate with monkeys, and this one does not appear to speak the Elven tongue."

Julian turned to Frank. "Maybe you could take him as your familiar."

# Critical Failures VIII

"If I wanted a familiar, I'd already have one."

"Not an animal lover?"

"I like animals just fine," said Frank. "But I saw how close the other spellcasters were to their familiars, and I didn't want to get that attached to anything of this world. I've been taken from the people I care about, and I never lost hope that I'd return to them one day. What's the point of forming that kind of bond here?"

"I've thought about that. I didn't realize how strong that bond was when I got Ravenus. I was new here, and Mordred guided me through the process."

Frank scoffed. "Of course he did. Anything to keep you docile and not thinking about going home, not to mention a potential hostage to keep you in line."

Julian thought about what Chaz had said when he decided to take his musical career seriously. "I still want to go home," he said quietly enough so that only Frank could hear him. "But have you given any thought to what you'll do if that turns out not to be an option?"

Frank glared at him, but Rhonda walked in before he could reply.

"The fire's all out and the crew is all tied up," said Rhonda. "We've got them in two cabins, with two of our guys monitoring each."

Frank kept his glare locked on Julian while Rhonda spoke, only turning to face her when she'd finished. "And what of the drunken excuse for an acting captain?"

"He's being escorted up now."

"Has he sobered up any?"

Rhonda frowned at the empty liquor bottles on the table. "Not really. It looks like he was hitting Captain Longfellow's booze pretty hard, like he wasn't expecting a sudden hostile takeover." She stood aside to allow the drunken former acting captain to stumble in out of the rain.

His clothes were just shy of being wet enough to hide the fact that he'd pissed himself, and his face was bruised and bloodied.

"Did you beat him?" Frank asked Rhonda.

"No, he had some trouble climbing up the ladders. He kept slipping and hitting his face on the rungs."

That was consistent with what Julian had witnessed when he came down from his cabin and tried to attack his own crew. It was amazing that he hadn't broken his legs falling from tier to tier, or anything else when Rhonda and two others finally tackled him.

He sprayed out a pink-spittled laugh when he saw Frank staring severely back at him. "I suppose you are the captain of this floating garbage heap now. Congratulations." He took off his hat and threw it like a Frisbee at Frank. At least, that's where Julian assumed he was trying to throw it. It went wide to the right and knocked some of Captain Longfellow's junk off the shelf. The monkey screamed and rattled his cage bars.

"Thank you," said Frank, either missing or ignoring the heavy-handed sarcasm in the usurped captain's voice. "Please sit down, Mr..."

"My name is Marcus," he said as he collapsed into the chair opposite the long table from Frank. Julian's nerves settled, as Marcus's drunken swaying had been making him dizzy.

"It doesn't matter who the captain is," said Frank. "You and I both know this ship isn't going anywhere anytime soon."

'That's right, *Captain*. You and your ungrateful band of fire-slinging fools have doomed us all."

"Ungrateful?" said Rhonda. "What were we supposed to be grateful about? You were going to sell us as slaves."

"A better fate than you deserve. You would have lived like royalty, and become masters of your craft. There is no better school for the arcane arts than Khalzhar."

"What do you mean, school?"

"Khalzhari wizards and sorcerers are known far and wide as the greatest magic trainers in all of Dalgar, and they're always looking for students with the arcane spark."

Julian had a question he felt was so obvious that he must have missed something. "If it's such a great place to learn magic, then why do they need to buy unwilling students from slave traders?"

Marcus shrugged. "There are downsides, of course. It is not for everyone."

"What are the downsides?" asked Rhonda.

"First, you would never be allowed to leave Khalzhar except to fight those who live beyond the grave in the Moor of Dread."

Julian nodded. "That certainly raises a red flag. What else?"

"You would almost certainly die in the Moor of Dread."

"Why does that name sound familiar?"

Marcus laughed. "Believe me, elf. You would know if you'd visited the Moor of Dread."

"Let's get back to Khalzhar," said Rhonda. "You say we'd be prisoners until we got ripped apart by the undead. Again, what part of that are we supposed to be grateful about?"

"The part *before* you get ripped apart by the undead," said Marcus without a trace of irony in his tone. "The accommodations for spellcasters in training are said to be quite luxurious. The Kingdom of Xanir funnels gold by the wagonload into Khalzhar to keep it as a buffer against the creatures of darkness." He spat on the floor next to Rhonda's feet. "At any rate, it would be a damn fine deal greater than starving to death on this sorry excuse for a ship! At least you'd get to live a little before you die."

"Mordred!" Julian blurted out as soon as it clicked in his

head. "Moor of Dread. Mordred. That can't be a coincidence, right?" He sat up excitedly in his chair. "How long has this conflict been going on?"

Marcus eyed him with confusion. "Conflict?"

"Between the Khalzharians and the... whoever. The Moor of Dread people."

Marcus rose from his chair, steadying himself on the table as he staggered toward Julian. He pointed to a spot on the map that was spread across the table.

Julian leaned over the map to see that Marcus was pointing to Khalzhar, located on a thin stretch of land connecting the vast Kingdom of Xanir to a long appendix-like peninsula.

"*Khalzhari*," Marcus corrected Julian. "They have been battling for centuries, neither side ever gaining any appreciable ground."

That poked a hole in Julian's theory. If this had only been going on for a couple of months, it would be a solid bet that one of Mordred's avatars was stirring up all the undead shit.

"How can a stalemate go on that long without eventually coming to a resolution?" asked Frank.

"By design, of course." Marcus sneered at Frank and Julian. "You lot aren't the brightest bunch of wizards we ever hauled into Khalzhar. That's the gods' honest truth if I ever did hear it."

"We had sheltered upbringings," said Rhonda. "Can you lay it out for us a little more clearly? Whose design is this? And for what purpose?"

"Everyone's design. The Xaniri could send in legions of soldiers to overrun the undead in a matter of weeks. In fact, they do sometimes lend some soldiers to the front lines when the wizards are scant."

"Then why don't they?" asked Julian.

"For the very same reason the ruling class wizards and the

## Critical Failures VIII

instructors don't blast the undead back to the Seven Hells themselves. They have grown accustomed to a certain quality of life. Without the ever-present threat of the Moor of Dread, Xanir would have a city-state full of powerful wizards on their doorstep and no justification to keep funneling gold and whores to them. The Xaniri common folk might start to ask questions."

"What about all the soldiers and wizard students they keep sending out to get slaughtered?" Julian knew the answer to his question even before he finished asking it.

Marcus laughed. "You truly did have sheltered upbringings."

"Frank!" said one of the Whore's Head elves as he suddenly appeared in the doorway. "You're not going to believe this."

Frank sighed, as if taking for granted that any news was bad news. "What is it, Roger? Is the ship sinking?"

"No." Roger paused to think about it. "At least, I don't think so."

"Have the prisoners escaped?"

"No."

"Is the ship on fire?"

"No."

"I don't know then, Roger. Did you lose your virginity? We're a little busy here."

Roger pointed outside. "I saw land."

That knocked the roll out of Frank's eyes. He stood up on his chair. "Are you sure?"

"One hundred percent sure. The storm's starting to clear, and I spotted what looked like trees through the mist. I waited for a bigger gap in the fog to confirm. We're only about a mile away from a shoreline!"

"Of course you are," said Marcus. He pointed at the map. "Here we are, just off the coast of the Moor of Dread. Makes navigation easier to follow the coastline."

"Awesome," said Rhonda. "We're a mile away from the coast of a peninsula full of the undead." She put her finger on the smudge Marcus had left on the map and ran it along the coastline to Khazhar. "The nearest port looks to be at least a week's journey on foot. And even if we somehow managed to survive the undead that long, we'd only get taken as slaves once we get there."

Marcus laughed again, and not in an encouraging or optimistic way. "That's not even where our troubles begin. Our mainmast is fucked beyond all hope of repair, and we do not have a dinghy."

"I'm telling you guys," said Roger. "We're less than a mile away. That's easily swimmable, especially if we grab some planks or barrels or whatever as flotation devices. I mean, I don't want to go to some ghoul-infested beach any more than the rest of you, but it's better than dying on this boat."

"You would not be all that is swimming in these waters. Just wait until the clouds clear and you can see all the black cock eels that slither just below the surface, then tell me how keen you are to go for a swim."

"Black cock eels?" said Julian. "Are they called that because…"

"They look like big black cocks."

Julian nodded his understanding, feeling a little sad that no one – including himself – found it within themselves to giggle. He missed Cooper.

"What would it take to fix the mainmast?" asked Frank.

Marcus slumped back down in his chair. "An act of the gods. Did I not make myself clear when I said that it was fucked beyond repair. It was barely hanging together with the shoddy repairs we made off the coast of Nazere." He nodded at Julian. "Your firebug here didn't do it any favors. It's cracked in two more places now. It must be completely replaced."

# Critical Failures VIII

Frank sighed.

"So we'll replace it," said Julian. "I mean, it's just a big pole, right? We don't have to win a regatta or anything. We just need something to hold the yards up so that the sails can harness enough wind to move us to a port before we die. Couldn't we substitute a tree trunk?"

Marcus raised his eyebrows at Julian. "Have you been hiding tree trunks up your arse this whole time? You might have mentioned that earlier."

"I was referring to the aforementioned forest full of trees on the peninsula over there."

"The peninsula full of ghosts and ghouls," said Rhonda.

"Yes."

"Beyond the sea of big black cocks."

"Correct."

"So what's the plan, then?" asked Roger. "We all gun it for the shore and hope to not get eaten by dick eels?"

Julian expected this kind of pessimism from Frank, but not from Roger. "You're the one who came in here all excited about spotting land."

"That was before I heard about the dick eels!"

"We've been through tougher challenges before. This whole game is about finding creative solutions to seemingly insurmountable problems, right?"

Rhonda cocked an eyebrow at him. "I'm eagerly waiting on what part of your creative solution involves a horse."

"I don't have a solution," said Julian. "At least, not yet. But I'm sure that if we put our heads together, we can figure something out."

Thunder rumbled softly in the distance while everyone spent a silent moment in thought.

Frank was the first one out of the gate. "We could cannibalize part of the ship to build a dinghy."

"There you go!" said Julian. "Way to think outside the box."

"Thanks, Dad."

Now that he thought about it, Julian supposed he had perhaps sounded a little condescending. "Sorry. I was just trying to be encouraging."

Frank nodded. "I know. So what about it?"

"We might be able to throw together something that will float and not fall completely apart the moment one of us steps onto it," said Marcus. "But I cannot see us crafting a boat so meticulously that half a dozen black cock eels can't slither through the cracks and send us all to an excruciating end."

Julian grimaced. "We'll come back to that. Keep thinking." After a longer moment of silence, Julian came up with a terrible idea. "I know this is going to sound bad, but maybe we can come up with something by taking pieces from different ideas."

Rhonda sighed. "Here comes the horse."

That was a decidedly unhelpful introduction to Julian's idea.

"What horse?" asked Marcus. "What good would a horse do us anyway?"

"Absolutely none," said Frank. "Let's hear it."

Julian took a deep breath. "So I summon a couple of horses." He waited through the expected collective groan, then continued. "They distract the eels while we row Frank's proposed dinghy as hard as we can."

Marcus's eyes focused on Julian like he was sobering up. "That's a horrible idea. I cannot even believe you'd propose it."

"It's called brainstorming," said Julian. "We're throwing out whatever we think of, and seeing what parts of those ideas we might be able to combine for an effective solution. Frank suggested the dinghy. You pointed out the shortcomings of that idea. My idea built on top of his. It's a small step up."

# Critical Failures VIII

"No, it isn't," said Roger. "We've got a mile of dick eel infested water to cross. Killing a couple of horses in addition to the rest of us won't make an iota of difference. We might as well go back to your original plan of jumping in and swimming like hell."

"I didn't suggest jumping in and swimming. You did."

"Well, unless you can fly, that's the only way we're getting to the shore."

Of course! Why hadn't that occurred to Julian before. "I *can* fly!"

Roger looked like he was cocked and ready to fire back with more unhelpful criticism, then he relaxed. "Oh. Cool."

"It's a Level 3 spell. I used it to get up to the Crescent Shadow. It should be no problem for me to cross a mile of open sea."

"Brilliant!" said Marcus.

Julian hadn't expected Marcus to be the one cheering on his idea, but he'd take what support he could. "Thank you. I don't know about *brilliant*, but I –"

"All you need to do is fly over there, chop down a tree by yourself while fighting off a bunch of zombies, ghouls, and wights, and then carry it back here."

Julian looked sternly at him. He wasn't getting through to these people. "I feel like I'm not making myself clear. The purpose of brainstorming is to –"

"You've made yourself plenty clear, elf. Now, please explain to the rest of us how you intend to combine your flying idea with horse murder and shoddy carpentry."

"Give him a break," said Rhonda. "It's not that bad an idea. So far, it's the only one that gets any of us to the shore alive."

"Thank you," said Julian.

"But it will still end with all of us dead."

"I'm not saying it's –"

"I know, I know," said Rhonda. "I'm just busting your balls.

It's a launching point. Can you cast Fly on only yourself, or can you cast it on other people as well?"

"I can cast it on other people."

"And how many Level 3 spells can you cast per day?"

"Four," said Julian.

Rhonda nodded while she thought, then turned to Marcus. "Do you think four of your strongest men could defend themselves for as long as it takes to cut down a tree?"

Julian cleared his throat. "We can only send two if they plan to come back."

"Shit, that's right."

"And one of them will have to be me, since I'm casting the spells."

"Double shit."

Julian shrugged. "We'll give it a shot. If the undead are too much to handle, we'll bail on the mission and either try again the next day or think of something else. In the meantime, we should all get some rest. I'll need to replenish my spells in the morning."

# CHAPTER 18

*R*andy was surprised at how little ceremony was involved with disembarking at Olan Meb. He wasn't sure exactly what he'd been expecting. Maybe having to go through customs and immigration or something. But there was nothing like that. Logan's men just marched them off the ship and led them by their chains straight into the city.

With few exceptions, most of the buildings were roughly cube shaped and made out of the same grayish-brown clay. They reminded Randy of Soviet-era eastern European apartment buildings.

Orc children dressed in patched-together scraps of recycled garments gawked and pointed at them, whispering excitedly to each other. It made Randy kind of feel like a celebrity. Maybe it was that, or maybe it was Captain Longfellow's infectious whistling or the lesser degree of sweat and poo smell in the air compared to down in the ship's cargo hold, or maybe it was a combination of any of those, but Randy was feeling unjustifiably cheerful as they marched toward the only landmark in the city that looked like any care or thought had been put into its design. The Colosseum-like structure stood high above the surrounding buildings at the center of Olan Meb. Even as they walked toward it, builders were busily adding to its grandeur. Towers were being erected on both sides of the entrance to welcome visitors.

"I will not be ignored!" said Denise. She had clearly not gotten caught up in the wonder of a new fantasy city, letting herself hang as dead weight between the two sailors she was chained to. "I demand to know where my baby is!"

There was more than enough manpower to drag her along, but her antics slowed the procession down enough to coax Rashad, the pirate flanking her, out of his feigned deafness.

"Halt!" he called ahead. The murmuring of orcish voices became clearer as the jingle of chains came to a stop, but Randy couldn't understand any of it. Rashad scowled down at Denise, sitting defiantly on her dwarven ass. "The crew picked through your *former* belongings, and we helped ourselves to what we wanted. Everything else, including that disgusting pet of yours, has been sent ahead for Zimbra to do with as he pleases."

"That ain't no pet," said Denise. "That's my baby! It came right out of my cooter."

Rashad's initial grimace turned into a sneer. "In that case, you might want to hurry. If I was Zimbra, I'd want to get rid of that thing as quickly as possible. His chimeras are always hungry."

Randy didn't know how plausible Rashad's speculations were, or exactly what a chimera was, and he suspected that Denise had no more insight than he did, but she got to her feet.

"You see this fist?" she said, shaking it at Rashad. "If little Fatty gets eaten by a Camaro, this is going right up your ass. I will hunt down every last one of you motherfuckers and pull your intestines out through your hiney holes." She pushed the man in front of her. "Come on, now. Move your ass!"

As gross as her threat had been, Randy was touched to see Denise's protective motherly nature shining through. He felt bad again about accidentally feeding the rest of her babies to Basil.

The rest of the walk to the stadium went quickly. Instead of entering through the large stone archway, they were led

# Critical Failures VIII

around back to enter underground through what looked like a root cellar entrance.

After a short walk through some dark corridors that smelled more like the inside of the ship, they came out again to bright light and fresher air. Randy now understood the unconventional way they'd entered. The big archway led to the seats above the arena pit and was meant for spectators. Randy and the others weren't there to see a show. They were down in the pit.

Ironically, the pit was one of the brightest and cleanest places Randy had been in quite a while. The sand covering the floor was bone white and combed flat. Aside from the B.O. they'd brought with them, the air was surprisingly fresh. It was almost exactly the opposite of *Nightwind*'s cargo hold in every way imaginable, except that they were all still prisoners chained together.

The arena seats were empty except for a group of five grinning goblins directly behind the spot where Randy and the others were instructed to stop. They were all dressed in what looked like potato sacks and armed with crossbows. One of them winked at Randy.

"Greetings!" cried a charismatic orc in a flowing bright orange toga as he sashayed toward them. He was flanked by decidedly less charismatic orcs wielding iron clubs the size of baseball bats. Dents and blood stains suggested the weapons had quite a bit of mileage on them. "Welcome to Olan Meb!"

"You Zebra?" asked Denise.

The flamboyantly cheerful orc's grin faltered briefly. "My name is *Zimbra*. And who do I have the pleasure of addressing?"

"I'm Denise. You have my –"

"That will do, thank you," said Zimbra. "It is an honor to meet you, Denise. I would like to introduce you to my friend, Rocco. Rocco, say hello to Denise."

The orc on Zimbra's left lumbered forward, then rammed the end of his club hard into Denise's gut, knocking the wind out of her and dropping her to her knees.

Zimbra put his cheerful face back on. "That's how Rocco says hello. He was once a gladiator here, just like the most fortunate of you will be. He used to be a lot more chatty, but that was before he learned how and when one speaks in the arena. Isn't that right, Rocco?"

Rocco stepped back from Denise and bowed slightly. "That is correct, Master Zimbra."

"Is there anything you'd like to add to that, Rocco?"

"No, Master Zimbra."

Zimbra sighed as he addressed his new recruits. "As for me, I like a bit of chit-chat. I want us all to have fun here. But it seems that the more lessons you learn, the less talkative you get. Rocco here had to learn a *lot* of very hard lessons before we finally got through to him. Now, before we move on, do any of you have anything else you'd like to say?"

Denise struggled to her feet. "I do."

Zimbra rolled his eyes. "What a shocking surprise. Rocco?"

"Wait!" cried Denise. "Where's my baby, you son of a – OOMPH!" She fell to her knees again and coughed up some blood on the otherwise pristine white sand.

"Did she say *baby*?" He turned to Ponston, the sailor Captain Logan had appointed as the acting captain of Katherine's ship. "Did you bring me a mother and child?"

Ponston laughed nervously. "Of course not, Zimbra. The dwarf is mad. There was no dwarven child with her when we took her."

Zimbra frowned at Denise. "Her nipples are leaking. This woman is lactating. Are you quite sure there was no child?"

"Fatty ain't a dwarf," said Denise, struggling to her feet again.

# Critical Failures VIII

Rocco glanced at Zimbra, who responded with a subtle shake of the head.

"Go on, dwarf. You have piqued my curiosity."

"I was impregnated by a scorpion woman," Denise explained. "She pumped me full of her fertilized eggs shortly before she passed away." She conveniently left out the details of Azhar's untimely demise. "When I finally gave birth to them, Randy here fed all but one to his pet Basilisk." She nodded up to Randy.

Both Zimbra and Rocco raised their eyebrows at Randy. It was the first hint of emotion he'd seen in Rocco.

"I ain't meant to," said Randy. "It was an accident!"

"Please," pleaded Denise. "Little Fatty's all I got left, and it needs my titty milk."

Zimbra stared thoughtfully at the well-manicured claws on his right hand. "So that's what that thing was. I thought it was a kraken louse you'd picked up at sea. Rocco, please go and see if the scorpion folk baby has already been fed to the chimeras."

"As you command, Master Zimbra." said Rocco. He started to walk away, then turned back to Zimbra. "If it has not been done, shall I do the deed myself and crush the chimera keeper's feet and hands?"

"No, you dumb motherfucker!" said Denise.

Zimbra let out an annoyed sigh. "Rocco?"

Rocco stomped back toward Denise.

"Where the fuck are you going, shit for brains? Hurry up and get my goddamn – OOMPH!"

"Someone has forgotten who gives the orders around here, it seems," said Zimbra. "Rocco, I want you to *fetch* the child. If it still lives, bring it back here to me." He turned back to Denise with a friendly grin as she panted on her hands and knees and spat more blood on the sand. "I simply adore babies."

"I mean no disrespect, Zimbra," said Ponston. "But there is the matter of payment to discuss."

"How can I pay for these recruits when I do not yet know what they are worth?"

"I can assure you that they are all strong and healthy. They will make excellent gladiators."

Zimbra shook his head. "How many times must I explain? Arena fighting is about more than two men beating the life out of each other. It involves showmanship and panache, a sense of drama and flair. Do any of these men have any theatrical training or experience?"

"Not to my knowledge," Ponston grumbled. "It appears we put the bard on the wrong ship. I thought you wanted men who could fight, not sing and dance."

"Perhaps a demonstration is in order. Draw your sword, Captain."

"I beg your pardon."

Zimbra hopped back a few steps and pirouetted, his toga swirling around him like a flickering flame. "Your sword. I want you to remove it from its sheath."

Ponston exchanged uncertain glances with his fellow crewmen, then unsheathed his sword. He held it down by his side. "Shall I bring it to you?"

"In a manner of speaking. I want you to attack me with it."

Ponston laughed. "You want me to *what*?"

"You do know how to use a sword, do you not?"

Now Ponston's crewmen were laughing and egging him on.

"Go on, Captain!"

"Get him!"

"Stick it up his arse!"

Ponston shot them a warning glare, then turned back to Zimbra. "You are as mad as the dwarf. I will not murder an unarmed man in his own arena. You have not even paid me yet."

# Critical Failures VIII

Zimbra yawned, then looked up with bored eyes at the goblins in the stands above Randy. "Huntak?"

"Yes, Master Zimbra," one of the goblins responded enthusiastically.

"I would like you to count down from five. If this man does not attack me by the time you finish, I want you to shoot him."

"Very good, Master Zimbra."

CLICK!

Randy recognized the sound behind him as a cocking crossbow.

"What?" cried Ponston.

"FIVE!"

Ponston looked desperately back at the goblins, then back at Zimbra. "Please!"

"FOUR!"

"Don't make me do this, I beg you!"

The goblins began hurriedly chattering in their own language, provoking an annoyed expression from Zimbra.

"I am sorry, Master Zimbra," said the one called Huntak. "Did you mean only me? Or do you want us all to shoot him?"

Zimbra's expression lightened. "Ah, that was my fault. I should have been clearer. I meant all of you."

The goblins chattered again briefly.

CLICK! CLICK! CLICK! CLICK!

"This is ludicrous!" cried Ponston.

"THREE!"

"YAAAAAA!" Ponston ran at Zimbra with his sword held out in front of him, less like he was fighting a person and more like he was trying to skewer a giant marshmallow.

Zimbra easily sidestepped the poor excuse for an attack and delivered a fist into Ponston's gut, causing Ponston to fall to his knees and drop his sword. Zimbra helped him back to his feet.

"You see?" he said, gesturing to Randy's group. "Look at them. They are bored. The very ship captain who ferried them in chains across the sea getting punched in the belly, and there is not a hint of emotion on any of their faces." He stepped back from Ponston. "Now, let us try again. This time I want you to come at me with –"

*POP!*

Ponston caught him by surprise with a jab to the snout. His men gasped as Zimbra staggered backwards covering his face. Randy looked up to the goblins, but they were watching the fight with amusement, their crossbows lowered.

"How does that feel?" asked Ponston, closing the gap between himself and Zimbra, his fists ready to throw another punch. "Is this how you orcs do business in Meb' Garshur? It is no wonder you –" He leaned back as Zimbra came at him with a wild desperate-looking swing, then drove his elbow down into his back, dropping Zimbra to his hands and knees.

Zimbra tried to stand up, but Ponston jumped on the advantage he currently held, kicking Zimbra repeatedly in the gut and ribs.

"You... prancing... dandy... fool!" he said between kicks. When Zimbra finally collapsed into a fetal position, Ponston circled him and continued berating him. "I sail across the sea to bring you good strong men. But instead of payment, you give me ridicule. Then you dare attack me in front of my own men!" He kicked Zimbra hard in the small of the back.

"Captain!" said Rashad.

Ponston smiled. "Have no fear, Rashad. We are merely having a little fun. This is what he asked for, after all, right?" He stomped on Zimbra's arm and kicked him in the ass. "Get up and fight, coward! Show us all how it is done."

"Should we do something?" Randy whispered to Captain Longfellow.

"Aye," said Captain Longfellow. "We should watch. I sense

a change in the winds be coming soon."

"What good is all your showmanship when you cannot even stand up?" said Ponston as he continued his assault. "You don't know what fighting is until you've boarded a ship and clashed swords with worthy men whose very lives are at stake. Do you know how many of you orcs I've sent to the bottom of the sea? Too many to count, and not a one of them pranced about the deck like a court jester before meeting his end. You are an embarrassment to your nation and your race. If these new recruits of yours learn anything from you, I hope it is how pitifully easy you are to –"

SWOOSH!

Zimbra's orange toga swirled around like a whirlwind of fire as he swept Ponston's legs out from under him. After a lightning-fast jab to Ponston's balls, he sprang to his feet and backflipped into an elegant-looking martial arts stance.

"Hot damn!" said Denise. "Y'all seen that shit?"

The punch in the balls hadn't been a hard one, more like just an attention getter. And it sure got Ponston's attention. He got back on his feet in no time, and ran at Zimbra like a pissed-off locomotive. Zimbra grabbed Ponston's fist, then used Ponston's own inertia to flip him onto his back. He hit the ground with an audible thud, kicking up a brief Ponston-shaped cloud of sand.

The prisoners cheered and rattled their chains. Even Ponston's men chuckled a little.

Any serious damage Ponston had suffered so far seemed only to have been to his pride. He was red-faced and sweaty when he got back up, but completely unbloodied.

Zimbra, on the other hand, was bleeding through his toga in several places, but he still carried himself gracefully.

Ponston approached more carefully this time, his forearms raised defensively like a boxer. "No more tricks, Zimbra. You want to fight? Let us fight like men."

"It is true that fighting for an audience differs from the ways many of you are accustomed to fighting," said Zimbra, addressing the recruits as he effortlessly bobbed, weaved, and ducked away from Ponston's increasingly frustrated swings. "What some of you will learn here is that which separates the artist from the common thug." He snatched Ponston's wrist as it flew by his head, twisted his arm around his back, and kicked him in the ass. Captives and crewmen alike shared a laugh at Ponston's expense.

"As you develop your art," Zimbra continued, "you will grow to cherish the cheers of the spectators more dearly than you cherish your own lives. And when you finally do meet your end, you will have lived a fuller life than the multitudes who squander their time away under the illusion of freedom."

Randy had to admit, this guy was making slavery sound pretty glamorous. He raised his hand as high as his chains would allow him.

Zimbra dodged a bull rush from behind at the last possible fraction of a second, extending his left arm as he did so to catch Ponston with a clothesline to the throat. Then he pointed at Randy. "You in the back row. Do you have a question?"

Randy stared at Ponston, who was writhing on the ground next to Zimbra and clutching his neck, until Captain Longfellow nudged him in the ribs. "Oh, yes. You mentioned freedom just a second ago?"

"The *illusion* of freedom," Zimbra corrected him.

"I seen a few gladiator movies in my time, and I was just wondering, if we do a good job, is it possible we might earn our freedom back?"

"Freedom to do what? To toil in some field until you are too old to control your bowels? To be remembered for only a short time after your passing by those few poor souls who are relieved to no longer be under the obligation to wipe the shit from betwixt your wrinkled ass cheeks? For your demise to not be mourned, nor your memory celebrated? No, sir. I am not so cruel a man as to deliver that fate unto you, nor that burden to your loved ones. Instead, I offer all of you the chance at immortality in the memories of those you entertain. Are there any other questions?"

Randy put his hand up again. "I got one more."

Zimbra gave him a doubtful look. "Is it about *freedom*?"

"Not exactly," said Randy. "At least, I don't think so."

"Ask, then. But do not try my patience."

"You said *some* of us will learn to be a fighting artist. What about the rest of us?"

Zimbra smiled. "Your question is less stupid than I had expected."

"Thank you."

"Sad as it may be, some of you simply are not cut out for this vocation. Despite your best efforts, most of you will prove incapable of entertaining an audience, even as your life depends on it."

"And what happens to them?"

"Their lack of dramatic flair will be offset by more spectacular opponents."

That didn't sound as bad as Randy had expected. "So they still get a chance, then."

Zimbra laughed like what Randy had just said was the most adorable thing he'd ever heard. "Watching one boring man stab another boring man to death is tedious. Watching a dire boar trample and gore five boring men to death is much more exciting. However, spectacular opponents are expensive and difficult to come by and care for. The risk we take to have them in the arena is a calculated one. But yes. In the most literal sense of the word, we give them a chance, albeit a very slim one. You would do well to keep that in mind when you –"

"Keep this in mind!" cried Ponston as he lunged at Zimbra with his sword he'd retrieved.

Zimbra smirked slightly as he caught Ponston's sword hand, wrapped it around Ponston's torso, then spun him around until both their arms were outstretched, like they were ballroom dancing. When he twirled Ponston back toward him, however, he ended the dance abruptly with a brutal head butt to the face. Ponston collapsed at his feet and did not attempt to get back up.

Randy, the other captives, and even most of Ponston's crew clapped politely. Harsh as it may have been, it was an entertaining end to the fight.

"FATTY!" cried Denise, suddenly ending all applause.

Zimbra stared at her in confusion. As lean and muscular as he clearly was under that toga, he was no doubt unaccustomed to being insulted in such a way.

But Denise's gaze was focused beyond Zimbra. Rocco was returning with Denise's baby in his arms. Randy didn't know what they'd been feeding him on the ship, but he'd grown about fifty percent of his original weight since he'd last seen him on Nazere.

"How delightful," said Zimbra. "The cockroach is still alive."

"Don't you talk about my baby like that!" said Denise. "Bring it on over here. Goddamn, Fatty. What they been feeding you?"

After a nod from Zimbra, Rocco set Fatty down on the ground and approached Denise with only his club in hand.

"The fuck are you doing? I don't want to see you. I want to see my – Hey, when did Fatty learn how to walk?" She glared at Rashad, the crewman nearest her. "I missed my baby's first steps, you sons of bi– OOMPH!" She dropped to her knees again, her eyes welling up with tears as she gazed lovingly between Rocco's legs at the baby scorpion person toddling about curiously on the sandy arena floor.

His tail was proportionally smaller than those of his biological parents, dragging behind him instead of curving upward and over his head. Likewise, the lobster claws at the ends of his lower set of arms were only about the size of bolt cutters. Not something Randy would ever wish to get pinched with, but a far cry from the massive claws he remembered the adult scorpionfolk having. The tail and claws would probably develop fully during puberty.

If his upper half was anything to go by, puberty was a ways off. The human-like part of him was still like that of a plump, red-skinned baby.

Zimbra cleared his throat. "If I may continue no further interruptions. As I expect most of you are interesting enough in your own right, I'll give you a little nudge in the right direction. I want each of you to think of yourselves as a character. Something bold and exciting, but simple enough for the crowd to understand with a simple introduction. For example, take the mouthy dwarf woman. She is built like a bull and has had relations with a mated scorpion woman. Mayhap she could be called Homewrecker." He smiled. "It is a double entendre, see? We could paint her face and dress her like a whore. It would be hilarious since she's so vile and offensive to look at."

"Hey, motherfucker!" cried Denise. "Don't talk that way about me in front of my kid! And I'll have you know that by dwarf standards, I'm sexy as – OOMPH!"

At this point, it would have been more merciful for Rocco to whack her upside the head and knock her out cold, but Randy got the feeling that Rocco was enjoying delivering his "lessons" in spite of the fact that Denise was clearly not learning anything from them.

"How about you in the back?" Zimbra continued, this time pointing at Randy. "You like to ask so many questions.

Mayhap you could be *The Inquisitor*. You could torture your opponents to extract information or confessions from them."

"Well, I don't much care for torture."

Zimbra stared at Randy with wide, shocked eyes. He was clearly not used to having his opinions challenged. Rocco looked to him for a nod, but Zimbra waved him back.

"No, no. If the slave thinks he has a better character idea than mine, I am keen to hear it. Speak, slave. Tell me about your character concept. Who are you?"

Randy hadn't actually put any thought into a character concept, but he didn't like the idea of getting clubbed in the belly. He opted to take the question at face value and see where it went from there.

"My name's Randy, and I'm a paladin of the New God."

Zimbra raised his eyebrows and frowned thoughtfully for a moment. "I will admit, you have surprised me. A holy warrior. I cannot say I am in love with the name *Randy*, but the concept has potential." He scanned Randy up and down. "Sadly, I am afraid that you are not right for the part. It requires someone with more passion, a larger-than-life personality. Then again, so would The Inquisitor. I picture you more in the role of... I don't know. Maybe a turnip farmer, or a target used in training dogs to attack. The latter might work as a concept if we could think of a catchy name for you. Something that says big, lumbering brute with a pea-sized brain and..." His eyes lit up. "I've got it! The Village Idiot!"

Denise snorted. Rocco narrowed his eyes at her but gave her a pass.

"You've been mocked since childhood," Zimbra continued. "All the other children used to spit on you and throw rocks at you. As you got older, those children's children spat on you and threw rocks at you while their parents laughed. Finally, you had enough. You flew into a rage and killed everyone in the village with your bare hands,

# Critical Failures VIII

because you are too stupid to understand how weapons work."

Randy wasn't sure how he felt about this being the impression of himself that Zimbra was picking up on. Also, he suspected Zimbra didn't appreciate how much science and skill there was behind getting an optimal turnip crop.

"We'll have you hauled out in chains," Zimbra continued with his vision of Randy. "Just like the ones you're in now, but we'll saw down one of the links. The other fighters will throw rocks at you and call you terrible names. The audience can even join in! We'll make sure every seat has a rock to throw. After a few minutes of that, you let out a horrifying scream, break your chains, and unleash your furious vengeance! How does that sound?"

"I appreciate how much thought you've put into my character," said Randy as politely as he could. The vision Zimbra had for him didn't sound too far off from his old life back in Mississippi. He didn't mind folks throwing rocks at him so much, but he didn't like all the mockery and ridicule. Besides, Zimbra had said himself that he liked the paladin character. Who better to play that than an actual paladin? "I wasn't talking about no character concept before. My name really is Randy, and I really am a paladin of the New God."

Zimbra sighed. "There are few things more irksome than a method actor who cannot act."

"But I –"

"However, I respect your dedication to the role and your commitment to –"

"YAAAAAAAA!" came a scream from ten yards behind Zimbra.

Zimbra rolled his eyes. "What is it now?" He turned around.

Ponston was awake again, screaming in agony with Fatty's stinger buried in his left ass cheek. As underdeveloped as his tail was, Fatty wasn't able to wield it overhead yet, so he had to attack while facing away from its target, which probably would have been difficult to do to a conscious victim.

"Oh, dear," said Zimbra, but neither he nor Rocco made any attempt to intervene.

The sailors exchanged glances, like they were wondering if they should do something, but none of them wanted to make a move without Zimbra's say so.

It took Ponston a few swats to grab hold of Fatty's tail, as if he was having issues with his coordination. He finally yanked the stinger out, rolled away, and tried to stand up, but his legs weren't working any better than his arms. He had only managed to stand high enough for it to look extra painful when he fell back down on his wounded ass. Randy guessed scorpionfolk venom must affect the victim's Dexterity score.

Fatty toddled backwards after Ponston, landing another hit with his tail, and eliciting another scream from Ponston. He tried to grab for the tail again, but his arms were flopping around like Willy Water Bug. They stopped flopping as Ponston's screams died down.

When Ponston was still and silent, Fatty removed his tail from Ponston's ass, then began cutting through his clothes and belly skin. Seconds later, he was devouring Ponston's intestines. His sweet, cherub-like baby cheeks glistened with blood and viscera as he snipped at Ponston's insides with his scorpion arms and used his human-like hands to stuff more of him into his mouth.

"That's my kid," Denise muttered with a mother's pride. "You go, Fatty. You eat that son of a bitch."

Rocco either didn't hear her, or he was so fascinated by watching a baby scorpion person disembowel and eat an adult human that it didn't register.

Zimbra turned back to his recruits. "There. You see that

## Critical Failures VIII

look on all your faces? That is what I was referring to earlier. Even the most boring man is fascinating to watch when being killed in a way you've never seen before. This is why it is important for you to put on a good show. Now, we have *Homewrecker,* and I have decided to let the tall one try his hand at *Randy the Paladin.* Do I have any volunteers for *Village Idiot?*"

# CHAPTER 19

"This is your room," said Yavin, the fellow inmate who had been assigned to show Cooper and Tim around. The sandy brown hair covering most of his body was very nearly the same color as his tanned skin, as was the loincloth he wore, giving him the appearance at first glance that he was furry and naked. He was a hulking beast of a man physically, but surprisingly friendly and good-natured. "It is not much, but it is home."

Cooper set Tim down and poked his head inside the room. It was small, with a bed on each side and a wooden table and chair between them. Judging by the smell, it hadn't been unoccupied very long before they arrived. Yavin was right about it not being much, but the beds alone put it a notch above sleeping on the floor at the Whore's Head Inn.

"Where the fuck's the door?" asked Tim, eyeing the entryway. Now that he mentioned it, that did seem odd. There weren't even hinges or anything to suggest there had ever been a door there.

Yavin smiled. "There are no doors here. You are free to roam about at any time."

"What kind of prison doesn't have doors on the cells?"

"That is precisely the reason we have no doors. The governor doesn't want you to think of this place as a prison, but as your home."

"My home had a fucking door," said Tim. "I'm not worried about roaming about. I'm worried about going to sleep in an underground complex full of trained murderers."

Yavin laughed. "You may sleep without worry, little friend. The only violence that happens here takes place in the arena."

"Why? Do they drug us or something to keep us docile?"

"Good evening, Yavin," said a cheery half-orc stepping out of an identical room across the hall.

"And a good evening to you as well, Hogarth." Yavin gestured to Cooper and Tim. "These are the newest of our fighting brethren. Cooper and Tim." He looked down at Tim. "Did I say that right?"

Tim gave him a thumbs up. "Yeah, you totally mastered all the subtle nuances and inflections of *Tim*."

"Greetings!" said Hogarth. "May your time here be long and full of –"

"Fuck you, fish lips." Tim glared up at Yavin. "What's going on? What's with all this Born Again bullshit? Is this a fucking cult or something?"

"I am sorry," said Yavin. "I do not understand your question."

"Why is everybody so goddamn friendly? And so help me fucking God, if you tell me some shit about how we're all a big happy crappy family, I will lose my shit, knock you the fuck out, and take a hot and steamy dump in your mouth."

Both Yavin and Hogarth glanced nervously up and down the hallway before Yavin answered.

"I do not know how much you know about arena fighting, but much of it is staged."

Tim nodded. "Yeah, we're in on your little secret."

"It is no secret," said Yavin. "The audience knows that we are putting on a show, and they enjoy it. But they would not return as frequently or spend their coin so freely if there was not an occasional act of genuine brutality."

"We heard about all that, too," said Tim. "If you can't put

on a good show, you get fed to monsters or whatever."

"Putting on a bad show is not the only misdeed you need fear committing, halfling. Many a gladiator meet their ends unexpectedly, only realizing their opponent's betrayal when their blood is already pooling at their feet."

Cooper felt like he was missing something important. "So sometimes people get a little overzealous in the heat of battle. That shit happens in prisons all the time. What the fuck do you expect if you actually give them weapons?"

"These betrayals are not the result of improvisations. They generally occur shortly after the betrayed stirs up trouble outside the arena. Perhaps they start a fight, attempt to escape, or get caught trying to organize a revolt. Zimbra will take the accused's opponent aside just before a fight and *alter the script*, if you understand my meaning."

"Shit," said Cooper. "Nobody said anything about a script. I can't fucking read!"

"I get that much," Tim said to Yavin. "Don't start no shit, won't be no shit and all that. But that still doesn't explain all the *How do you do, neighbor!* crap. There's a wide gap between keeping your head down and not causing trouble, and the way you guys seem to jerk each other off with your greetings."

Yavin laughed. "So it must seem. However, even when all is going smoothly down here, the audience in the arena still expects the occasional brutal death they laid down their hard-earned coin to watch. During these relatively peaceful times, lesser infractions become death sentences. A foul word or gesture, perhaps. Or even a grumbled hello might find you on the wrong end of a fellow gladiator's spear."

Tim looked up at Cooper, his face several shades paler than it had been a minute ago. "Dude, we are so fucked."

"Fear not, friend," said Yavin. "You will be given ample time to adjust to this new lifestyle. The kindness of your brother and sister gladiators will rub off on you, and your attitude about being here will change. After a few days, you will even grow to enjoy it. All of your needs are taken care of. Even the food is good, and you may visit the cafeteria to eat as often as you like."

"Fuck the cafeteria," said Tim. "What I need is the all-you-can-drink bar."

Yavin frowned. "I am sorry to say, there is no alcohol here."

Tim went even paler. "Are you fucking kidding me? How am I supposed to be friendly without booze?"

Cooper shrugged. "For what it's worth, you're not all that friendly *with* booze either."

"Again," said Yavin. "You will be given time to adjust. And even if you make the occasional slip-up, you have your reputation to fall back on. As long as the crowd loves you, you need not fear getting chosen as a sacrifice."

Tim laughed. "Loves me? The crowd isn't going to fucking love me. Nobody loves me. Cooper's my best friend, and I only managed to get him on my side by denying him lycanthropy treatment until he turned."

That sounded a little sinister when he put it that way, but Cooper remembered the fight he'd had with Tim on the road south of Cardinia. Hoping to set Tim on the right path, he'd had to lay down some shit that Tim didn't want to hear. Likewise, Cooper hadn't been thinking straight when he and Tim were in the desert. A lesser friend would have let him go "cure" his lycanthropy, but it took a true friend to leave him stranded in the desert until he could see clearly.

"How exciting!" said Yavin. Cooper was lost in thought for a moment there, but that seemed like a strange response to someone announcing they had what most people would liken to an STD. "I am also a lycanthrope! A werebear, to be precise. What is the nature of your gift?"

Again, this also seemed like an odd thing to ask. If he was

a lycanthrope, then why the fuck would he need them to explain the nature of it.

"We're wererats," said Tim.

"Oh," said Yavin, pretending he wasn't underwhelmed. Cooper knew that *Oh* all too well, having heard it whenever he ran into someone from back in high school and said he delivered pizzas for a living. If he followed the pattern, he was about to follow up with a hastily thought-up question in an effort to fake interest. "And how long have you had your... *gift?*"

What a dick. He had to force the word out, as if being able to turn into a rat monster was so much less extraordinary than being able to turn into a bear that it didn't even count as a gift.

"I've had it a couple of months now," said Tim. "Cooper's only been through one full moon so far." Why wasn't he telling this guy to go fuck himself? Surely he could sense the condescension as easily as Cooper could.

Yavin nodded. "That is quite a lot you two have to adjust to."

"Quite a lot indeed," said Tim. "So what do you all do for recreation around here?"

"Most of our time is spent training. We try to make the fights look as authentic as possible, which requires a great deal of practice."

"Say I wanted to do some sewing. Would it be possible to get some fabric, and a needle and thread?"

Maybe Yavin was right about this place rubbing off on them. Cooper didn't feel any different yet, but Tim had suddenly turned into a giant pussy.

Another thought occurred to Cooper. Maybe Tim was trying to Shawshank his way out. But of all the hobbies he could pretend to suddenly give a shit about, why sewing?

"Sewing?" said Yavin, sounding as taken aback by Tim's

request as Cooper.

"I want to make a costume for the character I'll be portraying."

Yavin smiled. "Have no fear of that. The tailor will provide you with a suitable costume."

"That's all well and good, but it's not the tailor's ass on the line if I'm not entertaining enough. I'd like to be in control of my own destiny, thank you very much."

Cooper was impressed. He had no idea Tim knew how to sew, but he was happy to see him taking some initiative for once.

"The tailor's name is Maurice," said Yavin. He pointed down the corridor past Tim and Cooper. "You can find him down there. Last room before the cafeteria."

Tim smiled. It was mildly unnerving. "Perfect. I just might grab a bite to eat as well."

That sounded good to Cooper. He was tired as shit from their forced march through the desert, but he was also really hungry.

Yavin smiled back at Tim. "Eat well, friends. And rest. Tomorrow, we will begin your training."

"Looking forward to it," said Tim with a friendly wave, then he turned around and started limping down the corridor.

Cooper followed him for a bit, then glanced back to make sure Yavin was out of earshot. "Dude, are you okay?"

"As okay as can be expected for a crippled midget about to start his first day of gladiator training. Why do you ask?"

"I was just surprised at how well you hit it off with Yavin."

Tim grinned up at him. "Are you jealous?"

"No, I'm not fucking jealous. But you're not usually as much of a..." Cooper had started the sentence without thinking through how he was going to end it. "What's the opposite of asshole?"

Tim shrugged. "Mouth?"

"That's not exactly what I had in mind."

"Don't even worry about that prick. He's the Ned Flanders of bear-men. But he's also a wealth of information. We need to warm up to people while we get a feel for the place if we're going to survive long enough to bust out of here."

Cooper felt some relief that Tim was acting like himself again. "You got something in mind?"

"I'm working on it." Tim stopped short of the last doorway before the corridor opened into a large room full of wooden tables. The smell of meatloaf wafted out. "Go on in and get something to eat. I'll join you after I get what I need."

"I can wait for you if you want."

"Go ahead. I won't be long." Tim took a step toward the tailor's doorway, then turned around. "And remember, we're in a place full of violent criminals. Don't talk to anyone."

"What if they ask me how many scoops of mashed potatoes I want or something?"

Tim rolled his eyes. "Then tell the person how many fucking scoops of mashed potatoes you want. All I'm asking is that you keep a low profile so that we don't get murdered on our first day. Do you think you can do that for the five minutes it takes me to get some goddamn fabric?"

"I mean, I think so. But if it's only going to take you five minutes, I can –"

"Jesus, Cooper. I'm not asking you to disarm a fucking bomb. Just keep a low profile. Go get some food, sit down at a table, and eat. You got this. I believe in you."

That gave Cooper a warm feeling inside that he hadn't felt since... He shook the thought out of his head.

"Thanks, man."

"I'll be right behind you." Tim hobbled into the tailor's room.

Cooper stepped nervously into the cafeteria. Tim was right

## Critical Failures VIII

in that it shouldn't be the biggest challenge in the world to get free food and sit down without pissing anyone off. He probably wouldn't be so jittery about it if Tim hadn't made such a big deal about telling him not to fuck it up.

Thankfully, the large room was nearly empty. Judging by when they'd arrived, it was probably somewhere between the breakfast and lunch rush.

It was laid out pretty much the same as his elementary school cafeteria. A bunch of wooden tables set out in rows filled the large main area. A serving station with large tubs of various foods stood at the far end. Even the orc attending the serving station reminded Cooper of one of the lunch ladies from back home.

"You must be new here," said the orc. He even sounded a little like the lunch lady from back home. "Do not be shy. Come in and help yourself. I'll be right back. I've got some fresh buns in the oven." With that, he abandoned his station and left through a pair of saloon doors into what Cooper assumed was the kitchen.

That was good. Cooper hadn't said a word so far, and it looked like he might not need to. His hunger took over his anxiety as he approached the serving station. He was surprised at how good the food looked and smelled, and was almost sure that it wasn't just because he was starving.

He grabbed a tray and two dishes, then filled the first dish with meat chunks in gravy. Most of the vegetables he gave a pass, having had enough of those in the Fertile Desert to last him a while. But he did like the look of the green stuff and the orange stuff that seemed to have the consistency of mashed potatoes. Gut-filling carbohydrates would be most welcome right now, and he bet that they would go well with the meat gravy.

At the end of the line was a bin of light wooden forks. He picked one up, and it felt like it might break if he looked at it too hard. It must have been made out of balsa. Certainly not something he had to worry about one of his fellow inmates stabbing him with. The only thing he could find to drink was a barrel full of brownish water. Giving it a sniff, he couldn't determine if it had been flavored with tree bark or dirt. He ladled some into a wooden cup and turned toward the tables to find a place to sit.

"Hot buns!" said the orc from behind Cooper.

So it was going to be like that. Cooper knew he should have waited for Tim. He didn't know how to respond in this sort of situation. Should he set an example with this motherfucker, or should he just bend over and take it?

No. A line had to be drawn somewhere, whatever the repercussions. Besides, that's the sort of shit you're supposed to pull in the showers. Everybody knows that. It's basic fucking prison etiquette. If he allowed himself to get cornholed in the cafeteria on his first day in the clink, he'd only be establishing himself as anyone's bitch for the taking.

Still, that didn't mean he needed to knock this guy's tusks out just yet. He'd start with a stern, flat rejection of his advances, and only resort to violence if he didn't take the hint.

Cooper turned around to find the orc holding a pan full of bread loaves. He gave him his best menacing glare. "No thank you, sir."

The orc smiled. "As you wish."

Cooper relaxed. That was easier than he'd anticipated. He was impressed with himself over the restraint he'd shown. That dude backed down faster than an erection when grandma walks into the room. Was he Cooper's bitch now? Only one way to find out.

"But I wouldn't mind helping myself to some of that bread you've got there."

"Please," said the orc, lifting the tray toward Cooper.

# Critical Failures VIII

"Take as many as you like."

Cooper nodded as he took a loaf. Then, just to make doubly sure that this motherfucker knew his place in the pecking order, he took one more. His would-be assailant just smiled and let him take it. Poor guy wouldn't last long in a place like this. Some folks just aren't cut out for a life in the joint.

Satisfied that he'd successfully established himself as someone not to fuck with, Cooper sat down at an empty table and enjoyed his meal.

The orange stuff tasted like some kind of pumpkin-potato hybrid, and the green stuff tasted like a mixture of pureed leftover vegetable parts. Neither was bad with a little gravy, which tasted like something between soy sauce and honey.

The meat he wasn't able to identify so easily, mostly because it was doused in so much gravy. It could have been roasted orphan for all Cooper gave a shit. He was hungrier and more tired than he could ever remember being. He thought he would go back for seconds, and possibly even thirds, but the bread was more filling than he expected. He got the first loaf down with no problem, but was only nibbling halfway through the second one, and even then because he had nothing better to do.

What the hell was taking Tim so long? Could he really be that engrossed in choosing the perfect shades and fabric patterns for his stupid –

"FIRE!" cried someone from inside the kitchen.

Two orcish cooks ran out wearing aprons with so many different colored stains they could have passed for art. Small but thickening tendrils of grey smoke followed them.

"Water!" said one of them, running for the water barrel. He tossed away the ladle in favor of a bowl. By the time they lugged the barrel back to the kitchen, smoke was billowing out the doorway and starting to fill the dining hall.

Cooper considered asking if there was anything he could

do to help, but fuck that. They'd probably end up blaming him for starting the fire. In fact, it was probably a good idea to get as far away from here as possible. Tim would have to eat alone.

He looked around for a bussing station where he could drop off his tray, but couldn't see the walls clearly through the smoke. Fuck it. The kitchen was on fire. Nobody was going to give a shit about his abandoned tray. Cooper stood up to leave when he saw a small dark blur slice through the smoke from the kitchen doorway to the serving station.

Squinting through the smoke as he approached, he found Tim wearing a royal blue silk scarf over his nose and mouth. He was hurriedly shoving loaves of bread into a temporary sack he made by holding all four corners of a square of yellow silk. When he'd taken as much bread as he was going to take, he shoveled meat and gravy into his mouth with his bare hand.

"Tim?"

"Sorry it took me so long," Tim responded through a mouthful of meat. "Maurice is a fucking prick."

"What were you doing in the kitchen?"

Tim almost choked on his mouthful of meat but managed to swallow it down. "Keep it down, asshole." He scooped up one more handful of meat and shoved it into his mouth. "Come on. Let's get the hell out of here."

When they were alone in the corridor and Cooper deemed it safe enough, he repeated his question.

Tim glanced back, then shot Cooper an annoyed scowl. "What the fuck do you think I was doing? I was starting a fire."

Cooper hadn't been sure, but he'd suspected as much. "Why?"

"Booze may be off limits to the inmates here." Tim's scowl softened to a grin as he separated the bundle of multi-colored

## Critical Failures VIII

silk he was carrying to reveal a brown glass bottle. "But it seems the staff is allowed to keep some hidden away."

"You put our lives at risk to score a bottle of fucking stonepiss?"

Tim turned his scowl back on and tucked his bundle under his arm again. "Would you keep your fucking voice down? And stop being so dramatic. I didn't put anything at risk. I know how to hide and cover my tracks. I'm a rogue."

"You're an asshole." Cooper had an overwhelming urge to fly into a Barbarian Rage and slam Tim against the wall like a dusty rug, but it was subdued by a long satisfying fart.

They walked the rest of the way to their room without saying a word to each other. Tim returned the smiles and greetings of other inmates as they passed, but Cooper avoided eye contact. He couldn't fake friendliness like Tim could. He was torn between wanting to drive a fist through every one of their faces and wanting to run away and hide somewhere. This mix of constant violent rage and fear was something he'd never felt before, and he didn't like it at all.

"I'm scared, Tim," he confessed when they finally reached the semi-privacy of their open room.

Tim unloaded his bundle of fabric onto his bed and took out one of the bread loaves he'd swiped from the cafeteria. "Scared of what?" He bit off a large chunk of bread and greedily chewed.

"I don't know. There's the whole gladiator thing. We're going to get killed if we're not entertaining enough, and I've got shit for a Charisma score."

"Leave the entertainment to me. We'll knock them dead out there."

"That was just an example," said Cooper. "I'm not really scared of any one thing in particular. I'm just scared in general. It's kind of like when we had a big test in high school that I didn't study for, except I give a shit about it. That kind of feeling."

Tim smiled. "I know exactly what you're talking about. It's the rat growing stronger inside you. Wererats are naturally cowardly and paranoid. You'll get used to it. Do you want some stonepiss? It might help take the edge off."

Cooper shook his head. "I think I'm just going to try and get some sleep." He lay down and yawned, welcoming the relative softness of the stained mattress.

"Suit yourself." Tim removed the bottle from his silk bundle and tucked it far under his bed, then sat down and started to thread a needle.

"You're not going to have any?" asked Cooper.

Tim closed one eye as he slid the thread through the needle's eye. "I've got work to do."

Cooper sat up. "Then what the fuck –" He glanced at the open doorway and lowered his voice. "Then what the fuck did you go to all that trouble to steal it for?"

"Relax, would you? It's not going to go to waste. But I've got shit to do right now, and I need a clear head."

Cooper lay back down. "You're a shitty alcoholic." He closed his eyes and went to sleep.

# CHAPTER 20

Stacy needed to think, and she needed to eat. There were plenty of options to choose from near the Temple of Life, but none of them looked particularly appealing. Her options were further restricted by the small amount of money she had tucked away separate from the coin purse she'd given Brother Mayfair.

"What are you in the mood for?" she asked Dave.

Dave looked up and down the street, sniffed the air, then pointed to a restaurant. "How about there?"

"The Stinky Pickle?" Aside from the name, it looked as clean and inviting as any other restaurant in the area.

"It smells good."

Stacy shrugged. "I wouldn't think they cater solely to rat monsters. We can give it a try."

When she opened the door, the smell was overwhelming. She'd caught a few whiffs of it outside, but assumed that someone had let some milk go sour or something. But once she acclimatized herself to the smell and mentally disassociated it with expired milk, it wasn't that bad. It wasn't something she'd call good either. All she could say for certain was that it was strong.

The interior was quaint but moderately clean. The round wooden tables were all scratched and scuffed, but at least they appeared to have been wiped down since they were last used.

There was one other customer in the place. A human man

dressed in earthy tones of green and brown. At his feet sat a leopard, which picked its head up and snarled at Dave.

Dave immediately hid his left arm behind his back.

"Easy, Lucia," said the man. He gave Stacy and Dave a quick glance, then resumed eating when his leopard laid her head back down. At least he seemed to be enjoying his food despite probably not being half rat. That was a good sign.

A large man with a meat cleaver for a left hand greeted them from behind the bar with a friendly smile. That, along with his blood-smeared apron, was far more alarming to Stacy than the leopard. She glanced back to make sure she knew exactly where the exit was.

"The name's Grimmond," said the man behind the bar. "Come in and make yourselves comfortable." He gestured with his prosthetic hand at the rows of jars behind him. "As you can see, we have a wide variety of pickled provisions to tempt your tongues."

Dave immediately started pointing to jars and asking to sniff them. Grimmond happily obliged, filling Dave's dish with a variety of animal parts that Stacy couldn't identify, along with a few pickled vegetables on the side.

Stacy spent the entire time wishing that Dave was discerning enough to ask exactly what was being slopped onto his dish, but ended up pointing to the only thing that looked at all familiar when her turn came.

"Are those eggs?"

"Indeed they are, m'lady."

"From a bird?"

Grimmond frowned. "I'm afraid we're fresh out of griffon eggs. Those you see there are from humble chickens."

"That's perfect!" said Stacy. "I'll have four, please."

"Very well." Grimmond laughed as he fetched the egg jar. "You remind me of some folks I had come here not long ago."

Stacy paid for their food from what little money she had

# Critical Failures VIII

on her, then took a seat at the table Dave had chosen. She devoured one of her eggs before getting down to business so that her stomach would have something to digest. It wasn't bad. A touch briny for her taste, but it got the job done.

"I was thinking," she said while she sliced her second egg into bite-sized pieces. "What if we raided the Rat Bastards?"

Dave laughed through a mouthful of something as some of it dripped down his beard. "Good luck with that."

"You don't think we can do it?"

"I *know* we can't do it," said Dave. "Because *we* aren't going anywhere near there." Before Stacy could respond, Dave held up a finger to indicate that he would elaborate after he swallowed his food. "Look, I know you've got me over a barrel, but you're just going to have to face the fact that there are some things I fear more than you. I'm not going back to the Whore's Head, and I'm sure as shit not going back to the Rat Bastards. They didn't even like me when I was part of the team, and I don't think they've warmed up to me any since Tim and I bailed after he shot one of them in the face. Oh yeah, and did I mention they're armed to the teeth with modern guns?"

"That's kind of what I was thinking. We could catch one or two of them alone with their guards down, jump them, and steal their guns."

Dave paused thoughtfully. "You think that lady at The Best Defense would give us a thousand gold pieces for one?"

"No, Dave! That's the last thing we need. I was thinking that if we armed ourselves, we could even the odds when we infiltrate their lair. We'd be doing just like Brother Mayfair suggested, except we can do it in one afternoon and we don't have to leave the city."

"Sure, if you call one or two guns against a dozen even odds. And those odds are going to get a lot less even when our clips run out of ammo while they're sitting on stockpiles of it.

Also, and I feel like I might have mentioned this, but I'm not going anywhere fucking near the Rat Bastards."

"Then what do you suggest?"

Dave shrugged as he put another forkful of food in his mouth. "We could do what Brother Mayfair actually suggested."

"What? Run off into the woods and hope to randomly run into a nest of evil monsters who are hoarding piles of gold? We need to get this done before the next full moon, or you'll be that much more difficult to cure. And no offense, but I'm not too keen to spend any more nights with you than I have to after your behavior last time."

Dave glared at her. "I thought we agreed not to talk about that."

"I'm sorry, but you forced my hand."

"If you're not going to sell the guns, then I don't see much point in making a raid. I highly doubt they've got a thousand gold pieces tucked away in a single cell. Most of what they pull in gets spent pretty quickly or funnels higher up in the organization."

Stacy swallowed the first half of her third egg. She knew Dave had every reason to lie to her, but what he was saying made sense. If they had that kind of money lying around, they probably wouldn't be holed up in sewers and abandoned shithole buildings.

"I guess we don't have much choice then."

"You could always go about your own business and let me go about mine."

Maybe Dave was right. Trying to save him from his affliction was taking time and energy away from trying to track down Tim, Mordred, or one of those dice, which would contribute to saving a lot more people. If she didn't have it in her to save everyone, then maybe it was best to cut her losses with Dave and –

## Critical Failures VIII

"I beg your pardon," said a man's voice from behind Stacy. He spoke softly, only as loud as was necessary to be heard clearly.

Stacy turned around to find the other customer and his leopard standing behind her. He smelled of sweat and dirt, like he'd been gardening all day. The leopard stared at Dave with hostility in its eyes, but remained silent. The man's eyes were calm, showing neither hostility nor warmth.

"Yes?" said Stacy, a little annoyed by having her thoughts interrupted.

"I could not help but overhear your conversation."

Stacy wondered what part of their conversation had inspired him to come and join it. Myrna, the shopkeeper at The Best Defense, had mentioned that a lot of people had taken up hunting wererats since the king put a bounty on them. If this guy had the right angle, maybe that was an avenue they could explore. Not wanting to give away her desperation, she continued to play more annoyed than interested.

"What do you want?"

"I am Alroth the Hunter, Protector of the Cedar Wilds."

Stacy didn't know where the Cedar Wilds was, but she was pretty sure it wasn't in this pickle joint. "Aren't you a little outside of your jurisdiction?"

"I have an arrangement with Master Grimmond." Alroth nodded to the man behind the bar.

Grimmond gave them a friendly wave with his meat cleaver hand. "Can I get you another egg, m'lady?"

Stacy smiled politely. "No, thank you. They're delicious though."

"I provide him with fresh meat from my kills," Alroth continued. "And he preserves a portion of it for me to bring back to the forest."

"That's fascinating," Stacy lied. Was he looking for

another distributor? Did she and Dave look like they worked at a deli? "But perhaps you didn't overhear our conversation as well as you thought you did."

"You seek to murder for coin."

"That's not what I said."

Dave shrugged. "Sounded like that to me."

"Shut up, Dave."

"I am a man of nature. It is not my place to judge or condemn your indifference to the lives of others."

Stacy jumped to her feet and got up in Alroth's face. "Well, that sounds pretty fucking judgy to me, and I am *not* in the mood." She backed out of his personal space when she heard the leopard snarl.

Alroth smiled as he patted his furry companion on the head. "Do not mind Lucia. She is a touch overprotective and unaccustomed to the ways of the city."

Stacy took a step back from him. "I'm sorry. I didn't mean to be rude. I just want to make it clear that I'm not some soulless murderer for hire. My friend and I have a situation. My intentions are good is what I'm trying to say."

"Your intentions matter not to me. The forest is neutral, and it is my responsibility to maintain the balance between what your foolish people refer to as *Good* and *Evil*."

"My foolish people?"

"A colony of ettins have recently settled in my wood."

"What are ettins?"

"Two-headed giants," said Dave before Alroth had time to respond, like he was trying to impress her with his nerd knowledge.

Alroth nodded. "That is mayhap an overly simplistic way to describe them, but your dwarf is not incorrect."

Dave stood up but kept his distance from Lucia. "I'm not *her dwarf*. My name is Dave."

"The tedious rituals you people waste so much time with."

# Critical Failures VIII

Alroth sighed. "I am Alroth the Hunter, Protector of the Cedar Wilds." He stared at Dave as if to ask if that was a satisfactory introduction. "Shall we rub our elbows together, or whatever it is you city dwellers do upon introductions?"

"What about the ettins?" said Dave without offering his elbow to rub. "How are they disturbing the balance of the forest or whatever? Do they have some kind of shaman who's cursing the land?"

Stacy knew what Dave was getting at. Might this be a lead on another Mordred?

"Nothing like that," said Alroth. "They are simply brutish and violent. They kill wild animals, eat their fill, then leave the rest to rot."

"That doesn't sound too bad. Nature reclaims it eventually, right?"

Alroth scowled at Dave. "At the rate they're destroying the trees, there will be no nature left to reclaim anything."

Dave chuckled. "If memory serves, ettins tend to be solitary creatures, only occasionally traveling in mated pairs. How can you call yourself *Protector of Cedar Wilds* if you can't even take down a couple of ettins?"

That line of questioning was decidedly unhelpful. Stacy was about to say something to set the conversation back on course, but Alroth spoke before she could think of anything.

"I am impressed. You know more about ettins than I would expect a sheltered city dwarf to know. It is true that the filthy beasts typically prefer only the company of their other head. But every now and again, a particularly strong or clever one will inspire others to band together, promising his followers that they can reap the *benefits of civilization* if they work together. It never ends well."

"Sounds like you've got yourself quite a situation there," said Stacy. "But I believe I've made our motivations plain. We can take care of your little ettin problem, but it's going to cost you a thousand bucks."

Alroth scoffed. "That is preposterous! Such a sacrifice would wreak havoc on the entire deer population of the forest. Even the ettins will not slaughter so many before they give up and disband."

Dave snorted.

Stacy sighed. "I apologize. I misspoke. What I meant to say was one thousand gold pieces."

"Please, woman. I have none of your silly coin. The forest provides all I need."

"Then why did you even come over here? I'm not a murderer for hire, but I'm not a murderer for charity either."

"Much like agriculture, government, and basic construction, ettins are aware of the concept of economics, but too stupid to put it into practice. They know that more civilized races trade coins and gems for goods or services, so they tend to keep what valuables they take from the bodies of those unfortunate travelers who cross their paths."

"How many ettins are we talking about?" asked Stacy.

"I have not been close enough to get an accurate count, but I would estimate around two dozen."

"There's no way," said Dave.

"As well as a few bears."

"Impossible."

"Perhaps half a dozen orcs."

"I don't think you're hearing –"

"And at least twenty goblins."

Dave sighed. "Is that all?"

"The orcs and goblins," said Stacy. "Are they loyal to the ettins?"

Alroth let out a small chuckle. It was the first hint of emotion she'd seen him betray. "Orcs and goblins are not even loyal to other orcs and goblins. The orcs are likely slaves. Goblins like to take advantage of ettins' ignorance. They find it amusing to request obscene amounts of coin for basic tasks. Sometimes it works, and other times they get clubbed into a bloody pulp. It is a calculated risk the goblins are willing to take."

Stacy thought for a moment.

"Stacy," said Dave. "What's there to think about? You and I can't take down two dozen high school football players by ourselves. Did you hear me when I said they were *giants*?"

"How giant are you talking about? Like, fifty feet tall?"

"Heavens no," said Alroth. "Thirteen or fourteen feet at the most."

Stacy shrugged. "That's pretty big, but manageable." She smiled at Dave. "Besides, we won't be by ourselves. We've got Alroth and Lucia."

Alroth nodded. "I shall assist you to the best of my ability."

Dave looked down at Lucia, who met his gaze with a low growl. "You can't be serious. The four of us together might be able to bring down one ettin, maybe two if we're lucky with our rolls. But we'd need an army to take on that many."

"That's kind of what I had in mind. If we can get the goblins and orcs on our side, then –"

"That's a pretty big fucking if!"

"Let's at least go check it out. If we get there and feel it's too big of a challenge, we'll abort the mission." Stacy turned to Alroth. "No hard feelings?"

"Of course not. I admire your courage and confidence."

He must have known that her willingness to even entertain any such endeavor was born much more out of desperation than courage or confidence, but Stacy appreciated his tact.

# CHAPTER 21

"This sucks," said Katherine. She'd said it a couple of times already, but she wanted to make sure her position on their situation was clear.

The Hollinites had been bailing out the ship's lower deck for hours, with little progress to show for it.

"You could speed this up any time you like." Chaz yawned as he leaned back against the bulwark. "Just saying."

He was referring, as he had on multiple occasions already, to using the Bag of Holding to bail the ship out.

Katherine wanted to tell him to go fuck himself, but she understood his frustration, especially since it was in response to her own complaining. Her crew was getting bored and antsy. There was little to eat or drink on the ship, and there was an inhabited island within a day's sail. It must have been infuriating to everyone that she was choosing to remain adrift at sea when they had such a simple alternative option at their disposal.

"I need to keep those Hollin freaks occupied and exhausted until we figure out exactly how we're going to get rid of them."

"You could always overpower them and shackle them below deck," said Captain Logan.

Katherine had a few reasons for having invited him to her little pow-wow at the back of the ship. The main reason was to keep him from consorting with his own crew and strategizing a counter-mutiny. Also, she wanted his crew to

# Critical Failures VIII

see him talking cordially with her and her crew, hoping that might make them less likely to stage a coup independently of him. A third, but still significant reason was that she wanted Logan to hear her and the others discussing their situation regarding the dice and their world. Naturally, it would sound crazy for one person to talk about it, but when a whole group discussed it, he'd at least have to weigh the odds of what they were saying as truth against the odds of them all being the same kind of crazy. If she could convince him of the danger that he and his crew would be in if Mordred got a hold of the dice, or even make him a little less likely to completely dismiss the idea, it was worth having him around.

"Thank you," she said. "I'll keep that in mind as a last resort."

Tony the Elf stared out at a cloud on the horizon blocking the setting sun. "If we can't handle a single boatload of these people, how are we going to get Mordred? He's bound to be surrounded by thousands of loyal fanatics."

That was at least five or six steps ahead of where Katherine's thoughts were, but it got her thinking in a different direction.

"We'll need help, of course."

"Logan's crew?" Tony the Elf turned around to face Katherine. "I wouldn't trust them as far as I could throw this ship." He turned to Logan and gave a small but respectful bow. "No offense, Captain."

"None taken," said Logan. "That is wise, considering the circumstances of our relationship."

Katherine smiled. "I feel like Captain Logan will come around once he realizes what's actually at stake, but they're not who I was referring to."

"Who, then?"

"The people who are already hurting from the spread of Mordred's cult."

"You mean, like, other ships' captains?" asked Chaz. "Sailors? Dockworkers? You want to start some kind of grassroots militia?"

That was something Katherine hadn't considered, but perhaps an idea worth exploring.

"Do any of you have any ideas on how we might go about doing that?"

Chaz shook his head. "Even if we did, they'd be just as susceptible to Mordred's magic as those guys." He nodded toward the Hollinites bailing out the ship. "As soon as we got anywhere near him, he'd turn our own army against us. Or even worse, he'd turn us."

Katherine nodded. "Yeah, yeah, I get it. That idea sucks. Sorry, Chaz."

"That wasn't my plan."

"It wasn't mine either. I was thinking about going higher than that. Sure, the farmers and cobblers and shit are the ones who do the real suffering, but the ruling class are the ones who stand to lose the most money. And they're also the ones who have the power to mobilize the people they rule over. Maybe they'll even have some idea about how we can defend ourselves against Mordred's influence."

"Who, exactly, are you talking about?" asked Tony the Elf.

"The drow."

Captain Logan laughed. "You would do better to put your faith in me and my crew than you would to trust the godsforsaken drow, and I say that while acknowledging the fact that moments ago I told you it was wise not to trust us."

"It's not right to paint a whole race of people with the same brush," said Katherine. "We have a word for that in our world. Stay focused. What do you guys think of my idea?"

Chaz shrugged. "Did you actually propose one?"

Katherine rolled her eyes. "Getting the drow to mobilize against Mordred's minions."

# Critical Failures VIII

"That's not really an idea. If they're under attack and have the means to defend themselves, then what the hell do they need us for? To give them permission?"

Shit. That was a good point. Katherine tried to think of something that would make everything she'd suggested up til now seem less stupid.

"Maybe the Hollinites haven't reached them," she said. "What if we got there in time to warn them?"

"What if we did?" said Tony the Elf. "You think they'll give us a medal or something? I still don't get what you're trying to ultimately accomplish."

"I don't know. I'm just thinking out loud. If we establish ourselves as valuable to the top tier drow on the island, maybe we'll be privy to information about Mordred. We could nail down exactly where he is, weaknesses in his defenses, come at him with some kind of strategy."

Chaz shrugged. "It's a longshot, but it's something. Anything beats sitting around on this fucking boat any longer than we have to."

"I don't know," said Tony the Elf. "Maybe it's not wise to bring a ship full of Hollinites with us when we're coming to warn the drow of invading Hollinites."

Katherine nodded slowly as she thought. "I can turn into a giant bat and fly there. Maybe I should go alone."

"I don't think that's a good idea. You should take at least one other person with you."

That sounded reasonable. Buddy system and all that. But who would she take? The person best suited for the job was dead in her Bag of Holding. She knew she would regret asking, but the silence was too awkward not to.

"Who did you have in mind?"

Tony the Elf smiled. "I could go."

Somehow, Katherine knew he was going to say that. Tony the Elf was a nice enough guy, but this puppy-dog crush he seemed to have on her kind of creeped her out.

"You're a ranger," she said. "You're better suited for a wilderness environment."

"You're a druid."

*Well played, Tony the Elf.*

"I'm also the only one of us who can turn into a fucking bat."

"I'll go," said Chaz eagerly.

Katherine was confident that his desire to tag along had more to do with wanting to get off the ship than it did with any feelings he might have toward her, but he was a bard. She tried to think of some way to let him down gently.

"I'm sorry, Chaz. But you're... useless." Julian might have been able to sugarcoat that a little better.

"Who does that leave?" asked Tony the Elf.

That was a good question. Katherine considered Captain Logan. It might put her mind at ease to know that he was with her – and away from his crew – while she was away from the ship. But she wasn't sure how well Logan would interact with the drow. He was coming off as a little bit racist. This situation called for some finesse, and she didn't know if it was a good idea to –

"Hey, guys," said a voice that derailed Katherine's train of thought. "What's up? Are you having some kind of secret meeting up here?"

Katherine turned around and smiled at the new guy.

His eyes darted left and right. "What?"

"Hi there, ..." *Shit. What was his name?* She knew it started with J. *Jaleel, Jamal, Jerome...*

"Jay."

"I know, I know. Give me a minute. It'll come to me." Finally, it came to her. "Jefferson!"

Chaz snorted.

Jefferson narrowed his eyes at her. "My name is Jay."

# Critical Failures VIII

"Oh…" Katherine shot Chaz a warning glance, then smiled again at Jay. "Yes, Jay. How would you like to accompany me on a little mission?"

"Him?" said Tony the Elf. "But he's a ranger, too."

"He has other qualifications unique to this particular mission."

Tony the Elf put his hands on his hips. "Such as?"

Katherine furrowed her brow at him. Was he really going to make her spell it out for him?

"I've also got a level in rogue," said Jay.

Katherine smiled, grateful that she didn't have to state the obvious. "There you go. He's a rogue. The perfect class for an urban assignment." Shit, did that come out wrong? "And by *urban*, of course, I mean in a city."

"Yes," said Jay. "That is what urban means."

"We've got some other rogues in the crew," said Tony the Elf. "More experienced ones, too. Unless, of course, there's something else about Jay that you feel makes him more qualified than anyone else…"

His playful tone wasn't lost on Katherine. He was toying with her, and Chaz was watching with a stupid grin like he wished he had a bowl of popcorn.

"Fine," she said. "You want me to say it? I'll say it. He's black. There, are you satisfied?"

Chaz nodded.

Jay frowned. "Well, this just got a little uncomfortable."

"I'm sorry. It wouldn't be if my crew didn't have the maturity level of a bunch of eight-year-olds."

"Are you really asking me to go with you on this mission because I'm black?"

"Yes, that's part of it."

"What, exactly, is the nature of this mission? I mean, if you need me to dance or play basketball or something, I should probably tell you that I've only had functional legs for –"

"It's nothing like that," said Katherine. "But we'll be interacting with drow."

Tony the Elf sighed. "And there it is."

"What's a drow?" asked Jay.

"They're black elves," said Katherine.

Jay perked up a bit. "Oh yeah?"

Tony the Elf shook his head. "No, they're not! I wish you would understand this. Drow aren't just elves with darker complexions. They're a completely different race of elves."

"I'm not trying to pass him off as one of them," said Katherine. "I just thought he might be more well-received than me. You know, like we're meeting them halfway."

"That's not halfway. The dead guy in your bag is halfway."

Jay looked down at Katherine's Bag of Holding. "You got a dead guy in there?"

Katherine shrugged. "I've got a few now. We should look out for a temple while we're on the island."

"I put my hands in that bag."

Tony the Elf looked pleadingly at Jay. "Listen to me. Drow aren't normal elves. Their skin isn't even brown like yours. It's actually black, like, jet black. And they have white hair. Oh yeah, and they're evil."

"Because they're black?"

"No! Because that's how their alignment is listed in the *Caverns & Creatures Monster Manual*."

Jay looked at Katherine. "That guy in your bag. Was he evil?"

"Tanner? Oh, no. He was really nice."

"Katherine," said Tony the Elf. "You're going to get this guy killed."

"You're coming off as a little racist, Tony the Elf."

"*Me?* You're the one who –"

"And I'd like to point out that I'm talking specifically about drow. Just because some book says they're evil, that doesn't make them bloodthirsty killers. I was technically evil while I was a vampire."

"And you were a bloodthirsty killer! You literally thirsted for blood."

"Also," said Chaz. "Don't you have a bit of a rough history with the drow? Didn't that Vivia woman try to murder you?"

Katherine sighed. "I really shouldn't have to explain this to you, Chaz. That was *one* individual drow, and there were extenuating circumstances. You were there. You know that."

"Extenuating circumstances?" said Tony the Elf. "How far do circumstances have to extenuate in order to justify someone trying to murder you?"

"I ate her cat."

"I'm sorry," said Jay. "You did *what?*"

Tony the Elf winced. "Yikes. That's pretty bad, but I don't know if it –"

"It was her familiar," Katherine explained.

"Oh, shit. That'll do it."

"For the record, I totally didn't know. I thought it was a stray."

"Merciful gods, woman," said Captain Logan. "Familiar or stray, what would possess you to eat a cat?"

"I was a vampire at the time."

Logan sighed. "Of course you were." He glanced toward the sun, which was almost touching the horizon now. "I see you got that sorted out, did you?"

Katherine rolled her eyes. "Listen, guys. I'm just saying that the drow on that island are the leaders of a community filled with different races. You can't lead effectively if you're going around murdering your citizens all the time."

"Historically speaking," said Tony the Elf, "that's not necessarily –"

"And besides, what makes you think you'll fare any better than Jay if the drow decide they want to kill us?"

"I've got more experience. I've spent more time in the game."

"You spent all that time in a pub. I'm the captain, and I've made my decision."

Tony the Elf sighed. "I guess that's that, then. Good luck."

Katherine removed her hat and put it on Tony the Elf's head. "You be captain while I'm away." She turned to Chaz. "I want to take the die with me."

Chaz's grin disappeared. "Why?"

"Just in case the Hollinites get any funny ideas. I'd rather them not be able to get their hands on it. Besides, I've got a special hiding place where no one will ever find it."

Chaz's gaze drifted down her body. "You're going to stick it in your –"

"Please don't finish that sentence. Just hand over the die, and I'll show you."

"Really?" Chaz glanced around. "Right here in front of Tony the Elf and..." He nodded at Logan. "Him?"

"If you don't agree that it's the perfect hiding place, I'll give it right back."

"I'm not sure I'll want it back." He reached into his pocket and pulled out the die. "But I'll admit, I'm curious."

Katherine took the die from him and placed it on the deck between them.

Chaz frowned. "If they just had to guess where it was hidden, I could maybe see the logic in –"

Katherine turned into a wolf, picked up the die with her mouth, then turned back into a half-elf. "Satisfied?"

"You ate it again? What if we need to use it? Do you even know how much digesting it can take before it stops working or explodes or whatever?"

"Relax. I didn't eat it. When I change forms, whatever I'm wearing or holding at the time gets absorbed into me. Next time I turn into a wolf, I'll have the die in my mouth."

# Critical Failures VIII

"Where is it in the meantime?"

Katherine shrugged. "Fuck if I know. It's just part of me."

"Very impressive," said Logan. "But if you plan on leaving the ship, it would be unwise to let *them* see you." He nodded down to the Hollinites. "If they suspect even a little that you've run off with their master's prize, you can be assured they will... How did you put it? ...*get some funny ideas.*"

"That's a good point. I'll wait until it gets darker."

Logan nodded. "There''s a small alcove at the rear of the ship one deck below. There is less of a chance you will be spotted if you leave from there."

"I know the place," said Katherine. "That's where I ate Bosley."

Logan's weathered eyes widened. "You *ate* Bosley?"

Jay turned to Logan. "Was Bosley your cat?"

"No. He was one of my crewmen."

Jay turned back to Katherine. "Damn, girl. You've got a hell of an appetite." He laughed, as if all the information he was taking in was too much to process and be properly horrified. "At least tell me this happened back when you were a vampire."

Katherine shook her head. "It was yesterday, and I was a shark."

"Is there anything you haven't eaten or been? The dead bodies in your bag, are those, like, snacks?"

"Do you want to come with me or not?"

"Will you promise not to eat me?"

Katherine smiled at him. "Would you trust me to keep that promise?"

Jay shrugged. "Still beats hanging around on this boat."

"What am I supposed to say if any of the Hollinites ask where you are?" asked Tony the Elf.

"I don't know. Tell them to mind their own fucking business and get back to work."

"I would not recommend that," said Logan. "On a ship, rumors spread faster than a fire in a rain-starved forest. You would do well to give those mad fools reason not to suspect anything amiss by your sudden lack of presence on deck."

Katherine hadn't thought of that. She had made herself pretty visible and vocal since she took control of the ship. Nobody was going to buy her suddenly deciding to go to sleep for a couple of days.

She hurriedly grabbed her hat from Tony the Elf's head and put it back on her own, then turned to Logan. "Do you have any ideas?"

Logan shrugged. "You could always claim to be sick, but they may take that as a sign of weakness and an opportunity to revolt."

"Shit." She turned to the others. "You guys got anything?"

Jay and Tony the Elf shook their heads, but Chaz's eyes lit up.

"PMS!" he said.

Katherine scowled at him. "This isn't the time for lame-ass jokes."

"I'm not joking," said Chaz. "Think about it. We could say it's hitting you really hard this month, and that you don't want to be disturbed."

She still felt like there was a shitty punchline coming, but Katherine decided to let Chaz's suggestion run its course.

"Let's say, for the sake of argument, that they bought that. Would they not take that as a sign of weakness?"

Chaz shrugged. "If I was looking to press my luck with a woman, that would be the absolute last choice of timing in which to do so."

Katherine thought about it. "That's a good point. But it's still a pretty flimsy excuse to explain my sudden disappearance."

"Then don't disappear."

# Critical Failures VIII

Tony the Elf sighed. "If she's just going to bail on the whole plan, then why are we even talking about this?"

Chaz stood up. "I'm not talking about bailing. I'm talking about maintaining visibility. May I borrow your hat?"

Katherine glanced toward the lower deck to make sure none of the Hollinites were looking at her, then took off her hat and passed it to Chaz.

Chaz held it out to Tony the Elf.

"That's your big plan?" said Tony the Elf. "Me in drag?"

"It's not drag. It's just a hat. You've got a similar body style to Katherine's, and your hair is nearly the same color."

"Are you out of your fucking mind? Nobody is going to believe I'm Katherine just because I'm wearing her hat!"

"Of course it won't pass a close inspection, but we just need it to pass a glance from the lower deck up through the dusty windows of the captain's quarters. Throw in some groaning, maybe smash a glass or something, and nobody will want to come even remotely close enough to be able to identify you."

Katherine snatched her hat back and nodded. "That could work. I like it."

# CHAPTER 22

Julian now had a better understanding of how Chaz must have felt when they were flying up to the Crescent Shadow. He didn't like the feeling of being dependent on Rhonda to hold on to him while she used his Fly spell for the first time. He wished it could have been the other way around, but Rhonda was considerably heavier than he was, and he didn't think he'd be able to hold her and fly at the same time.

The hatchet in his hand did little to soothe his anxiety as he scanned the sea below him for any signs of black cock eels. It wasn't a weapon he had any experience wielding, and he felt it would do him more hindrance than help if Rhonda dropped him. It would only slow his swimming down, and he doubted he'd get in even a single swing before the eels tore him to shreds. It didn't even seem like that formidable a weapon against a tree, which was what they needed it for, but it was the best tree-chopping instrument they could find among Captain Longfellow's belongings.

Julian kept his head down. Eels or no eels, watching the water rush by made him feel like he was moving faster. Every time he glanced up at the shore, it barely seemed any closer.

They'd decided that it would be best to wait until dawn if they were likely to face off against undead. Nobody knew exactly what kind of undead they could expect to encounter, but a daytime visit could at least rule out vampires. Julian didn't know if other types of undead were weakened by sunlight as well, but he figured they probably weren't

# Critical Failures VIII

strengthened by it. And at least they'd be able to see them coming from farther away.

Aside from the time he took to meditate and prepare his spells, he'd spent most of the night helping to disassemble the captain's quarters and turn it into a dinghy. They still had a lot of work to do before they had a finished product on their hands, but the progress they'd made when he and Rhonda left seemed to be leading toward something that Julian wouldn't trust to help him survive in a kiddie pool.

"Do you see any eels?" asked Rhonda, like she was just trying to pass the time.

"No."

The fact that he couldn't see any black cock eels comforted him about as much as his hatchet. The early dawn light didn't penetrate far into the choppy dark water. It could be teeming with eels a foot below the surface, and Julian wouldn't be the wiser.

"Steady as she goes!" said Ravenus, flying alongside Julian and Rhonda. "We're nearly there now."

Julian looked up, happily surprised to see that the shoreline finally looked significantly closer. He sighed with relief. The flight had taken longer than he'd expected, and he was afraid they might not –

"SHIT!" he said when he and Rhonda fell out of the air like a couple of rocks.

The water rushed up toward them. It was impossible to tell how deep it was. Too deep, and they'd be at the mercy of the eels for the entire time it took them to swim to shore. Too shallow, and he might get crushed to death under Rhonda.

Fortunately, Rhonda must have considered that latter scenario as well. She pushed him away before they splashed down.

An elf has a lot of time to think at night while other races sleep, and Julian had whiled away some hours considering what he would do if he was falling from a height into the sea. It came down to a choice between spreading his body out as wide as possible in order to lessen his terminal velocity upon impact and going full cannonball. The latter would make him more dense, which would make him fall faster, but ultimately be less painful. The only drawback he could see was plummeting too far down beneath the surface that he'd run out of breath before he could swim back up. But then he thought about TV shows in which forensics experts fire bullets into ballistic gelatin, and how quickly they slow down. Surely he would slow down even more quickly once he hit the water.

One variable he hadn't considered during his musings was uncertainty about the water's depth. In light of this oversight, he made a split-second decision to spread his arms and legs out as wide as he could. The last thing he heard before smacking into the water was Ravenus frantically telling him to flap.

SMACK!

It was a painful landing, something akin to what Julian imagined being bitch-slapped by Captain Logan's water elemental might have felt like. But the pain reassured him that he was, in fact, still alive. Even better, after a bit of panicked flailing, he found that he was able to stand up. The water was only up to his chest.

"Rhonda?" he called out as he searched his surroundings. But he couldn't see anything but water all around him. "Rhonda!"

"She landed over here," said Ravenus, flying in a circular pattern about twenty feet from Julian.

Julian started half-walking half-swimming that direction, but it was slow going. Fortunately, Rhonda surfaced.

"Damn, that hurt," she said after she caught her breath. The left side of her face was scraped and covered in coarse black sand. She must have opted for the cannonball approach.

"Are you okay?"

Rhonda nodded. "Just a bit of a headache." She raised her crossbow out of the water as she headed toward the shore. "We'll have bigger concerns than that if we don't get out of this water."

Julian followed her. The impatience and anxiety he'd felt while flying to the island was nothing compared to how he felt now that he was trudging there through eel-infested water. His gaze kept darting between the island ahead of them and the water behind them.

CLICK!

The sound of Rhonda's crossbow nearly made him piss himself.

"Did you see one?" he asked, whirling around and brandishing his hatchet. "Where is it?"

Rhonda laughed nervously. "It wasn't loaded. I just wanted to make sure it still worked after hitting the water." She loaded a bolt and cocked her weapon.

Julian sighed and let himself pee. That scare had primed his bladder, and there was still enough sea to wade through to dilute it down to nothing. Besides, maybe pee warded off eels.

A few minutes later, the water was only up to their waists. Julian started feeling optimistic.

"The shallower the water gets, the less likely we are to encounter anything big enough to eat us."

"Have you ever swallowed a pig?" asked Rhonda.

Julian appreciated her wanting to ease the tension with idle conversation, but had they really exhausted all worthier topics?

"No," he answered.

"Have you ever eaten a pork chop?"

That was a step in the right direction, Julian supposed. "Yes, I have."

"Well, there you go."

"I'm sorry," said Julian. "I didn't realize you were leading up to a point. What was it, exactly?"

"How big did you think those eels are supposed to be? They'd have to be as big as a bus to swallow us whole. My point is that there's still plenty enough water for a big-ass eel to swim up behind us and tear us to pieces."

Julian glanced back as he tried to wade faster. They might as well have been wading through ink for all he could see beneath the deceptively calm surface. "Sorry. I was just trying to stay optimistic."

"And I'm trying to stay alive. Don't let your guard down. Stay focused and let's get to shore before we – YAAAAH!" Rhonda jerked backwards. "Julian!"

"What is it?" said Julian, wading after her. He didn't think he'd be able to catch up, but Rhonda got her bearings and planted her feet down firmly in the sand.

"Something's got my robe!" she said, leaning forward in resistance.

Julian couldn't see anything behind her, but as he got closer, he noticed a trail of disturbance on the surface of the water running from about three feet behind Rhonda to about twenty feet behind her. Finally, a thrashing black tail broke the surface.

"EEL!" he cried. He reached for Rhonda, who grabbed him by the wrist. He had his hatchet ready to swing in his other hand, but no target to swing at. "What do you want me to do?"

"PULL!"

Julian dug his feet into the sand and pulled. They even made a little headway, but there was no way they would make it to the beach at this rate. He didn't know what kind of Intelligence score black cock eels had, but he was confident that it wouldn't take long for the thing to realize it was only holding on to a bit of fabric.

# Critical Failures VIII

"Master Julian!" cried Ravenus. "How may I assist you?"

"Stay up there! Don't come down here!" Julian peered at Rhonda's panicked face. "You need to turn around."

"Are you crazy? That's only going to pull it closer to me."

"Your legs are more powerful pulling backward than they are pushing forward. That's science." Julian was remembering that bit of science from a Saturday morning cartoon he'd seen as a kid, but Rhonda didn't need to know that. Instead, he focused on her crossbow. "Also, that will make it easier for you to shoot it in the face."

Rhonda turned just far enough so that she could point her crossbow down into the water, then pulled the trigger. The increased tail thrashing suggested she'd hit the eel, but it didn't let go.

If anything, it was closer now. Julian could make out its black head which was about the size of a cantaloupe and indeed dick-shaped. It opened its mouth, but instead of releasing Rhonda's robe, it further ingested it. When it closed its mouth again, its teeth grabbed a previously unbitten section of robe. Julian could imagine a gullet full of tiny barbed teeth rhythmically moving along esophageal muscles to trap and ingest whatever those first teeth latched onto. That made him dread the only idea he had even more than he already did. But it was either that or leave Rhonda to get eaten by dick eels.

"What are you doing?" shrieked Rhonda as Julian held the handle of his hatchet between his teeth and thrust his free hand under her robe.

A mouthful of hatchet made it difficult to explain, so he did his best to convey an apologetic look with his eyes before shoving his hand into the eel's mouth.

"AAAAAAHHHHH!" he cried as a thousand tiny hooks dug into his hand and wrist. The hatchet fell out of his mouth, but that was just as well since he needed to say his incantation.

"Fireball!"

He could feel the powerful magic flow through his body and release from his wounded hand, but he couldn't see any effect.

Then, a second later, the eel's body inflated in the middle, rising out of the water like a frog fellating the business end of a pressure washer. At its zenith, it looked like a three-foot-wide hot dog wiener, then it deflated as flames shot out of its anus about two feet away from the tip of its tail. After a few seconds, the entire tail disintegrated into charred lumps of flesh, creating an opening wide enough for the rest of the fire to escape in one large plume of flame. The eel lay still on the water, and Julian carefully opened its mouth and dislodged his bleeding hand.

After Julian retrieved his hatchet, he and Rhonda salvaged as much of Rhonda's robe as they could pull out of the eel's mouth, used its teeth to saw the rest loose, then picked up their pace wading toward the beach. The water was just above their knees when Julian heard more thrashing behind him. Looking back, he saw what must have been at least three or four more eels tearing into the first one. When he looked ahead again, Rhonda was halfway to the beach.

Finally, they collapsed onto the coarse black sand and caught their breath.

Rhonda tore off part of her robe and offered it to Julian. "I don't know how clean this is or if you're allergic to eel saliva, but it might help stop the bleeding.

Julian looked down at his hand. It hadn't seemed so bad while he was in the water, because the blood was continuously being washed away, but now it looked like he'd just pulled his hand out of a bucket of red paint.

"Thanks," he said, wrapping the soaked and partially shredded fabric around his wound.

"That looks really bad." She and Ravenus were both

# Critical Failures VIII

staring at him. He could feel his familiar's concern through their Empathic Link.

"I'll be okay. Injuries in this game are only a matter of Hit Point reduction. All I need is a long rest or a bit of magic, and I'll be good as new."

"I don't have any healing magic. We need to get you back to the boat and try this again after you're all healed up."

"That's going to be a problem," said Julian. "I only had two Level 3 spell slots, and I used the second one on that Fireball. We're stuck here until tomorrow."

# CHAPTER 23

"*I* will let you folks in on a little secret," said Yavin as he led Cooper and Tim from the cafeteria to the arena gate.

"We'd really appreciate that," said Tim. He was wearing the shittiest costume Cooper had ever seen. One sleeve was down past his hand while the other only barely came down past his elbow. The stitching was erratic and would be visible to a bat with cataracts . All that stuff he'd said about taking his destiny into his own hands had made sense when he said it. But if his destiny was related in any way to his choice of clothing, he would have been much better off letting Maurice shoulder that burden.

Yavin smiled down at Tim. "You have already been told that gladiatorial combat is more about entertainment than it is about trying to defeat your opponent. But it may ease your mind to know that there is only one person you need please to guarantee you live to see another fight."

That sounded like some woo-woo self-help bullshit to Cooper.

"Is it ourselves?" he asked just before letting rip a loud wet fart. "Sorry. That porridge is fucking with my insides." Until the damage from Tim's kitchen fire was repaired, their division would have to live on porridge hastily cooked up by the other division's disgruntled and overworked kitchen staff.

Yavin picked up his pace to keep ahead of Cooper's fart. "No, actually. I was referring to the governor, Yurog Lakha.

Please the crowd, and he will more often than not bend to their will. But please Gur Lakha, and you will enjoy a long and fruitful career in the arena."

"Who the fuck is Gur?" asked Cooper. "I thought you said his name was Yule Log or something."

"Yurog. Gur is his title." Yavin eyed Cooper nervously. "Should you ever have the honor of being asked to address the governor directly, always address him as Gur. He has shed much blood to earn the respect and admiration of his fellow orcs. Rumor has it the furniture in his home is upholstered with the skins of common folk who have committed far less grievous offenses than addressing him by his given name."

If that was such a huge offense, why had he even bothered telling them the governor's first name? Cooper knew himself well enough to know that he was bound to fuck that up. He needed a way to remember which nonsensical bullshit word was his first name, and which one was his title. Like in so many cereal commercials from his youth, Tony the Tiger came to the rescue.

*Gur is grrrrreat!*

That was simple enough. He could remember that.

"What sort of things is the governor into?" asked Tim.

"A wise question," said Yavin. "He bears the scars of many battles and prefers a more realistic and savage performance. The sight of blood excites him, so do not hold grudges if your fellow gladiators are a bit rougher with you under the governor's eye than they are otherwise, and none will be held against you for doing the same. It toughens us all up, and wounds heal."

"That *is* good to know," said Tim. "I'll certainly keep that in mind during our first performance."

"Mayhap you need not wait so long. I tell you this now because Gur Lakha is known to attend training sessions from time to time, especially when there are fresh recruits." He winked at Tim. "So do not hold back, halfling. Come at me with everything you've got."

"You can count on that."

When they arrived at the gate, it was closed. Zimbra was waiting for them on the other side. He was dressed in a loose-fitting multi-colored silk outfit that looked like what Tim's outfit might have looked like if it had been made by someone who knew what the fuck they were doing.

"Look sharp, gentlemen," said Zimbra. "Gur Lakha is in attendance, and he appears to be in a bit of a mood."

Yavin smiled down at Tim and raised his eyebrows, then stood at attention facing Zimbra. "I have prepared them for such a possibility."

Zimbra frowned disdainfully at Tim. "Have you?"

"Have no fear," said Tim. "We're going to put on a hell of a performance."

"We shall see."

Cooper didn't know what Tim was so confident about. He wondered if he'd missed a meeting or an orientation video or something, because he didn't feel prepared for shit. His anxiety leaked from his asshole.

"Mercy of the gods!" said Zimbra. "Pray the governor does not smell that." He backed away from the gate. "The gate will open shortly. Do not come out until you are introduced."

"Yes, Commander," said Yavin, standing straight and stiff like a soldier. When Zimbra turned away, he relaxed. "Are you ready?"

"Hell, yes!" said Tim.

"Fuck, no," said Cooper. "I thought this was supposed to be training. We haven't been given any instructions at all. What the fuck are we supposed to be doing out there?"

Yavin clapped a meaty hand on Cooper's shoulder. "Calm your nerves, friend. When they tell us to fight, we fight. Just try to make it look good. I shall let you land a few punches until it appears that the battle is decided, then come back and snatch victory from the jaws of defeat. Once the tide of battle has turned, you may continue to get up and fight as many times as you like, or choose to stay down until the guards drag you out of the arena. Of course, if you do choose to get back up, I'll have to –"

A blaring trumpet cut him off as the portcullis started to rise. Iron scraped against stone like teeth on a chalkboard.

"What the fuck was that?"

"They are getting ready to announce us," said Yavin.

"Lords, ladies, and our esteemed governor!" Zimbra's voice was as loud and clear as if he were standing right next to them. "It gives me great pleasure to present a match you will not soon forget. From the rugged hills of the Hemmelford Wilds, it took no less than twenty orcs to subdue and drag this beast of a man here to Meb Gar'shur. Powerful as he is wild, always a crowd-pleaser, I give you Yavin the Bear-Man!"

Yavin stomped out of the arena, roaring and pounding his chest. It was like he was a completely different person, completely caught up in his role. Cooper was a little annoyed at the paltry applause Yavin received, then remembered that they weren't playing for a full stadium.

Yavin roared ferociously as thick brown fur tore through his tunic and his body expanded to twice its normal size. His hybrid werebear form was a hell of a lot more impressive than any wererat Cooper had ever seen. The roar he bellowed after completing his transformation seemed to shake the whole stadium. Or maybe it was just Cooper that was shaking.

"Fucking hell," said Cooper. "I'm glad this is all staged. That dude's a fucking monster."

Tim snorted disinterestedly. "That dude's fucking dead."

"What are you talking about? You're not thinking about going off the script, are you?"

"Fuck the script. They want a show the governor won't

forget, and we're going to give them just that."

Cooper wondered if Tim might be giving him too much credit. "Listen, Tim. I know you think I'm strong as shit. But look at that fucking guy. Even with my Barbarian Rage, I don't know what you think we'll be able to do to him."

"I thought I'd made myself clear," said Tim. "We're going to murder him to death."

Cooper couldn't help but feel like Tim wasn't hearing his concerns. "Is this some kind of method acting shit?"

"What fool would face such a beast and hope to fight another day?" Zimbra asked the audience. "We searched far and wide for just such a fool, and finally found him in the humble village of Honeydew Meadows. A drooling imbecile, his tiny stature is matched only by his intellect. It is my distinct honor to present to you for the first time, Tim the Dim!"

Tim shook his head. "That motherfucker just went on my list."

"Dude," said Cooper. "What about the –"

"Just do like he said and go at him with everything you've got. You've got this."

"No, I haven't! Are you out of your fucking mind?"

As if to answer the question, Tim went suddenly cross-eyed, stuck out his tongue, and shoved a finger up his nose. Then he turned around and limped out into the arena.

That was... unexpected.

"Ah, there he is!" said Zimbra. "Just as advertised, a halfling so brainless he got lost on the way through a gate." Cooper sensed annoyance in his voice, but he got a small chuckle from the audience.

Cooper farted nervously as he considered his options. There weren't many, and he struggled to come up with a second one. Tim was going to get them killed. What the hell was he thinking? It's just not right to plot a murder alone when both of them would be taking the heat for it.

Fuck Tim. Cooper had stuck his neck out for that ungrateful little shit too many times, and Tim just continued to shovel more shit onto the fire. He'd thought he needed him to survive in this place. But if Tim was just going to keep actively trying to get them killed, then what the fuck use was he? Maybe it was time for that little cockroach to get stomped.

"You might be asking yourselves," Zimbra continued, "how does this tiny crippled moron stand a chance against Yavin the Bear-Man? The answer is, of course, he does not. But have no fear, Gur Lakha, for we would not insult you by making you watch Yavin pummel this cretin into halfling paste. He will be assisted by a creature nearly as vile and stupid as himself. Dragged to you straight from the putrid sewers of Cardinia, one of the very traitors who turned their backs on us under the ghastly light of the Phantom Pinas. The gods themselves have cursed this monstrous half-breed to wallow forever in excrement. It is said that one whiff of his rancid bowels can make a hill giant cower in disgust. I invite you to give a fitting welcome to Cooper the Pooper!"

What was all that shit about him being a traitor? He'd never been to this shithole in his life before now. Zimbra set him up to be hated before he even stepped into the arena. They were already booing him, and all he had ahead of him was killing their favorite champion. He was so fucked.

With a heavy sigh, he stepped out of the gate to boos and jeers, hoping that he'd at least be able to kill Tim before he was killed himself. At least the sunlight felt good on his head and back after having spent so much time underground.

The audience was indeed small. Seven orcs in all. The only one sitting on the bottom tier was older than most of the orcs Cooper had ever seen. Despite his wispy white hair and beard, he didn't look like someone to fuck with. His bare chest sagged, but it was big enough so that there was likely still a bunch of muscle under the flab. And something about him told Cooper that he'd love to add a few more scars to his collection if it meant getting to relive his old glory days of battle.

Half a dozen orcs stood surrounding him with spears long enough to reach down the entire height of the arena wall should the combatants come too close. They were the ones booing and jeering Cooper as he walked out to take his place next to Tim, who was dancing around Yavin like an asshole.

The governor wasn't booing, though. He stared at Cooper with what felt like mild interest. Of course, Cooper was probably reading his expression totally wrong. Guvvy was more likely just imagining Cooper's head displayed atop one of his guard's long spears. Cooper's shitty Charisma score was perfect for propaganda.

*You see this ugly piece of shit face? That's what a traitor looks like. See how it's been severed and mounted on a spear? That's what happens to piece of shit traitors. Don't be like this ugly piece of shit. Join the marines today!*

Or something like that.

The governor raised a hand, and his guards immediately stopped booing. Then he stood up.

Yavin stopped growling and dropped to one knee. Tim stopped dancing and did likewise.

"What's going on?" said Cooper. "Are you guys –"

A searing pain in the back of his knees dropped him to the ground. When he looked up, an orc in old leather armor was standing over him with a large iron club. Cooper had assumed from the lack of introduction that he was one of Zimbra's bodyguards, but this place didn't seem very organized.

"Asshole!" said Cooper. "I didn't know we'd started!" He swept a leg out, catching the orc by surprise and bringing him to the ground with him, then almost immediately felt a similar pain in his back. Glancing back, he found another orc beating him with a club. "Fucking hell, man! I thought I was supposed to be fighting Yavin!"

"Enough!" said Zimbra, and the two orcs stopped beating Cooper. He sashayed over and reached down to help Cooper to his feet.

Cooper wasn't sure how far he should trust Zimbra, but he figured if Zimbra wanted to do him harm, it would have been easier for him to just let his goons continue beating the shit out of him. He accepted the offer.

Zimbra was stronger than he looked. Cooper was back on his feet like he'd been put there by some kind of giant, spring-loaded device.

As jarring as that rise to his feet had been, especially after being unexpectedly beaten with clubs, Cooper was further unsettled by the fact that Zimbra was still holding his hand. Was he waiting for Cooper to say something?

"Uh... thanks?"

Zimbra stared at him intensely for a moment, still not letting go of his hand. Shit, was this dude into him?

"When the governor stands, you kneel," said Zimbra, still gazing intensely at Cooper and holding his hand.

"Okay."

Finally, Zimbra let go of his hand.

Cooper breathed out a sigh of relief, dropped to one knee, and waved at the governor. "Sorry, Yule... Shit! I mean... um... GRRRRREAT!" *Wait, that can't be right.*

The governor's bodyguards seethed at Cooper, and he could practically feel Zimbra's eyes burning a hole in the back of his head. But the governor himself just stared at him curiously for what seemed like a long time before finally nodding and sitting back down.

"Warriors rise!" called Zimbra from quite a ways behind Cooper.

Following Yavin and Tim's example, Cooper got to his feet. He turned back to see that Zimbra and his bodyguards had backed up to the edge of the arena.

Yavin gave him a small nod. "Fighting commence!"

*Fighting comments?* Was that, like, opening trash talk? Cooper really wished they'd given him more time to prepare for this. This wasn't a fucking improv show. How was he supposed to think up a good zinger on the –

"COOPER!" cried Tim.

"Huh?" Cooper turned to Tim but saw instead a mass of brown fur rushing at him a split second before getting jack-jawed and landing hard on his back.

It only took him a second to get his bearings again. Fortunately, Yavin used that second to extend his hairy bear arms and roar for the audience.

There was nothing like a good solid punch in the face to set a man's priorities straight. Cooper stopped worrying about whatever trouble he might get into for protocol violations or getting mixed up in whatever bullshit Tim was plotting. He was in a goddamn gladiator arena, a place specifically designed for people like him to channel their violent natures into something productive and entertaining. Zimbra wanted fighting comments? He'd give him fighting comments.

Cooper stood up and licked the blood from under his snout. "Hey, Yavin!" he shouted loud enough to be heard by the governor and his cheering bodyguards.

Yavin turned to face him. Unable to speak properly through his drooling bear maw, he growled and pounded his furry chest.

Cooper pounded his own chest, which sounded like someone slapping a raw steak against a waterbed. Fortunately, he had more than that in his response arsenal. He extended his arms, much like Yavin had, but with both middle fingers raised.

"I'M REALLY ANGRY!"

As his vision turned pink, he finally felt like he was truly in his element. This was the life he was meant for. One day he would die in this very pit, and he didn't give a fuck. He didn't care about money, or fame, or even if anyone remembered him after he was gone. His only wish was that he would be able to take as many lives as possible before someone finally took his.

As if able to read Cooper's feelings, Yavin staggered back a couple of steps. His bear eyes didn't look quite so ferocious anymore. It was like he knew the fight was over before it had even begun, but that wasn't going to stop Cooper from enjoying every brutal second of the carnage he was about to unleash.

He ran at Yavin, cocking his fist back to deliver the first crushing blow. The face was an obvious first target, a fitting retaliation. The gut was another option worth considering. Yavin's big bear gut an easier reach and broader target, and a gut punch was always satisfying.

But Cooper opted instead to go for the chest. Give that overtaxed ticker of his a wake-up call. He craved the crunch of sternum, smashing through to wrap his hand around this giant freak's still-beating heart. He'd pull it out of Yavin's chest, tear off a big bite, then hold up what was left for the governor to see.

THUD!

It felt like leather tightly wrapped around solid mahogany. Cooper had probably done more damage to his hand than he had to Yavin's chest. *Fuck, did Yavin even know he'd been hit?*

He drove his left fist into Yavin's presumably softer gut. It was softer, in the same way that pine is softer than oak, but still not something he'd advise someone to smash their fist into. If Yavin didn't kill him before he came out of his

Barbarian Rage, his hands were going to hurt like shit.

But instead of tearing Cooper's head clean off, Yavin took his human form, dropped to his knees, and let out a less-than-convincing groan of agony.

"You're doing great," he whispered. "Now hit me in the –"

CRUNCH!

Finally, Cooper felt something give a little. He was even more enraged now that Yavin had let on that he wasn't suffering even a little bit. Or at least he hadn't been a second ago. No matter how big of a badass a guy is, there's only so much he can do to toughen up his nose cartilage.

"That's it, Cooper!" cried Tim from a safe distance away. "Fuck that bear bitch up!"

Cooper landed two more punches on Yavin's face before he fell the rest of the way down. He wasn't faking it this time. Cooper was kicking his ass, and he was really enjoying it.

"FUCK YOU!" he screamed as he kicked Yavin repeatedly in the small of the back.

Yavin struggled to get up on his hands and knees. "Ease off a bit. I feel a little –"

Cooper took advantage of his compromised position by kicking him in the gut. He was relentless, stomping on Yavin's body when he was down, and kicking the shit out of him whenever he dared try to get back up. Every kick and stomp was more savage than the previous one. He might have broken every bone in his hands and feet, but it was worth it to put this smug motherfucker in his place.

"Am I still doing great?" he asked as he stomped Yavin's back. "You piece of shit! I'll fucking kill you! I'll... fucking..."

A wave of dizziness washed over him as he let out a long wet fart. He'd reached the end of his Barbarian Rage. Yavin was still alive, writhing on the ground and struggling to get up, but Cooper wasn't worried. Even in his post-Rage fatigued state, Cooper should still be in good enough shape to finish

## Critical Failures VIII

this asshole off. He'd only taken one hit, after all, and he'd been wailing on Yavin this whole time.

By the time Cooper had recovered from his fart, Yavin was back on his feet. He was a broken, bloody mess, hardly able to stand. Cooper could see in his eyes that he wanted Cooper to put him out of his misery. One or two more punches to the face ought to do him in.

Fists raised defensively, they staggered around each other like two retired heavyweight fighters drunkenly trying to settle an old score.

Yavin swung first, a left hook to the face. Cooper narrowly dodged, then returned it with a jab to the gut. His hands did indeed hurt like hell, but Yavin's human gut had a bit more give to it than his bear gut had.

He waited for Yavin to swing again. Yavin was moving slower now, and telegraphing his punches. This second swing might have missed Cooper's face even if he hadn't dodged. What's more, Yavin's clumsy follow through left him in the perfect position to get an uppercut to the face. Cooper gratefully took advantage of the opportunity.

The crunch this time was even more satisfying. It must have been loud enough to be heard in the stands, because the governor stood up and applauded.

As protocol dictated, Cooper took a knee. Maybe he hadn't quite killed Yavin, but that was probably for the best. He'd demonstrated to himself that he could take him, and it was a fun fight. But he was tired, and would appreciate a well-earned –

"Cooper!" shouted Tim.

"Huh?" Cooper looked up to find the wide black sole of a boot rushing toward his face.

CRUNCH!

The governor's bodyguards were cheering as Cooper rebounded from the sudden searing pain in his face.

"Get up, half-orc, traitor to your people!" said Yavin, shouting for the audience. He stood over Cooper, not looking nearly as shitty as he'd looked a few seconds ago. "Stand up and fight me like a man!" He winked as he reached down to help Cooper to his feet.

Cooper accepted his help because it was preferable to another kick in the face.

Yavin yanked him to his feet, then grabbed him by the throat and lifted him off the ground. "I'm sorry," he whispered as Cooper struggled to breathe. "I've got to hurry the final act a bit. I've suddenly come down with some terrible stomach cramps."

That son of a bitch had been faking all of it. No, not all of it. The blood still flowing out of his nose was real enough. He had vulnerabilities after all, and Cooper had a feeling he knew where he could find another one. He drove a foot hard up into Yavin's crotch.

Sure enough, Yavin let go of his throat.

The governor's guards let out a collective groan.

Refilling his oxygen-starved lungs with air, Cooper relished the look on Yavin's face as he stood there holding his crotch. He knew all too well what a hard kick in the nuts felt like, and it seemed like not too long ago he wouldn't have wished that kind of pain on anyone. But all he could think of at the moment was how sorry he was that Yavin's pain had to end. But as strong as his desire to continue staring into Yavin's wincing eyes was, even stronger was Cooper's desire to continue wailing on him until there was nothing left but a pile of broken bones and bloody pulp. His breathing back to normal, he stepped forward to finish the –

Yavin's eyes widened suddenly as his cheeks puffed out. Cooper was even more familiar with that desperate look than he was with getting kicked in the nuts.

"Dude, no," he said. "At least –"

# Critical Failures VIII

*BLEEEEGGGGGHHHHHH!*

It came at him like the stars when the Falcon went into hyperspace. It tasted like blood, porridge, and a bitter hint of something that Cooper couldn't quite identify.

In the shithole bars he used to frequent in Gulfport, he'd seen countless people take one shot too many and puke their guts out, and he'd gotten puked on once or twice. But it was usually on his shoes or the bottoms of his pant legs. No one had ever projectile vomited straight into his face before.

Then again, he'd never been in the position where he was about to murder the vomiter before. Maybe it was a defense mechanism hardwired into everyone's DNA, but seldom called into action. It was certainly effective. Between his fatigue and being showered in another man's puke, Cooper had lost the will to fight. All he wanted right now was a shower, and maybe to cry a little.

Yavin dropped to his knees, and Tim leaped onto his back and put him in a choke hold.

"This is what happens when you fuck with crazy," said Tim. "Crazy always fucks back harder."

Cooper felt like he ought to step in and help Tim finish the job, but he was kind of hoping to watch Yavin tear Tim away from his neck and beat the shit out of him a bit first. Instead, Cooper squatted down for a dump. Resting his hands palms-up on his knees, he tried to pass it off as meditation.

As it turned out, Tim was doing just fine on his own. Yavin made a couple of weak attempts to pull him off, but he was disoriented. His hand couldn't seem to find Tim.

"Would you please stop shitting on the ground?" said Zimbra with more than a hint of annoyance in his voice. He and his guards had moved close enough to where he could be heard while keeping his voice down. "Need I remind you Gur Lakha is watching?"

Cooper kept his attention focused on Tim and Yavin. "I

was trying to be discreet. It's only going to take longer if you break my concentration."

Zimbra sighed. "Feel free to fight back at any time, Yavin. I very much doubt the governor will believe a lone halfling is giving you this much trouble."

"Yeah, Yavin," said Tim. "Stop fucking around."

Yavin only groaned in response. It was a clear groan, his windpipe completely unobstructed by Tim's weak-ass choke hold. He followed that with a sharp juicy fart. A shotgun blast of shit sprayed the sandy arena floor behind him, inspiring Cooper to fire off what he had left in his chamber.

"Mercy of the gods," said Zimbra. "Could this battle get any more disgusting?"

"On it!" said Tim, then shoved a finger as far as he could up one of Yavin's nostrils.

Zimbra gasped. "What are you... I didn't mean... Pull them apart!"

His guards dropped their clubs and seized Tim from behind. They pulled as hard as they could, but Tim was holding on with both legs, one arm, and a deeply-lodged finger. Their efforts were only effective in pulling Tim and Yavin together, and certainly weren't doing Yavin any favors.

Tim's commitment to the role was more than Cooper had ever seen him give to anything. And while Cooper respected that, he thought this an odd set of circumstances to inspire Tim to turn over this new leaf. Kind of gross, too, if he was being honest. Cooper was well aware that he was generally viewed as gross by most people due to his low Charisma score. But while he'd been caught more than once two knuckles deep in his own nose, he'd never once picked anyone else's. This was true commitment to the craft.

"I'm Tim the Dim!" shrieked Tim as one of the guards wrenched his hand free of Yavin's face. Finally separated from Yavin, he turned his head to face the governor, who was

# Critical Failures VIII

being escorted out by his guards. "Are you not entertained?"

Perhaps the governor had sudden important governor business to attend to, but his departure before the end of combat probably wouldn't reflect well in the performance review of their first training. Fortunately, Yavin really dropped the ball hard with his performance. That should take some of the heat off Cooper and Tim.

"He's dead!" said Zimbra. He was kneeling next to Yavin, who was lying perfectly still flat on the sand, but Cooper glanced around, hoping that Zimbra might have been referring to someone else. Dying would be a pretty shitty move on Yavin's part when Cooper was counting on him to take the heat for this crappy fight. Unfortunately, everyone else present appeared very much alive.

"Are you sure?" Cooper asked, taking a tentative step toward Zimbra and Yavin. "He might just be sleeping. He said something about not feeling well."

Zimbra scowled at Cooper and lifted Yavin's head by the hair, revealing a puddle of blood underneath. Yavin's open eyes didn't have a trace of life in them. His face was covered in white sand, stuck there by his drying sweat and blood that had since stopped gushing out of his nose.

Could Tim have picked his nose hard enough to kill him? No, that was impossible. Cooper had probed farther into his own nose than even Tim's longest finger would be able to reach, and he hadn't stabbed himself in the brain.

That only left Cooper. Maybe it was that punch to the face he'd landed while in his Barbarian Rage, and it had just taken some time for Yavin to bleed out from it. Or it could have been any of the multitude of times he'd kicked him while he was lying defenseless on the ground. Several of those might have been Natural 20s, causing internal hemorrhaging. Maybe he'd ruptured Yavin's appendix.

Or maybe, just *maybe*, it was that kick in the nuts that did him in. It seemed highly unlikely, given the difference in their size. Sure, Cooper was strong as shit, but Yavin was a fucking beast of a man. It would be like if some high school kid from back home kicked him in the nuts. Yeah, it would hurt like hell for a while, but it wouldn't be nearly powerful enough to kill him... would it?

No. Cooper remembered all those YouTube videos of skateboarders smashing their balls against stair rails and shit. Those packed way more punch than some punk kid's foot, and those guys always managed to get back up eventually.

Then again, he'd only ever seen precious few of them take a hit in the nuts so hard that it caused them to vomit. None that he recalled had ever both vomited *and* shat themselves. Clearly, Cooper had achieved new heights of testicle devastation, but was it enough to kill a man? Perhaps, if he'd rolled a Natural 20, then another to confirm. He certainly wouldn't want to be on the receiving end of a double Nat 20 to the pills.

It didn't matter. In the future, whenever he told the story of this battle, it would be the kick in the balls that felled his opponent.

"What happened here?" demanded Zimbra, glowering accusingly at Cooper.

"I think..." Now was not the time to claim responsibility for this kill. He had to think of a plausible alternative explanation. "...Yavin sucked."

Zimbra's expression didn't change. "He was one of my best fighters, a born crowd pleaser. This was only meant to be a training exercise!"

"What are you shouting at us for?" asked Tim. "We didn't even have weapons. Yavin told us to come at him with everything we've got, so we did. You watched the fight. Hell, you even reprimanded Yavin for not giving it his all in front of the governor. Obviously, the problem was with him. Maybe

## Critical Failures VIII

he had a stroke or something."

Zimbra shifted his disgusted gaze to Tim. "Or maybe you stabbed his brain when you shoved your finger up his nose!"

Tim held up his pudgy little hand, still coated with Yavin's nose blood. "Yeah, right. Maybe if my finger was four inches longer and sharp enough to penetrate the base of the skull."

"Yes, yes. Obviously, I was being facetious. But whatever compelled you to shove your finger up his nose in the first place?"

"You did," said Tim. "I was merely playing the character you assigned me. And I don't mean to toot my own horn, but I really feel like I nailed it."

Cooper spotted an opportunity to likewise shift some of the blame for his own grossness back to Zimbra. "And you called me Cooper the Pooper. I'm not used to shitting for an audience, but I take my craft very seriously."

Zimbra turned to his guards, as if to question whether they could believe the bullshit flowing out of Tim and Cooper.

The larger of his guards shifted uncomfortably and avoided eye contact.

"Speak your mind, Rocco."

"The half-orc makes a valid point. He is called the Pooper. It is only natural that he would poop."

"So it would seem."

Tim gave Cooper an approving nod.

"I also found the halfling's performance very convincing," said the other guard. "My cousin is touched with dimness. He used to pick his nose all the time before he lost his hands for trying to pick a stranger's."

Zimbra grimaced, then turned back to Tim and Cooper. "Perhaps we need to rethink these roles."

That wouldn't do at all. Cooper the Pooper was a perfect cover for the inevitable. The only alternative he could imagine was incorporating a diaper into his costume, and that seemed like a better fit for Tim's character.

"If it's all the same to you," he said. "I'm kind of enjoying this role. I've grown an attachment to the character."

"Your performance is for the entertainment of the audience, not for your own."

"Shit can be entertaining," said Cooper, grabbing Tim by the back of the neck. "For example..."

"Cooper!" said Tim. "What are you –"

Cooper thrust Tim face first into his shit puddle. Tim writhed and flailed his arms and legs while Cooper smeared his face in the white sand, making sure it was completely coated.

When he was satisfied, he let go of Tim. "Now, watch this."

Tim hopped up, his face a furiously bewildered mask of shit and sand.

Zimbra's guards tried to stifle their chuckles, and even Zimbra himself cracked a small grin.

It might not have been as funny if he'd done it to someone like Gandhi or Martin Luther King Jr. or Robert DeNiro. But there weren't many people who'd spent more than five minutes in Tim's presence who wouldn't be entertained by watching him get his face shoved in shit.

"Very well," said Zimbra. "I shall consider it. Return to the dungeons and clean yourselves up."

Cooper sighed as he and Tim walked toward the arena gate, enjoying a small victory for once.

Tim wiped shit out of his face and flung it on the ground. "Fucking asshole." It was something he needed to say, but Cooper could tell he understood that it needed to be done. By the time they reached the gate, he was back to his old self again. "Ah well, it was worth it for the look on Yavin's face when the belladonna kicked in."

"The who?"

"Belladonna, otherwise known as wolfsbane. I ground

some up and spiked his porridge with it before the match. I don't know if you noticed or not, but he puked all over you."

"I noticed," said Cooper. "Where the fuck did you get belladonna?"

"I stole it from the kitchen when I started the fire. You didn't think I did all that just for booze, did you?"

"I kinda thought you did."

"That kick in the nuts was perfect, by the way. You couldn't have timed it better if you tried. I wasn't sure exactly how the belladonna would affect him, and I was a little worried that some sudden gastrointestinal issue might arouse suspicion with Zimbra. But you made it look like a perfectly reasonable reaction to getting his balls smashed."

Cooper wasn't exactly thrilled with Tim's praise. He'd been feeling pumped about taking down a werebear with his bare hands, and Tim was taking the wind out of his sails. "So you're saying the belladonna is what killed him?"

"Nah, that only fucked him up. He probably would have bounced back from that eventually."

That felt a little better. Crippled by poison or not, at least Cooper could say he'd killed a –

"It was the needle that did him in," said Tim.

Cooper wasn't sure what Tim was talking about. He stopped walking. "You're saying Yavin was a heroin addict?"

"Of course not, dumbass. I'm talking about the four-inch needle I stabbed his brain with."

"So, like... PCP?"

"This isn't a riddle, Cooper. While I was keeping the tailor busy picking out patterns for my costume, I swiped a few of his sewing needles." He held up his open palm to Cooper and grinned. "One of them was made of silver!"

Cooper thought Tim might be overestimating the value of a needle's worth of silver, but he slapped Tim's palm just the same. "Way to go, buddy."

Tim frowned. "What was that?"

"A high five?"

Tim looked at his palm, rubbed it on his pants, then held it up to Cooper again. "Look at my finger and thumb."

Cooper squinted as he leaned down to get a closer look at what appeared to be brown lines seared into the tips of Tim's thumb and index finger. "What are those? Tattoos?"

"Burns," said Tim. "That's how I knew the needle was made of silver. If it can burn my fingers just by touching it, imagine the effect it would have if shoved into a werebear's brain."

"So that shit you said to Zimbra about if your finger was four inches longer and sharp enough to..." He didn't remember exactly how the rest of it went.

"Sharp enough to penetrate the base of the skull." Tim smiled to himself. "I laid it all out before him, and he's totally clueless."

Cooper shook his head. "That whole time I was fighting and getting kicked in the face, and you were dancing around like an asshole and picking your nose, I thought you weren't pulling your weight in the fight, making me carry the whole thing." He thought about how Yavin had complimented Cooper's attack in the middle of his Barbarian Rage. "But I was the one wasting my efforts. Nothing I did made a lick of difference."

"You were having fun, though," said Tim. "I could tell."

"I feel a lot better about shoving your face in my shit," said Cooper. "I mean, I felt pretty good about it then, but I feel even better about it now."

"I'll feel better after I wash it off. Come on. Let's go hit the showers."

# CHAPTER 24

"Is that Cooper and Tim?" asked Randy, peering through the bars of the gate leading into the arena. He practically had to shout to be heard over Denise's screaming baby.

Gurok, the orc who had been assigned to train Randy and Denise, spat on the ground. "You know those fools?"

"That's highly unlikely," said Denise, sitting against the wall trying to shove a hairy nipple into Fatty's mouth. "Don't none of them half-orcs look any different from one another. And that dancing midget could be anyone. Those two ain't even together. Cooper ran off with that big-tittied bitch, and don't nobody know where Tim fucked off to."

"They fight without strategy or discipline," said Gurok. "The halfling does not even fight. He merely dances and picks his nose. What sense does that make?"

"Maybe he's got a booger lodged way up in there," suggested Randy. "And he thinks the dancing might help shake it out."

"Perhaps Yavin is the greatest disappointment of all. In my entire time here, I have never seen him make such a poor effort. With the governor attending, no less. With the South Pen's kitchen in dire need of repair, this is the time when we need to impress the governor most. And yet, Yavin stands there, sweating in his human form like some first month recruit."

"What's South Pen?" asked Randy, his eyes adjusting as he

turned from the glaring white sand back to Gurok in the shadowy tunnel.

"Where the other pigs are kept."

"Pigs?"

"We are all swine in the eyes of the citizens. As such, we are kept fat and healthy in our pens until it is our time to be slaughtered."

"And by pens, you mean our living quarters?"

"That is correct."

"I met most of the folks here over the past couple of days, but I ain't seen Cooper and Tim until just now."

"I'm tellin' you," said Denise. "That ain't them."

Gurok frowned as the half-orc in the arena seemed to fart out the end of a Barbarian Rage. "You would not see them here. We live in North Pen. Though they view us as animals, the citizens know that we will band together as brothers to protect each other against a common foe."

"Who's our common foe?"

"South Pen."

"Why?"

"Because we share no common bond."

"What do you mean? We're all slaves here in this arena just the same as they are, ain't we?"

"When both gates are opened at the next Full Moon Brawl, will you not defend your North Pen brothers?"

"Sure I will," said Randy, not exactly sure what a Full Moon Brawl was.

"Good. When both pen gates are opened, you can be sure that those from the South Pen will look after their own. Hopefully, these two idiots will be selected to represent them. They should be easy kills and will help shift the balance early in the fight."

Randy turned his attention back to the fighting pit. The large man who had been a bear monster a couple of minutes

# Critical Failures VIII

ago was now holding the half-orc that looked a lot like Cooper up by the throat. That is, until the half-orc kicked him between the legs.

Gurok chuckled. "Truly, Yavin is in poor – Mercy of the gods!"

The bear man threw up all over the half-orc, then even went so far as to spray poop all over the ground behind him. The halfling continued dancing and picking his nose, neither of which were activities that Randy knew Tim to be particularly fond of. He suspected that Denise might be right after all, and he'd misidentified these people.

"Is there nothing you can do to quiet that brat?" said Gurok. "I wish to hear what is happening out there."

"Fatty's hungry," said Denise. "My titty milk just ain't enough for her no more. What's that Full Moon Brawl you was just talking about?"

For once, Randy was relieved to hear something come out of Denise's mouth. It saved him from having to ask another question in a string of potentially annoying questions.

"We have more fighters brought in than the city can afford to house or feed. Once a month, during the full moon, the governor puts on a special fight. This is the only time those of us in the North Pen are allowed to meet those in the South Pen."

"That's nice," said Randy. "A little monthly social?"

"It is a fight to the death."

"Oh." Now that Randy thought about it, that aligned much better with the name of the event.

"Surplus fighters, usually between twenty and thirty, are selected randomly from each pen. Both gates are opened, and the fighting does not stop until everyone on one side is dead."

"Something don't add up," said Denise. "It sounds like you and your boy Yavin out there have been around for quite some time."

Gurok nodded. "Quite."

"If folks is selected at random for this big brawl every month, and it don't end until one side is completely slaughtered, how is it that you two have been able to hang on so long?"

"An astute observation," said Gurok.

Randy gave Denise a nod and a thumbs up. He was still trying to catch up mentally on her logic.

"Thank you," said Denise.

"The selection process is perhaps not as random as Master Zimbra would have us believe. Those of us who prove to be more valuable, whether in our ability to train novice fighters, to please the crowd, or to please the governor himself, seldom find ourselves selected for the Brawl."

Denise licked her lips thoughtfully for a moment. "What if someone wanted to get *randomly* selected?"

That took Gurok's attention away from the fight. He stared at Denise inquisitively. "For what purpose? Did I not make clear what is at stake? One group is entirely slaughtered, down to the last man. It is often the case that many in the winning group do not leave the fighting pit alive. There is nothing to be gained by participating."

"Maybe I phrased that wrong," said Denise. "Say someone was to step out of line, starting shit all the time and generally being a huge pain in Zimbra's ass. Would that put a person at higher risk of getting selected?"

Gurok nodded and bared his yellow teeth. "I understand. The selection process is not disclosed to us, but I have observed troublemakers being selected more frequently than random chance would account for." He turned his attention back to the fight. "I would bet my mother's soul that these two idiots will be selected for the coming Brawl."

Randy looked out at the fight again. The half-orc was squatted over, taking a dump on the ground while he watched

# Critical Failures VIII

the halfling shoving his finger up the bear man's nose and shouting something. Randy couldn't make it out clearly over Fatty's crying, but he thought it sounded an awful lot like Tim.

"Are you sure they ain't –"

"Randy," said Denise. "Shut the fuck up."

Randy had been making more of an effort these days to let Denise know she couldn't push him around anymore, but he didn't think it wise to get in a scuffle right before their first training session, especially since Gurok had just spelled out the potential consequences for causing a ruckus. Besides, it looked like the fight outside was wrapping up.

Gurok sighed. "The governor is leaving, and it appears that Yavin is dead. Those two fools are Brawl fodder for certain."

Randy felt a tug in his gut and hoped he was wrong about them being Cooper and Tim.

"That bodes well for us, though," Gurok continued. "Without the governor present, we need not worry about putting on a show. We can focus more on practical training."

When the gate closed behind the two surviving South Pen fighters, the North Pen gate opened.

Denise led Fatty out onto the fighting pit as Zimbra's guards were dragging Yavin's body away.

"Hold up, y'all!" she called ahead. "Do you mind if my baby eats some of that before you drag it away?"

Zimbra rolled his eyes. He looked like he was having a trying day, but he gestured for his guards to stop what they were doing.

"Very well. He might as well be of use to someone."

"I sure do appreciate that," said Denise. She bent over and scooped up a handful of the half-orc's poo and started smearing it all over her clothes.

"Denise!" cried Randy, as Gurok, Zimbra, and his guards

were all too dumbfounded to speak. "What are you doing?"

"Don't you mock my culture. This is how my people prepare for battle."

Zimbra turned his back on them and walked toward the edge of the fighting pit. "Never have I more looked forward to a Full Moon Brawl."

"Perhaps the scorpion child may be spared," suggested Gurok. "It is young enough so that its mother's influence may yet be –"

"These imbeciles are under your charge, Gurok!" snapped Zimbra, clearly at the edge of his rope. "I have had my share of disappointment from my trainers for the day. Fail me further, and the scorpion child will be feeding upon your corpse!"

Over the next couple of hours, as Fatty ate Yavin's entire left calf, Randy and Denise learned the basics of how to take kicks and punches in a theatrical way. Unlike theater as Randy understood it, the kicks and punches were all too real. While they hurt quite a bit, at least that took their lack of acting experience out of the equation.

"Ugh!" said Randy when Gurok shoved a fist into his gut.

Gurok nodded. "Very good. But I need you to project your voice more." He punched Randy again.

"UGH!" repeated Randy.

"Much better."

In Randy's opinion, Denise was the better performer of the two of them. Projecting her voice came naturally to her, and he imagined that the audience would be entertained by all her swearing.

But whether Gurok found Denise to be a worthier clay to mold into a gladiatorial champion, or because he enjoyed beating the crap out of her more, Denise definitely got the lion's share of that day's training. If her poop stunt had been intended to discourage Gurok from getting too close, it had

## Critical Failures VIII

failed miserably.

"Enough!" said Zimbra after Gurok had spent a sufficient amount of time beating the snot out of Denise. "You have done well, Gurok. My faith in your abilities as a trainer has been restored, and my mood elevated." He shifted his gaze to Denise. "Gurok has taught you well, dwarf, and I hope you will drink in his tutelage."

Denise glanced back to check on Fatty, who was still eating Yavin's leg. "Yeah, all right." She coughed up a gob of bloody phlegm, then got down on her knees in front of Gurok. "But make it quick. My kid's right over there."

Gurok drove his knee into her face.

"Ow!" cried Denise, falling back on her ass. "What the fuck was that for?"

"When you are chosen for the Full Moon Brawl, I shall pray to the gods for a South Pen victory." With that, Gurok turned his back on Randy and Denise, then walked with a slight limp back to the gate. He must have overdone it a bit while kicking Denise.

Randy helped Denise to her feet. "You okay?" He left the question ambiguous so that Denise could respond either with her feelings about the physical trauma she'd just suffered or her feelings about Gurok's rejection.

"Fuckin' queer," she said. "No offense, Randy. I was talking about Gurok."

"You know, Denise. Just because a man don't want to put his –"

"Jesus Christ, Randy! Can you stop thinking about cocks for one goddamn minute?" She glanced past Randy to where Zimbra and his guards were talking, then whispered, "We got more important shit to discuss."

"We do?"

"Your training is over," said Zimbra when he noticed them still standing there. "Do you need Rocco to show you the way to the gate?"

Denise shook her head. "Come on, Fatty!" she called to her child. "It's time to go!" When Fatty started scuttling toward them on her eight spindly arachnid legs, Denise pushed Randy toward the gate. "You heard the man, Randy. Get your dick warmer moving."

"Okay, okay!" Randy waved goodbye to Zimbra and his men as Denise continued shoving him toward the gate.

When he, Denise, and Fatty were in the North Pen corridor, and the gate started closing behind them, Denise turned around and looked back in the direction they'd just come from.

"Did you forget something?" asked Randy.

Denise stared out across the fighting pit. "Nah. I'm just checking on something. Find your boy Long Dong Silver."

"You mean Captain Longfellow?"

"Whatever. Get him and his crew together for a private meeting pronto."

Randy frowned at Denise. "Do you want to take a shower first?"

Denise sighed. "Goddammit, Randy. What's the point of rubbing shit all over my body if I'm just gonna turn around and wash it off?"

"I don't rightly know. I just thought maybe you'd be more –"

"Focus, Randy! I got the beginning of a plan to bust us the fuck out of this shithole. But I'm gonna need some help fleshing out the finer details."

Captain Longfellow and his crew weren't hard to find mingling with the other residents of South Pen in the cafeteria. And once Randy pulled the captain aside and relayed Denise's request, he was intrigued. The captain wandered the room, making brief small talk with his highest ranking crew members. Then they did likewise, disseminating the information to the rest of the crew.

Before long, all of them had casually disengaged with

whoever they'd been chatting with and filtered out of the cafeteria so subtly that Randy wouldn't have noticed if he hadn't been paying such close attention.

With no doors in any of the rooms, it was impossible to have total privacy, but one of the captain's crewmen found a suitably sized empty room at the end of a corridor. It appeared to be used for storing old furniture and set pieces for special arena battles.

"That be all of us," said Captain Longfellow when the last of his crew entered. "Avery, Milton. Go outside and suck each other's cocks in the hallway to keep wanderers at a distance."

Two of his men saluted. "Right away, Captain!" They hurried out of the room.

"I don't mind standing guard outside," said Denise.

Randy scowled at her. "You're the one who called the meeting."

"Shit, that's right."

"So what be this big plan of yours?" asked Captain Longfellow.

Denise glanced cautiously at the open doorway. Satisfied that all she could hear were the sounds of slurping and heavy breathing outside, she spoke.

"Well, it ain't so much a plan as it is the first couple of steps, and a basic framework for the rest."

"Sounds to me like ye be walking eight feet out on a four foot plank."

"I ain't walkin' fucking nowhere yet," said Denise. "That's what I called you motherfuckers in here for. Randy, why don't you whip out that big ol' lizard of yours?"

He supposed that, after all this time, he shouldn't be surprised by anything Denise said, but Randy was truly taken aback by the request.

"Your plan involves me exposing my wiener?" He hoped he wouldn't have to do it in front of a full audience.

"There's more to life than dicks, Randy. You and your friends can jack off all over each other when we're done with the meeting. In the meantime, would you please summon Basil?"

Randy felt a little uneasy about summoning Basil in the arena when none of the masters were aware of his existence yet. But he missed him, and he was relieved that he wasn't being asked to pull out his junk.

"You may want to take a step back," Randy warned everyone.

They crowded together near the doorway, not needing to be told twice.

Randy pointed to the corner furthest from the crowd. "Basil."

The crowd gasped, suddenly in the presence of the massive glowing basilisk. Even Randy had to admit Basil looked bigger in such a confined space.

"Hey there, buddy," said Randy as he placed a calming hand on Basil's head. "How you been?" He closed his eyes to better receive Basil's thoughts in his head.

*I'm hungry. Are they food?*

Randy followed Basil's gaze to see that he was staring at Captain Longfellow and his crew. "No. I'm sorry, but you can't eat them."

"I'm gonna approach," said Denise, taking a tentative step toward Basil. "You tell that big son of a bitch not to eat me."

But Basil turned his head away and flared his nostrils as Denise stepped closer. If there was anybody in the room who didn't need to worry about being eaten, it was her.

*Tell the dwarf to go away. She smells like shit.*

"I don't mean to be rude," said Randy. "But Basil doesn't like the way you smell. It ain't nothin' personal. It's the poo you smeared all over yourself."

Denise stepped even closer to Basil's face, deliberately

waving her poo scent at him with both hands. "Tell him to take a big whiff and commit it to memory."

"Why?"

"This ain't just any shit, Randy. This is Cooper's shit, and we need Basil to deliver him and his little bitch buddy a message."

"You mean that was really them out there?"

"Of course it was. Are you fuckin' blind?"

"But you said –"

"Never mind what I said. We don't need Gurok blabbing our business to Zimbra. If Zimbra gets wind that we know folks in South Pen, the whole plan falls apart."

"And what plan might that be?" asked Captain Longfellow.

Denise scowled at him. "I'm getting to that." She turned back to Randy. "How far away from where you're standing can you summon Basil?"

Randy thought about it for a moment. "I ain't never tried any long distance, but I reckon I can summon him to appear anywhere I can see."

"I was hoping you'd say that. From the gate that leads out to the fighting pit, there's a clear line of sight to the South Pen gate on the other side. If you was to summon Basil on the other side of that gate, he'd be free to sniff down Cooper and deliver a message."

"But I'm the only one Basil can communicate with," said Randy. "Even if he can find Cooper without getting killed, how's he going to deliver a message?"

"Ain't nobody gonna fuck with a big-ass glowing basilisk, Randy. You seen how terrified folks are of a normal one on the street. Basil will be free to roam wherever that scaly-ass nose leads him. As for the message, we'll have to write something down and shove it up his butthole. He can shit it out when he finds Cooper."

Randy was surprised to hear what sounded like positive

murmuring from Longfellow's men. They actually seemed to think this crazy idea had merit.

"What will the message say?" asked Gort, one of Captain Longfellow's senior crewmen.

Denise shrugged. "How the fuck should I know? I can't even fuckin' read. That little scrotum-snipping halfling motherfucker seems clever enough. Let him think up the rest of the plan, write it down, and send it back up Basil's butthole."

The murmuring from Longfellow's men was now decidedly less positive.

"That's your plan?" said Gort. "Send a message asking someone else to think of a plan?"

"I came up with the first part," said Denise. "I told you it weren't fully developed, ain't I?"

"If the message is all covered in basilisk shit, how can we be sure they will even recognize it as a message?"

"Are you fuckin' kidding me? Picture yourselves in their situation." Denise spread her arms dramatically. "You're imprisoned in a gladiatorial arena, in a foreign land, forced to fight for the entertainment of orcs who see you as nothing more than pigs."

"We are all quite literally in that very situation."

"I wasn't finished yet. Then, from out of nowhere, a giant magical lizard appears before you and shits on the floor. Would you not see that as a sign from the gods?"

Gort shrugged. "Maybe, but –"

"And would you not carefully sift through every ounce of that magical lizard shit to discover what it is the gods wanted to tell you?"

"I don't think I would." The other crewmen murmured their agreement.

"No," said another. "Honestly, I do not think that would even occur to me."

## Critical Failures VIII

"Then you're all a bunch of fools," said Denise. "Last time that basilisk took a shit in front of me, it turned out to be a very dear friend of ours. If I hadn't scooped up that lizard turd, our friend wouldn't be alive today."

There was a long moment of silence while nobody knew exactly how to respond to that.

Randy got the conversation rolling again. "So maybe we'll find something conspicuous to put the message in. Right now, I think we should focus on fleshing out other aspects of the plan."

"A basilisk shan't go unnoticed roaming the corridors of South Pen," said Gort. "Even if nobody is equipped to deal with it immediately, the masters have people who are trained at wrangling large and dangerous beasts. This brute may have time to deliver a message, but it surely won't be sticking around long enough to wait for a response, much less a fully formed escape plan."

"Then we keep it one way and simple," said Denise. "We tell them to make sure they're selected for the Full Moon Brawl, and we'll do the same."

"And what, exactly, be a Full Moon Brawl?" asked Captain Longfellow.

While Denise explained the Full Moon Brawl to the captain and his crew, Randy tried to think of why Denise would want them all to participate in it. Did she have so much faith in Longfellow's crew that she thought it would be an easy win for them? Maybe build their gladiatorial reputation a bit and take credit as their leader in the hopes that she would rise to a similar station as Gurok and not have to participate in future fights? The selfishness of the idea certainly fit Denise, but it was too forward thinking. Denise was a lot of things, but Randy had seen no evidence that she was a brilliant strategist inclined to think so many steps ahead. And besides, why would she insist that Cooper and Tim be there, knowing it was a fight to the death, unless... Was all this just a plot to kill Tim because he cut off her balls?

"But if it is a fight to the death," said one of the crewmen now that Denise had finished explaining the general concept of the Full Moon Brawl. "Why would we invite our allies to be a part of our opposition?" It was like he was reading Randy's mind.

Denise sighed. "Again, and I feel like I've made this abundantly clear. I don't fuckin' know. I just figure it's the only opportunity we're likely to get to all be together at the same time. So if we're gonna come up with an escape plan, that would be a good time to set it in motion."

Maybe she wasn't setting up Tim to be slaughtered after all. Maybe there was more to her idea than Randy thought.

"I like it," said Randy. "Division is the whole point of the Full Moon Brawl. As long as they can set us up to kill each other, we have no power. But what happens if we turn the tables on them and decide to work together?"

Several of the crewmen looked hopeful. Captain Longfellow did not.

"So we lay down our arms and refuse to fight," he said. "Surely, we would not be the first lot to try such a stunt. They'll just set their goblin snipers on us, picking us off one by one until we start fighting proper again."

"I wasn't talking about laying down shit," said Denise. "I ain't got much of a plan in mind, but I certainly wasn't thinking about no fuckin' peace strike. One way or another, I aim to fuck some shit up. Otherwise, I wouldn't want to get Cooper and Tim involved. Cooper's strong as shit and dumber than a sack of dog dicks, and Tim is a ruthless motherfucker. Any plan that involves those two ain't gonna end in no holding hands in peaceful protest."

And just like that, with nothing but a vague promise of mindless violence, she had won the crowd over.

# Critical Failures VIII

Captain Longfellow tore off the entire left sleeve of his shirt and handed it to the half-orc sitting next to him. "Hammercock, take dictation."

"Yes, Captain." Hammercock sliced open his chest with one of his clawed fingers. "What shall I write?"

The captain scratched his chin thoughtfully for a moment before beginning. "Wipe the orc jism from yer eyes and heed me words. Get ye yer cock scabbards to yon fighting pit for the –"

"I'm sorry to interrupt," said Randy. "That might be a little too... *eloquent* for our purposes. I was thinking something a little more to the point. How about this? Cooper and Tim. Planning escape. Full Moon Brawl. Be there."

"It be a touch drab for my tastes, but I suppose it will serve its purpose." Captain Longfellow nodded to Hammercock.

Hammercock dipped a claw in his own fresh blood, then began scrawling out Randy's message onto Captain Longfellow's sleeve. When it was done, he blew on it until he was satisfied the bloody words were dry, then rolled it up nice and tight.

"Shall I insert this into the beast's arse?" Hammercock turned to Randy. "Or would you prefer to do the –"

"Somebody's coming!" said Avery, one of the two sentries the Captain had posted outside. His penis was large and erect, glistening with his partner's saliva. His partner, Milton, stood beside him, rubbing his jaw.

All of the murmuring stopped. The pirate crew was dead silent, as if they were sneaking up on a merchant vessel under the cover of darkness.

"Who is it?" whispered Randy.

"I don't know, but he looked big."

"Did he see you?"

Avery shrugged.

"I saw you go in there," called a familiar voice from out in the hall. "Don't be shy."

Denise locked eyes with Randy. "Gurok."

"He must have seen what they was doing out there," said Randy. "Maybe if we just stay quiet, he'll respect their privacy and go away."

"I saw what you were doing," said Gurok. He was closer now. "It is nothing to be ashamed of. All I want is a piece of the action."

Denise clapped a hand on Randy's shoulder. "Sit tight, buddy. I got us covered." She shoved her child into Randy's arms. "Mind Fatty, and make sure your fuckin' lizard don't eat her." By the time Randy got a comfortable hold between the baby's multitude of limbs, Denise had waddled halfway to the doorway.

"You must be from the new group." Gurok's voice was coming from almost right outside. "There's a certain hierarchy here that you will have to get used to. It may be more fun for me to come in there and take what I want, but I can all but guarantee it won't be as much fun for you."

"That won't be necessary," said Denise in what Randy assumed was supposed to be a seductive tone as she stepped out into the hall. "I'll give you shit you ain't even known you wanted."

"Yeegh," Gurok responded like he'd been propositioned by a sentient pile of roaches. "Stand aside, dwarven whore, before I finish what I started in the fighting pit."

"That's right, big boy. Finish in my fighting pit. I want it in all my pits."

Randy and Captain Longfellow exchanged a sour grimace.

"I saw two human men enter that room," said Gurok. His voice sounded a little farther away. Randy had to hand it to Denise. Even though Gurok had proven decisively a short time ago that she was no match for him in a fight, there was just something about her when she was trying to be seductive that

## Critical Failures VIII

a man couldn't help but back away from. But was her offensiveness so powerful that it could make Gurok go away?

"Is it true what they say?" asked Denise. "Orc hard, play hard?"

"Who says that? Nobody says that."

"Let's just reach under that pretty skirt and see how hard that big orc sausage of yours –"

SMACK!

"How dare you touch me, you disgusting hairy bitch!"

All Randy could make out after that was Denise's grunting and the repeated thunk of hard leather against flesh. He might have suspected that Gurok had succumbed to Denise's wiles, and that they were now engaged in angry rough intercourse, but Gurok's words suggested that he was kicking the shit out of her again.

"Get this... through your... thick... dwarf... skull!" said Gurok between kicks. "I would never... in a thousand lifetimes... put my cock... anywhere near... your rancid... whore... cunt!"

Gurok had already messed her up pretty bad during the training, and Randy wasn't sure how much more punishment Denise could take. Should he go out there and interfere? Or were they still hoping that Gurok would go away? Captain Longfellow seemed to have anticipated his concern. When Randy glanced his way again, he shook his head and raised his finger. Wait it out and see what happens.

"It seems you learned little in training today," said Gurok. "Perhaps your friends shall prove better at projecting their voices." He was getting closer again. "Listen for their squeals as I shove my cock up their –" He'd backed three steps into the room, his entrance obviously meant as a show of indifferent bravado, still facing in Denise's direction to show how little he feared the two scared men he expected to find cowering in here.

Instead, he found more than a dozen angry pirates, a paladin, and a basilisk when he turned around. An almost imperceptible trace of fear flashed in his eyes, but his training kicked in quickly. He shot Randy a steely-eyed glare.

"Whatever this is, the masters will hear of it." He took a step back, keeping his eyes on the crewmen nearest him. Imagining himself in the same situation, Randy could practically read his thoughts. He didn't want to turn tail and run away from a bunch of rookies, but he knew he couldn't face so many at once. Instead, he would back away slowly and confidently. It was not his duty to deliver the masters' justice, after all. Whatever bed they were making, they would soon have to lie in. But for now, they could at least go on living a few more hours as long as they didn't try anything stupid.

But even if he did bolt out of there right now, two or three of Longfellow's crew might be able to give chase while the rest were bottlenecked in the doorway. He would quickly dispatch them and easily find help before anyone else could hope to catch up to him. Gurok was by no means assured an escape. But the way Randy saw it, the odds were definitely in his –

"I'm... really... angry." The words sounded weak through labored breathing, but the hulking silhouette of a she-dwarf darkening the doorway looked anything but weak.

Gurok turned around. "Mercy of the –"

CRUNCH!

Randy didn't know balls could crunch when kicked. Denise must have gotten a piece of Gurok's pelvic bone as well.

Longfellow's men joined Denise like a pack of jackals. Gurok was in as much danger of suffocating as he was getting beaten to death.

"Stop!" said Randy. "This ain't right. Let me tend to his wounds. When he feels the healing power of Jesus, we can part ways in peace!"

# Critical Failures VIII

Longfellow's men quieted down, got to their feet, and backed away from Gurok. Even Denise came out of her Rage and shrunk back down to her normal size.

"Well, how about that?" said Randy, quite pleased with himself. "I honestly didn't think that would work."

The nearest crewman turned to face him. "You didn't think what would work?"

"That stuff I just said about the healing power of Jesus and how y'all should stop fighting."

"I didn't hear any of that. We stopped fighting because the dwarf snapped the orc's neck."

Randy looked down to find Denise lying on the floor next to Gurok. They were both lying face up, but the rest of Gurok's body was facing the other direction.

"How about passing some of that healing power of Jesus my way?" said Denise.

Realizing there was nothing he could do for Gurok, Randy took Denise's outstretched hand in his. "In Jesus Christ's name, I heal you." He gave her all the healing power he had for the day. It wasn't enough to bring her all the way back to full health, but it stopped her bleeding and significantly lessened the swelling in her face.

"What are we going to do with the body?" Avery asked Captain Longfellow.

The captain shrugged. "I suppose we feed it to yon beast."

"But Gurok was a trainer. He will be missed long before the next full moon. The masters will search every room in the dungeon for evidence of his murder."

"All the more reason to make sure there be none to find." Captain Longfellow turned to Randy. "Feed yer beast all but one of the orc's arms up to the shoulder.."

"I don't know how I feel about using Basil to dispose of a body," said Randy. "Or about whatever it is you intend to do with its leftover arm."

Captain Longfellow smiled. "And that be why I did not tell ye me plan."

"That doesn't make me feel any better about it."

"That's part of having a pet, Randy," said Denise. "You got to take care of it, and that means feeding it when it's hungry. Gurok ain't getting no deader. All you'd be doing by not feeding him to Basil is starving that poor fucker to death."

"I know, but –"

"Think about where we are. You can't go to fuckin' Rouse's and buy fifty pounds of ground beef to feed this thing. You got exactly one source of food available to you, and that's the remains of folks who've been murdered. I reckon it's gonna take some time before you work out a system for smuggling body parts out of the fighting pit, so you best take these opportunities when they present themselves. For Basil's sake."

Randy nodded. "That's very insightful of you, Denise. Thank you."

"What can I say? I s'pose it's just them motherly instincts kicking in."

The immense gratitude Randy felt through his Empathic Link with Basil made him feel guilty for having let him get this hungry in the first place. Having to deny him an arm made him feel even worse. He didn't relish the thought of smuggling body parts out of the fighting pit, but he would do what had to be done.

At least it was over quickly. Basil gulped down Gurok's body in three bites.

Captain Longfellow backed away from Basil with the leftover arm, then pried its lifeless fingers open.

"What are you doing with that?" asked Randy.

"What need be done. Keep that beast of yours calm."

# CHAPTER 25

"You ever been to Port Town?" asked Elramar, Grimmond's half-elven delivery driver. Since they were all heading southward anyway, Grimmond offered to have Elramar take them as far as they needed to go. Alroth, Lucia, and Dave sat in the back with the cargo of pickled meats, and Stacy sat up front with the chatty driver.

"No," she lied, hoping to avoid any further questions about it. She felt bad for possibly coming off as rude, and for not taking this opportunity to learn more about this strange fantasy world from one of the locals. She was normally quite the chatty gal herself. At least she used to be. Had she changed since coming here?

She had a lot on her mind right now, traveling with a man she didn't know from Adam and who she wasn't sure she could trust, and Dave who she knew she absolutely couldn't trust. Together, they were diving headfirst into a mission that they had very little hope of accomplishing for the dubious hope of attaining what would likely be too little reward. It made sense that she wouldn't want to get distracted by idle conversation.

But was there more to it than that? Had something more fundamental about herself changed since coming here? Was there something about her rogue character that preferred to keep things close to the chest, carefully analyzing every sparse word that escaped her lips, lest she let slip dangerous information to the wrong ears? She didn't want to be that person. She always thought of herself as a cheerful and bubbly person who brightened other people's days with her sunny disposition. But she didn't feel very sunny right now.

A large grey cloud drifted across the sky, casting a shadow over them. The resulting drop in temperature reminded Stacy that the reluctant summer was finally giving way to autumn. Now that she took the time to look for them, she spotted more signs of the coming change of season. Small bursts of yellow in the otherwise green forest, flocks of migrating birds, a certain crispness in the air.

"It's a lovely little town," said Elramar. "Maybe a bit less so after those hog-faced orcs trampled through it. But they'll bounce back, mark my word. Mr. Grimmond is providing his meats at a steeply discounted price to help with the rebuilding effort."

"Is that right?" Stacy's tone was a little more curt than she'd intended it to be. The hog-faced orc comment had rubbed her the wrong way. Maybe a group predominantly made up of orcs had wreaked destruction on their way through the town, but she sensed that Elramar was using that to fuel a predisposition toward hating orcs. It made her skin crawl the same way it always had when overhearing conversations between extended family members over Thanksgiving dinner.

Elramar laughed. "Is that a touch of cynicism I hear in your voice?"

"No, I –"

"I suspect the same as you. Mr. Grimmond is a fine man, to be sure, but he is also quite the savvy business person. Always looking for a new angle. If you ask me, those pig fuckers did that town a favor. They'll rebuild it bigger and better than ever. And when the dust settles, I would not be at all surprised to see a second Stinky Pickle open up there."

*Let it go. Don't engage. You have more pressing concerns right now.*

"Pig-fuckers? Really?"

"I meant orcs, of course. Pardon my vulgarity." He was decidedly less jovial now, seeming to understand that he'd touched a nerve with her. "It just burns me up to think of what they did."

"Fucking pigs?"

Elramar breathed a sigh of relief, then laughed. "Too right, you are! Fucking pigs indeed, every last one of them!"

Great. Now he felt like they were on the same page. That was exactly the opposite of what she was going for.

"That's not what I meant," she said. "You called them pig fuckers. I was asking you if you'd ever seen an orc fucking a pig."

"I meant their faces look like –" He stopped short when he saw what *her* face looked like. "No, m'lady. I have not."

"You do realize that a large number of orcs gave their lives to defend Cardinia during the invasion, don't you?"

"I was unaware of that."

"Are you aware that one of my best friends is a half-orc? Would you call him a fucking pig?"

Elramar shook his head. "I'm sure he is lovely."

"You might want to think about your own people before you cast judgment on other races." That felt wrong even before she finished her sentence.

"My *people*? I take it you mean half-elves?" He was trying to turn the tables on her, and she'd given him the leverage to do it.

"I meant they way you're looked down on by other races."

"You look down on me because of my race?"

"No, not me. I meant, like, generally speaking."

Elramar rolled his eyes. "I suppose one of your other best friends is a half-elf."

"As a matter of fact, that's true." Stacy heard Dave snort from behind her. "Something wrong, *Dave*?"

"No," he said. "I, um... swallowed a bug."

So Stacy and Katherine weren't exactly best friends. That had nothing to do with Katherine being a half-elf, and everything to do with her being a bitch.

"This will do, driver," said Alroth. "We shall part ways here."

Stacy looked around but didn't see any landmarks or side roads heading into the forest. Was this actually where they needed to get off to get to get to the Cedar Wilds? Or had she made the trip too uncomfortable by getting into a racial argument with Elramar?

"Are you quite sure, sir?" asked Elramar. "Master Grimmond is not the only vendor contributing to rebuilding Port Town. Have you tried that new place on Wizard's Alley?"

Dave stood up next to Alroth, barely able to peek over the front of the cart. "Do you mean Arby's?"

"That's the one."

"Goosewaddle opened another Arby's in Port Town?"

"Not yet. Much like Master Grimmond, he has been shuttling carts full of his roasted beef sandwiches and seasoned potato curls to sell to the Port Town workers at a fraction of what you'd pay for them in Cardinia. Whether or not he decides to open a second restaurant there probably depends on how well his wares are received."

Dave chuckled. "He's doing market research under the guise of charity. Classy."

"What is this Arby's?" asked Alroth. "Who are the Sand Witches?"

"Sandwiches," Elramar corrected him. "They are a new culinary phenomenon. Thinly sliced roasted beef between two bread circles."

"That does not sound very phenomenal to me."

"It's something you need to experience to fully appreciate," said Stacy. "If it's not too far out of the way, it

## Critical Failures VIII

might not be a bad idea to swing by there first."

Dave's eyes widened over the front of the cart. "Why would you think that's anything but a bad idea? How many times does the man have to tell us to stop visiting his place of business?"

"That was specific to his Cardinia Arby's."

"He never said that."

"He also didn't not say it," said Stacy. "So that's the interpretation I'm going with. Besides, what are the odds that he's even there? A fully functioning restaurant requires a lot more supervision than some schlub slinging pre-made sandwiches from the back of some cart. And you know as well as I do that he's probably on Earth again sampling the finest fast food southern Mississippi has to offer."

"You noticed he's looking a little pudgier too?"

Stacy nodded. "Little bit."

In the pause that followed, she noted that Elramar hadn't stopped the horses, nor had Alroth asked him to. It was like both of them were interested to see how her and Dave's conversation would end.

Finally, Dave sighed. "I mean, I guess he can't expect us to avoid a place if he doesn't even tell us it's there."

"I completely agree."

"How were we supposed to know he opened a second Arby's in Port Town?"

"Right?" said Stacy. "We're not mind readers."

"What are we supposed to do? Send scouts ahead to every remote village we travel to just to make sure there isn't an Arby's?"

"That would be ridiculous."

Dave narrowed his eyes at Stacy. "But if he is there and pissed to see us, I'm telling him that you forced me into it."

"I can live with that."

"Maybe he'll kill you, and I won't be a slave anymore."

"That's the spirit!" Stacy turned to Alroth. "That is, of course, if it's okay with you."

Alroth shrugged. "No deal has been struck, nor coin changed hands. You are under no obligation to follow me. All I can do is hope that you will assist me once you have concluded your business in Port Town. For that hope, I shall delay my journey home by an hour or two. Also, it would be dishonest of me to say I am not intrigued by these curled potatoes you spoke of. How does one even curl a potato?"

"I wouldn't get too excited," said Dave. "Those things have a shelf life much shorter than the time it would take to transport them from Cardinia to Port Town."

Stacy felt bad for Alroth. Back at the Stinky Pickle, she'd been thinking that she was the one in the desperate situation. But while hers was definitely desperate, his was much more so. She hadn't thought about it until now because of the way he spoke and carried himself. He didn't give off any trace of a desperate vibe.

But this was a man who reached out to two complete strangers in a restaurant to join him in the almost certainly futile task of fighting off an entire tribe of giants. Not only that, but now he was resigned to delaying his mission so that the assholes he'd recruited could do an Arby's run first. That was a lower place than Stacy ever hoped to be, and now she felt extra bitchy for the whole Arby's thing.

It wasn't about getting a lukewarm hours-old roast beef sandwich and a pack of soggy fries. Stacy believed in paying close attention to seemingly innocuous connections. If fate had placed her on this path to Arby's, there must be a reason for it. Maybe they'd run into Professor Goosewaddle, and he would be moved by Stacy's continued dedication to curing Dave's Lycanthropy and offer to pay for it himself. After all, what's a thousand gold pieces to him? He was loaded, and his business was booming.

# Critical Failures VIII

Stacy laughed quietly to herself. Who was she kidding? Dave was right in that they'd probably be lucky to get out of there without being fireballed to death.

On the bright side, at least she wouldn't have to feel even more bitchy with regard to Alroth. If, by some miracle, the professor did see fit to fork over the thousand gold pieces she needed, she and Dave were absolutely going to ditch him. She felt a sense of relief knowing that it was almost certainly not going to come to that. Still, she couldn't help but wonder what fate had waiting for them in Port Town.

"We're nearly there now," said Elramar, snapping Stacy out of her contemplation.

At first glance, the stretch of road ahead of them didn't look any different from what she'd been idly staring at for hours. But now that she was looking for it, she spotted the sign that Julian and Dave had tried to steal when they first encountered Mayor Merriweather.

WELCOME TO PORT TOWN

She knew they wouldn't be staying long, but she hoped she would get to say hi to the mayor while she was –

*Oh my God, that's it!*

It all made sense now. The Mayor seemed like he was doing pretty well for himself, and Dave had saved his life last time they were together. Fate hadn't brought them to Port Town to hit up Professor Goosewaddle for cash. It brought them here to hit up Mayor Merriweather!

# CHAPTER 26

"This is going to be tricky," said Katherine as she considered the possible ways that she could get herself, Jay, and Butterbean from the ship to the island. The alcove where she'd sneaked aboard the ship and eaten Bosley wasn't roomy enough to launch herself from in bat form. "The way I see it, we have two options."

"Options are good," said Jay. "Lay them on me."

"We could both jump in the water. I turn into a shark, and you hold on to my dorsal fin while I swim to shore. I can see a few potential problems with that right off the top of my head."

"Such as me being dragged by a shark."

Katherine nodded. "That's one of the problems. I don't think I'd try to eat you, but it's weird being a shark. They're so primitive and prone to letting their basest instincts guide them. Some of that rubs off on me, and I don't always have the best impulse control."

"And what's the other potential problem?"

Katherine stared down at the inky black water, barely sparkling with the thin waxing moon's reflection. "There are probably scarier things than sharks in there, especially at night."

"Agreed. Option Two it is. So... What's Option Two?"

"When I take an animal form, anything I'm wearing or carrying gets absorbed into my body. Just like I did with the die earlier."

Jay nodded. "Very cool." He looked at her like he was still waiting to hear what Option Two was.

"So that's it, really. I could hold you and Butterbean while I turn into a giant bat. You'd be absorbed into my body until we reach the island and I change back into a half-elf."

"Oh," said Jay.

Katherine sighed. "Yeah."

"That sounds..."

"Too intimate?"

"I was going to say gross and terrifying, but intimate works."

"Well, that's all I've got. Unless you've got a better idea, take your pick."

Jay thought for a moment. "I guess you're not strong enough to carry me while you're in bat form?"

Katherine scoffed. "Guess again. If I could carry Cooper, I can sure as hell carry your scrawny ass."

"Then why didn't you list that as one of our options? That sounds a shit ton better than getting eaten or otherwise absorbed into your body."

"That would be no problem if we were up on the main deck," said Katherine. "There's not enough room for me to spread my wings here. If you jumped in the water, I could try to swoop down and grab you with my feet. But taking off from the water is hard enough with my wings slapping the surface. I'm not sure I'd be able to do it with your added weight."

"We're really close," said Jay. "There's got to be a way to make this work. What if you stood on my shoulders, turn into a bat, then I jump off the railing? Would you have enough time to start flapping before we hit the water?"

"That could work, except for Butterbean."

"Can't you just absorb him like you were going to do with me?"

"Sure, but I can't climb up onto your shoulders while I'm

carrying a goddamn wolf!"

"So absorb him before you start climbing."

Katherine took a second to think about it. "I guess that could work. I've got these neat little hooked thumbs at the leading edge of each of my wings. I feel like I could probably climb up your back with those. You ready to try this?"

Jay shrugged. "I guess. If it doesn't work, we can just do the shark thing." As if to solidify his commitment, he climbed up onto the railing and stood with his back to her. "Ready when you are."

Katherine took a deep breath. It was go time. She sat on the floor and gestured for Butterbean to come sit on her lap.

"Don't worry. It'll be just like before, but this time I'm sober."

"What?" said Jay, but Katherine was already starting to change.

When it was done, the alcove felt a lot smaller than it had just a second ago. Her body wasn't particularly huge, but her giant leathery wings scraped against the side walls as she instinctively tried to expand them.

She couldn't help but feel amused by Jay. He could obviously hear her clumsily scraping around as she tried to orient herself, but also obvious was the fact that he was very deliberately not looking back.

Climbing onto his back wouldn't be necessary. Her wings were big enough so that she could latch onto the overhang above his head with her thumbs and pull herself up onto his shoulders.

"Stay calm," he whispered to himself as her massive wings flanked him on both sides. "You knew she was going to turn into a giant bat. This is nothing to freak out about."

Katherine pulled herself up and grabbed his shoulders with her feet.

"Oh my God! I'm freaking out!"

# Critical Failures VIII

"Keep your shit together!" said Katherine, but it came out as a series of squeaks and an echolocative sensory map of her surroundings.

"I'm sorry. Everything's cool. Please don't eat – Oh shit!"

Katherine didn't wait for him to jump. Now that he was firmly in her grasp, she pushed forward with her wings until they were falling away from the boat. As soon as she cleared the alcove, she spread her wings wide and started flapping.

It wasn't a long fall, and Jay's feet dragged in the water a bit, but she got her rhythm down and began ascending.

Every two hundred yards or so, Katherine let out another barrage of squeaks to track her progress. The island only seemed to get marginally closer with every squeak, and her wings were getting tired. Evidently, bats weren't meant for long-distance flying... or for passenger transport.

She desperately wanted to look back at the ship to see if it was farther away from her than the island, but her bat head couldn't turn back and she didn't want to waste what precious little energy she had left to loop around.

Surely she was past the point of no return, though. She'd been flying for a while, and she was picking up more details on the island. There was no choice now but to persevere, ignore the burning in her muscles, and make it to the island. Lives were at stake. Jay, Butterbean, and everyone who was counting on using that die would be doomed if she succumbed to her exhaustion and got devoured by sea creatures.

The best way to take her mind off the flying was to think about something else. For example, now would be an excellent time to think about what she would say to the drow when she encountered them.

*'Sup, dawgs. This here's my boy, Jay. Fo shizzle.*

Now that she'd gotten that out of her system, it was time to think of something less stupid.

*Hello, your eminence. We've come to warn you about an*

*imminent attack on your island.*

No. She had to speak from the heart. If she went in there trying to use flowery words like eminence and imminent, she'd fuck it up for sure. She'd probably just end up calling their leader Eminem, and that wasn't likely to go over well. Be yourself, Katherine.

*Hello, drow friends. We've come to warn you about a group of cultists who are on their way this very minute to invade your island.*

That was much better. Now, how would they most likely respond?

*Do you honestly think we don't know that, idiot mongrel? They've been here for weeks. We're totally fucked. Wait a minute... Aren't you that bitch who ate my sister's cat?*

Okay, so maybe it wouldn't go that catastrophically bad, but the odds of that happening seemed like better odds than any good coming out of this mission. What were they doing out here? Had she just wanted so badly to get off the boat that she convinced herself this was a good idea? What did she have to offer the drow, and what could she reasonably expect to get from them in –

"Katherine?" shouted Jay. "You think maybe you could fly a little higher?"

Katherine looked down. Jay had his knees pulled up to his chest to avoid dragging his feet in the water.

"Shit!" she said as she tried to flap her tired wings harder. The resulting squeak revealed the shoreline to be only about a quarter of a mile away. She could make out individual trees and man-made structures. Distracting herself by musing about the futility of their mission had worked. They were going to make it.

Redoubling her efforts, she flapped for all she was worth, lifting Jay safely away from the water. The burning in her shoulders and chest intensified, but she flapped even harder as if to say "Fuck you" to the pain.

# Critical Failures VIII

The pain said "Fuck you" right back to her, and she wasn't sure she had anymore flaps to give. She let out one last shriek to see how far they'd need to swim and discovered that they were only about twenty yards away from the beach. She'd done it! They had made it safe and –

"Katherine!" cried Jay as Katherine felt a strong tug halting her forward progress. "Something's got my leg! Pull up! PULL UP!"

Katherine flapped as hard as she could, but it was no use. She was getting pulled backward. Looking down, she let out a loud squeak to see what they were dealing with.

As cool as it was to be able to sense her surroundings with echolocation, it was useless for seeing through water. Sound bounced back from the surface as opaque as if she was trying to look through pudding. All she could make out was a tentacle wrapped around Jay's right leg. Probably an octopus or a giant squid.

She was losing the tug-of-war battle as a bat. The only hope they had was for her to change back into a half-elf and hope she could reach Jay before the creature pulled him under.

"Keep flying!" said Jay. "I got this."

Katherine was a little relieved to hear him say that; she'd been almost sure he would be dragged out of reach in the time it took her to change forms. But she didn't know how much longer she could flap her wings. She already felt like she was dipping into some reserve tank of adrenaline that was quickly running out.

Jay grabbed her left ankle with his left hand and wrested his shoulders out of her feet. Fearful of losing him completely, she wrapped her toes tightly around his wrist.

"What are you doing?" she asked, knowing full well that Jay couldn't understand her. She needed to keep squeaking to be able to see what was going on. "Blah! Blah! Blah! Blah! Blah!"

With his free hand, he drew a serrated hunting knife and started sawing at the tentacle that was holding him. "Let go of me, you slimy son of a – SHIT!"

The creature loosened its grip on his leg, but flung out another tentacle to wrap around his knife-wielding arm. It was a good idea, but he'd been outplayed.

"Katherine!" he called up to her as he desperately tried to kick at the second tentacle. "I could use some help!"

Fighting while flying wasn't going to cut it. She had no choice now but to change.

Jay tried to hold on as her bat foot turned into a normal foot. But without her toes gripping his wrist, his hand slipped away.

She and Butterbean splashed down into the brisk water, which she discovered only came up a little past her waist when she stood up.

"Jay!" she cried, but he was nowhere to be seen. Except for where Butterbean was swimming, there was barely so much as a ripple on the surrounding water.

"Shit!" she said, scrambling for an idea. "Shit shit shit shit shit!" Then she remembered the Summon Nature's Ally spells she had at her disposal.

"SHARK!" she shouted, pointing at the water toward her best guess where Jay was.

A dorsal fin sliced through the surface of the water. It quickly darted forward, then submerged. She hoped that it would recognize the squid monster as her enemy and not go after Jay.

"Come on, shark," she said as she stared out at the water for any sign of... well, anything. "You can do it."

Finally, she spotted some disturbance on the surface, as if something below was thrashing. Then Jay burst out, sucking in as much air as his lungs would hold. He had his knife in one hand, and a length of severed tentacle in the other.

# Critical Failures VIII

"There's a goddamn shark down there now!" he said when he finally caught his breath. "This is a violent fucking ecosystem!"

"That's my shark," said Katherine. "Come on. He won't be around for long. We have to get to the shore."

Jay didn't argue. Tossing the tentacle aside, he and Katherine waded as fast as they could for the beach while Butterbean paddled between them.

"What do you mean, *your* shark?" he asked. "Like, you carry a shark around in that magic bag of yours with all the dead bodies?"

"Of course not." Katherine thought back to the shark she'd captured to feed her crew. "I mean, not usually. I summoned one with a druid spell."

"You can shapeshift *and* summon sharks? This is bullshit! My special powers amount to hiding and hating animals."

Katherine pulled her scythe out of her Bag of Holding as she continued wading, grateful that she was using her legs now rather than her exhausted arms. It probably wasn't the best weapon for fighting in the water, but the reach it provided gave her some comfort.

"It's not a very big shark, if that makes you feel any better," she said. "And it only sticks around until it dies or the spell duration times out."

"How long's its spell duration?"

"Only a few seconds, so keep moving. We've come too far to – FUCK!" As soon as she felt the slimy tentacle wrap tightly around her left leg, Jay disappeared back under the water. It had both of them.

The creature pulled her leg out from under her, sending her face first into the water and pulling her back.

Instead of attacking, she dug her scythe's curved blade into the sand and tried to pull herself forward. If they could drag it to shallower water, they might be able to get the upper hand. It seemed to be working, as she wasn't losing any more ground, but she could only maintain it until she ran out of breath. Fortunately, the tentacle let go of her.

Rising to her feet again, she found Butterbean snarling as he tussled with something just below the surface.

Jay emerged from the water with another severed tentacle in his hand. "Keep it coming, motherfucker. You've only got but so many arms."

Katherine drove her scythe down near where Butterbean was fighting. She wasn't sure what she hit, but she definitely met some resistance.

"Come on, Butterbean," she said. "Fall back. Go to the beach!"

Butterbean disengaged with the creature, and Katherine soon felt another tentacle around her leg.

"Goddammit!" said Jay.

"It's got you too?"

"Asshole just doesn't know when to quit." Jay adjusted his grip on his knife for downward thrusts rather than sawing.

"Wait!" said Katherine when it occurred to her that she wasn't being dragged underwater. She tried to move toward the shore. It was a struggle, but she was moving the right way. "It's weak. We can just drag it back with us."

Jay started moving with her. "Or we could just finish it off here and not have to bother with it."

"This is good eating. We don't always know where our next meal is coming from. If we catch something edible, it's always best to chop it up and throw it in the Bag of Holding."

Together, they dragged the beast onto the black sand beach and discovered that it was, in fact, a giant squid. Its body was easily as big as hers. Its tentacles seemed to go on forever.

"Is there any particular way you want these cut?" asked Jay, looking doubtfully into the soulless round eyes of the dying squid as he sawed off the tentacle wrapped around his leg.

Katherine dragged a large chunk of driftwood to the middle of the beach. "Produce Flame." When her hands burst into flames, she held them against the bottom of the damp wood, then turned to Jay. "Just cut them into small enough pieces to fit in the bag. And maybe cut us a couple of steaks from the thick part of the tentacles to eat as soon as I get this fire going."

Jay gawked at her. "Just so you know, your hands are on fire."

"It's a first level spell. The fire doesn't hurt me."

He shook his head and resumed dismembering the squid. "This is bullshit."

A few minutes later, Katherine had boiled all the moisture out of the wood and had a strong enough fire going to ignite more wood. By the time Jay had cut off all the squid's legs, the fire was roaring nicely.

Jay threw two thick cross sections of tentacle straight onto the fire, and they sat in silence as they watched it cook. Butterbean preferred his squid raw, and he seemed to enjoy the challenge of tearing pieces from the rubbery head.

"This isn't bad," said Jay through a mouthful of chewy squid steak. "Beats the hell out of rat."

"Huh?" Katherine was so tired she barely heard him. She jerked her head up. "Oh. Yeah, it's good."

"That was quite an experience. There were a few times back there where I didn't think we were going to make it."

"Next time, I'm absorbing you into my body, and I don't want to hear shit about it."

Jay laughed, then looked around. "So what now? Are we staying here for the night? Or should we try to find a hotel or something?"

"I honestly don't know if I can move. Are you okay with

spending the night on the beach?"

Jay shrugged. "It's a hell of a lot nicer than anywhere I've slept since I've been in this world."

"Good. It's probably not wise to go skulking around some place we know nothing about in the middle of the night. Especially since this place is run by drow."

"What's so bad about these drow people, anyway?"

Katherine didn't know how to answer that in a way that didn't make her extremely uncomfortable. "I don't know. Everyone says they're just evil."

"The only thing I've heard anyone say about them is that they're black. So I'm wondering, are they actually evil? Or do folks in this world just not like black people?"

"They're not black like you're black," said Katherine. She scooped up a handful of volcanic sand. "They're *black* black, like this sand. I mean, like, if I rubbed this sand all over my face, I might be able to pass for one."

Jay laughed. "That's probably not a good idea."

Katherine forced out a small laugh and dropped the sand. "Of course not. That would be incredibly offensive."

"Maybe. I don't know the historical context for blackface in this world. I just meant it would be stupid. It would take a huge moron to think they could pass themselves off as being part of a different race of people just by painting their face a different color."

"I don't know if that's necessarily true," said Katherine. "Maybe if they didn't interact with anyone. Say, for instance, if they just wanted to walk around without calling attention to themselves."

"Where do you think you're going to walk around with your face covered in sand and not call attention to yourself?"

Katherine knew she was creeping close to sounding like a talk radio host, but she didn't like being called a moron, even if it was unintentional. Furthermore, she still didn't understand why her previous attempt to impersonate a drow hadn't worked.

"Forget sand. Let's say we dug the ink sac out of that squid. If we –"

"Let me stop you right there," said Jay. "Before you go on any further, I need to ask you one thing. Are you about to suggest that I put on blackface?"

"Absolutely not!" That was technically true. She wasn't *about to* suggest that. She was going to test the waters a bit first and gradually lead up to it, hoping that maybe he'd be the one to suggest it. Now she saw that it was probably best to steer clear of that line of thinking altogether. "I was just playing Devil's Advocate. You know, trying to kill some of our down time with silly conversation."

"We might do better using this time to discuss what our next move is going to be, or at least to get some rest."

Rest sounded great to Katherine. Her arms were sore from flying, and it was well past the time she should have gone to sleep for the night.

"Do you want me to take the first watch?"

Jay shook his head. "I got in a couple hours of sleep on the boat, and you don't look like you could stay awake another five minutes if you were on fire."

Katherine wanted to laugh, but it came out as a yawn. "Thanks." She called Butterbean over to act as her pillow. Not only was his fur soft and comfortable, but the rhythm of his breathing and knowledge that he was there with her helped her sleep easier.

Wondering what the hell they were going to do tomorrow, she closed her eyes and fell asleep.

# CHAPTER 27

"This will never work," said Tony the Elf. "I don't know why I ever agreed to it."

Chaz did his best to pretend like Tony the Elf and Captain Logan weren't in the cabin with him while he peed in the steel basin against the wall. It was tricky enough trying to keep from pissing all over the wall with the swaying of the ship, but doing that while keeping one eye over his shoulder to make sure the others had their backs turned was even more of a challenge.

"You couldn't have put this in a corner?" he asked. "Maybe put a stall around it?"

"This cabin was made to accommodate but one inhabitant," said Captain Logan. "And I am not so bashful about the size of my member."

"My *member* is..." Chaz looked down at his member. "Adequate. But it's perfectly normal to want some privacy when I pee."

"They're going to see right through it," Tony the Elf continued whining. "And then they're going to come up here and murder us. I'm going to die in drag."

His business concluded, Chaz turned around and grabbed a cleanish-looking glass and a bottle of some dark brown liquid. He started to help himself to a few drops of their rapidly dwindling supply of booze, but he felt it might be good form to first consult the man they'd stolen it from. He turned to Captain Logan. "You mind?"

# Critical Failures VIII

Logan chuckled mirthlessly from a chair in the corner of the cramped room. "I am but a passenger aboard this vessel now. Drink as you see fit."

"Thanks," said Chaz. He poured himself a quarter glass of dark brown liquid and turned back to Tony the Elf. "You're not in drag."

"I'm dressed as a woman, aren't I?"

"You're wearing Captain Logan's hat and a Grim Reaper cloak. I guess the Grim Reaper probably doesn't have genitals." He gestured to Captain Logan. "But Logan's definitely a dude, so I'd say you're at least leaning male."

"I'm impersonating a woman."

"A woman going through PMS. And I've got to tell you, your attitude is really selling it." Chaz raised his hand for a high five. "Up top!"

Tony the Elf merely continued glaring at him. "This is the dumbest thing I've ever heard of."

Chaz took a sip of his dark brown beverage and winced at the bitterness. It tasted like it had been infused with the essence of scorched ass. No wonder it was one of the last to go. Still, it was potent. He took another sip.

"You're getting all worked up for nothing," he said. "This is the easiest role you'll ever have to play. Think about *Home Alone*."

Tony the Elf sighed. "Why do I think you're about to set a new record for the dumbest thing I've ever heard of?"

"Kevin put a cardboard cutout of Jordan in the window to fool the crooks. Why did that work?"

"Because it's a movie."

"Sure, that's part of it. But to be plausible to the audience, it needed to at least seem like it *could* work. And why is that?"

"I'm really not in the mood. Just speak whatever idiotic drivel is on your mind and be done with it."

"It was plausible because it filled in gaps in the crook's

minds. The mind interprets what it perceives in the way that makes the most sense to it. If something doesn't quite add up, the imagination fills in the gaps. It's this whole psychological thing. I saw this documentary once about babies who looked at a series of –"

"What the fuck are you talking about?" Tony the Elf turned to Captain Logan. "Does any of this make sense to you?"

Captain Logan scratched his chin. "You mentioned *Jordan*. Do you speak of Jordan Knight?"

Tony the Elf buried his face in his hands and started either laughing or crying. It was hard to tell.

Chaz nodded. "Okay. Back on track. Harry and Marv saw silhouettes in the window that looked enough like people moving around. If they had reason to suspect there was some little asshole in the house trying to trick them, they would have seen through the ruse right away. But they didn't know Kevin was left behind. It was a lot less of a stretch for their imaginations to think they'd made some sort of mistake about when the McCallisters were leaving for their trip, or to assume they'd changed their plans at the last minute, than to imagine that some ten-year-old sadist was pulling a fast one on them."

Tony the Elf looked back up at him with a sharp scowl. "Again, that's a *movie*. The idiot criminals will believe whatever the screenwriter needs them to believe. No real person would be fooled by a cardboard cutout drifting across the window in predictable cycles."

"Maybe they would, and maybe they wouldn't," said Chaz. "But you've got a much easier job than Kevin had."

"How's that?"

"For starters, you don't need to fake a whole party's worth of people. You just need to fake a single ship's captain."

"I don't look like Katherine!"

## Critical Failures VIII

"From down there, through these grimy-ass windows, all they'll be able to make out is a black cloak and a blur of blond hair. Honestly, we could pull this off with a mop if we had to."

"But what if you're wrong? Or what if the Hollinites decide they have business with the captain that's more pressing than her period? I mean, who knows how long they'll even be gone? The PMS story won't hold up for more than a day or two. We're going to get found out, and what happens then? You gave Katherine the only leverage we had. What's to stop them from commandeering the boat again, slitting our throats, and going after her and their master's precious die?"

"Would you just chill the fuck out, man? The Hollinites don't know Katherine's got the die. Even if they did, what are they going to do? They're unarmed and exhausted from all that bailing. They won't be any match for Logan's crew."

"That's taking for granted that Logan hasn't switched sides again." Tony the Elf turned to Captain Logan. "No offense."

Captain Logan shrugged.

"Have you?" Chaz asked Logan.

"No."

Chaz smiled at Tony the Elf. "See?"

Tony the Elf sighed. "Well, I guess that's that."

"Katherine knows what's up. She and that other guy are just going on a quick diplomatic mission. They'll be back before anyone knows they were –"

KNOCK KNOCK KNOCK

Chaz and Tony the Elf turned to Captain Logan. His face looked as alarmed as Chaz felt. He shook his head.

"Turn around," Chaz whispered to Tony the Elf. "Pretend you're sick."

When Tony the Elf was doubled over facing away from the door, Chaz opened it just wide enough to look outside.

"Permission to speak to the captain," said a large, bare-chested half-orc with a list of names tattooed down one of his muscular arms. One of Logan's men.

"Now's not a good time," said Chaz.

"Uuuunnnggghhh," Tony the Elf groaned as if he was trying to force out a difficult shit.

The sailor frowned as he tried to peer past Chaz. "Is Tony the Elf all right?"

"That's not... How did you... Shut up and come inside!" Chaz opened the door wider to allow him to enter the captain's quarters, then shut it quickly behind him.

"Uuuuuuuuunnnnnngggghhhhh!"

Chaz rolled his eyes. "Knock it off. He knows."

Tony the Elf sat up and glared at Chaz. "Of course he fucking knows. I told you this was a stupid idea." He waved to their visitor. "Hey, Lug."

Lug nodded. "Hey."

"What brings you to my former quarters, Lug?" asked Captain Logan.

"I kicked Sadler in the balls last night."

Logan laughed. "So you finally got Sadler, did you? Well done. He is a hard one to sneak up on."

Lug didn't look nearly as pleased with his accomplishment as Logan did. "So then I went to find Higgins so he could tattoo Sadler's name on my arm, but he was already asleep. When I woke up this morning, I couldn't find him anywhere."

"Did you ask around? Mayhap he is making use of the alcove."

"*I* was in the alcove," said Lug. "That's where I fell asleep." He frowned. "And Higgins isn't the only one missing."

Captain Logan sat up straight. "Who else?"

"As far as I can tell, everyone but me."

"What do you mean, everyone but you?" said Chaz. "Was there a fight? A plague? Did they fall off the side of the ship?"

Lug shrugged. "They just went missing during the night."

# Critical Failures VIII

"How thoroughly did you search the rest of the ship?" asked Captain Logan.

"Not very. I only checked the spot on the deck where Higgins went to sleep, then I thought it was suspicious that I didn't see anyone, so I came here to report."

Captain Logan nodded. "You were right to do so."

"Where are the Hollinites?" asked Tony the Elf. He turned to the window but dared not approach it and reveal his face.

Chaz went to the window instead. Two of the Hollinites were visible above deck, passing buckets from the cargo bay door to the side of the ship where they could be dumped over the side. They seemed to have quite a stride going, and nothing looked out of the ordinary.

"I'll go see what I can get out of them with Diplomacy."

"How many ranks do you have in Diplomacy?"

"A few." Chaz cocked an eyebrow. "But if that doesn't work, I'll whip out the ol' RazzmaChaz."

Tony the Elf grimaced. "Is that what you call your dick?"

"That's my stage name," said Chaz. He picked up his lute case and slung it over his back. "This is a music-loving crowd. If they got all shook up over *Hangin' Tough*, maybe they'll be receptive to some of the songs I've been working on."

Tony the Elf sighed. "Fantastic."

"Just stay here and don't go near the window." Chaz slipped through the door, then quickly closed it behind him.

The sky was transitioning from purple to blue. Chaz had to admit he was impressed with the Hollinites' work ethic, starting work so early in the morning. He supposed that was the power of cults, though. Anyone who said they wanted to sleep for another fifteen minutes was probably reprimanded by the others for not having enough faith or whatever.

"Good morning!" he said cheerily to the men above deck.

"And a good morning to you as well, sir," said the man receiving full buckets from below deck, just as cheerily and without missing a beat. He reeked of seawater and sweat. "I've not seen you down here in quite some time. To what do we owe the honor?"

Chaz shrugged, trying to come off as if the interrogation he was about to perform was just a natural flow of conversation. "Rumor has it that some of Logan's crewmen went missing during the night." That didn't come off nearly as naturally as he'd meant.

"Is that so?"

As long as he'd blown his Diplomacy roll, he might as well just be straight with them. "I wondered if you good people might have seen or heard anything amiss last night?"

The Hollinite shook his head as he accepted a bucket of water and passed it to the next man in line. "We know nothing of that. All night we have toiled to empty the ship's hold so that we may continue on our master's quest."

"Seriously?" said Chaz. "You've been at this all night?" He couldn't think of anything that could motivate him enough to work through an entire night. "You guys must be exhausted as fuck."

"Knowing that we are moving toward our master's goals gives us strength, as does his song in our hearts."

"You're going to wear yourselves out. Don't you think you should take a little break every once in a while?"

"Aye. A break sounds nice." He looked below deck and gave a shrill whistle. One of his fellow Hollinites hurried up the stairs to take his place.

"I was actually talking about all of you," said Chaz. "But that's cool. Whatever works for you."

"I would much like to speak with your captain. I wish to share news of our progress."

"She's not feeling too hot right now. Why don't you tell me the news, and I'll relay it to her. What's your name?"

"Jahmir," he said with a grin that made Chaz a little uncomfortable.

# Critical Failures VIII

"It's a pleasure to meet you. My name's Chaz. You might know me better by my stage name, RazzmaChaz?"

"I am afraid the name fails to ring a bell."

"Give it time. My career's just getting started. Just you wait and see."

Jahmir cleared his throat. "It would be better if the captain heard this news from me. Mayhap it will soothe whatever ails her."

Chaz laughed. "I don't think so. She's got PMS."

Jahmir's grin disappeared. "She does?"

"You bet your ass she does, and it's a big one. Trust me, you don't want to be anywhere near that right now."

"So she is..." Jahmir paused, as if he was considering his next words carefully, "*tending* to it?"

"Oh yeah," said Chaz. "Don't even worry about it. Captain Logan's up there helping her through it." He winked at Jahmir. "Better she's a pain in his ass than ours, am I right?"

"Jahmir," said one of the other Hollinites, stepping away from his bailing duties to join them. He was accompanied by three of his peers, and more were emerging from below deck. "What is the holdup?"

Jahmir tore his confused gaze away from Chaz to address his companion. "Oh, Fenwick."

"Is there a problem?"

"Not so much a *problem*, so to speak. But you know that lady captain who took over the ship?"

"I am aware of her, yes."

Jahmir pointed his thumb at Chaz. "This bloke says she has a cock."

"Excuse me?" said Chaz. "I don't believe I said anything of the –"

"He said that other captain, the one she deposed, is up there wanking her off."

While Chaz tried to think back on what Jahmir could have

possibly misinterpreted, the Hollinites exchanged uncomfortable glances.

Fenwick cleared his throat. "Other cultures assert dominance over their rivals in different ways. It is not our place to judge. All that matters is acquiring our master's die."

Finally, Chaz figured it out. His *Home Alone* theory had played out just as he'd predicted it would. The term "PMS" hadn't been coined yet in this world, so Jahmir's mind interpreted it as the closest phonetic match to a word he knew. *Penis.*

He laughed nervously. "I'm afraid there's been a big misunderstanding."

Jahmir grinned again, seemingly in response to Chaz's nervous laughter. "It is you who is misunderstanding if you think you're getting away without handing over that die."

*Shit.*

They thought he still had the die on him. He *should* still have the die on him. In his relief from not bearing the burden of their only leverage, it had completely escaped him that he could and should still be pretending to bear that burden. Maybe he could still fake it.

"Take it easy, fellas," he said, tucking his hand into his pocket and stepping back from Jahmir. "Let's not forget what happens if I toss this die over the –" Two things suddenly occurred to him at once. The first was that they had him surrounded, and the second... "Where did you guys get weapons?"

Chaz had spent long enough in this world that the sight of a dagger or sword on someone's belt didn't even register as unusual. It was only when they drew said weapons that he remembered the Hollinites were all supposed to be unarmed.

"Send our condolences to Captain Logan," said Fenwick, brandishing a mean-looking curved blade. "Last night, some of his men came down with a case of..." He paused to think of something to follow that with. "Death!"

Jahmir and a couple of the others grimaced, like they were a little embarrassed for him.

"Hollinitis," said Chaz.

Fenwick narrowed his eyes at him. "What did you say?"

"Hollinitis," Chaz repeated. "You could have said Hollinitis, as in 'Some of his men came down with a case of Hollinitis.'"

"What in the Seven Hells does that mean? Inflammation of the Hollin?"

"No, it's just a... You know, with the disease metaphor. You guys killed Logan's men. You're Hollinites. Hollinitis. I don't... Are none of you getting this?"

All of the Hollinites either shook their heads or stared blankly at him.

"Enough of your nonsense!" said Fenwick, brandishing his curved short sword. "Surrender the die, or I shall be handing our master your testicles instead."

"I can't imagine he'd accept that as a suitable replacement. You know what? It doesn't matter." He made a fist, then removed his hand from his pocket. "You think I can't throw this over the side of the ship from here? If you knew what was good for you, you'd take a step – DOOF!"

One of the Hollinites tackled him from behind, sending them both crashing onto the deck. The others immediately piled on top. Chaz got in a few initial kicks and elbows, but they paid him back tenfold. There were only so many punches he could take before he decided that his best chance of not getting beaten to death was to just go limp and hope they stopped.

They didn't. Instead, they continued pummeling the shit out of Chaz until he regretted not trying harder to fight back. If he was going to die, he could have at least taken one of them down with him. But now, a few punches away from death, he kind of wished someone would just stab him and get it over with.

"Enough!" said Jahmir. "Do not kill him until we have the die."

"What shall we do with him, then?" asked Fenwick.

"Get the die! Cut off his hand if you have to!"

Having no reason to believe they wouldn't do just that, even if they didn't have to, Chaz quickly opened his hand. "I don't have the die!" He spat out a large gob of blood. "I was bluffing!"

"Do you take us, the devoted followers of Jordan Knight, for fools?"

Chaz would have laughed if he didn't feel like he'd just been run over by a fleet of trucks. "No, of course not."

"Search him! Leave no cavity unprobed."

When it was done, Chaz wanted a shower and a cigarette more than he had ever wanted either before. To their credit, his friskers and probers didn't appear to enjoy the experience anymore than he did, but he really hoped that Tony the Elf didn't chance a peek out the window while it was happening.

They were also gentle with Chaz's lute when they removed it from its case to inspect it, which Chaz was grateful for.

"He's clean," said Fenwick, who had thoroughly searched Chaz's groin and ass area with a clinical disinterest that Chaz appreciated. It was more than Chaz could say for Fenwick's fingers.

Jahmir glared intensely at Chaz, pressing the point of his sword against his throat while the others held him down. "Where is it?"

Chaz's loyalty to his friends had a limit, and the very believable threat of death was well beyond it.

"I gave it to Katherine, our captain."

"The lady with a penis?"

"She doesn't have –"

# Critical Failures VIII

"Morris, Dolan, Hograth, and the Weston brothers. Go retrieve our master's prize. Gibbon, Sabor, Flint, and... you three. Stand by with me in case the first group meets unexpected resistance. The rest of you stay with him and make sure he doesn't go anywhere."

Chaz let out a shallow laugh and spat out more blood. Where the hell would he go?

The first and second groups took their position at the bottom of the stairs leading up to the captain's quarters, while the remaining four Hollinites stayed with Chaz. Fortunately, they got off of him first.

Jahmir raised his left hand, prompting the first group to ascend the stairs quickly, but relatively quietly.

Morris, the leader of the first group, nodded to his team, then kicked the door open. Chaz had apparently not shut it all the way, as it gave no resistance whatsoever.

There were a few shrieks from inside, but none of them sounded half as horrified as Morris's face looked.

"Mercy of the gods!" he cried, then turned back to Jahmir. "She really does have a penis!" Evidently, he caught Tony the Elf taking his morning whiz.

Reactions from his fellow Hollinites were varied.

"Impossible!"

"I never would have guessed!"

"I suspected it all along."

"You did not!"

"What does it look like? How big is it?"

Morris looked back inside the cabin. "It's like an albino garden snake."

"Get the fuck out of here!" shouted Tony the Elf, not even attempting to alter his voice.

"Come to think of it," said one of the men who'd stayed back with Chaz. "You can kind of hear it in her voice if you listen carefully."

Chaz noticed that the four of them had all stepped forward to try to get a peek. They all had their backs turned to him. If he had any strength left in him, and if there was anywhere to escape to, he could totally bail right now.

"Stop gawking at her cock!" shouted Jahmir. "Get her!"

Morris and his group jammed into the captain's quarters. Chaz was a little disappointed to not hear any fighting, but relieved that he also didn't hear any telltale sounds of people being stabbed. They must have known they were outmatched and surrendered peacefully. But how long was that peace going to last once they discovered that neither Tony the Elf nor Captain Logan had the die on them?

Armed only with his lute, Chaz crawled back away from his captors, hoping that he might spot a place to hide that would be difficult to find despite the trail of smeared blood he was leaving in his wake.

No such luck. He'd barely made it five feet when Fenwick, who'd been sniffing his fingers, turned around.

"Where do you think you're going?"

It was a question Chaz honestly couldn't answer.

"Nowhere," he said. "I was just… um… getting out of the sun. I burn easily." He changed course, crawling into the shadow of the bulwark, and leaned against it.

Fenwick glanced past him and seemed satisfied that there wasn't anywhere to escape to, then turned his attention back to the goings on in the captain's quarters.

Resigned to his fate, but not wishing to hear any sounds that Tony the Elf, Captain Logan, or Lug might make while being searched, Chaz sought solace in his music.

Lodor, the owner of the venue where Chaz had played his first gig, had given him some advice, suggesting that he alter his songs to appeal to the local audience. He may have been batshit crazy when it came to forcing bugbears to lick his testicles while their families watched, but Chaz took his

# Critical Failures VIII

entertainment advice to heart. He strummed his lute and started singing a reworked version of John Mellencamp's *Pink Houses* he'd been working on.

*There's a black man with a black axe*
*Choppin' up some firewood.*
*I said some rude things to his old lady.*
*You know, he didn't take it so good.*

"Quiet, you!" snapped Fenwick, stepping toward Chaz.

Chaz hoped that he only intended to beat the shit out of him some more, but one of his companions stopped Fenwick with a hand on the shoulder.

"Wait," he said. "Let him keep playing."

Chaz was happy to oblige.

*'Cause she's a wizard with a cauldron summoning a dragon flock.*
*And I look at her and say, 'Hey darling, come on over here and suck my cock.'*

The four men assigned to watch over him shot each other uncomfortable glances.

It was a work in progress. Chaz kept singing, hoping the chorus would bring them back around.

*Oh but ain't there a cleric to come heal me?*
*Ain't there a cleric for my HP, baby?*
*Ain't there a cleric? I'm at negative three, yeah.*
*A little divine magic from you to me, oh from you to me.*

"I am a cleric," said the man who had stopped Fenwick from approaching. A look of horror came over his face. "Dear gods! What have I done?"

"What are we doing here?" asked another, looking equally horrified.

Chaz wasn't sure what was happening, but he strummed his lute more fervently and sang even louder.

*Well there's a fighter in a chain shirt*
*Workin' out his frustration*
*On a grizzly bear, with a grisly smile.*
*I say, "Hey! You ever try masturbation?"*

"I have tried masturbation," said Fenwick. "Indeed, I found it to be very therapeutic."

*'Cause I found out, when I was younger*
*I was more chill when I was spent.*
*But just like everyone else, that crazy old fuck*
*Misunderstood my intent.*

One of his captors grabbed the self-proclaimed cleric by the front of his shirt. "Do you not see? We are the crazy fucks he sings of! Jordan Knight seduced us with his song and caused us to do unspeakable things!"

*So ain't there a cleric to come heal me?*
*Ain't there a cleric for my HP, baby?*
*Ain't there a cleric? He fucked up my knees.*
*A little divine magic from you to me, oh baby from you to me.*

"For the love of the gods!" cried the man who was assaulting the cleric. He shoved him toward Chaz. "Heal his wounds! Undo this small part of the damage we have caused and pray the gods forgive us."

# Critical Failures VIII

The cleric proved himself to be the genuine article when he placed a hand on Chaz's head and mumbled some words that made his pain instantly subside.

Chaz didn't miss a strum as he got to his feet and smiled at the cleric, then at Fenwick. They parted, allowing him to walk toward the front of the ship. He sang louder.

*Well there's monks in their temples.*
*What do they know, know, know?*
*Made one joke about their lifestyle,*
*And they hit me with a Flurry of Blows. Oh yeah!*

"What is this?" demanded Jahmir. "I told you to..." He dropped his sword as his face turned a shade paler. "Why are we..." He turned back toward the captain's quarters. "Morris! Stop!"

Chaz walked freely on the deck now as he sang, the Hollinites all staring at him in awe.

*And there's hookers, and loose women.*
*I love how they feel.*
*'Till the next morning, baby, when I wake up*
*With something that doctors can't heal.*

Morris peeked out from the cabin doorway. "What was that? We can't find the..." His eyes widened. "Oh, dear." He went back inside. "Stop! Remove your fingers! Let them go!"

*So ain't there a cleric to come heal me?*
*Ain't there a cleric for my HP, baby?*
*Ain't there a cleric? It hurts when I pee, yeah.*
*A little divine magic from you to me, ooo ooo yeah.*

A few of the men on deck joined in as Chaz sang the chorus one last time.

*Ain't there a cleric to come heal me?*
*Ain't there a cleric for my HP, baby?*
*Ain't there a cleric? How much is your fee, yeah.*
*Yeah yeah yeah yeah yeah yeah yeah!*
*A little divine magic from you to me, ooo yeah ooo yeah.*

# CHAPTER 28

While Julian lay on the sand trying to ignore the pain in his bleeding arm, Rhonda picked up the hatchet and surveyed the edge of the dark forest. It loomed over the beach like an impenetrable wall of shadow.

"As long as we're stuck here, we might as well make good use of the time."

Julian suspected she just wanted something to keep her mind off the cold. The day had been pretty warm, but the temperature dropped severely after the sun went down. It didn't help that they were both soaking wet.

There was plenty of dead wood around, much of it dry, and Rhonda had suggested they build a fire. But Julian thought that might call attention to them. With the damage he'd already taken from the black cock eel, and without a spell to get them out of harm's way, it was better to suffer through the night than to alert any nearby undead to their –

*THWACK! THWACK! THWACK!*

Julian sat up and turned to where the noise was coming from. He saw Rhonda chopping at the base of a tree on the edge of the forest.

He wanted to shout at her to stop, but that wouldn't be any better than all the noise she was making. Wincing at the pain in his arm, he struggled to his feet, then jogged over to her.

*THWACK! THWACK! THWACK!*

"Rhonda!" he said when he was close enough to be heard.

Rhonda stopped chopping and turned to him. "What's wrong?" She eyed the tree she was chopping. "You think this one's too thin?"

"Keep your voice down," Julian whispered. "The tree's fine. But what happened to not drawing attention to ourselves?"

"Do you know of a quieter way to chop down a tree? I mean, isn't that the whole reason we came here?"

"Sure, but have you forgotten that this stretch of peninsula is reportedly crawling with undead?"

"That's not likely to change anytime soon, but the ship still needs a new mast."

"I'm just saying that I'd prefer to have an exit strategy ready and more skin on my arm before we start chopping. If we get attacked right now, we're in no shape to defend ourselves."

"I'm freezing, Julian," said Rhonda. Her skin was pale, and her lips were purple.

"Why don't you try doing some jumping jacks?" Julian immediately regretted the suggestion when Rhonda glared at him. She must have taken it as a criticism of her weight. "I meant, as a way to keep warm."

"We can light a fire, or I'm chopping down this tree. The choice is yours."

Julian thought about it for a moment. "Maybe if we dig a hole in the sand, the fire won't be too visible." There was still the smoke to consider, but Rhonda looked like she wanted to swing that hatchet at him.

"Fine, we'll dig a hole."

Because of Julian's arm wounds, Rhonda ended up doing most of the digging. But she was motivated, and had a decent hole dug in about half an hour. Julian hoped that the exertion might have warmed her up to the point where she would be more reasonable and see that a fire wasn't necessary to their survival.

She stood up in her hole and shot Julian an annoyed look. "You could at least gather some sticks or something."

"I was thinking maybe you might..." Julian could see in her face that she wasn't going to back down. "Okay. I'll do that."

While they gathered wood, Julian held out a final hope that Rhonda was depending on him to have the means necessary to start a fire, which he didn't. He'd considered mentioning it before now, but thought it was better to let Rhonda use up as much time and energy as possible so that she might be too exhausted to go back to chopping when she realized the fire wasn't happening.

She dumped some larger chunks of wood on top of the pile of sticks that Julian had tossed in the hole, then pointed both hands down at them. "Scorching Ray!"

Jets of flame shot out of her hands and ignited the wood almost instantly.

"That's a second level spell!" said Julian. "Don't you think it would have been wiser to save that in case we get attacked?"

"It's a new spell. I wanted to try it out."

"Why didn't you try it out on the eel?"

Rhonda shrugged. "I didn't know if it would work in the water." She sat down next to the hole and rubbed her hands over the fire. "Stop pouting and warm yourself up. You'll feel a lot better."

Julian sat down but continued pouting. His mood lightened, however, when he warmed his hands over the fire. He hadn't realized just how cold he was until he felt warmth returning to his numb fingers.

They both jumped slightly at a sudden flapping sound that seemed to come out of nowhere, then Julian realized it was Ravenus.

"You started a fire, I see," said Ravenus.

Julian sighed. "Yeah, we did."

"I thought we agreed not to do that."

"We had a change of heart. Get closer to the edge. It feels good."

Ravenus stepped closer to the edge of the hole. "I'm actually not terribly cold, sir."

"Did you get bored up in the tree?" asked Julian. He smiled at Ravenus. "No lady birds to bump cloacas with?"

"Ew," said Rhonda.

"Sorry. Guy talk."

"You asked me to keep an eye out for anything suspicious approaching," said Ravenus.

*Shit.*

"Did you see something?"

"Several somethings, sir. Humanoid figures coming this way."

Julian glanced at Rhonda, but did his best not to look too judgmental. "This is what I was afraid of."

"We don't know they're hostile," said Rhonda. She looked down at Ravenus. "Did they look hostile?"

Ravenus stared dumbly back at her.

"Did they look hostile," Julian repeated once he realized that Ravenus couldn't understand her.

"It is difficult to say. If I had to guess, I would say they looked injured."

Julian sighed in relief. Injured was good. Obviously not for the injured people, but it meant they wouldn't be as much of a threat if they were hostile. And if they were stranded on the beach like Julian and Rhonda, they might appreciate a warm fire to sit next to. Strength in numbers and all that.

"I'm out of spells," said Rhonda. She didn't look as relieved as Julian felt. "Maybe we should throw some more wood on this fire."

# Critical Failures VIII

"That's a thoughtful idea, but I'm still concerned about drawing unwanted attention. If there are too many to sit around the fire, I'll step away for a while."

Rhonda stared at him in confusion for a moment before something clicked. "I think we've already drawn the unwanted attention. I'm suggesting we beef up the fire in case we need to throw someone in it."

"Jesus, Rhonda!" said Julian. "We don't even know who these people are. But whatever their intentions, they're hurt. I think a nice warm fire and a half-decent Diplomacy roll will go a long way toward turning them into friends. And when you're stuck next to a forest full of undead, who couldn't use more friends?"

Rhonda dropped a large chunk of wood on the fire. "What if they *are* the undead?"

"And they're still injured? Then the afterlife sucks."

"I'm talking about zombies, Julian. You've seen a movie before, right? Think about what zombies look like when they walk. Isn't it possible that what Ravenus thought looked like a group of injured people might actually be a group of animated corpses?"

Julian chucked a couple more sticks onto the fire. "Now that you mention it, that actually sounds a lot more likely." He looked down at his quarterstaff and decided that he should really invest in a better weapon.

Rhonda picked up the hatchet. "Let's go see exactly what we're dealing with."

"Which way are they coming from?" Julian asked Ravenus.

Ravenus lifted his left wing.

"Okay. You go wait up in a tree where it's safe. We're going to do a little recon."

Julian and Rhonda jogged as quietly as they could along the beach. Traveling too close to the forest would provide them cover, but make them vulnerable to any creatures that might be waiting to ambush them. Going along the water would give them ample time to avoid being surprised by anything that leaped out of the forest, but would make them much easier to spot. Instead, they opted to traverse the beach halfway between the forest and the water, which offered them neither of their advantages and both of their disadvantages.

"Stop!" Julian whispered when he heard the first groan. He pointed ahead of them. "They're right around that next bend."

Creeping forward, Julian heard more groans. There must have been at least three of them. He spotted the first one shambling out from around the bend. It looked like it might have been a formidable warrior in life, but the heavy pieces of metal armor that hadn't yet fallen off were only serving to weigh it down now. Another one staggered into view right behind the first.

"Get down!"

Julian and Rhonda dropped and flattened themselves against the sand as best they could.

"How many are there?" whispered Rhonda.

What kind of question was that? Could she not count? Then Julian remembered his elven Low-Light Vision. As a human, Rhonda probably couldn't see more than ten feet in front of her. But Julian could make them out just fine in the dim light of the waxing moon.

He waited until new ones stopped appearing. "Unless there are some stragglers falling behind, I count six."

"Can we take six zombies?"

"I don't know. I guess we're about to find out."

"Is there any way to separate them?" asked Rhonda. "I'd feel better about our chances if we could fight them one at a time."

# Critical Failures VIII

Julian noted how they were moving. They looked like a group of drunks stumbling home from the bar at four in the morning.

"They shouldn't be too hard to outrun," he said. "I'll see if I can distract one of them and draw it away from the group."

He crawled to the water's edge, then crept forward to sneak past them. They didn't even glance in his direction.

Once he was behind them, he let out a small whistle, trying to get the nearest one's attention without the rest of them hearing. It didn't work.

He cleared his throat, which also turned no heads.

They were getting a little too close to where Julian had left Rhonda, so he ramped up the decibels a couple of notches.

"Hey!"

All six zombies turned toward him. They groaned louder as they shuffled on the sand toward him.

*Shit.*

It only now occurred to Julian that he'd just done exactly the opposite of what he'd set out to do. He was on a thin stretch of beach with a group of zombies separating him from his only ally.

All of his instincts told him to gun it back toward Rhonda, but that would mean he'd have to beat every single zombie either to the edge of the water or the edge of the forest, neither of which he was confident he could do. They were slow, but they weren't *that* slow. He could go wider around them if he were to enter the water or the forest, but neither of those options appealed to him either.

Instead, he ignored his instincts altogether and backed away from the approaching zombies.

"Come and get me," he said, feigning confidence more for himself than for the zombies, who he suspected wouldn't be at all swayed by it. "Warm juicy elf, ripe for the nibblin'."

*Ripe for the nibblin'? Where did that even come from?*

He was just saying words to distract himself from pissing his serape.

His hastily thought up plan was working, though. All six zombies were moving toward him, congregating closer and closer to the water. When he decided it was safe to make his move, he bolted for the trees, then veered left to run back to Rhonda.

In retrospect, he would have been wiser to hold out a little longer. One of the smaller zombies, unburdened by armor, nearly caught up to him. He could barely keep it at bay while he ran past frantically batting at it with his quarterstaff.

"Rhonda!" he called out. There was no point in trying to be stealthy with six corpses already on his tail.

"Julian?" Rhonda cautiously got to her feet, squinting to try to make him out in the darkness.

"It didn't work. They're right on my tail."

Rhonda turned and started running. "I've got a better idea, anyway. We can divide them around the fire hole."

Julian thought about it as they ran. It would work better if they had planned on it while digging the hole. They could have dug it longer, like a trench. Then, when the zombies were chasing them, they could each run along either side of the trench, splitting up the zombies.

Unfortunately, there wasn't time for that now. They'd just have to hope that their fire hole was big enough to divide the zombies enough to give them at least a little bit of an edge.

"Master Julian!" said Ravenus, flapping down to intercept him.

Julian and Rhonda stopped, then looked back to check on their pursuers. The zombies were a good fifty yards behind them.

"Yes, Ravenus? We're kind of in a hurry."

"I have excellent news to report, sir."

"What is it?"

## Critical Failures VIII

"I spotted another group of injured people coming from the other direction."

"That news sucks, Ravenus."

"Oh, dear. I'm terribly sorry."

"It's not your fault. Those aren't injured people. They're zombies, and we're in no shape to fight so many."

"I shall assist you with talon and beak down to my very last breath, sir!"

"No," said Julian. "You stay up in a tree where it's safe. Rhonda and I will think of something."

"But sir, I –"

"That's a direct order, Ravenus! I don't want to hear another word about it. Whatever happens to us, you stay up in a tree until it's safe to come down."

"Very well, sir."

Julian didn't need an Empathic Link to tell him Ravenus's feelings were hurt as he flew out of harm's way. He felt pretty shitty for snapping at him, but it had to be done. Brave as he was, he was still a bird. One bite from a zombie might very well do him in.

"Julian?" said Rhonda. "If we're going to think of something, we'd better do it quick."

Looking back, Julian saw that the zombies had closed in to within twenty yards of them.

"Come on," he said as he started running again.

"What are we going to do?"

"Same plan as before. We'll just have to do it twice. The key will be getting there in time to take out one group before the other group gets too – Shit."

Just beyond the fire, Julian saw the second zombie group approaching. They weren't as densely herded together like the first group, but there were at least a dozen of them. And the last ones he could see were on the far end of his Low Light Vision range. Who knew how many more were coming?

"What's wrong?" asked Rhonda.

Julian didn't have time to answer. They needed to take down as many zombies as possible before they all crowded in on them, and he spotted a perfect target approaching near the fire hole.

He sprinted toward it, holding his quarterstaff in front of him like a lance. This was another zombie weighed down by a heavy steel breastplate, and Julian aimed for the center of it.

His timing was perfect. Julian knocked the zombie off its feet and straight into the fire hole. It briefly tried to get back up, but the flames consumed its decaying flesh almost instantly. Somehow, that managed to smell even worse. The sudden surge of illumination revealed another half dozen zombies approaching from behind the ones Julian had already counted.

"There's too many," he said as Rhonda caught up to him. "And they'll all be converging right here from both sides." A zombie moved in on him, and he could barely keep it at bay by jabbing at it. He had neither the right angle to push it into the fire, nor the force of momentum that he'd taken advantage of with his charge, and his injured arm was screaming with pain from all the exertion he'd just put it through. "We can't handle this many."

Rhonda buried her hatchet in the back of its head. "We have to try!"

The hatchet attack wasn't enough to kill it, but it did draw its attention from Julian to Rhonda, giving Julian a clean shot at it.

He swung his staff like a baseball bat, whacking the zombie in the side of the knee. It fell to the sand, and Rhonda stomped its face, forcing the hatchet deeper into its head. Two more stomps later, it stopped trying to get up, but the others were closing in.

## Critical Failures VIII

Julian dug his feet into the sand as he tried to shove another zombie into the fire, but he was barely keeping it at bay. Rotted strips of flesh and sleeves flailed wildly as it reached out to grab him. The vacant sockets where its eyes used to be seemed to gaze longingly at him as it snapped its black-toothed jaws.

"Help me!" he shouted to Rhonda, who was still trying to dislodge her hatchet from the last zombie's head. He realized, of course, that she was trying to help him, and didn't know what he expected her to do without a weapon, but horrible gross death was staring him in the face.

Rhonda let go of the hatchet and grabbed Julian's quarterstaff with both hands. For a second, he feared that she was trying to disarm him, and he resisted when she started moving it.

"Push!" she cried, and it finally occurred to Julian what she was trying to accomplish.

With their combined Strength, they were able to push the zombie backward until it fell into the fire hole.

Julian took a couple of deep breaths. "Nice work. Way to think on your – Behind you!"

Rhonda dropped like a sack of rocks just as another zombie lurched forward to bite the back of her head. Julian knocked it back a step with a jab to the face, then batted its head sideways. Unfortunately, that barely seemed to faze it, and it turned its attention from Rhonda to Julian.

She used the distraction he'd provided to pull a leg out from under it, and Julian drove his quarterstaff down into its open mouth, relishing the crunch as it broke through the back of its neck. Once again, Rhonda helped secure the staff while they both stomped the zombie until it stopped moving.

It might have been an effective strategy if the rest of the zombies were thoughtful enough to continue coming at them one at a time, but Julian wasn't holding out much hope for that.

"I've got an idea," said Rhonda, pulling Julian's quarterstaff out of the zombie's mouth.

Julian was glad to hear that. "What is it?"

"We need to push one back into the fire."

As zombies closed in on all sides, Julian's brief flicker of hope was extinguished like a birthday candle in a hurricane.

"I don't know if you've been paying attention, but we've already done that. We can't do it fast enough to get them all. Besides, the fire hole is filling up." The fire was consuming the rotted flesh quickly enough, but the bones were piling up too high to effectively keep the zombies from climbing out.

"I'm not talking about shoving them all the way into the hole. If we push one just close enough to catch fire, maybe we can corral it close enough to the others to catch them all ablaze."

It wasn't a bad idea, and it was far better than any idea Julian could come up with.

He nodded. "Sounds good. Let's do it."

With one last zombie far enough away from either of the approaching packs, they only had one chance to get it right. It was a larger one, a little over six feet tall. A half-orc, judging by the lower tusks fully exposed from the rotted tendrils of lip hanging down from its mouth. It would be a little harder to push, but Julian felt that, with their combined effort and the adrenaline rush from not wanting to be eaten alive, he and Rhonda were up to the task. Hopefully, a bigger corpse would burn longer and hotter, increasing the odds of it igniting its fellow zombies.

"Ready?" said Rhonda as they both held Julian's quarterstaff out in front of them.

Julian's palms were sweating, so he gripped the staff as tightly as he could. "GO!"

## Critical Failures VIII

They ran at the half-orc zombie and drove the staff as hard as they could into its chest. Unfortunately, it pierced straight through its sternum and out of its back.

The zombie didn't even seem to notice it had been skewered. And now, instead of setting it on fire, they had tethered themselves to it if they didn't want to let go of their one remaining weapon.

"NGUUUUHH!" shouted the zombie as it swiped a large rotted hand, catching Rhonda on the forearm she'd raised to defend herself and knocking her into Julian. They both fell over and lost their grips on the staff.

Even if they could pull off some miracle, the others were too close. This was it. They were done for. As the hulking corpse lurched over to grab him, Julian curled into a ball and prepared to deliver a futile kick or two before he was torn apart and devoured.

"FUCK YOU!" cried a shrill avian voice from above.

Julian uncovered his face and looked up to find Ravenus clawing at the top of the zombie's head, removing sizable chunks of flesh with each swipe of his talons.

"Ravenus!" said Julian. "I told you to stay in the –"

"NNNGGGGUUUUUUHHHH!" shouted the zombie, slamming its hand down on its head and grabbing Ravenus.

It tore him away from its head, but Ravenus held on, peeling away most of the zombie's scalp, leaving two thirds of its massive skull exposed.

"RAVENUS!" cried Julian. He scrambled to get to his feet, but the zombie would easily shove Ravenus into its mouth before Julian could do anything to stop it.

Then, strangely, Julian's quarterstaff plunged into the zombie's chest. It was like the opposite of toast popping out of a toaster. Julian barely had time to register what had just happened when his staff reappeared again. Only this time it was poking up through the zombie's forehead like the world's grossest unicorn.

When the staff retracted again, the zombie fell over, revealing a woman who was standing behind it, Julian's quarterstaff in her hands. She was as incomprehensibly beautiful as she was incomprehensibly naked.

After giving Julian and Rhonda the slightest of glances, the mysterious woman smashed another zombie's face in with the staff, then planted it in the sand to support her as she jumped up and side-kicked the head clean off of another.

"Did I kill it?" asked Ravenus, squirming his way out of the dead half-orc hand.

Neither Julian nor Rhonda answered as they watched the naked woman kick the unliving shit out of every zombie on the beach. She didn't have the build of an Olympic weightlifter, but her Strength score must have been off the charts. Grabbing one zombie by the foot, she used it like a club to beat other zombies to permanent death until the leg she was holding separated from the rest of the body.

She kicked and punched wildly, but not with the desperation of a person who's getting attacked by dangerous monsters. It was more like a kid wailing on Styrofoam targets he'd set up in the garage to practice the sweet kung fu moves he'd seen on TV.

When the massacre was done, and the dead were resting in pieces, she turned to Julian and Rhonda.

"This place is not safe for you."

"I..." Julian was at a loss for words. The nearby sound of scratching and slurping turned his attention to Ravenus, who was greedily trying to put down a large strip of rotting half-orc scalp. "Ravenus! Don't eat that!"

Ravenus coughed up the flesh he'd half swallowed. "I apologize, sir. But I'm hungry."

# Critical Failures VIII

"Is it not common for ravens to feast upon carrion?" asked the stranger. "Why do you deny your friend this food?"

That was really none of her business, as far as Julian was concerned. But she had just saved their lives, so he supposed he could cut her some slack. "I don't want him to get infected or whatever and turn into a zombie."

The woman laughed giddily. "Silly elf. Zombies are created through magic, not contagion. These bodies are no different than a festering rat corpse on the forest floor."

Julian looked down at Ravenus. "Go ahead. But don't eat too much. You're putting on weight."

"Thank you, sir!"

"And cut your food into smaller pieces. I don't want you choking."

"Very good, sir," said Ravenus, then started clawing at the flesh he'd been trying to swallow.

Rhonda cleared her throat. "Excuse me, Miss..." She paused to give the woman a chance to fill in the blank, but all she got was a blank stare.

"Yes?" responded the woman as she walked toward the fire hole. Being naked, it was understandable that she might be feeling a bit of a chill.

"My name's Rhonda, and this is my friend Julian."

The woman gave them both a smile like an awkward kid getting his class picture taken. "It is a pleasure to meet you both." She hopped down into the hole.

"JESUS!" said Julian. He and Rhonda ran over to help her out of the hole. When they got there, they found her squatting, completely undisturbed by the fire she was peeing on.

She looked up at them. "Keep your voices down. There are more dangerous things than zombies lurking in these woods."

Julian averted his eyes. "Do you, um... need some help?"

"Thank you, but I believe I have it under control. It was unwise of you to build a fire. It attracts attention." Her pee sizzled on the burning logs as the firelight slowly dimmed.

Julian and Rhonda stood there for about a minute, neither of them knowing the proper etiquette for such a situation. It felt wrong to walk away from someone who was squatting in a fire, but it felt a different kind of wrong to hang out and listen. Julian hoped that in the time it took to ponder the dilemma, she would have stopped peeing, thus resolving the situation. But no such luck. It was still flowing out of her with no sign of slowing down.

"What's your name?" he asked, mostly so that he could hear something besides the hiss of her pee on flames.

"Akane."

"That's, um... pretty."

"Thank you."

Julian didn't have anything to follow up with, so they stood there awkwardly for about another thirty seconds before Rhonda spoke up.

"Would you excuse us, Akane?" Without waiting for a response, she grabbed Julian by his good arm and led him away from the fire hole. She didn't stop until they were at the water's edge.

"What's wrong?" whispered Julian. He guessed that if Rhonda had dragged him this far away from Akane, she probably didn't want them to be overheard.

"Do you think that could be one of Mordred's avatars?"

Julian shrugged. "The thought had crossed my mind," he lied. Nothing remotely close to that thought had even begun to occur to him.

"It just seems like a hell of a coincidence that this woman showed up just in the nick of time to rescue us."

# Critical Failures VIII

"Wouldn't it also be kind of coincidental for Mordred to be hanging out in a zombie infested forest so close to where we got stranded on the beach?"

"He could have been tracking us with magic or something, waiting for the perfect opportunity to strike."

"But she didn't strike," said Julian. "At least not us. Did you see how she took out those zombies? If that's Mordred, he could have taken us down easily."

"What's the point of taking us down? We don't have what he's after. Wouldn't it be more beneficial for him to take the form of an attractive naked woman to make you let your guard down, then have you lead him to our friends who might have acquired one of his dice?"

"I don't know. That sounds kind of far-fetched. If she was trying to seduce me, would her first move really be squatting down to take a piss in front of me?"

Rhonda shrugged. "Some guys are into that, right?"

"Mordred doesn't know me that well. It's a pretty big gamble to assume that I get turned on by watching some woman piss like a trucker after forty-seven cans of Red Bull."

The light from the fire was completely extinguished, but Julian could still hear the strong and steady cascade of Akane's urine against scorched wood and bone.

"Maybe I'm just being paranoid," said Rhonda. "But I think the circumstances warrant a bit of paranoia. Just mind what you say to her until we're both in agreement that she isn't Mordred, okay?"

That sounded reasonable. Julian nodded.

"What should we do now?" he asked. "Should we go back and wait for her to finish? Or does it look suspicious if we're hanging out way over here?"

"Not if we're busying ourselves with something useful. We could be digging holes to bury the bodies in."

Julian sighed. "That sounds like a lot of work just to keep her from being suspicious. I mean, once we start, we can't very well stop until all the bodies are actually buried." As soon as he finished talking, he noticed that Akane's stream had slowed to a faint trickle. "Shit! She's almost done. Start digging!"

He and Rhonda dropped to their hands and knees and started raking their fingers through the damp sand.

"What are you doing?" asked Akane, plodding toward them, still dripping pee from between her legs. If this was Mordred trying to seduce him, he didn't seem all that committed to the idea.

Julian focused slightly to her left, trying not to be rude by looking away, but also trying not to gawk. "We're digging graves for the bodies."

Akane laughed. "Don't even bother. I have not had a workout like that in quite some time. I am famished." She picked up a zombie leg that had been separated from the rest of its body and bit into the thigh, pulling away an impressive chunk of decaying flesh.

Rhonda doubled over and threw up into the hole they'd been digging.

"You still think that's Mordred?" Julian muttered out the side of his mouth.

Rhonda heaved a couple more times, but she had nothing left to give. "I'm beginning to have my doubts."

"Oh, no!" said Akane after swallowing the meat she'd bitten off. "I can see now how you might find this disturbing." She dropped the zombie leg. "And to think, I took this human form specifically so you would not be alarmed when you saw me."

Ironically, Julian found what she'd just said far more alarming than the zombie leg thing.

## Critical Failures VIII

"I'm sorry," he said. "But what do you mean by *human form*?" The cards were all out on the table. There was no point in acting coy.

"I am a dragon. I have found that frightens some people. Are you afraid of dragons?"

"I have a healthy respect for anything that can kill me. You've demonstrated that you could easily do that in human form, so I don't see why I'd be more afraid of you as a dragon."

"It pleases me to hear that. Would you mind, then, if I change into my true form? These mammalian nipples are quite sensitive to the cold."

Julian couldn't help but stare directly at her nipples. She wasn't wrong. They looked hard enough to cut diamonds with.

"Please do," said Rhonda. "I think we'd all feel more comfortable."

"Thank you," said Akane. She dropped to her hands and knees, and her skin began to turn green. Her whole body grew as her hands turned into clawed talons and her face grew more elongated and reptilian. Batlike wings sprouted out of her back, unfolding to show off their orange-green membranes.

"I submit," Rhonda whispered. "I don't think this is Mordred."

When Akane was finished, she was about the size of two horses. Her green metallic scales shimmered in the faint moonlight. From the front of her snout to the tip of her tail, Julian estimated her to be about thirty feet long. He'd been premature to say that he wouldn't be more frightened of her in her true form. He was absolutely terrified.

"Can you speak?" asked Rhonda, more fascinated than scared.

"Of course I can speak." Aside from being a little louder, Akane's voice was no different in her dragon form. "That is, if one can count this as speaking. Your Common Tongue is so basic and barbaric. It lacks the rhythm and subtle nuances of our ancient Draconic language. Do you mind if I eat while we talk?"

Julian willed himself to speak calmly, hoping that she was still satisfied with feasting on the undead. "Not at all."

Akane picked up the zombie leg she'd bitten, shoved it into her mouth thigh first, and closed her mouth just above the knee. When she pulled it out, there was nothing left but femur. "Fresh meat tastes a lot better, but I like the way that long dead meat falls right off the bone."

Julian had learned long ago that the secret to making tender ribs was low heat over a long period of time, but he didn't think it was in his and Rhonda's best interest to share this knowledge. Perhaps a change of subject was in order.

"So... Do you live here?"

"Yes. I moved out this way about thirty years ago when I left my mother's lair. It has everything a young dragon could hope for. The forest looks gloomy now, but it is very pretty during the day. There's always an ample supply of food. And most importantly," she swung her head toward Julian and Rhonda and narrowed her greenish-gold eyes at them. "I don't often meet a lot of living intruders."

"We didn't mean to intrude," said Rhonda. "We didn't think anyone lived here."

"Those poor souls who are forced to do not tend to live very long. Most of them are poorly trained criminals ostensibly sent to clear the wood of zombies. But they inevitably create more zombies than they destroy. I try to only eat the surplus to keep my primary source of food sustainable." She stared at Julian as if expecting a response.

"That's very sensible of you."

Akane's scaly lips stretched back in what Julian hoped was an appreciative smile. "Thank you." She turned back to her meal, trying to claw the calf meat out from between the bones of the zombie leg. "But you two do not appear to have even the poorest of training, which begs the question... How did you come to arrive here?" Having scraped most of the meat from the leg, she tossed it aside and picked up a headless torso.

"We came by ship," said Rhonda.

"For what purpose?" Akane tried to bite the torso in half but found the rib cage too difficult to break through. "I hope you are not foolish enough to come here seeking my treasure." Cupping the torso in both hands, she took a deep breath, then breathed out a long barrage of white lightning bolts at it. The zombie flesh sizzled as the bones snapped and popped like acorns in a fire. When she was done, she found the body much easier to bite through.

"I assure you we seek no such thing," said Julian. "Our ship was damaged in a fire, and we came here hoping to cut down a tree to replace the mast."

Akane scrutinized him as she swallowed her second half of zombie torso. "Where were you headed?"

Something about her tone made Julian hesitate. Was she trying to catch him in a lie? Or was she simply that starved for conversation? He tried to remember the name of the ship's intended destination before he'd set fire to it.

"Khalzhar," said Rhonda.

"Oh?" Akane had been idly scanning the carnage for the next best chunk of meat, but now she devoted her full attention to Julian and Rhonda. By what he could read from the look on her face, Julian wasn't sure that was a good thing. "You are slave traders then? Mayhap I shall have some fresh meat after all."

"No!" said Julian. "We're totally not slave traders. Quite the opposite. We were going to be sold as slaves, but we overpowered the crew and took over the ship."

Akane raised her scaly eyebrows. "You expect me to believe the two of you overpowered a crew of slave traders? You do not look like you could overpower a one-legged kobold, and the fat one looks like she would get winded by the effort it takes to stand up."

Rhonda jumped to her feet, which unfortunately didn't leave her winded. "What the fuck did you –"

"Rhonda!" said Julian. "Please." When he was satisfied that Rhonda wasn't going to attack a dragon with her bare hands, he turned his attention back to Akane. "The ship was under-manned, and we had help from the other captives. And of course, we had magic." Julian cast a Prestidigitation spell, causing purple and orange trails of light to follow his hands as he waved them around.

Akane frowned. "I cannot imagine that would fetch much of a price at the slave auction."

Julian deactivated his spell. "We had somewhat of a difficult time with the eels on our way from the ship to the shore. That took up most of our more powerful spells."

"So you are both wizards?"

Julian had already failed to impress her with his Prestidigitation spell, and the general consensus of people he'd spoken to seemed to be that sorcery was viewed as 'playing with magic', so he decided to lead with their best foot forward. "Rhonda is a wizard."

Akane continued staring at Julian, not even glancing Rhonda's way. "And you?"

Julian shrugged. "I'm just a sorcerer."

"*Just* a sorcerer?" said Akane. "Do you not realize your noble lineage? The blood of dragons runs through your veins."

That was news to Julian. "Does it?" Julian tried to think of how that could be the case. He'd just seen a dragon take human form, so it wasn't a huge leap to imagine they could

# Critical Failures VIII

take elven form as well. But would that give a male dragon elven sperm? Would a female dragon have to remain in elven form during the entire pregnancy? Would he be able to breathe lightning at some point?

"Silly elf," said Akane. "Every sorcerer has dragon ancestry. That is where the magic comes from. Wizardry is but a cheap imitation by those who envy what comes naturally to our kind. It is insulting how they mock our –"

Ravenus interrupted with a loud belch as he waddled toward them. "Oh my! I humbly beg your pardon, sir! I may have overdone it on the zombie meat, but it has been ages since I've had anything so delectably rotten."

Julian smiled at him. "Hey, did you know I have dragon ancestry?"

"I did not, sir." Ravenus looked up suddenly at Akane. "Oh heavens! Is this your mother? And look at me, a gluttonous pig with entrails all over my face!" He drove his beak into the sand and shook his head. But instead of scraping away the rotting viscera, all he managed to do was get a bunch of sand stuck to his face.

"Take it easy," said Julian. "This isn't my mother. This is our friend, Akane." He hoped that was received as more friendly than presumptuous.

Akane smiled at Ravenus. "And what is your name, little bird?"

"He can only understand –"

"Ravenus," said Ravenus with a slight bow. "It is a pleasure to meet you."

"How could you understand her?" Julian looked up at Akane. "He only knows the Elven tongue. How were you able to communicate with him?"

"I can speak with any animal," said Akane. "I have been able to since I was very young." She frowned. "I do not use this ability very often, as I usually tend to eat most of the animals I encounter. Also, it is rare that I find an animal that has anything worthwhile to talk about. More often than not, they just beg me not to eat them. Then I feel bad for doing it." Her eyes brightened as she smiled at Julian. "But you and I can talk. You are a sorcerer. We could talk for days about that."

"We don't have days," said Rhonda. "We need to get back to the ship as soon as possible."

"Why are you in such a hurry to get back to a slave ship?"

"We took over the ship," Julian reminded her. "But we were separated from our other friends, who were put onto other slave ships, and we need to repair this one so we can go rescue them." The seed of an idea sprouted in Julian's head. But if it was going to bear any fruit, Julian would have to be subtle about bringing it up. He had to make Akane think it was her idea. "That is, of course, unless you know of a faster way for us to get to Hollin."

Akane spread her huge wings wide. "There is no faster way to get anywhere than by air."

*Hook.*

"It's too bad we don't have wings like those."

"We are friends," said Akane. "Is it not the custom for one friend to help another in need?"

*Line.*

Julian feigned confusion. "Wait a minute. You're not suggesting..."

"Let me fly you to Hollin. It would only take a couple of days, and think of all the great conversation we will have along the way."

*Sinker.*

If anything frightened Julian more than the thought of being eaten by a dragon, it was the thought of riding on one's back at ten thousand feet in the air. But this was an opportunity he couldn't let slip by, not while his friends were in danger.

# Critical Failures VIII

"Thank you so much!" Julian laughed. "Imagine the look on their faces when we show up with a big green dragon!"

Akane's nostrils flared, then she vomited lightning bolts at Julian's feet. He barely jumped out of the way as the heat from the lightning singed the tiny hairs on his legs.

"Julian!" cried Rhonda and Ravenus over the loud crackle of lightning as Akane shifted her lightning breath to a nearby zombie corpse, setting it on fire.

Scrambling to think of what he'd said to offend Akane, he nodded at Rhonda to let her know he was okay. *Rhonda! Of course!* She'd given him that same look earlier in the evening when he suggested she do jumping jacks. Akane must also be sensitive about her weight.

"I'm so sorry!" Julian pleaded. "I only meant that you're big compared to us, which is perfectly natural considering that you're a dragon and we're –"

"Look closely at my scales, elf!" she demanded, thrusting her hand into the flames rising up from the charred remains of the zombie. "Do these look green to you?"

"No," Julian lied. They definitely had a metallic greenish tint to them, but examining them more closely, he could see the edges were more of a metallic brown.

"I am a *bronze* dragon," said Akane. She grabbed the flaming corpse and blew out the fire, then sulked as she tore its limbs off. "My scales have not yet transitioned all the way."

"That's no reason to throw a tantrum!" said Rhonda. "It was an honest mistake, and you could have killed him."

"If I was a *green* dragon, I would have killed you all by now. Horrible disgusting creatures, breathing that putrid acid gas. Good luck having a conversation with one of them. Count yourselves lucky you met me instead. A green dragon would have melted the skin off both of you by now and been feasting on one while watching the other writhe in agony."

"Again, I'm very sorry," said Julian. He had to find out if Akane's offer was still good. "Those green dragons sound like dicks. I can't imagine one of them being kind enough to offer us a ride to Hollin."

Akane scoffed. "I am rescinding my offer." She tossed the scorched corpse aside. "And now I've lost my appetite."

*Oh no.*

Julian started to put some pieces together in his mind, and he didn't like the picture that was forming. Akane was moody and prone to tantrums. She liked to talk shit about other dragons. Her scales were in the process of transitioning. She was an adolescent dragon.

Maybe he could use this. If there was one thing teenagers wanted more than anything else, it was to be taken seriously as an adult. Unfortunately, he couldn't think of an angle that made giving two strangers a ride across the continent seem like an adult thing to do, so he had to go the other direction and possibly risk being electrocuted by dragon breath.

"It seems kind of childish to have such a big change of heart over a simple misunderstanding," he said, trying to look more casual than a man bracing himself for electric death.

"Quite the contrary," said Akane. "It was irresponsible of me to have made the offer in the first place. I should not leave my treasure unguarded for so long. I barely have enough gold to sleep on as it is."

There wasn't another living soul for miles in any direction, and Julian didn't imagine that zombies cared about treasure at all. But in spite of that, Julian didn't think he would get anywhere by arguing that abandoning her life savings was the responsible thing to do. However, that did give him a new angle to explore.

"What if we offered you money?" he asked, knowing full well that neither he nor Rhonda had any to offer, and there wasn't likely enough on the ship to make it worth Akane's while.

Akane raised her eyebrows. "How much money?"

"I honestly have no idea how much something like this should cost," Julian admitted rather than aim too high or insult her with a lowball offer.

"Very well. I will do it for one thousand gold pieces."

Julian had certainly been in no danger of aiming too high.

"That seems a little steep," said Rhonda. "A few minutes ago, you offered to take us for free."

Akane spread her wings as if to show off the goods they'd be paying for. "And then I changed my mind. You are asking me to do something I would prefer not to do, and I have given you a price that would make it worth my bother. You can take my offer, or you can leave it." She sneered at Rhonda. "Also, just to be clear, I offered to take *Julian*. My poor wings can only flap but so hard."

"You can take your offer and shove it up your scaly –"

"We'll take it!" said Julian before Rhonda could sour the deal. Their friends needed help. And as long as the starting offer was impossible for him to pay, he didn't see much point in trying to nickel and dime Akane for a few gold pieces off.

Rhonda gave Julian a hard, frustrated glare, then turned back to Akane. "Do you mind if I speak to my friend privately for a moment?"

"Not at all." Akane folded her wings and picked up the charred corpse that she'd previously discarded. Apparently, duping some suckers out of a hefty sum of cash brought her appetite back.

Rhonda dragged Julian back to the water. "Where the hell are you going to get a thousand gold pieces?"

"I don't know," said Julian. "I'll figure it out."

"Do I need to remind you that that's a dragon?"

"I know, but –"

"You'd be better off ripping off the Russian mob. She already nearly killed you for calling her green. What do you think she'll do when she realizes you can't pay her what you promised?"

Rhonda made an excellent point. He wouldn't be any help to his friends if he was roasted and eaten by a dragon.

"I'll just have to level with her."

Rhonda scoffed. "What are you going to say? *I'm flat broke, but if we happen to come upon a sack of gold coins along the way, they're all yours.*"

"I've got an idea."

"Is it better than the one I just mentioned?"

Julian sighed. "A little bit. But just like she said, she can take it or leave it." He walked back to make his offer to Akane.

"If it is all the same to you," said Akane, "I would prefer to be paid upfront so I can add it to my pile now rather than have to carry all that gold back here.

Julian cleared his throat. "Here's the thing. I don't have the money on me."

"Oh?" Akane narrowed her eyes at him. "Then where is it?"

"I don't have it at all. Actually, neither of us have any money. We were about to be sold off as slaves if you recall."

"Did you seek to deceive me?"

"Absolutely not," said Julian. "You are clearly much more powerful than me, and I have no doubt that you're much smarter than me as well."

Akane smiled and relaxed as she resumed eating her charred corpse. "Go on."

"I know how to get the money. One of the friends I'm trying to rescue is a bard. I'm his manager, actually."

"Oh?" Akane stopped nibbling on her corpse. "Is he a juggler? I do enjoy a good juggling performance."

"No, he's a musician."

# Critical Failures VIII

"Does he sing in Draconic?"

"I don't think so. I'm pretty sure he only knows the Common tongue."

Akane went back to her meal. "If I wish to hear the screeching of baboons, it is a shorter flight to the Balqoray Jungle."

"I think you might be surprised. I can guarantee you've never heard songs like his before. Anyway, we did a couple of gigs on the Crescent Shadow not too long ago, and –"

"I have always wanted to visit the Crescent Shadow. Is it as nice as everyone says?"

Julian shrugged. "It's a little noisy for my taste, but I can see the appeal. My point is that we made quite a bit of money doing shows there. And if you're willing to hang around a few extra days after we rescue my friends, I'm sure we'll be able to make enough money to pay for your service." He wasn't as sure as he was claiming. Pulling this off was hugely dependent on a wide range of variables, not least of which being whether or not Chaz was still alive. But it was a gamble he had to make.

"And what happens if you can't afford to pay?"

"I'll definitely be able to pay," said Julian. "It might just be a matter of time." Technically, he was telling the truth. Thirty years of washing dishes in a tavern was a matter of time, after all. If things didn't pan out with Chaz, he hoped Akane would accept that letter-of-the-law reasoning.

"I admit that I am intrigued by your proposition," said Akane. "Shall we state our agreement formally? I will deliver you to your friend in Hollin, for which you will pay me one thousand gold pieces."

"There's one more condition I'd like to ask of you."

Akane scoffed. "You admit to having no money to pay for what you already ask of me. How is it that you see yourself in a position to ask for more?"

"It's true," said Julian. "I need you more than you need me, but the reason I need you is to save my friends' lives. It doesn't do me much good to fly off and save one group of friends while I leave another stranded at sea. All I'm asking is that you help us take one of these trees to our ship so we can repair the mast."

Akane sulked on it for a moment, clearly not relishing the thought of giving any more than she'd already agreed to for a dubious promise of getting paid. Julian couldn't blame her for that.

"Fine," she finally said. "That doesn't sound like too much of a bother." She swung her head back and blasted lightning at the base of the tree Rhonda had started to chop. After ten seconds, the top of the tree began to tilt. After a series of loud cracks, it fell onto the sand with a loud thud.

"The undead will have heard that," she said. "Let us get to your ship."

# CHAPTER 29

Cooper sipped on the bottle of liquor Tim had stolen while he watched Tim work on his costume. He was hoping Tim would ask for the bottle so he could refuse him in retaliation for the unnecessary ass-kicking he'd received earlier in the day, but Tim barely looked up from his handiwork.

"What is it with you and that dumbass costume?" Cooper finally asked.

"Anything worth doing is worth doing right."

"When the fuck did you get a work ethic? If you'd put as much effort into the Chicken Hut as you are into this shitty clown costume, you'd be fucking Colonel Sanders by now."

"Why would I want to fuck Colonel Sanders?" Tim pulled the thread tight through the seam he was working on, then bit off the excess. "As long as we're imprisoned, it makes sense to develop what skills we can. If you were smart, you'd be doing the same."

"Sewing?"

"Not necessarily, but something." He held up the shirt he'd been working on. "What do you think?"

Cooper didn't know what to say. He wasn't a fucking seamstress, after all. But if he was forced to have an opinion, he supposed this shirt was a drastic improvement from Tim's first effort.

"It's beautiful," he said. "You'll be the belle of the fucking ball." He took a swig from the bottle. It was weaker than the stonepiss they stocked at the Whore's Head, and it had a weird aftertaste. He suspected it might be meant strictly for cooking, but it was getting the job done.

Tim smiled, admiring his work. "It's not bad, right? I feel like I'm really improving."

"I'm really happy for you," said Cooper. "But I don't get what you're so excited about. I mean, it's great that you want to improve yourself, but we're in a goddamn gladiator arena. Wouldn't your time be better spent doing push-ups or some shit? Maybe practice a fight choreography or –"

Screams echoed through the subterranean corridors from some distance away.

Tim hurriedly bundled his shirt and tucked it away behind his bed. "Lose the bottle."

"What's going on?" asked Cooper.

"How the fuck should I know? I was sewing."

"So what are you so spooked about?"

"Do you not hear that screaming?"

Cooper shrugged. "We're in prison. Maybe someone's trying anal for the first time."

Tim shook his head. "That's definitely more than one person."

"Maybe they're having an orgy."

"Would you get your mind off of butt sex for five minutes."

"I'm just saying, it could be anything. I don't see why you're making such a big deal out of it."

"It's unexpected, that's why." Tim got up from his bunk and poked his head out of the open doorway. "A place like this has strict rules and routines. It's predictable, which is crucial when you're planning a breakout."

"We're planning a breakout?" Cooper remembered Tim mentioning something about that before, but he hadn't brought it up since. "Is that what all the sewing is about?"

"Kind of."

# Critical Failures VIII

That wasn't an unheard of trope in prison shows and movies. Cooper had definitely seen more than one breakout involving a protagonist making himself a convincing prison guard uniform out of shit he picked up in the laundry room and dye brewed up in the toilet, then just casually stroll out through the front door. But Tim would have to sew like a motherfucker if he expected to pass for an orc. That is, unless the uniform he planned to make wasn't for himself.

"Holy shit!" said Cooper. "Are you going to make me a prison guard uniform?"

Tim scowled at him. "What the fuck are you talking about? The guards here don't even wear uniforms."

Cooper nodded thoughtfully. That was definitely a flaw in their plan that would need ironing out. That's why Tim was the brains of the operation. But if not a prison guard uniform, that could only mean one thing.

"You're going to cross-stitch a tapestry of Raquel Welch?"

"Shut up, Cooper. The less you know about it, the better." He looked back outside. "That shouting is getting closer. Whatever's getting everyone all riled up, it's coming this way."

Cooper didn't know how to react to that, except to gulp down one last swig of stonepiss before tucking the bottle behind his cot.

Tim pulled his head in and pressed his back flat against the wall. His face was as white as an albino baby's ass.

"What did you see?" asked Cooper, alarmed at seeing Tim so shaken. "What's out there?"

"I don't know what the fuck that thing is," Tim whispered. "Just keep your voice down until it passes."

But it didn't pass. That is, unless Tim had been referring to something other than the massive glowing lizard-like creature that stopped in front of their open doorway.

It sniffed the air, then squeezed itself inside.

It stuck its snout right in Tim's crotch, then quickly backed off when Tim pissed his pants. Turning its attention to Cooper, it stepped further into their cell. Cooper counted four legs on the side he could see and assumed it must have an equal number on the opposite side. What the fuck was this thing? He could only think of two eight-legged animals off the top of his head, but he was pretty sure this was neither a spider nor an octopus.

The creature sniffed repeatedly at Cooper's crotch. He wasn't any less terrified than Tim, but he had already pissed himself a few minutes ago.

"Can I, um... help you with something?"

Apparently, the beast had satisfied its curiosity with regard to Cooper's crotch. After some intense sniffing, it slowly backed out of the cell, then continued on its way.

Tim moved to the back wall next to Cooper. "What the fuck was that about?"

"Beats the shit out of me," said Cooper as he watched the monster's tail drag past the doorway.

But then the tail stopped, and the monster started backing up. It was entering their room again, only this time it was doing so ass first. As if that wasn't strange enough, there appeared to be something poking out of the creature's ass.

"Is that a hand?" asked Tim, a little more relaxed now. Having a dinosaur ass in their face wasn't exactly more pleasant, but it was certainly a whole lot less threatening than the toothy end.

Cooper looked at his own hands, then at the fist poking out of the monster's asshole. It was rougher than his, with slightly longer claws.

"It looks like an orc hand."

"How did it get up that thing's ass?"

The answer seemed pretty obvious to Cooper. "I guess it ate an orc."

## Critical Failures VIII

"I don't think so," said Tim. "When you eat a chicken, you don't shit out whole sections of its anatomy. That hand hasn't been digested at all."

"Maybe it sat on an orc."

Tim glared up at him. "And the entire orc went up its ass?"

"Yeah!" said Cooper, excited that the pieces of the puzzle were falling into place. It was just like an episode of *CSI Miami*. "Then he tried to get out, but only managed to reach one hand out before he died."

"Honestly, sometimes I wonder how that brain of yours has the capacity to keep your heart pumping."

Cooper was fine-tuning a reply involving an orc fist and Tim's mom's asshole when he heard a wet splat on the floor in front of them.

The monster had taken a dump that could have filled the trunk of a small car. Resting atop what looked like a puddle of extra-chunky chili was not only an orc hand, but an entire arm all the way up to the shoulder.

Having delivered its payload, along with a couple of wet bonus farts, the creature disappeared. It just winked out of existence like one of Julian's ill-fated horses.

"Thanks for that, asshole!" Tim said to the empty air between them and the doorway. "Seriously, what the fuck?"

Cooper squatted over the shit puddle and examined the arm more closely. "Dude, I think there's something inside the fist." He picked it up and pried the fingers open one by one until he could remove the rolled-up length of fabric it was holding. He suspected it had once been white, but had seen too much wear and too few washes. At this point, there wasn't enough Tide in the world, especially with the smudges of what looked like dried blood all over it. "It looks like a shirt sleeve."

"Give me that," said Tim, snatching the fabric out of Cooper's hand.

"Look, man. I know you've suddenly got this weird textile obsession, but –"

"Shut the fuck up for a second, Cooper. This is a note. It's addressed to us." He held the filthy sleeve stretched out in front of him, scanning slowly from one side to the other. "Listen to this. *Cooper and Tim. Planning escape. Full Moon Brawl. Be there.*"

"Who's it from?" asked Cooper.

Tim shrugged. "I have no idea. They didn't sign it."

"You think it's a trap?"

"That was my first thought, but that doesn't sit right with me. If someone was trying to lure us into getting caught trying to pull off some cockamamie escape plan, they'd just wait until we weren't around and drop off a letter. They wouldn't go to all the bother of delivering it via dinosaur ass, which leads me to believe it's legit. The question is, who do we know who has a big-ass magic dinosaur?"

Cooper thought back to something he'd heard last time he was in the Whore's Head. "Was that thing a basilisk?"

"How the fuck should I know? I always thought of basilisks as being more snakelike, but whoever wrote that entry in the *Monster Manual* could have gone with an eight-legged lizard. Who's going to argue with them? What difference does it make, though? We don't know anyone with a pet basilisk either."

"Randy," said Cooper.

"The pedo we picked up in Gulfport? What about him?"

"He's a paladin. I think he got a basilisk as his Special Mount."

Tim laughed. "I guess nine-year-old boy wasn't an option."

"How did he know we were here?"

"Who gives a shit? What matters is that he knows we're here and he wants to help." Tim sighed. "It's too bad we can't trust him."

# Critical Failures VIII

"Why not?" asked Cooper. "Because he's gay?"

"Of course not. I'd suck ten orc dicks to get out of this shithole. We can't trust him because he's dumber than a sack of dildos. How the hell is he going to mastermind some big escape?"

"Shouldn't we at least hear him out?"

"I suppose it couldn't hurt," said Tim. "We've got about a couple of weeks until the full moon. We'll see what he's got in mind, and I should have a solid Plan B ready by then."

# CHAPTER 30

"It's done," said Randy, peering through the bars at the gate on the other side of the arena. "Basil delivered the message to Tim and Cooper. At least, he thinks he did." It gave him a great sense of relief to send Basil back to the Celestial Plane. Through their Empathic Link, he could feel his simple-minded but fiercely loyal steed's discomfort as he sniffed his way down unfamiliar corridors to a cacophony of terrified screams. He imagined that shitting out an entire arm played no small part in that relief either.

"What do you mean, he *thinks* he did?" asked Denise. "Our lives depend on that dumb motherfucker delivering that message to the right people."

"He did his best with what he had to work with. You smeared a lot of poo on yourself, so I'm confident that he had enough scent to go on."

"I pray ye be right," said Captain Longfellow, keeping a wary eye behind them for patrolling guards who might be suspicious of the three of them hanging around by the gate. "I have gambled me life on countless foolish gambits, but never one quite so senseless as a dwarven whore slathered in half-orc shit."

Denise turned around and got up in his face, or at least his chest. "Who the fuck are you callin' a whore, you semen slurping mother–"

"Denise!" said Randy. "That's enough."

Denise folded her arms and pouted. "He started it."

# Critical Failures VIII

"What's done is done. All we can do is hope for the best and go forward. Presuming Basil delivered our message correctly, what's our next move?"

"That be clear enough," said Captain Longfellow. "We would do well to actually come up with an escape plan."

Randy nodded. "That's certainly high on the list of priorities. And we also got to make sure we're all picked for the Full Moon Brawl."

"That should be the easy part."

"Damn straight," said Denise. "Gurok laid it out plain and simple. You start talkin' shit and causin' trouble, and you get dumped in the Full Moon Brawl."

"I don't know," said Randy. "I reckon we still got about two weeks before the full moon. If we cause too much trouble before then, they might just kill us."

"Aye," said Captain Longfellow. "A sudden change in behavior by all of us at once may arouse suspicion. I propose we take a more subtle approach."

Denise grabbed a bar of the gate as she squatted for a pee. "Fuck subtle. Who gives a shit if they get suspicious and decide to kill us? That's the whole point of the fuckin' Brawl, ain't it? Thin the herd, rout out the troublemakers."

"I get what you're saying," said Randy. "But we should listen to Captain Longfellow's idea. Captain?"

"If there be one thing that spooks those who hold the power, it be the masses huddled together whispering of mutiny. I propose we continue doing as we did tonight, gathering together for secret meetings. The others be bound to pick up on it, and rumors will no doubt start to spread. As long as they have no reason to suspect we actually want to be selected for the Full Moon Brawl, that be exactly where they'll send us."

Randy appreciated the subtlety of the captain's plan. "That's perfect. We'll make them think it was their idea all along. The best part is that we got to have those secret meetings anyway to come up with our escape plan."

Denise shook her head as her pee puddle expanded around her feet. "I don't like it. What if folks think we're just a bunch of queers lookin' for a private place to hold our orgies? No offense, Randy."

"I don't think –"

"You there!" said a gravelly voice from behind them. "What are you doing here?" It was Rocco, Zimbra's second in command and a real hard-ass. He was armed only with a small club, but he looked like he was itching to use it.

"Nothing," said Captain Longfellow amiably. "Just stretching our legs a bit. We thought we heard –"

"What the fuck does it look like I'm doing, pig face?" said Denise. "I'm takin' a fuckin' piss."

"Denise!" cried Randy.

"You think we're afraid of you, you fat sack of hog shit?" Denise stood up and stepped out of her puddle toward Rocco. "I'll pull those rotten tusks out of your bitch-ass mouth and make you cry wee wee wee all the way home."

"Wee wee wee?" said Rocco, looking more confused than angry.

"You're one ugly motherfucker, you know that? Honestly, what kind of barnyard reject swine whore did your daddy have to poke his pecker in to make such a limp-dicked retard of a –"

CRACK!

With a blur of Rocco's club across her face, Denise was out cold on the floor.

Rocco shook his head. "Are you *trying* to get sent to the Full Moon Brawl?"

"Yes," said Randy before he could stop himself. His compulsion to always speak the truth had betrayed them.

Rocco stepped over Denise and eyed Randy. "Is that so?"

## Critical Failures VIII

"We are men of the sea," said Captain Longfellow. "This life of confinement does not suit men like us. I do not mean to complain, mind ye. We have been treated well enough during our time here, but we yearn to breathe the air of free men. Be that impossible, we would prefer to perish by the sword in the heat of battle than to have our spirits crushed little by little with each passing day."

Rocco stared at him for a moment, then nodded. "Your request is a noble one. I shall relay it to Master Zimbra. Now, take your dwarf and get back to your quarters at once."

Captain Longfellow bowed. "May the gods bless ye."

# CHAPTER 31

Dave had gotten a few badly needed hours of sleep on the road to Port Town, and his head was finally clear enough to put some thought into his next escape attempt. The temptation to hop out of the moving cart and make a break for the surrounding wetlands was strong. It wasn't a great habitat for a dwarf, but he might be able to tough it out in hybrid or rat form until he managed to lose Stacy and make his way to a different city with a wererat population that didn't want to kill him.

But he knew he wouldn't be able to outrun Stacy. If he couldn't do it when she was alone, he didn't have a chance when she had a ranger and his fucking leopard to help hunt him down. He had to be patient. If the perfect opportunity fell into his lap in Port Town, he would jump on it. But failing that, he knew his best chance at freedom was waiting for him in the Cedar Wilds.

Stacy was a clever bitch, but she was overconfident. While she was recklessly attacking a band of orcs and ettins, all he would have to do is not help. He'd just stay back and enjoy the show. If he was lucky, they'd kill Alroth and his stupid cat but merely knock Stacy down to a few negative Hit Points and leave her for dead. He would tie her up, just like she'd done to him, then bring her back to consciousness again with a Cure Minor Wounds spell before standing over her and rubbing one out. And this time he wouldn't turn away at the last

## Critical Failures VIII

second. The last thing she'd see before she went to Hell would be blurred through a thick coat of dwarf jizz.

His dick was hard just thinking about it. And with Alroth standing right next to him, he was not in an ideal position to remedy that situation.

*Calm down, Dave. Think of something else.*

"The journey was long and hard," said Elramar, the driver. "But finally, we are coming to the end."

That wasn't helping Dave's situation at all.

Alroth took in a deep breath and smiled. "Truly, it has been too long since I have tasted the sea's warm salty spray."

Stacy looked back at Alroth. "Have you ever been to Port Town?"

"Not since my youth."

*Thank God. A change of topic.* Dave was afraid he might –

"She has blossomed much since then," said Elramar. "Taking in galleons of seamen night and day."

*Oh, for the love of –*

"I dislike traveling by sea," said Alroth. "As a man of the wood, I prefer to enter her by the backside, nice and dry."

Elramar shrugged. "To each his own, I suppose. As for me, I dream of the day when my big vessel delivers huge loads onto her –"

"SHUT UP!" cried Dave, closing his eyes to focus on not ejaculating. It was no use. He hadn't had a moment of privacy since Stacy had him on a leash, and he felt like he'd just pumped out a quart. When he opened his eyes, Stacy was glaring back at him.

"What the hell crawled up your ass?"

"Nothing." Dave sniffed. He faced the corner of the cart so Alroth wouldn't be able to see the big wet spot that was surely forming around his crotch. "I have a headache. I haven't eaten in a while, and it's making me irritable."

Stacy pulled a baseball-sized bundle of white fabric out of her bag, which Dave recognized as one of the leftover pickled eggs she'd taken from The Stinky Pickle. She held it out to him.

"Here. Eat this and keep your shit together. We're almost there."

Dave wasn't really hungry, but that gave him an idea. "I don't want an egg." He turned around and grabbed the first jar within reach. It was full of thin purple sausages sloshing around in dark green liquid. "I want this."

"Well, that doesn't belong to us, *Dave*." Stacy was talking to him like a child, and he really wanted to hurl the jar into her condescending face. "Do you have money to pay for that?"

Elramar glanced back at him. "Pig penises? Don't even worry about it. Those come cheap enough. Grimmond won't miss one jar." He winked at Stacy. "I can just tell him it broke in transit."

"Thank you," said Stacy. "That's very kind of you." She scowled back at Dave. "Enjoy your pig dicks."

She and Alroth were both looking at him, which made it difficult to fake an accident.

"Do you mind?" he snapped, pressing himself up against the front of the cart to hide his wet spot. His dick felt like it was glued to his clothes. "Is there nothing more interesting you can gawk at than me eating?"

Alroth politely turned away, but Stacy continued staring.

"Honestly, no," she said. "I've never seen anyone eat a pig's penis. I wish I'd known you were such a big fan of them."

"Why don't you grow up?" he said, then crouched down in the corner to open the jar without anyone seeing him. Breaking the wax seal, he removed the lid and dumped the whole jar onto his crotch. Pig dicks spilled all over the cart floor.

# Critical Failures VIII

"Dammit!" he said as he stood up. "Look what you made me do!" He stepped back to show her his wet clothes.

Stacy laughed. "I didn't make you do that. Stop being such a crybaby and eat."

"I can't eat those. They fell on the floor."

"Since when are you so picky? First you turn down my egg, and now you're put off by food touching the floor? Weren't you the one who ate a half-eaten turkey leg you found on the ground?"

"That was different! I was –"

"Elramar was kind enough to let you have that jar of pig dicks, and you're going to eat them if I have to shove them down your throat myself."

Dave didn't doubt for a second that she would do just that. The sadistic bitch would probably get off on it.

Fortunately, Alroth's leopard, Lucia, seemed to have quite a fondness for pickled pig dicks. She was lapping them up left and right.

But Dave knew that Stacy wasn't going to let him get away with not giving her the satisfaction of watching him eat at least one. That was fine. Later, when he got his revenge on her, he'd make sure it was worth having eaten a pig dick.

Under Stacy's smug stare, Dave picked up a pickled pig penis and held it up to examine it. Thin and curly, it resembled what Dave had always thought a pig's tail was supposed to look like. Maybe it was a pig's tail. Elramar only glanced back for a second to identify what was in the jar, after all. And how could he be so certain with all that dark murky pickle juice obscuring the so-called pig dicks within?

Alternatively, Elramar might have just been messing with him, or even flat out lying. If he wanted to dissuade Dave from stealing his employer's food but didn't want to come off as a stingy prick, that was the perfect cover. *Sure, you can eat all you want... if you like pig dick.*

Confident now that what he was holding was actually a pig's tail, Dave looked Stacy straight in the eyes and took a big bite. His confidence faltered as he bit down. He'd been expecting it to be tough and leathery, like tearing off a piece of beef jerky, but this felt more like ground beef stuffed into a used condom. The fact that it squirted pickle juice into the back of his throat didn't ease his queasiness at all.

He tried to maintain the facade of confidence as Stacy watched him chew. Or at least he tried not to throw up. He told himself that it was all in his mind, that it was just like eating any other pickled meat.

*Focus on the taste, not the texture. Does that taste like dick?*

Dave had never tasted dick, but he'd sniffed his fingers after scratching his balls enough times to have a vague idea of what he expected dick to taste like, and it certainly wasn't anything close to dill seed and vinegar.

Whatever he was eating, it was a food that people paid money for. It was childish, and perhaps a little culturally insensitive, to let the dick thing go to his head.

"How is it?" asked Stacy.

"Great," lied Dave. If he did throw up, he hoped at least that it would project far enough to get on her.

"I am surprised to hear that," said Elramar. "I have never seen anyone brave enough to put a pig penis in his mouth. They are more commonly used for dog treats."

Stacy laughed, but Dave didn't give her the satisfaction of gagging or spitting out his mouthful of dick. Instead, he swallowed what he'd been chewing and shoved the rest of it into his mouth.

"You don't know what you're missing," he said. "You want to try one?"

"No thanks," said Stacy. "I'll eat my egg. You enjoy your dog food."

## Critical Failures VIII

Dave gulped down his mouthful with as little chewing as possible. "What's your problem, Stacy? I mean, you say you're trying to help me, but all you've done so far is be a huge bitch."

Stacy scoffed. "*I've* been a huge bitch to *you*? Need I remind you that –"

"No, you needn't remind me." Dave didn't need the whole world to know about his indiscretions back at the inn. "I thought that was behind us now, but you're still riding my ass without any provocation. It's not bad enough that you make me spill pickle juice all over myself, but you need to also tell me I deserve to eat dog food? Why are you even bothering to help me at all?"

"I'm just messing with you, Dave. When we get you back to normal, we'll laugh about all this." She turned around to face forward again. "Besides, if I did make you spill that pickle juice, I was doing you a favor. You can hardly make out that come stain now."

Dave looked down at his crotch to discover that Stacy was a goddamn liar. His pickle juice plan hadn't worked at all. Most of it had soaked right through his clothes, leaving them a shade darker than before. But whatever was in there that gave it its dark green color had coalesced around the edge of his jizz. The Australia-shaped blob on his crotch would be visible from fifty yards away.

"That's sweat!" said Dave to anyone who was listening. "Dwarves get really sweaty down there, and it leaves a ring of salt deposits. I didn't... I mean, when would I have..."

"Look!" said Elramar. "We have arrived."

Dave decided to quit while he was behind, hoping that no one would bring up his soiled clothes again now that they were in Port Town.

The town was bigger than it had been when Dave and Stacy last visited, which surprised Dave. When the Phantom

Pinas had passed over it, most of the buildings, which were built on barges, had gotten out of its way. It made sense that they would all return, making Dave expect the town to look about the same as before. Maybe they spruced up the Merriweather Inn with a fresh coat of paint after the fire damage, but he hadn't expected much more from these backward fisherfolk.

But Port Town was bustling, with building barges he could have sworn hadn't been there last time. A small army of carpenters and shipwrights were busily building more.

"Tiger!" said Alroth, picking up his bow and pulling an arrow from his quiver. He was calm but alert as a vicious-looking tiger bounded toward them through the parting crowd.

Even Dave, who knew it was Mayor Merriweather, was more alarmed at the sight than Alroth sounded.

"Put down your bow," said Stacy. "He's not going to hurt us. That's a friend of ours."

Alroth lowered his bow, but the horse pulling their cart flipped out, screaming and backing up on its hind legs. Fortunately, it calmed down when the tiger stopped and morphed into a naked old man.

"I thought I smelled pussy!" said Mayor Merriweather as he walked around to Dave and Stacy's side of the cart.

Dave smirked at Stacy until he remembered their first encounter with the mayor and realized he was referring to him. He looked at the band of leopard fur on his forearm and sighed.

"Hello, Mayor Merriweather."

"And what brings you good folks to our fine city this evening?"

Dave still wasn't quite clear about the purpose of their visit. "Arby's?"

# Critical Failures VIII

Stacy climbed down from the front of the cart, and Alroth followed her lead. Dave struggled to do likewise, but Mayor Merriweather picked him up under the armpits.

"Thank you for the ride, Elramar," said Alroth. "Go forth and deliver your load."

Mayor Merriweather sniffed at Dave's crotch. "It would appear as though someone has beaten him to it."

"Would you please put me down?" asked Dave.

The mayor set him down gently, but Dave acted like he'd been dropped. Feigning a loss of balance, he staggered off the boardwalk and fell into the murky swamp water. Fortunately, it wasn't very deep. He grabbed a handful of mud and rubbed it vigorously on his crotch, then stood up.

"Easy, Mayor!" he said. "Looks like you don't know your own strength."

Stacy rolled her eyes, clearly seeing through his ruse. But Dave didn't care as long as he could walk through the town without everyone staring at his –

*Why is Alroth staring at my junk?*

Dave looked down. Instead of finding his splooge stain hidden by mud, it was now a distinct and bright shade of green.

"What the hell is that?"

"Algae," said Mayor Merriweather, reaching out to help Dave climb back up onto the boardwalk. "It is attracted to the nutrients found in semen."

"Fantastic."

Now he wasn't merely a walking billboard of filth and sperm, but he also had billions of microscopic whores guzzling down his Davy gravy.

"After an ejaculation like that, you must be starved," said the mayor. "Let us go forth and partake of some roasted beef sandwiches together. It will be my treat." He started walking into the town, full of people hauling building materials to and fro, busily expanding what was once a humble little fishing village.

"That's very kind of you," said Stacy, following him.

"After you saved my life, it is the least I could do for you."

"That's kind of what I wanted to talk to you about. We ran into a bit of a –"

"Good evening, Mayor!" said a man as he hurried past with a heavy-looking sack slung over his back.

The mayor waved. "Indeed it is, Eli. The new gardens are coming along quite nicely."

"It is kind of you to say so."

"Pass my compliments on to the others!"

"Doing the rounds again, Mayor?" said a half-elf carrying a bulky wooden toolbox.

"No, just welcoming some old friends."

The half-elf's smile wilted as his gaze fell to Dave's crotch. "Isn't that lovely."

It was the same with everyone they passed. Nobody gave a second glance to the naked geriatric with his dong flopping around in the breeze, or Stacy's amazing tits, or even to the guy with a goddamn leopard following him around. Instead, every eye in the town seemed to be as irresistibly drawn to Dave's crotch as that fucking algae. It was like his own personal Scarlet Letter.

"I'm sorry," Mayor Merriweather said to Stacy when he got a break from his adoring citizens. "What were you saying?"

"You'd mentioned us saving your life. I was wondering if you would consider that when I ask you for a favor."

The mayor sighed. "My gratitude has limits." He scowled down at Dave. "Were my gifts not adequate to compensate you for a simple healing spell?"

How the hell was Dave taking the heat for this?

# Critical Failures VIII

"No!" he blurted out. "I mean, yes! That was totally adequate!" That didn't come out right either. "I mean, it was extremely generous of you!"

"And yet you seek to shake me down for more, even as my people toil to rebuild what was lost."

"We're not trying to shake you down," said Stacy. "But Dave's been cursed with lycanthropy. We need a thousand gold pieces before the next full moon to get him cured, and I didn't know who else to turn to."

Mayor Merriweather stopped to glower at Stacy. "Need I remind you that you are speaking to a lycanthrope?"

Finally, Dave got the satisfaction of seeing some egg on Stacy's face.

"I'm sorry," she said. "I didn't mean to –"

"What you refer to as a curse, others would consider a blessing."

"Right?" said Dave. "That's exactly what I've been trying to tell her, but she refuses to hear it."

Mayor Merriweather smiled at Dave. "And what is the nature of your new gift?"

"I'm a wererat."

The mayor's smile vanished as he took a step back from Dave. "Oh, dear. No, that is most definitely a curse. Those are vile and filthy creatures. You should get that sorted out as quickly as possible. In the meantime, keep your disgusting sperm away from my citizens."

"So you understand our problem," said Stacy. "All I'm asking for is a loan, and that's only because we don't have much time left. I promise we'll pay you back."

Mayor Merriweather started walking again. "I am sorry, good lady, but I have invested nearly all of my coin into rebuilding and improving this city. Look around and see how far we have come!"

"It's very impressive."

"Would that I could see it through your eyes. I have almost forgotten how small and quaint this town used to be." The mayor sighed. "But I am afraid I cannot allow you to stay here. I have promised you roasted beef sandwiches, and I shall honor that promise. But after that, I must insist you leave immediately. I shall not risk having my citizens turn into cowardly, foul-smelling abominations."

Dave didn't even bother trying to argue with this old prick set in his racist ways. Fuck him and his shitty town.

"You've got some sway around here," said Stacy. "Are there any clerics here that you might persuade to lift Dave's curse?"

Mayor Merriweather chuckled. "It is true that we are growing swiftly, but this town is not yet large enough to support a temple. The way I see it, you have two options. You can kill him before he escapes and infects other people, or –"

"Fuck this," said Dave. "I think we've heard enough. Let's get out of this shithole."

The mayor scowled at him. "I shall have none of that kind of talk in my town, young man. I have half a mind to rescind my offer of a roasted beef sandwich."

"It's *roast* beef, and you can shove your offer up your wrinkled asshole."

"Dave!" said Stacy. "You're being rude!"

"He just suggested you kill me!"

"That wasn't a suggestion. It was merely an option."

"To be fair," said Mayor Merriweather. "It is the safer of the two options, so I would lean toward suggesting it."

"Still, that's no excuse for interrupting." She stared coldly at Dave. "Especially when he was about to present an alternative to killing you."

Dave sighed. "Fine. What's the second option?"

"You could sell that Immovable Rod I gave you. That should easily fetch three or four thousand gold pieces.

# Critical Failures VIII

Perhaps a little less since you are in such a hurry to get rid of it, but certainly more than enough to cover the cost required to remove your curse."

"That would be a great option if I still had it."

The mayor's muscles tensed under his papery sun-weathered skin. "You fat, ungrateful oaf! Mere weeks have passed since I gave you such a valuable gift, and you have already given it away to some sewer-dwelling rat whore!"

That was quite an assumption he was making. In truth, Dave had last seen his Immovable Rod when Katherine's half-drow friend used it to kill a dragon outside of Cardinia. Craftsmen, butchers, alchemists, and opportunists had swarmed on the dragon corpses within hours of the end of the battle, stripping them of their hides, meat, bones, and whatever else they thought they might be able to sell. No doubt someone had discovered what was keeping one of the dead dragons suspended in the air.

But the truth wouldn't get Dave any closer to not getting murdered, so he let Mayor Merriweather keep thinking his own theory was correct.

"So what if I did? She's probably got it all the way up her furry rat snatch right now while she waits for me to come back and give her the real thing."

"Dave!" said Stacy.

Mayor Merriweather laughed. "I hope for her sake that you are able to remove your trousers first."

Stacy covered her mouth as she stifled a laugh at Dave's expense. Even Alroth, who hadn't said shit this entire time, let out a little snort.

Dave wanted to hit back with something scathing, but he was too flustered to think of anything. The moment was slipping away when Stacy pulled it right out from under him.

"Oh, look. There's the Arby's. That's adorable."

# Robert Bevan

It was little more than a lemonade stand with a glowing neon Arby's sign that Goosewaddle must have swiped from another location. A small gathering of would-be customers impatiently waited while Paul, the assistant manager of Goosewaddle's Cardinia restaurant, argued with the goblin driver of a delivery cart that appeared to be empty.

"I was promised ten gold pieces," said the goblin. His voice sounded familiar to Dave. But while he was wearing an Arby's uniform shirt that was too large for him, Dave was pretty sure he wasn't one of Goosewaddle's Scooby gang.

"You are an hour late with the delivery," said Paul. "If you want to be paid in full, I suggest you show up on time. Consider yourself lucky I'm offering you five gold pieces. That's more than your average gobber makes in a month."

Several people in the crowd whispered and exchanged uncomfortable glances. Dave remembered hearing that *gobber* was the goblin equivalent to the N-word.

"Very well," said the goblin, hanging his head and reaching under his shirt. "I shall take it."

Paul gave him a smug grin and held up a small coin pouch. "That's more like it. I should dock you another gold piece for talking back to me, but I'm feeling –"

"I apologize," said the goblin, pulling something out from under his shirt. "I was not finished. I meant, I shall take it up with Professor Goosewaddle."

"What? No!"

The shiny black object in the goblin's hands turned out to be a flip phone. He grinned as he began pressing the keys with both thumbs.

"There's no need to get Professor Goosewaddle involved!" said Paul. "How about six? I'll give you six gold pieces!" When the goblin stopped typing and looked up from his phone, Paul sighed with relief.

"Is *gobber* spelled with one 'b' or two?"

## Critical Failures VIII

"Please!" pleaded Paul. "Eight gold pieces!"

The goblin laughed. "I was only jesting with you."

Paul sighed again. "Thank God."

"I know how to spell gobber." He grinned at Paul as he pressed a final button, and Dave remembered where he'd seen those beady little goblin eyes before.

"Shorty?" he said.

The goblin's grin vanished as his giant head pivoted in Dave's direction. "Who are you?"

"Do you know this person?" asked Stacy.

Dave ignored her, stepping closer to the mule-drawn cart. "You were my friend's jailer in Algor. He helped you escape."

"Oh yes. You're one of *that* group. Funny, I do not seem to remember you. I remember the halfling, of course. And there was a half-orc."

"That's Cooper," said Dave.

"And an Elf. Julia, was it?"

"Julian."

Shorty thought for a moment. "And I think I remember a half-elven woman with a wolf and a sickly human who I was not allowed to eat."

"You remember Chaz, but you don't remember me?"

"Good evening, Paul," said Mayor Merriweather. "I would like to procure four of your roasted beef sandwiches, and two large boxes of curled potatoes. You may charge it to my account."

"I'm afraid I can't do that, Mr. Mayor. You see –"

"We have been waiting here for an hour!" shouted one of the waiting customers. "The cart has arrived! What is the delay?"

"I'm very sorry!" said Paul. "But it's not my fault. The driver is being uncooperative."

Shorty grinned at Paul, then hopped down from his wagon and approached Dave and Stacy. "I am certain I would have remembered your friend." He grinned at Stacy. "What is your name?"

"I'm Stacy. I must have arrived after the two of you met. Hey, listen. I wonder if you'd be interested in accompanying us on a little recovery mission."

"What?" said Dave. "Stacy, I don't know if it's such a good idea to –"

"Quiet, dwarf!" snapped Shorty. His gaze fell to Dave's crotch. "You have already had your emission. Let the lady state her proposal."

Stacy smiled at him. "Thank you. This is my friend Alroth and his Animal Companion, Lucia."

"How do you do?" said Alroth.

"They're from the Cedar Wilds, where they claim to have witnessed some of your people enslaved by ettins."

Dave appreciated the angle she was going with. Instead of straight up asking for help with her own goals, she was trying to appeal to his feelings as a goblin.

"Impossible," said Shorty. "I have no people."

"I meant goblins."

Shorty shrugged. "I have no goblins either. When I am able to afford a slave, I will buy a fat stupid dwarf. He shall carry me upon his shoulders and tell me stories while I fall asleep."

Stacy might have had as high a Charisma score as Julian's, but she clearly hadn't put as many ranks in Diplomacy as he had. And she severely overestimated how much of a shit goblins gave about the well-being of other goblins.

"I was wondering if you'd be interested in coming with us to rescue them," said Stacy.

Shorty scratched his chin. "It sounds dangerous."

"I won't lie. It could very well be dangerous. But we'll have Alroth's fighting skills and knowledge of the terrain, which should give us an upper hand. Dave is a skilled... Dave has healing magic. You will be our inside man, preparing the goblins to revolt. And I'm pretty much just awesome at everything."

"So your plan involves me getting captured by ettins?"

Stacy frowned. "We don't really have much of a plan yet. I just came up with that on the spot."

"Very impressive. I like it. How much?"

"I can offer you fifty gold pieces."

Dave could practically see dollar signs in Shorty's eyes, despite his poor attempt to hide his excitement.

"I wish to be paid upfront." Shorty nodded back toward Paul. "I have been cheated by humans before."

"We completely understand," said Alroth, a hint of hopeful desperation in his voice. When Stacy was hitting up Mayor Merriweather for the money she wanted, he probably suspected they were going to ditch him. But now that Stacy seemed resigned to going along with him, he wanted to be as accommodating as he could toward whatever scheme she had in mind. "However, if we pay you now, the ettins are just going to take it away from you when they take you prisoner. It is better if we hold on to the money until after we have taken care of the ettins."

Shorty folded his arms. "I am afraid those terms are unacceptable."

"No hard feelings," Stacy said with a smile. "You're probably better off working for Paul. We'll just have to find ourselves a different goblin." She turned as if to walk away.

"Wait!"

Stacy turned back to him. "Yes?"

Dave had to admit, she was a hell of a lot better at playing it cool than Shorty was.

"May I ride upon the dwarf's shoulders?"

Dave laughed. "Like hell you –"

"Sure," said Stacy.

"What?" Dave objected. "I didn't agree to –"

Shorty removed his Arby's uniform shirt. "You have yourself a deal." He crumpled the shirt into a ball and threw it at Paul, who was still trying to calm the hungry crowd.

"Please!" said Paul. "If you'll just be a little more patient, we'll have this resolved in a matter of – AUGH!" He swatted at Shorty's shirt like it was a bat attacking his face. "What the... Where are you? What is the meaning of this?" He scanned the crowd, looking for Shorty as he held up the Arby's shirt.

Dave looked down to find that Shorty had indeed disappeared. "Where'd he go?"

"I don't know," said Stacy. "He was here just a second ago."

"OW!" cried Paul as a shiny black flip phone bounced off his head. "Filthy little gobber!"

"PAUL!" shouted Professor Goosewaddle, emerging from the back of the crowd with Jennifer, his second in command. "What is going on here?"

Dave tried to hide behind Stacy.

"Professor Goosewaddle!" said Paul with a nervous laugh. "To what do I owe the pleasure?"

"Why is the food not unloaded? Where is Shorty?"

"Here I am," said Shorty, climbing back up onto the delivery cart.

"He's a quick one," whispered Stacy. "And he's got some moxie. I think we did well to recruit him."

"Open the stasis portal at once," demanded Professor Goosewaddle.

Shorty nodded. "Right away, Professor." He pulled the cart up about an inch away from the side of the Arby's stand. From the back of the seemingly empty cart, he produced a couple of ten-foot wooden poles and a rolled up canvas sheet. Quickly and efficiently, he set up something that looked like an old-timey projector screen.

"We have the meats," he said triumphantly as the canvas screen became a doorway to a pile of foil-wrapped roast beef sandwiches and the freshest looking curly fries Dave had ever seen.

"Very good," said Professor Goosewaddle. "Jennifer, you take over." He levitated high enough to grab Paul by the ear and drag him to the other side of the stand. "Now, please explain to me the message I just received on my cellular telephone!"

"Whatever he said, it was a lie!" said Paul. "I promise!"

"He said you refused to pay him."

"He was an hour late, so it didn't seem right to pay him the full amount. I offered him half." Paul held up the pouch meant for Shorty.

"Meanwhile, all these people waited even longer to eat!" Professor Goosewaddle snatched the pouch from Paul's hand and weighed it in his own. "Where is the rest?"

Paul dug in his pocket. "I wasn't going to keep it, I swear. I was just holding onto it until I could return it to you."

Goosewaddle held the coin pouch open for Paul to drop the remaining coins in. "Shorty!"

"Yes, Professor?" said Shorty, peeking out from behind the inter-dimensional projector screen.

Goosewaddle tossed him the coin pouch. "Thank you for your service. Jennifer, see that he gets a roasted beef sandwich, on the house."

"You got it," said Jennifer as she busily swapped sandwiches for coins to the mass of hungry customers.

"I'm very sorry, Professor," said Paul. "I was only trying to –"

"I have been too soft on you," interrupted Goosewaddle, seizing him by the ear again. "I shall have to instruct Fred and Daphne to be more diligent in your sensitivity training."

"NO!" cried Paul, wincing from Goosewaddle's vice-like ear pinch. "Not sensitivity training! Anything but –"

With a few sparks of electricity and a puff of green smoke, they both vanished. Dave guessed that Paul was mere seconds away from being beaten with sticks by the goblin crew of Cardinia's Arby's.

"I hope everyone is hungry," said Mayor Merriweather, returning from the booth with four sandwiches and a big smile. He handed the sandwiches out. "One for the lady, one for the ranger, one for me." He stared coldly at Dave. "And one for the leopard." He tossed the remaining sandwich on the ground in front of Lucia.

Dave rolled his eyes and sighed.

"Thank you, Mayor," said Stacy. "That's very generous of you." She tucked her sandwich into her bag. "I think I'll save mine for –"

"Who do you think you are coming around here looking like that?" said Jennifer, her sharp tone cutting through the din of the crowd. Several nearby customers apologized before the crowd went completely silent, but her smoldering glare was focused downward.

"I believe I was promised a roasted beef sandwich," Shorty responded uncertainly, as if now rethinking whether or not redeeming the compensation was worth it.

"You represent Arby's. Where is your uniform?"

"I am afraid I have decided to tender my resignation."

"After I worked so hard to see that your people were paid a decent wage," said Jennifer. "How could you just turn your back on us like that?"

"My skills were more highly valued elsewhere."

*No no no. Don't look this way. Don't look this – Shit!*

Jennifer's gaze pivoted to Dave and Stacy like the barrel of a high-caliber rifle. The crowd parted so as not to be caught in the line of fire. Shorty, now visible, looked apologetically at them.

"You!" said Jennifer. "Weren't you warned to stay away from Arby's?"

# Critical Failures VIII

"I - I took that to mean the Cardinian Arby's specifically," Stacy explained with a slight tremble in her voice. "We didn't even know you'd expanded."

"That tubby piece of shit hiding behind you is the only one expanding around here." That got a few nervous chuckles from the crowd, and it pissed off Dave.

"I'm not hiding!" he said, stepping out from behind Stacy. "And you don't own Port Town. We were just minding our own business, just like you ought to mind yours." He felt emboldened by his confidence that Stacy would stall her at least long enough for him to turn into a rat and run away.

"Minding your own business?" said Jennifer. "You're poaching my employees!"

Dave had to admit she had a point there. "I know this doesn't look good," he tried to explain, unsure of how he was going to follow that. "But we didn't come here with the intention of –"

"You're dead, dwarf." Jennifer pulled a cell phone out of her pocket and started to tap furiously at the buttons. "When Professor Goosewaddle hears about this, you're getting a fireball right up the –"

"Enough!" said Mayor Merriweather, causing Jennifer to cease texting. "This is my town, Jennifer. If you and the professor would like to continue doing business here, you would do well not to threaten my guests."

Jennifer slipped the phone back into her pocket and bowed her head. "Yes, Mayor Merriweather. I apologize."

Weretiger or not, Dave had no doubt that Jennifer would chase down the mayor and beat him savagely with a broom for talking to her like that if he wasn't an integral part of their business expansion into Port Town, but such was the nature of capitalism.

Mayor Merriweather frowned at Stacy. "They were just leaving, anyway." He no doubt also had a financial stake in a thriving Port Town Arby's.

Shorty glanced up timidly at Jennifer like he was waiting for her permission to leave.

Jennifer threw a sandwich at his head. "Go on, get out of here."

"Thank you." Shorty picked up his sandwich and hurried toward Dave and Stacy.

"Enjoy working for the dwarf!" Jennifer called out after him. "Have fun washing the jizz out of his pants!"

The crowd had themselves a nice hearty laugh at that, then commerce resumed.

It was all the humiliation Dave could take for one day. He stomped back toward the rear end of town while Stacy and Alroth said their thank yous and goodbyes to the mayor.

He didn't know if he had it in him to go the distance with regard to taking vengeance on his enemies and coming out on top. As appealing as the fantasy was, maybe that just wasn't him.

He'd judged Tim's decision to quit school to run a chicken restaurant to be a mistake. As it turned out, he was probably right, but did Dave really have so much more to show for his decision to stay in school and be some cog in a corporate machine? The Chicken Hut was crap, but at least Tim had tried and failed at something. The ability to make bold choices, both middle fingers raised to improbable odds, was what it took to achieve greatness. But that wasn't Dave. The best he could ever hope to achieve was the high end of okayness. It was almost laughable to think he'd ever be respected by anyone.

"Dave!" Stacy called out behind him. "Wait up!"

Dave continued walking. He'd be lagging behind them soon enough.

# Critical Failures VIII

"These roasted beef sandwiches are amazing!" said Alroth. "Truly, I must travel to Port Town more often."

"Come on, Dave," Stacy said cheerily when she caught up to him. "Buck up. You can't let them get to you like that."

"Them?" He glared up at her. "If I recall correctly, it was you who started laying into me about... Just leave me alone."

"You have to admit, you kind of had it coming."

Shorty stifled a laugh.

Stacy shushed him. "I was still upset by the other night in the inn, and you dropped an opportunity to ridicule you right in my lap."

"That is better than what he dropped in his own."

"Shut up, Shorty!"

Dave sighed. "Of course you're going to bring up the inn again. Am I ever going to live that down?"

"Sorry, Dave, but that was fucked up. And it's kind of hard for me to forgive you when I don't think you'd feel in the least bit ashamed of yourself if I hadn't witnessed the whole thing."

"You have no idea how I feel." In truth, Dave felt pretty fucking disgusted with himself.

"But I know it's not completely your fault," said Stacy. "That's why I'm trying to help you. From now on, I'll try to go a little easier on you until we can get you cured."

Cured. That was more insulting than any of the jizz comments, because he knew she meant it. Like he was crawling with AIDS or something. Why couldn't anyone see that what he had was a gift? Who wouldn't want the ability to shapeshift? It's not like he had to get in some quota of rat time. It was just an option. Admittedly, it came with a few personality kinks that he still had to work out, but that would be much easier to do if everyone would stop being such an asshole to him all the time. Otherwise, he was no different than he'd ever been.

"I got you something," said Stacy, reaching into her bag. She pulled out the roast beef sandwich Mayor Merriweather had given her and offered it to him.

Dave scoffed. "Keep your guilt burger. I'm not hungry."

"Suit yourself. Alroth, would you like another –"

Dave snatched it out of her hand faster than he knew he could move. He was actually very hungry, and he longed to get the taste of pickled pig dick out of his mouth. Closing his eyes as he bit into it, he let himself drift back to a memory of his former life, sitting in a booth at Arby's and enjoying a roast beef sandwich and an order of curly fries.

Neither the memory nor the sandwich lasted nearly as long as he would have liked. All too soon, he opened his eyes to find himself a shitty dwarf on the outskirts of a shitty town in a shitty game world, and he was still hungry.

# CHAPTER 32

Katherine woke up to the soothing sound of heavy rain. The cool morning air smelled pleasantly of sea salt and wood smoke. Had she left the window open all night? She hoped the neighbor's apartment wasn't on fire as she pulled her blanket up over her shoulder and dug her hand under her pillow to squeeze out some of the lumps.

When the pillow gave her a low warning growl, she opened her eyes.

"What the fuck?"

"Good morning," said a skinny, half-naked, pointy-eared black man sitting next to a campfire.

"Jay?" Memories of her current life flooded in, muddying the image of the real world she'd been dreaming about. She pushed herself up and looked down at her pillow. "Butterbean?"

"Did you have some nice dreams?" asked Jay.

Katherine yawned, trying to recall what she had been dreaming about just a few seconds ago. "I think so, but I can't remember."

"Something about chicken?"

She must have been talking in her sleep. Had she really been dreaming about the Chicken Hut? Maybe it wasn't such a great dream after all. Her mind had just needed to retreat to somewhere familiar for a while.

"Yeah, maybe." Looking down, she discovered that her blanket was actually Jay's shirt. That explained why he was topless. She balled it up and tossed it over the fire to him. "Thanks, but you didn't have to do that."

"It seemed like the chivalrous move. Chivalry is still a thing in this world, isn't it?"

Katherine shrugged. Most of the interactions she'd had here had been with a bunch of mopey drunks in a shitty pub. The closest she'd come to experiencing anything like chivalry was when she lived with Millard, and he murdered her.

"Thank you," she said. "It was thoughtful of you, but you could have taken the clothes off one of the bodies in my Bag of Holding so you wouldn't be cold."

Jay grimaced. "I think I'd rather be cold." He pulled his shirt on and stood up. "I'll be right back. I've got to step away and answer Nature's call."

Katherine watched him for a couple of steps before she realized he wasn't stepping as far away as she'd expected. When he stopped abruptly at the edge of the dry sand, she turned her gaze toward the sea. Only then did it occur to her that she was a lot drier than she ought to be with all the rain falling down around her. Looking up, she discovered that they were all under a rocky outcropping jutting out over the sand. She was sure she would have remembered such a prominent feature no matter how tired she'd been the night before.

"How did we get here?" she asked. "I don't remember there being a giant rock over our heads when I fell asleep last night."

"I dragged you here when it started to rain," Jay answered to the trickle of pee on wet sand. "You're quite the sound sleeper."

"Did you get any sleep?"

"A little. Butterbean and I took turns keeping an eye out for –"

# Critical Failures VIII

"You there!" shouted a voice to Katherine's right. Turning that direction, she saw two human men approaching through the rain. They were armed with long spears and wore identical white tunics, suggesting that they were part of some military organization. But their flabby physiques, betrayed by their wet clothes clinging to their skin, didn't reflect a great deal of intense physical training. "Who are you?"

"I'm Katherine," she said. "This is my friend, Jay." It couldn't hurt to casually point out that they were also accompanied by a wolf. "And this is my Animal Companion, Butterbean. Who the hell are you?"

They stopped about fifteen feet away from Katherine and Butterbean, spears at the ready in front of them.

"We are Knights of Jordan," said the one on the left. "It is our sacred quest to retrieve and return the artifacts which have been stolen from our master."

Katherine sighed. "These fucking guys again."

"No ships were seized last night," said the one on the right. "By what means did you arrive on this island?"

Katherine tried to think of a lie, but Jay beat her to it.

"Our ship was boarded by some of your men," he said. "They demanded the captain's surrender, but the captain said he'd be damned if he would surrender to a band of dickless zealots."

"You dare call the Knights of Jordan dickless zealots?"

"His words," said Jay. "Certainly not mine. Your men put up a hell of a fight. But when the captain saw that the fight was lost, he put a hole in his own hull. He said he would rather let it rest for eternity on the ocean floor than be used to further the ends of some pansy ass semen guzzling bard."

"Semen guzzling bard!" shouted the man on the left. "How dare you speak of the magnificent Jordan Knight in such irreverent terms!"

Katherine appreciated the way Jay was embellishing on actual events to sell his story, and how he added the part about the ship sinking to keep them from searching for corroborating evidence to back up their claims, but she shared a bit of the Knights' feelings about how he was insulting Jordan Knight. She'd gone through a New Kids phase in elementary school.

"Again, those were the captain's words," Jay explained. "He wasn't a nice man. As for us, we're huge fans of Jordan Knight."

"I do not believe you," said the man on the right. "How did the two of you and this wolf escape the battle?"

"We escaped in one of the ship's boarding vessels."

Anticipating their next question, Katherine chimed in. "That's the last of it, burning in our fire."

Jay let out a nearly inaudible sigh. He'd almost slipped up with that one.

The man on the right looked convinced, but the one on the left narrowed his eyes skeptically at Jay. "If you are truly fans of Jordan Knight as you claim, then perhaps you can sing us a bit from one of his songs."

Katherine and Jay looked at one another, then back at the Knights of Jordan. "Oh, oh, oh, oh, oh."

Both Knights smiled as if their hearts were melting like warm butter.

"That is one of my favorites," said the one on the right.

"Mine too," said the skeptical one.

Kathrine smiled. "It's a classic!"

The Knight nodded. "Indeed, it is. Now, we shall have a quick search through your belongings, and then you may go on your way."

"Why do you want to search through our belongings?" asked Katherine. No amount of singing would get her out of having to explain the dead bodies in her Bag of Holding. The

## Critical Failures VIII

very best she could hope for was that their greed might overshadow their fanaticism, and they'd offer to keep the bodies their little secret if she agreed to give them the bag.

"We reserve the right to inspect anyone's belongings for our master's stolen treasure."

"The right under whose authority?" asked Katherine, trying her best to sound more curious than argumentative. "It was my understanding that this island is governed by drow."

The two Knights chuckled, then the skeptic stopped abruptly.

"Those abominations of darkness may think they are in control, cowering inside their tower, but the Knights of Jordan keep the peace over the streets and harbors." He wagged his spear at Katherine. "But these give us all the authority we require. Now hand over your bag at once."

Her hope for finding a peaceful resolution dwindling, Katherine held open her Bag of Holding with her thumbs tucked on the outside of the mouth and hoped Jay and Butterbean would be quick to follow her lead.

"Here," she said, holding the bag in front of her and taking a step closer to the skeptical Knight, who was also the smaller of the two and seemed to have the stronger personality. "I don't think there's anything in here your master would be even remotely interested in."

The knight righted his spear to let her approach and smiled smugly at her. "I shall be the judge of that."

"Fine." When she got close enough, she flipped the bag over his head and pulled down as hard as she could. "Have a look for yourself!"

"Huh?" said the other Knight, who had been keeping a wary eye on Butterbean.

"Katherine!" said Jay. "What are you doing?"

"What does it look like?" Katherine kept all her Strength and weight on the bag as the Knight dropped his spear to use both hands to try to pull it off of his head. "Help me!" She tried to maneuver so that he was between her and his companion, but she only moved fast enough to catch a spear in the upper arm that had been intended for her heart.

"Fuck!" she cried, letting go of the bag. Her captive dropped to his knees and pulled the bag off his head as Katherine stood defenseless for a second stabbing.

The larger knight brought his spear back for another thrust, but Jay and Butterbean charged at him from the side. Jay hit him like he was sacking a quarterback, clearly intending to prevent further violence rather than to cause harm. Butterbean was less forgiving, and the Knight had his hands full trying to keep from getting his face torn off.

"Bodies!" cried the smaller Knight as he scrambled on his hands and knees for his dropped spear. "Her bag is filled with dead bodies!" He grabbed for the spear, but Katherine stepped on it. With her other foot, she kicked him in the face.

When he fell back on his ass, Katherine snatched up his spear before he could get up again.

"You mongrel whore!" he said as he got up to charge at her.

Katherine twirled the spear around and planted the butt end in the sand just in time to catch her attacker in the gut with the business end. He was charging at her so hard that it went straight through him.

He slid further down the shaft as he fell lifelessly on the sand.

"Rickel!" cried the other Knight. His face and arms were bleeding from tooth and claw wounds, but Butterbean had broken off his attack when he saw someone else going after Katherine. "You... you killed him!"

# Critical Failures VIII

Katherine frowned down at the dead man on the beach. "I was just holding the spear. He ran into it."

Jay leaned over the other side of the Knight he was sitting on and threw up.

"Oh, come on," said Katherine. "It was self defense. They were trying to do the same thing to us." She pointed to the bleeding gash on her arm. "Look. They drew first blood."

"I know," said Jay. "I just wasn't prepared for…" He gagged at the sight of the bloody spear shaft sticking out of Rickel's back. "Oh God, that's so gross."

"Well, you'd better turn away again, because this isn't going to be any less gross."

Jay turned back toward the sea. "What are you going to do to him?" His tone sounded accusatory.

"I'm just pulling the spear out of his gut. I meant that it won't be pleasant to watch."

It wasn't pleasant to listen to either. The shaft slid out quietly enough, but the barbed head grabbed some guts on the way back through. Katherine was able to muscle it out eventually, but she took half of his small intestine out with it. It sounded like she was trying to pull her leg out of knee-deep mud.

"Can't you just break it in half and pull out both ends?"

"I could have, but who knows when an extra spear might come in handy. It's not like he's any deader now. Anyway, what's done is done."

Jay turned around to look at her, then glanced down at the entrails on the beach and quickly turned away again before he added to his vomit puddle.

"Help!" cried the remaining Knight of Jordan. "Murderer! MURDERER!"

"Shut him up!" said Katherine.

"How?" asked Jay, trying to force his hand into the Knight's mouth when he opened it to keep shouting.

"MURDER–mph!"

"Ow!" Jay jerked his hand away. "Dude bit me!"

"What did you expect?" said Katherine. "I meant knock him out."

Jay punched his head a few times, but Katherine could tell he was holding back.

"Get out of the way." She walked over to the Knight. "Subdual." She raised a knee, then brought her foot down hard on his head.

Jay stared up at her. "Subdual?"

"It's a little trick I picked up from the guys. Unless you're using a weapon, you won't kill a person you're attacking if you specify that you only want to subdue him."

"So he's..."

"He'll be fine. Help me stuff him into the bag."

"What? Why?"

"We can't very well leave him here," said Katherine. "He'll rat us out as soon as he wakes up."

"Can he survive in there?"

"As long as we replace his air every ten minutes." Katherine put the unconscious Knight's feet in the bag and started pulling it up his legs. "Don't worry. I've done this before."

It took a bit of struggling, but they managed to get him in the bag.

Jay sat on the sand and stared glumly at the dead Knight. "What do we do with him?"

"What do you think?" said Katherine. "We stuff him in the bag."

"What for? Shouldn't we bury him?"

"We don't have time for that right now. We've got shit to do. We'll bury him later."

Jay looked away while Katherine used the spear to pile the Knights intestines onto his body. To spare Jay any more emotional trauma, she took the bag up chest deep before asking him to help with the rest.

After she put the spears in the bag, Katherine washed her hands in the sea, scrubbing them with a handful of sand. The heavy rain felt good on her skin after that little workout. She couldn't remember the last time she'd had a proper shower. Hopefully the rain would flush out some of her acquired funk.

When she returned, she found Jay sitting by the fire roasting a pair of squid steaks.

"What are you doing?" she said, kicking some clean sand over spots that hadn't completely absorbed all the blood. "Pack it up. We've got to get moving."

"I'm sorry. I just puked up all the sustenance I had in me. I imagine we've got a busy day ahead of us, and I'd rather not do that on an empty stomach."

Katherine had to admit he had a good point. "Okay, but let's take them to go. I think I cleaned up most of the evidence that there was a fight here, but I'd like to be as far away as possible if anyone should happen to notice anything."

"These should be done in a minute."

Katherine picked up her Bag of Holding and reached inside. "Carbon dioxide." After she felt the stale warmth of the bag's exhalation, she held it wide open and waved it up and down.

"What's that you're doing?" asked Jay.

"I'm replacing the air in the bag so that guy can keep breathing. We've got to do this every ten minutes."

"Is that not going to look incredibly suspicious in a populated area?"

"It's a hell of a lot less suspicious than leaving this guy free to rat us out to the rest of Jonestown. We'll just have to duck into alleys or something. We'll figure it out."

When Jay finished cooking, he smothered the fire with sand, then looked up and down the beach. Not much was visible beyond a hundred feet in either direction.

"You got a preference for which way to go?" asked Katherine.

Jay swallowed a big bite of roasted squid. "Those guys had to have come from somewhere. I figure the way to town is probably that way."

Katherine smiled at him. "Look at you, putting those Rogue and Ranger skills to good use."

"A four-year-old could have come to that conclusion."

Katherine hadn't come to that conclusion. But rather than take that as an insult, she reassured herself that she would have eventually come to that conclusion if she'd put any thought into it.

Beyond the rocky outcropping, the beach ended at an ancient stone wall. Plants grew through most of the cracks, and most of the mortar between the black stones had eroded away.

"This doesn't look too hard to climb," said Jay. "It might save us some time."

Katherine looked doubtfully up at the fifteen foot high wall. "Wouldn't it be better to go in through a gate, though? What if we get caught trying to sneak in over a wall? These guys are pretty paranoid as it is, and that's going to look really suspicious."

"If they're that paranoid, they'll have guards posted at the entrance who are also going to want to look through our shit. If you thought a few random dead bodies looked bad, how do you think they're going to react to finding two of their own?"

"That's true." Katherine was glad he brought this up before they arrived at a gate. She needed to start thinking about how she could talk their way through.

# Critical Failures VIII

"Let me at least climb up and take a peek over the wall," he said. "I'll be discreet. That's, like, literally the only thing I'm any good at."

Katherine nodded. "Okay, but make it quick."

After a few seconds of testing, Jay found some adequate hand and footholds to start climbing. When he reached the top, he pulled himself up until his head was just over the wall. Katherine kept a watchful eye out for another patrol. However well-hidden Jay might have been to anyone on the other side of the wall, he was anything but discreet-looking with his whole body dangling from the top of this side.

More than two minutes passed before Katherine finally lost patience. What the hell was he looking at that was so goddamn interesting?

"Well?" she whispered. "What do you see?"

Jay hopped down from the wall. "Good news and bad news."

"What's the bad news?" asked Katherine.

"This place is crawling with Knights of Jordan. Maybe there aren't so many people out because of the rain, but I counted about one Knight for every two regular townsfolk walking around. This island must be pretty important to them."

"It's a trading hub. Lots of boats coming in for them to seize. What's the good news?" Katherine really hoped the answer to that question would outweigh the bad news.

"I've got two pieces of good news, actually," said Jay.

"I'll take all I can get. Hit me."

"I saw a good spot for us to climb over unseen about twenty yards back."

"That's something." Katherine was more concerned with how they were going to maneuver through all those Knights of Jordan, but hopefully Jay was saving the best for last. "What else?"

"The Knights are made up of diverse races and genders."

Katherine nodded. "Okay. Go on."

"That's it."

"How the hell does that count as good news?" asked Katherine before she could stop herself.

*Oh, no! I've done it again!*

"I'm sorry," she said. "I didn't mean it like that. Of course I think it's important for organizations to strive for diversity and equality, even cults. There's no reason why you people..." *Shit, you're not supposed to say you people.* "...by which I mean half-elves..." *Shit, I'm a half-elf!* "I mean, *we* people, should be excluded from any cult we wish to join." After a second or two of uncomfortable silence, she smiled apologetically. "Has it been ten minutes?" She reached into the Bag of Holding. "Carbon dioxide." Spinning around with the mouth of the bag held open, she hoped he wouldn't still be staring at her with that exasperated look on his face when she stopped.

He was.

"I was thinking that it might be easy for us to pass ourselves off as Knights of Jordan," he said. "You know, hide in plain sight. We could walk around town without getting stopped every five minutes."

"That's a great idea!" said Katherine, hoping her enthusiasm would help them get through the awkwardness more quickly. In truth, she didn't know how they were supposed to pass themselves off as Knights of Jordan without even having – She had an idea of her own. "Hey! We have two of their tunics and spears in my bag!"

Jay gave her a confused look. "I know that. How would that have been a great idea if we didn't have those?"

"I don't know. We're brainstorming. Any idea's a great idea, right?"

Jay laughed. "I'm not so sure about your squid ink blackface idea from last night."

# Critical Failures VIII

It was effectively the same idea, only now he was taking credit for it while making her out to be a racist.

But Katherine decided to be a bigger person and keep those thoughts to herself. She put her hand inside the Bag of Holding.

"Knight of Jordan tunic." When she felt the wet fabric in her hand, she pulled it out and tossed it to Jay. Then she pulled out the second one for herself.

"So," said Jay, staring at the bag. "Are they naked in there now?"

Katherine shrugged. "I guess that depends on if they were wearing anything underneath these." She slipped the tunic on over her regular clothes. "How do I look?"

Jay shrugged. "It's not very flattering."

"Can I pass for one of those assholes or not?"

"I guess we'll find out." Jay slipped on his own tunic, then frowned at the blood all over the front of it. "I'm not sure this is going to work."

"You'll be fine," said Katherine. "I'm sure these guys get stabbed all the time. Just act injured."

Jay sighed. "I guess that's the best we can do." He led her back along the wall twenty yards. "This should be the best place to go over. There are some thick bushes growing a few feet away from the wall. If we can drop behind those, we'll be able to wait for an opportune time to walk casually into town."

"Sounds good."

Jay climbed the wall more confidently this time. He was on the other side in no time, leaving Katherine feeling alone and exposed.

*Calm down, Katherine. He's not going anywhere. He's a black man covered in blood in an unfamiliar town. A less enlightened person might jump to the wrong conclusion. Anyway, he needs you way more than you need him.*

"Jay?" she called out just over the sound of the rain.

"Come on," he responded. "It's all clear."

Relieved at the sound of his voice, she held her Bag of Holding open for Butterbean. "You won't be in there long, I promise. I just need to get you over this wall."

Butterbean whined a little but obediently crawled into the bag.

"I'm sending Butterbean over," she said.

"Huh? Oh, okay."

Katherine tossed the bag over, then tried to find the holds Jay had used to climb the wall. Jay had made it look so easy that she was determined not to blow a Spider Climb spell so early in the day. But the wall was wet and slippery, and she had a hard time finding her footing. It would be easier if she had one of those...

"Jay?"

"What?" He sounded a little annoyed now.

"Can you toss me over one of those spears?"

A couple of seconds passed before he responded. "How do I do that?"

"Put your hand in the bag and say 'spear'."

"Spear. Oh, shit! That's so cool!"

Katherine laughed to herself until a spearhead passed within an inch of her face. "A little warning next time."

She backed away from the wall, then ran at it, using the spear to vault herself just high enough to grab the top. It was enough. She dropped the spear butt-first over the side, then grabbed the wall with both hands and pulled herself over.

Safely on the ground and concealed by bushes, she took a moment to catch her breath, then noticed something was out of sorts.

"Where's Butterbean?"

"How should I know?" asked Jay. "You said you were going to send him over, but then you... Oh wait, was he in the bag?"

## Critical Failures VIII

"Shit!" Katherine thrust her hand into the Bag of Holding. "Butterbean!"

Her Animal Companion spilled out with an annoyed growl, but no worse for the wear.

"Sorry," said Jay.

"It's not your fault. But it's time you learned how to use this bag. Our prisoner could probably use some fresh air. Why don't you give it a try?"

Jay nodded. "Good idea. So I just put my hand in the bag and say 'carbon dioxide', right?"

"Yes. That will cause all the carbon dioxide to be released from the bag. Then you need to wave it around to refill it with oxygen."

"You should put some plants in there."

Katherine thought that was an odd suggestion. "I'm not trying to make it a bed and breakfast. I'm just trying to keep this guy alive. Ideally, I'd rather not have anyone in there at all."

"Plants produce oxygen," said Jay. "And they absorb carbon dioxide. If you had some plants in there, you might not need to replace the air so often."

"That's actually a pretty good idea. But for now, give it a try."

Jay reached into the Bag of Holding. "Carbon dioxide." He jerked his hand out. "Whoa. That was weird. It was like the bag breathed on me."

Katherine smiled. "That's how you know it worked." She peeked up over the bushes. There were a few people milling around in the rain, including at least two with spears and white tunics, but nobody was looking their way. "The next part is going to be a little trickier, because it's hard to casually wave a bag around in the air without looking suspicious, and you need to get as much oxygen in there as possible."

Jay stood up, scanned their surroundings, then quickly waved the bag back and forth a few times before dropping back down behind the bushes.

"I don't think anyone saw me. But yeah, you're right. That's a lousy way to keep a low profile. We need to move fast and keep an eye out for the next place to switch out this guy's air."

"Agreed." Spears in hand, they stepped out into the town streets.

Hardly more than dirt paths where enough foot traffic had dissuaded grass from growing, the town's streets didn't appear to have any planning behind them. The mud and wood structures that passed for homes and businesses seemed equally haphazard.

The only structure Katherine could make out that appeared to have been built with any sense of permanence was the black stone tower atop the hill at the center of the island. At around four stories tall, even that wasn't terribly impressive compared to what she was used to seeing in Cardinia.

"That must be where the drow live," said Katherine. "That's where we need to go."

The dirt paths got wider as they went further into town. And while the buildings mostly looked like they'd been constructed by the first two Little Piggies, there were a hell of a lot of them. This was no bumpkin village. If it hadn't been pissing down rain, Katherine imagined these shitty roads would be bustling with all sorts of people coming and going to and from the harbors.

Some of the townsfolk they passed scowled at them with contempt, while others just kept their distance, seeming to hold their breath while they waited for Katherine and Jay to pass.

"I guess the costumes are working," Katherine whispered.

# Critical Failures VIII

Jay nodded. "The Knights of Jordan must have really done a number on this town. Let's duck between these two buildings and swap out the air while we've got the chance."

"Go ahead. I'll stay out here and keep watch."

"Carbon dioxide!" Jay bellowed a few seconds later like he was announcing the winner of Best Motion Picture.

"Shh!" Katherine snapped at him. "A whisper will do."

A few swishes of fabric later, Jay returned to the street and held out the bag to her.

"You hold on to it for now," she said, still preoccupied with what exactly they were going to say to the drow. "Roll it up and tuck it down the back of your pants."

"Will he be okay? That won't squish him?"

"The inside of the bag is made of extradimensional something or another. He won't know the difference. Hurry up. We've only got ten minutes before we have to do this again."

Jay did as he was instructed, and they started up the twisting dirt roads again, zigging and zagging their way toward the top of the hill.

"Hail Jordan!" proclaimed one of a pair of Knights approaching from the other direction. He raised his right palm in less of a Hitler salute and more like a 'talk to the hand'.

Katherine and Jay did their best to mimic the gesture.

"Hail Jordan," they repeated awkwardly.

"Fellow Knight!" said the other, staring at the blood streak running down Jay's tunic. "You are injured!"

"It's nothing, really." Jay quickly lowered his hand to cover the hole in his tunic. "It's just a scratch."

"Who did this to you?" demanded the one who'd spoken first. "Was it one of the drow?" He sounded like he was looking for an excuse to tangle with the drow.

"No," said Katherine. "It was just some drunk sailor." She quickly thought up a description that she hoped would send them on a wild goose chase. "A minotaur, with a peg leg."

"Did you search him?"

"Of course we did, very thoroughly. That's what we were doing when Jay–" Maybe it was best not to use their real names. "–braham caught a horn in the gut."

The Knight rubbed his stubbled chin. "If he put up a fight, it stands to reason he might be hiding something. Did you check his rectum?"

Katherine didn't know how to respond to that. She didn't want to come off as a lazy Knight of Jordan, but neither was she comfortable going on record that she'd fisted a minotaur ass. "Um..."

"Katholemew!" said Jay. "There *is* one place we didn't search!"

It took Katherine a second to realize that she was Katholemew. "Huh?"

"What if he had hollowed out a section of his peg leg? Surely, that would be large enough to smuggle away our master's prize."

"You didn't think to check the leg?" shrieked the second Knight. "Incompetent fools!"

"I'm sorry," said Katherine. "I got distracted. My friend had just gotten gored by a man-cow."

"You lack the Right Stuff to call yourselves Knights of Jordan!"

"Easy, Kaduin. We are but humble servants of Jordan Knight. To expect perfection is to claim to be his equal."

Kaduin nodded. "You are right, Madal. But it is vital that we remain diligent in our quest. Step by Step, just as our master has taught us."

Jay started to turn back, then doubled over in pain. "He couldn't have gotten far. We must go back."

## Critical Failures VIII

"You will only slow us down. How many one-legged minotaurs could there be on this island? We shall hunt this suspicious character down. You get to the temple at once and demand to be healed."

That worked out nicely. Katherine needed to go to the temple, anyway.

"I'm sorry," she said. "Which way is the temple located?"

The testier of the two Knights, Kaduin, rolled his eyes, then pointed back in the direction they'd come from. "It is only one of the two solid structures on this gods-forsaken pile of mud. Now stop wasting our time."

The other Knight, Madal, raised his open palm toward Jay. "Hang tough."

Jay glanced at Katherine, who nodded encouragingly, then slapped Madal's palm. "Right on."

Ten minutes and two air exchanges later, they were standing before a brick structure that looked more like a small town DMV than a holy temple. It was surrounded by marble pedestals that might have been meant for statues of gods or saints or whatever but seemed to have been unburdened for quite some time.

"Is this it?" asked Katherine.

"If there are only two solid structures on the island, I'd guess this is the other one." Jay looked up at the black tower looming overhead another hundred yards up the hill.

At the very least, they could ask whoever was here for directions. If they were lucky, they might even be offered a drink. Katherine walked up and knocked on the door.

"Enter," called a tired voice from inside.

Katherine pushed the door open into a dimly lit square room that smelled like mildew and incense. Five men in identical orange togas sat cross-legged on the floor in the same formation of dots on the 5-side of a die. In front of each of them stood a lit candle, and two golf ball sized polished granite orbs orbited each of their heads. Most of their concentration seemed to be focused on keeping the orbs in the air, but their eyes were all on her.

"Hi," she said uncomfortably. "I didn't mean to interrupt. My friend and I were looking for the Temple of..." It only now occurred to Katherine that she didn't know the name of the temple.

"This is the Temple of Oxlos," said the man in the center, a bit snippier than Katherine would have preferred. He rose to his feet and let his orbs descend gently into his open hand before tucking them into a pouch hanging around his waist. If the testicular imagery was unintentional, it had been a huge oversight.

"Oxlos," repeated Katherine. "That's just the temple I was looking for."

The monk stared disdainfully at Jay. "I trust you are in need of healing?"

Katherine stepped forward. "That would be fantastic. I've got a pretty nasty cut on my upper arm."

The monk's gaze moved from the bloody hole in Jay's tunic to Katherine's arm. He shrugged.

"Very well," he said, stepping forward and placing a hand on Katherine's shoulder. "Forgive me, blessed Oxlos, and shed your mercy on this unworthy stain upon your glory."

"That's not very –" Katherine forgot what she was saying as the healing power of Oxlos surged into her, making her weak in the knees. Her upper arm seared with pain for just a second as her wound fused together, then she felt better and more refreshed than she'd felt in a long time. "Holy shit, that was great. Thank you, Mr..."

"My name is Thibil," he said curtly. "You are healed and may go now."

"We actually had another favor to ask."

# Critical Failures VIII

"Have the drow not taken enough from us?" Thibil completely let go of his tenuous facade of politeness. "They removed our statues, claiming they could not bear the sight of them. They plundered our sacred relics while they told us we should be thankful that they allow us to continue practicing our faith. And now, as they cower in their miserable black keep, clinging to the illusion of power while the island falls to ruin, they strike a deal with you idol-worshiping fools. We have agreed to their demands that we heal you cretins, but we shall do no more than that!"

These guys really had it in for the drow. If Katherine had known that, she would have asked Jay to wait outside.

"Carbon dioxide," said Jay, still waiting near the doorway. Great. Now he was calling even more attention to himself.

The stones orbiting around the seated monks' heads wobbled in the air as their concentration faltered. Even Thibil's angry eyes turned confused as he looked past Katherine.

"What is he doing?"

Katherine glanced back to find Jay waving the Bag of Holding wildly up and down. Effective, but distracting.

"Nothing," she said. "It's a black thing."

"I think there's been a misunderstanding here," said Jay, stepping up to stand alongside Katherine. "We're not who you think we are."

Katherine shot him a warning glare. "I've got this, *Jaybraham*." He should know better than anyone how useless it was to try to reason with someone who couldn't see past the color of his skin.

He returned her glare with the slightest of eye rolls, then turned to face Thibil. "We're not Knights of Jordan."

"Jay!" They were on shaky enough ground as it was. Why would he blow their cover like that? It was their only leverage.

"Oh?" said Thibil. He actually sounded intrigued.

"We stole these uniforms," Jay continued. "It was the only way we could walk around town without getting harassed by those crazy zealots."

Thibil frowned. "In that case, I should have required a donation for the healing. Who are you, then? What is your business here?"

"My name's Jay, and this is Katherine."

As long as their cover was blown, Katherine decided she might as well see if she could use her reputation to her advantage.

"You might have heard of me," she said. "I killed the Ice Queen of Nazere and returned the Eye of Russia to the temple in Cardinia." *Wait, something was off about that.*

"The Eye of *Rasha*?" asked Thibil.

"Yes, that's it! Anyway, the gods were so pleased with me that they brought my friend back to life as a way to say thanks. I hate to have to hit them up again, but I was wondering if they might be able to do that again."

"Do what again?"

Katherine wasn't sure exactly what this guy was having trouble understanding. Then it hit her. She was asking for a resurrection, but there wasn't a body to resurrect. She took the bag from Jay and reached inside.

"Dead body."

A dead naked man covered in fresh red blood spilled out onto the floor. Katherine didn't recognize him for a second until his intestines spilled out on top of him.

The squelch of wet viscera was followed by the clatter of eight stone orbs hitting the floor. Their concentration finally broken, at least two of the monks threw up.

"I'm sorry," said Katherine. "This is the wrong one." She reached into the bag again, making a mental note to name a specific dead body this time. "Tanner."

# Critical Failures VIII

As Tanner's stiff and lifeless body fell onto the Knight's like brick on an uncooked meatloaf, Katherine felt a tug in her gut.

She also felt a little guilty for prioritizing him over her companions from Earth, but he had proven himself loyal and competent on countless occasions. If she could only choose one person to bring back right now, and that choice was based on who would be the most likely to help get the others resurrected in the future, then Tanner was by far the most practical choice.

Jay sighed. "Of course, you'd choose a drow."

Katherine suddenly remembered everything Thibil had said about the drow, but she was still surprised at Jay's reaction.

"You of all people should..." *Shit. I'm doing it again.*

"Go on," said Jay. "I'd like to hear where you were going with that."

Thibil laughed in spite of the macabre scene at his feet. "This is no drow."

Jay furrowed his brow at Katherine. "Didn't you say drow are black elves? That guy looks like he fell into a vat of toner. So if he's not a drow, then –"

"He is half drow," said Thibil. "No full-blooded drow would claim him as one of their own. And that is just as well. He is not tainted with the same darkness that corrupts their black souls."

"Oh."

"Oh?" said Katherine. "You don't find that just a little bit racist?"

Jay shrugged. "He's clearly not judging them by the color of their skin."

Katherine was frustrated about the eggshells she had to walk on while this monk got a free pass, but there were more important matters to discuss right now.

"So," she said to Thibil. "Can you bring my friends back to life?"

"I am afraid I do not have that authority."

"Oxlos isn't good enough?" *Yikes, that didn't come out right.* "I mean, what higher authority do you need?"

"The gods meddle little in the affairs of mortals. We faithful servants shoulder the burden of spreading their divine light, and we are often limited by certain practicalities. This temple, humble though it may be, has stood here for over five hundred years. It existed long before this island became a trading hub."

"That's very impressive," said Katherine, unsure of what this had to do with her dead friends.

"Before that, Blacktalon Point was the destination of choice for seafaring merchants to hawk their wares. The drow who controlled the Point amassed great riches with their whores, games of chance, and even slaves. Cursed by the gods of Light, they burrowed underground to bask in their unholy decadence. Opulent subterranean chambers for their orgies and dark rituals. And as they grew in number, they required more space. They dug farther and farther into the bowels of the planet until, so it is said, they tore open a hole into Hell itself!"

"You mean, like, *literal* Hell?" asked Jay. "Did they release a bunch of demons or something?"

Thibin laughed. "Would that they were so fortunate. They no doubt would have gotten along well. But no. Truly did they reap the rewards for their debaucherous lifestyle, for the dark gods of the Abyss spewed forth a torrent of molten rock with which to reseal their cursed domain. It filled every chamber and corridor, instantly snuffing the life out of every dark-hearted man, woman, and child within before erupting through the surface and leveling the whole town. Those who managed to escape the gods' wrath moved here to start anew."

"That's all really interesting," said Katherine. "But we really need to –"

"Without any provocation, they began ruthlessly slaughtering island folk. When they were satisfied that their dominance had been established, they forced those who remained to construct that blight that sits atop the hill. In exchange for tribute, they allowed our people to continue practicing our faith as long as they did not have to look at statues of our gods. Over time, people grew to accept their tyranny, and to accept the drow as the ruling class. Here at the temple, we were allowed to channel Oxlos's power to keep the islanders healthy enough to work. But greater acts, such as resurrections, were expressly forbidden without explicit permission from the High Drow. That is why I cannot bring your friends back to life."

"How are the drow going to find out?" asked Katherine. "I'm certainly not going to tell them."

"Divine magic of that nature requires certain materials that are expensive and difficult to come by."

Katherine sighed. The last thing she needed right now was to run off on another side errand. They were tedious enough on land, but now she'd have to deal with a boatload of impatient cultists as she sailed off to wherever-the-fuck in search of the Lost Scrotum of the Ancient Pharaoh, or whatever bullshit this guy was going to come up with. But she supposed she didn't have any choice.

"Fine," she said. "What do you need, and where can I find it?"

"I have already told you. The drow took everything from us. They allot to us only what is required for the divine favors they need performed." Thibil frowned down at Tanner's body. "It is rare that they ask me to resurrect anyone outside of their own race. They will never agree to have me resurrect a half drow. I am sorry, but perhaps it is the gods' will that your friend remains dead."

Katherine wasn't ready to accept that.

"If that was their will, then they wouldn't have resurrected him last time."

"This half drow is the friend you had resurrected at the Temple of Life?"

Okay, now they were getting somewhere.

"That's right," said Katherine.

"But the Eye of Rasha was returned only a few weeks ago. How could you let him die again so quickly?"

"I didn't let him die." Katherine tugged on her tunic. "He died trying to save my life from that son of a bitch these jackasses are all worshiping."

"Jordan Knight?" Thibil almost looked like he was cracking a hint of a smile. One of the other monks snorted as he stifled a laugh.

"My friend is dead on your floor," said Katherine. "What the fuck is so funny about this?"

"Forgive me, good lady. I trust you meant to say you were attacked by his followers."

"No. Jordan Knight killed my friend, and he very nearly killed me as well." Now that she said that out loud, she could see how it could be taken as funny. But that should only be true from her perspective.

All the monks were laughing now.

Katherine looked at Jay, who just shrugged.

Thibil was the first to compose himself. "We mean no disrespect. It has been too long since we have had reason to laugh. But how is it that two of you were not able to overpower one bard?"

There were several truthful ways Katherine could have answered that. She could have explained that they were

# Critical Failures VIII

fighting a different manifestation of the person they knew as Jordan Knight, but she didn't have that kind of time and they most likely wouldn't believe her. Or she could have said that not only did she overpower him, but she also ate him, but that would inevitably lead to her having to explain the whole Mordred thing, anyway. Or she could tell them –

"We'd just finished fighting a pack of werewolves," said Jay. "And he got the jump on us."

"That's right," said Katherine, backing up his bald-faced lie to a bunch of monks who she needed to revive her friends. She hoped to grease the wheels a bit by leveraging their disdain for the Knights of Jordan. "And we mean to deliver some payback. But for that, I'll need my whole team. We're going to go have a little chat with the drow. We'll return with whatever you need to bring my friends back to life."

Thibil raised his eyebrows. "And may I ask how you intend to persuade them?"

Katherine narrowed her eyes. "We can be very persuasive when we want to."

"Carbon dioxide!" said Jay. He waved the Bag of Holding up and down like a plastic grocery bag he was trying to open all the way.

# CHAPTER 33

*T*rue to her word, when the sun rose the next morning, Akane had towed a tree trunk back to the *Maiden's Voyage* and assisted the crew as they replaced the mast. Julian had no idea how they'd intended to do that at sea without the help of a dragon. As it was, Akane wasn't strong enough to hold the tree up by herself. Between her and as many of the crew as could get their hands on it, they were only just able to get the mast upright.

But it was done. Rhonda, Frank, and the others were now headed slowly back to Nazere with a crew that had been informed that if they tried anything funny, they would be eaten by a dragon. Akane hadn't agreed to this arrangement as part of her deal with Julian, but she was sporting enough not to call him out on his bluff.

Julian was miles away now, about two thousand feet above the sea, trying not to strangle Akane as he clung tightly to her neck. Like any long flight, it had been both terrifying and exhilarating at first, but quickly grew tedious. Unlike flights Julian was more familiar with, the tedious part was also terrifying, because he had no pressurized cabin, SkyMall crossword puzzle, or in-flight movies to keep him distracted from the constant knowledge that his life might end abruptly in less than a minute.

Ravenus, who was tucked into the back of his serape, did his best to assuage Julian's fears by explaining how wings work. Rather than talking about lift, and thrust, and air pressure like Julian had learned in high school physics, he likened it to swimming on air. But while Julian appreciated the effort, it didn't make him forget that he didn't have any wings.

He did, however, have two Fly spells, which he'd prepared specifically to ease his mind. If he lost his grip, he should have plenty of time to cast a spell before smacking into the sea. But rational thought seldom eased irrational fear, so he spent most of the flight thinking about how he might stretch out his serape between his arms and legs like a flying squirrel if he should happen to lose his grip.

"That is Nazere up ahead," Akane shouted over the rushing wind. Julian, keeping his face pressed firmly against her scaly skin, would take her word for it. "I can hardly believe it. The Ice Queen is really gone."

A few minutes later, Julian was relieved to feel the wind slow down and the air begin to warm as Akane stopped flapping. They were gliding now. Soon, Julian would be able to plant his feet on solid ground once again.

The descent seemed to take forever, but Julian finally breathed in the rich earthy scent of decay. It seemed stronger than he remembered. Risking a peek over the side, he lifted his head and saw the forest of dead trees below. Their trunks were darker now, and it looked like only about two-thirds of them were still standing upright from the bright green undergrowth teeming beneath them and crawling up their trunks. Decay was setting in. The remnants of Old Nazere were giving way to a brighter future. The island was recovering.

It really was a breathtaking aerial view, and Julian almost wished he could take in more of it. But there was nothing he wanted more right now than to get off this dragon's back and crawl around on the ground for a little while.

And it would indeed only be for a little while. Nazere was the third island they'd landed on so that Akane could rest and refuel, but it wasn't their ultimate destination. The next flight was likely to be the worst, because they had no idea where to find Chaz. All they had to go on was that he was on his way to Hollin. If he'd arrived there already, that would make him even more difficult to find. But if that was the case, at least they could remain on land while they searched.

"There does not seem to be much in the way of fauna on this island," said Akane.

That had totally slipped Julian's mind. What was she going to eat?

"All the animals were killed off in the ice. Are you going to be able to make it to another island without food? Can you catch fish?"

Akane glanced back at him with one big reptilian eye. "Fear not, for the island will provide. I smell something."

Ravenus fidgeted under Julian's serape. "I smell it too!"

With so much rotting organic matter surrounding them, there was no telling what Ravenus was so excited about. Maybe bugs had reestablished a foothold on the island. It seemed unlikely, given the short amount of time and no nearby island to swim from. Was it possible that some could have come over with the ships? Could their population have exploded that rapidly? Julian supposed that, with no natural predators on the island to stop them, the exponential growth of a species of insect that reproduced frequently and laid enough eggs could fill up an island in pretty short order.

But did Akane eat bugs? And if so, shouldn't those bugs be all over the place? Why were they still flying? One spot should be just as good as any other, so where were they going?

Julian got his answer a few minutes later when they finally touched down among a forest of foot-tall saplings. Their green stems only just beginning to turn into brown trunks, they were growing far too close together for all of them to survive. Before long, their roots would be battling for dominance over the island's limited space. Only the strongest trees would mature to bear seeds for future generations.

Thankful as he was to be on the ground, Julian's appreciation for the rebirth of the island was spoiled by the putrid stench of a small round puddle of water they'd landed next to. There was some kind of man-made wooden frame standing over it, which Akane and Ravenus both seemed very interested in.

"That looks like the beginning of a house," said Julian. "Probably an entryway. My guess is that it dates back to just before the Ice Queen arrived and froze everything. Are you interested in archaeology?"

Akane took a deep breath, then breathed out a torrent of lightning at the structure. It immediately exploded into flaming wooden chunks.

Julian shielded himself with his serape. "I guess not."

The dragon's next move was even more peculiar. With the pesky clue to a past civilization out of her way, she plunged her head into the foul-smelling puddle of water. What Julian thought was simply a slight depression where some water had collected and stagnated turned out to be much deeper than it looked.

He'd winced when he thought she was about to slam her face into solid earth below, but half of her neck disappeared into the water.

"It must be a well," said Julian. That went some way toward explaining the powerful stench it was giving off. Any number of animals might have fallen in there, preserved in ice for decades, then all thawed out at the same time. Was that what Akane was fishing for?

But when Akane finally pulled her head out of the water, she wasn't holding a dead rabbit or baby deer. She pulled out a human corpse. Bloated, pale, and naked, it landed on the ground with a wet plop like a waterbed mattress made out of flesh.

"I want the eyes!" cried Ravenus as he flew over to join Akane.

Knowing what was coming next, Julian turned around so he wouldn't have to watch. Listening was almost just as bad, though. His highly sensitive elven ears picked up every squelch, tear, bite, and gulp as Akane and Ravenus devoured the body of some poor schmuck who'd drowned in a well.

When the carnage subsided, Julian turned back around to witness an even more disturbing scene than the one he'd just avoided.

For whatever reason, Akane had decided to take her human form to squat for a dump. She was facing away from him, and it was gushing out of her like a busted hydrant.

Ravenus wasn't helping matters either. The only part left of the corpse was its junk, and Ravenus was taking that dead dong down his throat like a hooker who sucked dick competitively.

"Ravenus!" said Julian, but he was too late. Ravenus looked at him with a testicle stuffed in each cheek before he finally swallowed.

"Yes, Master Julian?"

Julian sighed. "Nothing. Never mind." It wasn't the first set of testicles Ravenus had swallowed, and probably wouldn't be the last. He wondered if his instinctive revulsion might have been rooted in some repressed homophobia. If he'd suddenly walked in on Ravenus eating a dead woman's vagina, would he be so disgusted? Yes, now that he thought about it. He absolutely would. Perhaps even more so. He felt better about that.

"I apologize, sir. Did you want some? I could regurgitate some of it if you like."

# Critical Failures VIII

"No, thank you. I'm not hungry." Between Ravenus's cock swallowing show and Akane's record setting dump, Julian wasn't sure if he'd ever be hungry again.

If Stacy were to catch him in the company of this beautiful naked woman, he hoped it would be at a time like this. He wondered where Stacy was right now, and if she was okay.

"We can start flying again soon," said Akane, looking back at Julian and snapping him out of his thoughts about Stacy. "I should be finished in a few more minutes."

Julian realized with sudden horror that while he was thinking about Stacy, his gaze had been focused roughly in Akane's direction. She must have thought he was watching her shit.

He quickly looked away. "I wasn't... I didn't mean to..." *Change the subject! Change the subject!* "I, um, couldn't help but notice that you chose to take your human form." Not as sharp a subject change as he'd intended, but it provided a good cover excuse for why he seemed to be gawking at her.

"I prefer to defecate from a mammalian anus," she said. "It takes longer than if I were to use my much larger cloaca, of course, but I did not think we were pressed for time. I could use a few more minutes to rest my wings."

"By all means, take your time," said Julian, relieved to be discussing anything other than Akane's shitting preferences. "We don't want your wings giving out over the open ocean, do we?"

"I enjoy the sensation of how it feels flowing out of a tighter orifice."

"Sure," said Julian, hoping he would never hear the words *flowing* or *orifice* come out of her mouth ever again. "Who doesn't?"

"I find it cathartic and slightly arousing."

Julian didn't have nearly enough ranks in the Diplomacy skill to know how to respond to that.

"Okay."

Akane let out a long satisfied sigh. "I feel fifty pounds lighter now."

Judging by the pile of shit she was now standing next to, Julian found that to be a conservative estimate. He had so many questions he wasn't sure he really wanted the answers to. How did the whole mass thing work between her dragon and human forms? She'd clearly just shat out more than any human rectum could hold. Where had it all come from? Did she weigh the same in each form? Had she wiped?

Akane addressed that last question when she morphed back into her true form. Lifting one of her huge reptilian legs, she swung her head around and licked her cloaca clean.

Julian felt like he'd done well so far by not overreacting to some of the more shocking cultural differences he'd just witnessed from Akane and Ravenus, but this was the straw that finally broke him. He dropped to his knees and heaved, but his stomach had nothing left to give. He'd emptied what little he had during the ascent of their first flight.

"What is the matter?" asked Akane. "Are you ill?"

Julian shook his head. "Just pre-flight jitters, that's all. I'm better now. Ready to go when you are."

# CHAPTER 34

The night of the Full Moon Brawl was approaching, and it couldn't come fast enough for Cooper. The gladiator life was really starting to get to him. He hated everything about it. The dull food, the lack of booze, even the friendliness of his fellow inmates. No, *especially* the friendliness of his fellow inmates.

That was a constant reminder that he was trapped. He wanted so badly to grab one of these assholes by the throat, pin them against a wall, and punch them in the face until their head turned to jelly, just to know that he could. Instead, he had to live with the constant struggle to contain his rage.

Not even the fighting helped. Every time he went out to train, he thought about how refreshing it would be to go out in the sunlight and open air and beat the shit out of people. But even that did little to appease his urges. Ever since that first training, when Tim had poisoned Yavin, Tim had instructed Cooper to lie low and pull his punches. Follow the script, and they could make their move during the Full Moon Brawl.

Cooper still didn't have any idea what that move would actually be, but he was looking forward to a real fight. If they somehow managed to pull off an escape, great. If he died in battle, so be it. But the most satisfying result would be going out there, giving it his all in the arena, and slaughtering every last one of his opponents. He only hoped that satisfaction would hold him over to next month's Full Moon Brawl.

Zimbra's personal bodyguard, Rocco, had been put in charge of training, and he was a real no-nonsense hardass. That was fine with Cooper because he got to punch him. But Rocco had clearly been living the gladiator life for quite some time, and Cooper's attacks didn't seem to cause quite as much suffering as he would have liked. More often than not, Rocco would just criticize his form and whack him like a dog. Only instead of using a rolled-up magazine or newspaper, Rocco used a club. Cooper was sure he could take him down a few pegs with his Barbarian Rage. But using that would involve a loss of control that Cooper couldn't afford to risk. Instead, he just took his beatings like a bitch and stared through the arena gate bars every night, watching the moon grow fuller and fuller.

Today's training hadn't been so bad. Rocco's heart didn't seem to be in it. He and Cooper were pretty much just going through the motions.

Tim wasn't even doing that. He'd put so much effort into his costume, which was now looking more fabulous than any gladiator attire had any business looking. But he put sweet fuck all effort into his training, mostly just standing around impatiently while Cooper got the crap knocked out of him. And Rocco just let him get away with it.

Cooper suspected that rumors were spreading about Tim regarding the sudden disappearance of one of the trainers in North Pen so soon after Yavin's untimely passing. He hadn't heard anything directly, but he'd noticed a lot of sideways glances in Tim's direction. At first, he chalked it up to Tim's ridiculous clothing, but that didn't explain the abruptly halted conversations or changes of subject whenever he and Tim entered a room.

Maybe there was something to Tim's costume after all. Some psychological bullshit. If he couldn't be the biggest badass, he could at least be weird enough for people not to want to fuck with.

At any rate, Cooper had every confidence that, whether they wanted to or not, he and Tim would definitely be selected for the coming Full Moon Brawl.

"That will do for today," said Rocco after dropping Cooper with a blow to the side of his knee. Cooper was still no match for him without a proper weapon or using his Barbarian Rage, but he'd been getting in a few more hits lately with the training club he was provided.

"Thank fuck," said Tim. "I thought I was going to die of old age out here. Come on, Cooper. Move your ass."

"Fuck you." Cooper winced as he got to his feet and started limping toward the gate. Tim, on the other hand, was a bit faster on his feet these days. He'd stuffed some fabric into one of his sequined boots to make up for the lack of foot to occupy the space. It wasn't a perfect prosthetic, but it certainly helped.

"What's up your ass?"

"Rocco's foot. Did you actually fall asleep out there this time?"

Tim looked back to make sure Rocco was well behind them. "Just because you can't see it doesn't mean I'm not doing my part to get us out of this. In fact, my part *depends* on total secrecy and discretion."

Cooper had walked off the worst of the pain and was walking normally again. "Your part depends on total bullshit. I've seen what you've been doing this whole time. Fucking sewing. How is that going to help get us out of here."

Tim smiled up at him. "I've been doing more than that. Just wait until you see what I've got waiting for us back in our room."

That sounded more ominous than exciting. What the hell could Tim have possibly gotten in here that he thought would ease Cooper's mind?

"Is it a hostage?"

Tim laughed. "Why is that the first place your mind went?"

"Because it's reckless as fuck and almost guaranteed to get us murdered, which seems to be your end goal. Do you have any idea how terrifying it is for me to feel like *I'm* the smart and responsible one of the two of us?"

"Believe me. If you were the smart and responsible one, we would have been dead a long time ago. Put a little faith in your best friend, would you? I've got this shit under control."

Despite having seen no evidence to support that claim, Cooper desperately wanted to believe it. Maybe Tim had been Shawshanking a tunnel this whole time. That also seemed like a reckless move, but as long as they were trapped in this place for life, maybe a measured risk was the only hope they had of ever escaping. He followed Tim in silence all the way back to their room, half cautiously hopeful and half dreading what was there waiting for them.

When they arrived, Cooper could see nothing that warranted either hope or dread. Nothing looked out of the ordinary at all. He scanned the walls for something that might be covering the start of an escape tunnel, but they were completely unadorned.

When Tim crawled under his bed, Cooper thought the tunnel might go down through the floor. That would be smart. But Tim backed out, dragging a wooden crate behind him. It was covered with a sheet of green silk left over from his costume creation.

"What's that?" asked Cooper.

"Just a little reward for all the hard work we've done and sacrifices we've made over the past few weeks."

# Critical Failures VIII

Cooper couldn't remember Tim doing either of those things. "But... What *is* it?"

Tim pulled away the silk to reveal twelve full bottles of stonepiss.

"Holy fucking shit!" said Cooper. "Where did you get that?"

"I have my secrets."

Cooper understood Tim's reluctance to share all the details of his plans. Loose lips suck dicks and all that. But it would be nice to know that acquiring this booze hadn't involved something that was going to get them both killed before they got to find out whatever plan Randy was brewing up for the Full Moon Brawl.

"Can you at least tell me how fucked we are because of this? Last time you scored booze, you burned down the kitchen for it."

Tim laughed as he opened a bottle for himself. "This is nothing like that. They don't stock this stuff in the kitchens here." He took a swig from the bottle, then sucked air between his teeth. "Oh God, it's been so long. You've got to try this shit, Cooper. I guarantee you it's better than that orc piss I swiped from the kitchen."

"First, I want to know how you got it. I don't need to know all the details. Just enough to reassure me that you didn't do anything that's going to get us killed."

"Dude, would you fucking relax?" Tim grinned up at him. "I've got a man on the inside."

That was certainly a step up from arson, but still potentially problematic.

Cooper took a bottle from the crate. "Are you sure you can trust him?"

"One hundred percent sure," said Tim. "In fact, I've got him delivering a message back to Randy tonight."

That wasn't good enough for Cooper. In fact, it was pretty far from good enough. But it was as good as he could reasonably expect to get. He pulled the cork out of his bottle of stonepiss and took down half of it in his first series of gulps. Tim was right about one thing. It was indeed some good shit.

# CHAPTER 35

"Son of a bitch, that hurts!" cried Denise. "You ain't got to bite my goddamn titties off!"

Randy yawned, not sure if he was prepared for whatever he was about to open his eyes to. Then he heard the familiar clicking of arachnid feet against the wall and floor and realized it was just Denise breastfeeding Fatty.

He opened his eyes and was relieved to discover both that his guess had been correct, and that he'd paused to think about it before opening his eyes. Fatty had grown quite a bit over the past couple of weeks, and Randy could have easily mistaken the scene he was waking up to as some horrible cavern-dwelling beast overpowering and devouring Denise.

"Good morning," he said.

"The fuck are you looking at?" said Denise. "This ain't no fuckin' peep show. What kind of paladin are you?"

Randy turned his head toward the ceiling, thinking about all the men Denise had flashed her boobs to since she'd had boobs to flash. What was she so sensitive about now? It's not like he wanted to see them.

"Sorry."

"If you need something to keep them dirty eyes occupied, you might want to take a look at that letter."

"What letter?" asked Randy.

"How many fuckin' letters are there in this room, Randy? The letter I'm pointing to!"

"I'm sorry. You told me not to look at you."

## Robert Bevan

"Goddammit, Randy. I'm sure even you can tell the difference between a lady's finger and a lady's titties. Now, if you'd pay attention to your own titties instead of mine, you'll see the fuckin' letter I'm talking about."

Randy lifted his head to find that there was indeed an envelope sitting atop his chest. "Who do you think it's from?"

"How the fuck should I know? If I could read, I would have read the letter by – OW! Son of a... All right, Fatty. That's enough. Time to switch titties."

Careful not to look in Denise's direction, Randy sat up and inspected the envelope. There wasn't a mark or seal or anything to identify who it was from. When he opened it, he discovered that it wasn't an envelope at all. The letter itself had been folded to resemble an envelope.

"I'll bet it's from that elf guy," said Denise. "You remember? The one who hangs out with that bird."

"Julian? What makes you say that?"

"'Cause he used that *oraguchi*."

"*Oraguchi*?" Randy repeated, looking up briefly before he was unpleasantly reminded of Denise's breastfeeding. He quickly looked down. "What's *oraguchi*?"

"You know how them Chinamen fold paper into swans and frogs and shit."

Randy opened the letter the rest of the way and looked at the bottom to see if there was a signature.

"It's from Tim."

Denise scoffed. "Figures. Racist little piece of shit. That's called *cultural procreation*."

"I don't reckon he meant no harm by it."

"Who gives a shit?" said Denise. "What's the letter say?"

Randy brought his gaze up to the top of the letter, cleared his throat, and read aloud.

*Dear Randy and the other pedo whose name I can't remember,*

# Critical Failures VIII

"I call bullshit," said Denise. "He remembers my name. I guarantee you he only wrote that to be hurtful."

"Do you want me to read it to myself first?" asked Randy. "In case there's anything else that might upset you?"

"Fuck, no. I'm a strong woman. I can take whatever that little jizz stain can throw my way. Go on and read the rest of it."

*I'm assuming you're together, and that you're the ones who sent me the message I received via dinosaur ass. Thank you so much for that, by the way.*

Randy smiled. "It's nice to get a little appreciation for a change."

"I reckon that's sarcasm, Randy."

"You interpret it how you want to. I'll take it at face value."

"Jesus Christ. This is gonna take all fuckin' day. Keep reading the letter, will you?"

*I'm also going out on a limb and assuming that at least one of you two hillbilly retards can read.*

Denise laughed. "You still feel appreciated?"

Randy ignored her and continued reading.

*Cooper and I are intrigued by your proposal, but we would like more details about what you have planned, and to know if there's anything we can do to help. Please write back as soon as possible. Leave future correspondence under the large brick just outside the North Pen gate. I have a man on the inside who will retrieve it for me.*

*Looking forward to hearing from you soon.*
*Tim*

Denise snorted. "Sounds like Tim's movin' in on your turf."

"What are you talking about?"

"He said he's got a man on the inside."

Randy shook his head. "That ain't as funny as you think it is."

"Lighten up, Randy. It's a double *intendray*, a play on words. The man inside is like you taking a dick in your –"

"I understand it. It just ain't funny. Now, put your clothes on. We got to round up Captain Longfellow and his men and decide once and for all which one of them plans we been discussing is the one we're gonna go with."

Denise sighed. "If any of them was any good, it would be an easy choice."

"I'm sure we're all open to new suggestions if you got a good one. But we got to write something now that we got a means to communicate with Tim and Cooper."

"And what means might that be?" asked a voice from the doorway.

Randy quickly shoved the letter down the front of his pants and thought up a lie. "It's a letter from Tim regarding our plans to escape during the Full Moon Brawl!"

*Oops.*

"Shut yer bleatin' cock scabbard!" said the man who Randy was relieved to discover was Captain Longfellow when he turned around. "A fine lot of good those plans will do us if ye blurt them out to all of Meb'Garshur!"

"I'm sorry," said Randy. "I forgot I'm unable to lie. What are you doing up so early?"

"It be hard enough to sleep without the floor swaying under me feet. How could I hope to sleep through the howling fornications of a bear and a giant cockroach?"

"I am *breastfeeding*!" snapped Denise. "How dare you come in here and mock a perfectly natural activity between a child and his mama!"

# Critical Failures VIII

Captain Longfellow's eyes widened like he'd only just now realized Denise was there. "I was actually referring to a disturbing dream I had while nodding off to –"

"Mama," said a small voice from somewhere in the vicinity of Denise's titties.

Denise gasped. "Y'all hear that? This little freak just called me mama!" She smiled at Fatty and held it tight against her bruised and bite-marked titties. Tears welled up in her eyes as she gently removed a coarse curly tit hair from the side of its mouth. "I'm a goddamn mama."

"How very touching," said Captain Longfellow. "Remind me ne'er to fire me cannon into a wench's berth. Now, what be that bit of scribbling ye shoved down yer bloomers?"

Randy sheepishly pulled Tim's letter back out. "We was just coming to talk to you about this. It's a response letter from Tim."

"How did he manage to deliver a letter?" asked the captain.

Randy shrugged. "I just woke up and there it was, sittin' on my chest, all folded up like uriguchi."

"I beg yer pardon?"

"It's *oraguchi*," snapped Denise. "You fuckin' retard."

Captain Longfellow frowned at the crumpled paper in Randy's hand. "Smells fishier than a merman's puckered cloaca if ye ask me. Might it be a ploy by Zimbra and Rocco to discover why our peckers be so hard to fight in the Full Moon Brawl?"

"I don't think so," said Randy, offering the letter to Captain Longfellow. "Some of the phrasing in here is very... well, Tim."

Longfellow grimaced at the letter as he hesitated to accept it, but finally snatched it from Randy's hand. He snickered a couple of times as his eyes moved back and forth across the paper, then he finally nodded.

"Aye, I'd wager me mizzenmast that this be not the writing of any Meb'Garshur orc. So, how do ye propose we respond?"

"That's what we was coming to see you for. I figure we need to decide on a course of action. Only question is, which one?"

"A conundrum indeed. I say our best shot is taking the governor for ransom and demanding we be set free. Between my crew and whoever Tim can wrangle together, we can form a pile high enough to send one or two of us over the wall. If ye summon that big beast of yours, he can keep the others at bay."

While Randy agreed that was the best plan they'd come up with so far, he didn't like it. "That puts too many people at risk, and I don't think one or two people is gonna be enough to overpower the governor's guards and take him hostage."

"And what makes you think any of them other orcs give a shit about the governor, anyway?" asked Denise. "I bet there's a whole bunch of them just itching for him to kick it so they can take his place."

Longfellow sighed. "I did not say it be a good plan. Merely the best we have managed to think of so far."

Something the captain said gave Randy a new worry. "North Pen will be solid on account of we got your whole crew, but I ain't sure how many folks Tim is gonna be able to wrangle. He ain't the nicest feller in the world, and Cooper ain't exactly the most charming. I reckon they're like to be the only two in on the plan. Everyone else from South Pen will be actively trying to kill us. We got to take into account a certain level of chaos that Basil might not be able to contain as effectively as you think. Them folks will be thinking they're fighting for their lives. Getting turned to stone might not inspire as much fear in them as it does to regular folks."

# Critical Failures VIII

Captain Longfellow frowned. Randy felt bad to see such a strong and brave man so disheartened.

"Chaos!" said Denise. "Fear! Regular folk!"

Randy wasn't quite sure what she was getting at. "Them's all words I said."

"Goddammit, Randy. Don't you see? We been focused too much on the people working against us inside the fightin' pit that we ain't even considered all the people who could be working *for* us on the outside!"

"You mean the folks from the Whore's Head Inn?"

"Fuck, no! I wouldn't count on those bunch of fuckwits to help me suck off a seven-dicked goat."

"I don't reckon it would be unreasonable for them to refuse to –"

"Would you shut the fuck up while I'm musing? I think I got somethin' here."

"What is it?" asked Randy. "Who do you think is gonna help us from outside Meb'Garshur?"

"I ain't talking about outside Meb'Garshur. I ain't even talking about outside the stadium. I'm talking about the audience."

Randy's heart sank, his hopes pulled right out from under him again.

"You're thinking about *Gladiator* again, ain't you? Building up the love of the crowd takes time that we ain't got. And besides, that don't lead to nothing in this place besides maybe getting promoted to a trainer. They don't let folks leave this place."

Denise grinned up at him. "Who said anything about love? I distinctly remember saying fear."

"How do you reckon you're going to scare the audience from the fighting pit?"

"I ain't gonna. *You* are."

"And how am I supposed to do that?"

"The same way as Longfellow just said. You summon Basil. But you don't summon him down in the fighting pit. You plop his fat ass down up in the fuckin' bleachers. The audience will lose their shit."

While Randy agreed it would be an effective means to scare people, he wasn't sure how that was going to save them, and there were ethical issues as well.

"I can't send Basil up there to eat innocent people."

"Innocent? Those motherfuckers is coming to watch us butcher each other for their fuckin' entertainment! How do you call that innocent?"

"It ain't nice, but it don't justify killing nobody neither."

"And I never said nothing about killing nobody," said Denise. "You can tell Basil beforehand not to eat nobody. All we need for him to do is put the fear of God into them and let the chaos ensue. Everyone will be screamin' and hollerin', and when the South Pen folks see that some major shit is going down and we ain't killing them, we can get them on our side."

"Aye," said Captain Longfellow. "And the governor's guards will have no choice but to go confront the beast. That be when we make our move. We can take the governor hostage and send some men down to open the dungeons."

It almost sounded crazy enough to work. At the very least, they'd put on a show that the audience wouldn't soon forget.

"I guess that's as good as we're gonna get," said Randy. "What, exactly, should we write back to Tim?"

Denise snatched the letter out of Captain Longfellow's hand. "We ain't gonna write him shit." He handed the letter to Fatty, who sniffed it curiously before beginning to eat it. "All they got to do is show up, and they already know that much. Each one of these letters we send back and forth is another chance for us to get caught. I don't know who his *man on the inside* is, but I don't trust him no further than I could spit out a wad of elf jizz."

"The dwarven whore be right," said Captain Longfellow. "The best course of action be no course at all. The fewer folk who know what we be scheming, the less likely it be that information be leaked into unfriendly ears. I say we keep this between the three of us. I'll tell me crew the morning of, and those in South Pen will find out as events unfold."

Randy could understand their reasoning, but he didn't like the idea of not responding at all.

"It don't feel right to just leave them in the dark completely. Couldn't we leave a small response? It don't have to include any details or names or nothing. Just something to acknowledge that we got their letter and let them know we still got a plan. Otherwise, they might think something went wrong. They could panic and do something that might put us all in danger."

"And what sort of message did ye have in mind?" asked Captain Longfellow.

Randy shrugged. "Nothin' fancy. Just something to make them put their minds at ease, let them know that we got everything under control and all they got to do is show up."

"There's your message," said Denise. "Just show up."

Captain Longfellow nodded. "Nice and simple. Those who it be meant for will understand its meaning, but it shan't mean more than a sack of collie cocks to a cuttlefish to anyone else who chances upon it." He tore off the remaining sleeve of his shirt. "Do either of ye happen to have a blade on ye?"

Randy and Denise shook their heads.

"Never ye mind. We'll do it the old-fashioned way." He squatted in front of Denise. "Hit me."

Denise shrugged, then slapped Captain Longfellow across the face.

"Son of a sea whore!" shouted the captain. "I did not say to slap me as ye would a cabin boy's bare arse. Hit me like ye just caught me up to me elbow in yer dear mother's poop deck. She be moaning with pleasure as I slide it in and out, slick with her –"

CRUNCH!

Randy winced as Denise's fist broke Captain Longfellow's nose.

Captain Longfellow grabbed a handful of Denise's hair.

"What the fuck, man?" cried Denise. "You done told me to hit you!"

Captain Longfellow ignored her panicked slapping and shoving as he put the end of a lock of her hair in his mouth. "Hold still, ye crab-infested sperm lagoon!" When Denise stopped struggling, he licked her hair to a point, dipped it in the blood running down from his nose, and scrawled the agreed-upon message onto his former shirt sleeve.

When it was done, he let go of Denise's hair and blew on the message to dry the blood.

"You want I should heal your nose?" asked Randy when the captain handed him the rolled up fabric.

"Aye, lad. That would be lovely."

# CHAPTER 36

Stacy was beginning to understand why Alroth hadn't been too bothered about a small detour to Port Town. She'd incorrectly assumed that the Cedar Wilds would be just a little hike off the main road. Now that they'd been trekking through the forest for three days straight, a couple of extra hours to eat some Arby's didn't seem like such a big deal.

She wouldn't have minded under normal circumstances. The forest was beautiful and smelled a lot better than the Whore's Head Inn. Alroth proved himself to be quite an accomplished outdoorsman, providing Stacy, Dave, and Shorty most of the comforts of home. A skilled hunter, forager, and cook, he put together meals from what the wilderness provided that made Stacy feel ashamed about taking him to Arby's.

He was also a huge help with keeping Dave in line. Between the two of them splitting the watch, and Dave being a plump, slow-moving morsel for any woodland monster that should happen to catch him alone, Dave didn't dare make any attempts to escape.

The first night had been a little rough since she couldn't be entirely certain that she could trust Alroth or Shorty until she woke up the next morning neither molested nor murdered. But the next two nights gave her some of the best sleep she'd had in a very long time.

Unfortunately, however, she was racing against the coming full moon, less than a week away, and a three-day journey to the Cedar Wilds would mean at least a three-day journey back to Cardinia.

"How much farther away is the Cedar Wilds?" asked Dave.

Stacy was grateful for his whining, as she'd been wondering the same thing.

"Look around you," said Alroth, gesturing up at the trees. "We are among the cedars now."

Dave looked up. "Oh. Is that what these are?"

Alroth laughed. "Did you take them for ficus trees?"

"Excuse me. I guess I don't know my trees all that well. I must have been too busy not giving a shit."

"Are you saying we're in the Cedar Wilds now?" asked Stacy before Dave's bitching could get any more hostile. "How long have we been here?"

"We do not recognize strict borders the way you do," Alroth explained. "The Cedar Wilds is not a political entity. It is merely the area of land that I prefer to call my home."

"So where are we going now?" asked Shorty.

"There." Alroth's tone was grim as he pointed at a fallen cedar blocking the way ahead of them.

"Thank the gods! Does that mean we can finally stop walking?"

"That is not the work of any god. The once noble tree you see lying dead before you was felled by an ettin. See how they do not even use it for timber or fire."

"Then why do they tear down the trees?" asked Stacy.

"From what I have observed, it is simply because they can. They wield clubs of walnut, and –"

"How do they make clubs out of walnuts?" Dave interrupted.

Alroth frowned at him thoughtfully, as if he was trying to decide whether or not that was a serious question. "Mayhap it is generous to call them clubs. They are simply the trunks or branches of walnut trees. The wood is much harder than that of a cedar, and it seems to give them fleeting satisfaction to knock down a tree."

Dave walked up to the trunk of the fallen tree and examined the break point more closely. "Are you telling me that those freaks chopped down a tree with another fucking tree? And you want us to fight them?"

Now that she witnessed the destruction firsthand, Stacy was leaning toward agreeing with Dave. They might be in way over their heads.

Alroth caressed the bark of the fallen trunk. "Powerful though they are, ettins are weak of mind and can be easy to manipulate if you find one who is willing to talk to you instead of immediately attacking. I am a simple ranger, not skilled in the arts of trickery and deceit. It is my hope that you may use your cunning and charm to turn the ettins against each other."

"I appreciate your confidence," said Dave. "But I'm more of a Wisdom guy, and I think it's wiser for us to get the hell out of here before we run into one of those things."

Alroth chuckled. "I apologize for the misunderstanding. I was referring to Stacy. You have as much cunning and charm as the scrotum of the boar we ate for dinner last night."

"That's just great. Dump on Dave again. We'll see how hard you're laughing when you need –" He stopped himself mid-sentence like he'd accidentally let slip something he'd been mulling over in secret for quite a while.

"Nobody's laughing at you, Dave," said Stacy. "Alroth was just saying that he doesn't have very good people skills. I'm sure he wasn't trying to insult you." She hoped Alroth would take that as a warning to mind what he says about Dave from now on. "But you have to admit, you haven't exactly been a barrel of laughs since we left Cardinia."

"You mean since you kidnapped me?"

"I'm not going through this with you again. Look at it however you want until the full moon. But in the meantime, you could at least try to make the best of –"

"RAAAAAAAHHHHHHHHH!"

The roar sent a shiver up Stacy's spine. It sounded like an angry god had stepped on a LEGO, shaking the needles of every surrounding tree.

"What the hell was that?" she whispered.

Alroth frowned. "That would be an ettin."

"*An* ettin? Are you sure that wasn't, like, a dozen ettins?"

"I mentioned that they are quite large, did I not?"

When she'd asked him more about ettins during their walk, he'd told her they averaged about thirteen feet tall. Stacy had been relieved by that estimate, fearing that "giant" might have entailed something more akin to something the size of a skyscraper. Thirteen feet was a bit more than twice as tall as she was, which made it feel a lot more manageable.

But now that she heard one of the monster's actual roar, she mentally reassessed how much of a threat a thirteen-foot tall two-headed giant might actually be.

"We should move in for a closer look," she said, carefully avoiding leaves and twigs as she made her way toward the direction the roar came from.

"Did you miss the part when he said they fight with tree trunks?" asked Dave. "Have you ever been hit by a tree trunk? I'm going to assume that, because you're alive, you haven't. We need to turn our asses around and get out of this forest while we still can."

Stacy acknowledged, to herself at least, that Dave might be right. But she had to see with her own eyes what one of these things actually looked like.

"Stay here and be quiet," she said, then pulled the hood of her Cloak of Elvenkind over her head. As long as the ettin had no reason to think anyone else was around, it would make her effectively invisible.

Compromising a bit of speed to focus on Stealth, she climbed to the top of a nearby hill. What she saw on the other side almost made her fall back down.

Height alone was not an adequate metric with which to convey how massive this thing was. His torso the size of a small car, he easily weighed a couple of tons. Alroth hadn't been exaggerating about their preferred choice of weapon either. Stacy could see the worn remains of a root network on the business end of the club he was wielding in his right hand.

The heads looked more orcish than human, with flat noses, prominent lower jaws, and yellow tusks. The simple brown strip of hide he wore as a loincloth, combined with his apparent lack of personal hygiene, gave off a strong primitive vibe. Alroth's idea of using their wits to turn them against each other had sounded kind of far-fetched at first. But if they really were this simple-minded, and as hot-tempered as Alroth claimed, Stacy thought she might be able to find some way to make it work.

"My turn!" the ettin's left head said to its right.

"NO!" the right head responded as he raised its huge club. "Your turn finished!" He swung for a nearby cedar, which Stacy had no doubt would have snapped in half upon impact if the ettin's left hand hadn't intercepted it.

Forcing the club upright, but unable to wrest it completely free from the right hand, the left hand smashed it repeatedly into the right head's face.

"No hit yourself!" said the left head. "No hit yourself!"

"Stop it, Gurlog!" cried the right head, letting go of the club to brace them for a fall as the right leg kicked its heel hard against the left leg's shin.

Stacy felt the ground shake when the ettin fell. She wasn't sure what the right head had in mind, but he'd definitely put his side of the whole at a distinct disadvantage now that they were on the ground.

The left head, Gurlog, doubled down on the verbal and physical abuse, laughing and drooling as he slammed the club repeatedly into the right head's face.

"No hit yourself! No hit yourself! No –"

"UUUUNNNNGGGGHHHH!" they groaned together as the left hand dropped the club.

Apparently, both heads were vulnerable to the feeling of being punched in the balls.

Stacy continued watching with interest, wondering if maybe this problem wouldn't sort itself out if she just stayed out of it.

"Why you punch stones?" asked Gurlog when the pain subsided enough for him to speak.

The right head spat out about a gallon of blood. "I ask for choke, but you put club in butthole. My turn no count."

Stacy hoped she had misinterpreted something in that, but she now had an even stronger reason to not want to get hit with that club.

"You want choke? I give choke!" The left hand grabbed the right throat and squeezed until the right head's eyes started to bulge out.

But instead of fighting back, the right hand reached under the loincloth and confirmed what Stacy had hoped in vain that she'd misinterpreted.

"You like?" shouted Gurlog as it strangled the other head. "You like that? You like..." His gaze drifted up as the corresponding hand loosened its grip. "Oh, I like."

"Harder!" croaked the right head, seemingly angry that he was able to breathe while he manhandled their quite substantial man handle.

Feeling like she might throw up if she witnessed any more of this, Stacy turned away. If she and Dave were going to go through with this, then fate had just dropped a gift in their laps that would be extremely unwise to let slip away. How often would they be fortunate enough to encounter a lone ettin, much less one that's already beaten the shit out of himself and is distracted with make-up masturbation?

This one was a freebie, or at least it would be if Stacy had any ranged weapons at her disposal. She wasn't really a fan of violence, but preferred to take a foe on face-to-face if a brawl was inevitable. Still, it would have been wise to invest in a bow at some point in the event that she should ever have to face off against a two-headed giant with a shit-slathered tree trunk. But that was an oversight she'd have to resolve at a later date. For now, she had to work either with what she had or with what the forest could provide.

Fortunately, the forest had quite a lot of rocks to offer. She picked up the six in her immediate vicinity most ideal for hurling, about the same size as baseballs and three times the weight, and put them in her bag. He was a big bastard, sure. But Stacy was strong and fast, and she had a nice big stationary target to aim at.

Of course, to get the most bang for her rock by using her Sneak Attack, she'd need to get within thirty feet of him. As chilling a prospect as that was, this was as good an opportunity to reduce the ettin population as she was likely to get. She picked up a seventh rock and hoped that Alroth was telling the truth about how evil these things were.

"Is he doing what I think he's doing?" whispered Shorty, suddenly standing right beside her.

Stacy jumped. "You scared me."

"Sorry."

"How did you know where I was?" Stacy felt her hood to make sure she was wearing her Cloak of Elvenkind properly. "Am I that easy to spot?"

"Easy for one who knows where to look. I saw you don your cloak." Shorty frowned at the rock in her hand. "You were not, by chance, entertaining the idea of attacking a creature of that size armed only with a rock, were you?"

"Of course not."

"That is a relief."

Stacy lifted her bag. "I've got more rocks in here."

"If I recall correctly, Alroth claimed to have recruited you because of your intelligence."

"Look," said Stacy. "I know this doesn't look very bright on the surface, but the math checks out. The odds of me taking down this lone ettin are high enough to justify the increase of our odds of taking out the rest of them down the line. Besides, he can't hit what he can't see, right?"

"Your cloak does not make you invisible," said Shorty. "The ettin will spot you with ease as soon as you throw your first – and quite possibly last – rock."

"Uuuunnnnnggghhhhh," groaned Gurlog. "Lagra. Lagra!"

It looked like things were ramping up. Stacy remembered Dave's little performance back at the inn. If that was anything to go by, she didn't have a lot of time to act before the ettin finished the deed.

"Lagra!" Gurlog continued, lost in his fantasy. "Lag–" The right hand stopped pumping the primer, then Gurlog loosened his grip on the right head's neck. "Why you stop?"

"I no want think about Lagra."

"But I like Lagra!"

"Good for you," said the right head. "But then I stuck with Mugmug. Besides, they have tits like Elders' jowls. My turn. I pick girl."

Gurlog sighed. "Fine. Who you pick?"

The right hand started stroking again. "Cressa."

"Sirrug and Hucsol's daughter?" said Gurlog. "But she is only a babe. She and Migar not yet grow hair on meatflaps!"

# Critical Failures VIII

The right head laughed. "They will scream like humans. You cannot tell me it no excite you. I feel your hardness in my hand."

Stacy felt like she was going to be sick again. At least now she had solid justification for putting this thing down. It might be a different story if they ever encountered Cressa and Migar, though. It hadn't occurred to her until now that these ettins might be traveling with innocent children.

"Sirrug and Hucsol have large member," said Gurlog. "If they hear of this, they will take us in the butthole before the whole tribe. Then the elders will have us flogged to death!"

"Then they will not hear of it," said the right head. "My turn, my choice!"

When they resumed strangling and stroking, Stacy looked down at Shorty. He looked justifiably uncomfortable.

"I have an idea. If you help me, I think I can easily get in two solid hits before they even know I'm there."

"How can I help?" asked Shorty. "I can barely lift one of those rocks."

"You don't have to. But we do have to hurry. Follow me and keep quiet."

The grunting, groaning, and stifled breathing grew progressively louder the closer they made their way to the masturbating ettin. As sickening as it was, it made up for Shorty's lack of ranks in the Move Silently skill.

There was no such silver lining for the stench, though. Stacy didn't know what goblins might smell like when left to their own devices, but that Jennifer girl ran a pretty tight ship at Arby's. The goblin crew under her was cleaner than most of the people at the Whore's Head, and those were the only goblins Stacy had ever encountered. But even at their worst, she couldn't imagine they'd smell a fraction as bad as this thing. He smelled like something you'd have to dilute with water to achieve the essence of a bus station bathroom.

Breathing as little as possible, she led Shorty behind the ettin where he had dropped its club. She had a clear shot at the back of both heads. Now the question was which was was it wiser to hit.

The obvious answer was the right head. Being strangled would make it more difficult to alert the other head that they were under attack.

But the right head controlled the hand holding the dick. And if Stacy had learned anything from Dave, it was that the dick could be very persuasive when it came to making regrettable decisions. It would be better to let the head controlling the arm that was holding the dick – the dick head – keep doing what he was doing for as long as possible.

Disturbing the dick head was inevitable. But if, rather than disturb him directly, she attacked Gurlog, that extra step in the process might stall them long enough for her to remain unseen.

She crouched down next to Shorty and took her pack of caltrops out of her bag. "Are you ready?"

"Ready for what?" asked Shorty. "You have not yet told me what we are doing."

"I apologize. That was an oversight on my part." While she explained her plan, she carefully shoved one prong of her caltrops into the part of the walnut trunk the ettin had been using as a handle, leaving three prongs exposed. "I'm going to throw this rock, and you're going to run like hell. When they turn around, they'll think you threw the rock, and I can get in one more shot. Got it?"

"And then?"

Stacy impaled a few strategically placed leaves on some of the caltrops to camouflage them. "And then we'll take it from there. Hopefully, those first two hits will take him most of the way down, and –"

# Critical Failures VIII

"Most of the way down?" Shorty was making an effort to keep himself at a whisper. "Two rocks?"

"By then, Alroth and Dave will have heard us and come to join the fight. The ettin will be confused and overwhelmed. We'll finish him off easily."

Shorty shook his head. "You are insane. That is the only plausible explanation. I should have stayed at Arby's. What mad devil possessed me to –"

"Kiss me," said Gurlog.

Stacy and Shorty turned to the two-headed monstrosity. Had they been spotted?

Dick Head was craning his neck away from Gurlog, who had let go of his throat and was leaning in with his dripping tongue hanging from his open mouth.

"No, Gurlog! Stop it. I no want do that again."

"We almost finish," said Gurlog. "You pretend I am Cressa. I pretend you are Lagra."

"No! My turn! I no want –" Whatever he was going to say after that was lost when Gurlog grabbed him by the back of the head and shoved their faces together.

It didn't take long for Dick Head to get over his reservations. He started jerking more rapidly. Their face sucking sounded like two snarling dogs fighting over the remains of a giant slug.

"Mercy of the gods," said Shorty. "Throw the rock, already."

Stacy didn't need to be asked twice. She took aim at Gurlog's head, wound up, and hurled her rock. It struck him hard in the back of the head just above his left ear.

"YAAAH!" cried Gurlog, pulling back from Dick Head and looking straight at Stacy.

*Shit.*

"No stop!" said Dick Head. "Almost... there!"

Gurlog ignored him, glaring fiercely at Stacy. "You hit me with rock?"

Stacy shook her head and pointed to Shorty, who was running like hell, just as she'd instructed him.

When Gurlog turned to look, Stacy saw a bright crimson stream of blood flowing down from where she'd hit him. Her Sneak Attack damage had clearly made a difference. She ducked behind a tree and quickly pulled the hood of her cloak down, then back up again.

"Hey!" said Gurlog, whipping his head back in Stacy's direction. He looked madder than a sack of badgers, but his gaze failed to meet hers.

"What wrong?" asked Dick Head. "Why stop?"

"Stupid goblin hit me with rock."

Dick Head spotted Shorty running away and laughed. "We rub his guts on happy stick. Make slippery."

Gurlog laughed in agreement, then they got up.

Stacy grabbed two more rocks from her bag. She would have preferred to hit Gurlog again, hoping that knocking him out might cause the ettin to lose control of half of its body. But she had a clearer shot at Dick Head and took it.

The sound of the rock connecting with the back of his skull made her wince.

"YEEEOOOOOW!" cried Dick Head, stumbling to his knee as he turned to face her. "Who is human girl?"

"I kill her!" said Gurlog, reaching down to grab his club. "I cut off tits and use for – OOOOOOOHHH!" He gawked in pain and confusion at his bleeding palm.

Stacy used the distraction to hurl another rock, striking Gurlog square in the forehead. Unfortunately, it didn't leave a gushing wound like the previous two hits had. She wouldn't get her Sneak Attack bonus until she was hidden again, or until the ettin was engaged in combat with someone else. Even more unfortunately, Dick Head was clever enough to grab the club by the other end, which not only failed to hurt him, but also meant that the weaponized end was full of embedded caltrops.

Both heads grinned as he stepped toward her, Dick Head wielding the club and Gurlog stroking his still erect penis. What was it with guys in this world? First it was the lamia in the desert, then Dave, now this thing. In fairness to the ettin, he was just continuing a process that she'd interrupted, but this behavior was still far from appropriate. She drew her dagger and readied herself to dodge the coming attack.

He swept the walnut trunk wide and low toward her. She dropped flat against the ground and felt the wind of it passing inches over her. Anticipating his next move, she rolled to the left just in time to avoid being smashed into a puddle of lube.

The third swing was another sweep, and it looked too low to duck. Her only hope was jumping it. She pushed off the ground as hard as she could, but it wasn't enough. She felt her sudden change in direction more than the pain in her right leg, but she definitely heard her femur crunch.

As the ettin raised his club for the killing blow, Stacy lay crippled on the ground, unable to move her legs. She was completely defenseless.

The last thing she would see before she died was an ettin scrotum swinging like a leather sack of potatoes. She would have preferred a nice sunset, or the loving faces of grandchildren, but she found herself unable to look away. How many testicles did these things have? She could make out at least –

"YAAAAAAAAHHHH!" cried the ettin. When he turned around, two arrow shafts were sticking out the small of his back.

*Alroth!*

The fight wasn't over yet. Stacy pulled up the hood of her cloak and picked up her dagger by the blade. She could still make out the generous collection of balls between the ettin's legs and was tempted to aim for that. But she was messed up pretty bad already and about to lose her only means of defense. His massive back was like the side of a barn as far as targets went, so that's where she aimed.

*Sneak Attack, motherfucker.*

The dagger hit dead center, penetrating all the way to the hilt. She must have severed the spine, because the ettin stopped dead in his tracks and fell forward, making no attempt at all to brace himself for hitting the ground.

Alroth winced at the impact. He had a better vantage point to see the ettin fall on his erection.

Stacy didn't want to think about that, which was fortunate because her leg suddenly started screaming for all of her attention. Now that the shock and adrenaline from the fight had subsided, her right leg let her know just how fucked up it was. Every tiny movement amplified the pain in her leg. Even breathing hurt.

"Are you hurt?" asked Alroth, jogging down the hill toward her.

Stacy let out a shallow laugh through her pain. "You could say that. Where's Dave?"

"Here he is!" said Shorty, dragging Dave by the arm behind him.

"Thank God. I'm pretty sure my leg's broken. Can you hit me with a healing spell?"

Dave was breathing more heavily than that little stroll down the hill should have warranted. He looked nervous, his eyes darting left and right. "I... I don't know. I mean, I might not have any prepared."

"Did you use any today?" asked Stacy.

He took a step back. "Maybe. I think so. I don't –"

# Critical Failures VIII

"I have a potion," said Alroth, digging through his bag. "It may not restore you completely, but hopefully it will be enough to mend your –"

"No!" said Dave. "I just remembered. I have one left." He reached for her hand, and Stacy grabbed his. He flinched at her touch, as if he wanted to jerk his hand away, but Stacy had a firm hold on it. "I heal thee."

"Nnnnnnnnnnggggg!" Stacy groaned as her femur fused back together.

"Yeeeeeeoooooowwwww!" cried Dave as Stacy squeezed his hand even tighter.

After a moment of the most intense agony Stacy had ever felt, her pain dissipated entirely like a fart in a hurricane.

"Thanks, Dave," said Stacy. "I owe you one."

"Can you let go of my hand?" When she released it, he let out a long sigh and started massaging it with his other hand.

"Sorry about that. That was pretty intense."

"Don't mention it."

Stacy used the trunk of a nearby cedar to support herself as she got to her feet and found that not all the pain had dissipated after all. She would have to remove her pants to see how injured she still was, but that could wait. For now, she was grateful to be able to walk.

"Whatever possessed you to attack an ettin alone?" asked Alroth.

"It was distracted, and I had to make a split-second decision." She looked over at the dead ettin. "It all worked out in the end." She limped toward him, yanked her dagger out of his back, then cut the rope securing the ratty leather pouch around his waist. "Let's see how much one of these things is worth."

Solidarity was vital, especially after all the bad blood between her and Dave, so she wanted to be as transparent as possible when it came to discovering treasure. To that end, she dumped the pouch out on the ground in plain view of everyone.

The contents were underwhelming. Four gold coins, eight copper, a small orange gem, half a clam shell, and what appeared to be an ettin tooth. The top was riddled with cavities like a termite-infested tree stump, and the bottom half of one of the roots had snapped off, but it was definitely a tooth.

"What is all this crap?" asked Dave.

Alroth picked up the clam shell and examined the inside. "Ettins do not understand currency as you do. They collect anything they perceive as interesting or believe others might find valuable."

Stacy sighed. "At this rate, we'll have to kill at least two hundred of them before we have enough money to pay the temple."

"Or we could just forget about the temple," said Dave. "Quit while we're ahead."

"Not helpful, Dave."

"Isn't it? You nearly got yourself killed, and for what? Less money than you paid for that dagger. You're putting all our lives at risk for something I don't even want."

Stacy wasn't about to get roped into this cyclical argument again. She picked up the coins and the gem, put them in her bag, then limped to the ettin's club to pry out her caltrops.

"This ettin's purse does not necessarily represent what you can expect to find with any others we manage to kill," said Alroth. "Having no concept of the value of what they possess, the contents of their purses can be quite unpredictable."

"Do you think it's possible that the group has a communal treasure with them?" asked Stacy.

Alroth shrugged. "Who can say? Ettins are solitary creatures by nature. I believe it unlikely that such a concept would even occur to them. However, the one who acts as their chieftain may have amassed a considerable collection of treasure by demanding tribute from those under him."

"You see, Dave? Never give up. There's always hope."

Dave sighed. "Wonderful." He waddled over and extended his hand toward her.

"What's this? Like, a truce or something?"

"I think I might have one more healing spell left in me."

Stacy took his hand. "Well, thank you, Dave. I really appreciate that." Being a rogue, she had no spellcasting abilities, but she couldn't recall any time when Julian hadn't known exactly how many of those horse spells he had left in his head. Maybe it was different for clerics, but Stacy suspected he'd been holding out on her until now.

"I heal thee," Dave said again.

Stacy felt a small surge of pain this time, but it quickly turned into a rush of... *arousal?* She jerked her hand away from Dave's. Healing or no healing, that wasn't a feeling she was comfortable having while touching him.

"Thanks," she said, trying to smooth over her reaction. "I think that did it. My leg feels great."

"I'll bet," said Dave with the slightest hint of a smirk.

"Excuse me?"

"You bet. No problem at all. That's what I'm here for."

"We should rest," said Alroth.

Stacy looked up at the sky. It was barely evening. "It's kind of early, don't you think?"

"The other ettins will not be far from here, and we must prepare for the challenges that lie ahead."

Stacy frowned at the giant two-headed corpse on the ground. "You want to rest *here?*"

Alroth pointed up the hill where they came from. "Over there. We will have a better view of our surroundings. If we should be so fortunate that another lone ettin comes to loot the body of this one, we would be better positioned to ambush it from up there."

Stacy put the last of her caltrops back in their pouch. "You had me at 'over there'."

# CHAPTER 37

Katherine would have preferred not to look like a drowned sewer rat when they met with the drow. But if anything, it was raining even harder when they left the Temple of Oxlos. Fortunately, it wasn't a very far walk from there to the keep at the top of the hill.

Stopping at the large wooden front door to mentally prepare herself for the inevitable confrontation ahead, she could see the entire village spread out before them, each tier outlined with a small brick wall like a topographical map all the way down to the beach. Contrary to what those two Knights of Jordan had said, she spotted a couple more substantial buildings down near the harbor. Nothing like the black stone tower looming over her, but a few notches above the mud huts she'd passed on her way up the hill. The rain obscured her view of anything beyond the harbor. On a clearer day, she wondered if she might be able to see her ship from here.

"What, exactly, do we have to offer these people?" asked Jay. "We're too late to warn them of a coming invasion."

"I've been thinking about that, and I think the only card we've got left to play is to tell them the truth. We're on a mission to capture Jordan Knight. If we're able to do that, then maybe we can get him to call off his cultists. Our goals line up with theirs. It would be in their best interests to help us."

"If they believe us. And that's a pretty big if. Would you hand over a bunch of money to some rando who showed up at your door and offered to solve all your problems?"

Katherine shrugged. "Maybe if I was desperate enough. But we're not asking them for money."

"Thibil said the stuff we need to resurrect your friends is expensive. Asking for that is pretty much the same as asking for money."

"Then I guess we'll just have to hope they're desperate enough," said Katherine. "They must know they're outnumbered, and not just by the Knights of Jordan. If the townsfolk see this as an opportunity to run off the ones who slaughtered their ancestors, they might be tempted to make a temporary alliance. Even if they're not, the drow can't be sure of that. Maybe we blow some air on that fire."

"And if that doesn't work?"

"I don't know. Then I guess we're fucked. Why are you so focused on the worst-case scenario? We've come all this way. Doesn't it make sense to save our moping until after it doesn't work?"

"I'm not trying to be fatalistic. I was just thinking that we do have one ace up our sleeve that we could play if we had to."

Katherine knew exactly what he was talking about. "Absolutely not."

"You didn't even hear what I was –"

"Don't even say it." Katherine scanned their surroundings for listening ears, then leaned closer to him. "We're not showing them the die."

"Why not?" asked Jay. "That would go a long way toward convincing them that we might actually have some insider knowledge that will help us take down Jordan Knight."

"Or they might just pull a Logan and steal it from us in the hopes that if they give the Knights of Jordan what they want, they'll go away."

# Critical Failures VIII

"That is a possibility," Jay admitted. "But this is kind of a different situation. Captain Logan didn't realize how powerful a force Mordred had created, and he didn't know there were several dice. I think it's safe to say the drow have a healthy understanding of what they're up against, and they're probably smart enough to realize that the Knights of Jordan probably won't stay true to their word for very long. If they surrender the die to the Knights, that will only serve to make the Knights suspect that they might have information as to where the rest of the dice can be found. Then this tower turns into Guantanamo Bay. That's the fire we should be blowing air on."

Katherine shook her head. "It's too risky."

"The drow aren't the only ones who are in a desperate situation right now."

"You there!" shouted a voice from above. "What do you want?"

Looking up, Katherine saw a black elven head scowling down at them from a small window about twenty feet up. Butterbean growled, but Katherine put her hand on his head to calm him.

"We would like to speak to the head drow," she said.

"His Eminence has heard enough from you. We have held up our end of the bargain. Whatever other problems you have are yours alone to deal with. Now, go away!"

Katherine sighed. "Not off to a great start."

"I disagree," said Jay. "They're acting petulant because they're not used to being in a position of weakness. Let me try."

"That's what I brought you along for. Knock yourself out."

Jay cleared his throat and peered severely up at the drow looking down on them. "You may tell *His Eminence* that he may grant an audience to the two of us, or he will grant an audience to every Knight of Jordan on this island."

The drow stared back at them with hateful, narrowed eyes for a moment before speaking. "I shall relay your message to His Eminence." He disappeared back inside the keep.

Katherine laughed. "He did *not* like being talked to like that."

"That got us in the door, but it might come back to bite us in the ass once they know we're not actually Knights of Jordan."

With a loud thud from inside, the doors opened outward a couple of inches.

Katherine and Jay waited a moment to see if they were going to open any further before Katherine looked between the crack.

"Hello?"

"You may enter," said the same voice they had just been talking to.

Katherine grabbed one door, and Jay grabbed the other, and they pulled the doors open just wide enough to slip through.

The air inside was nice and dry, and a good twenty degrees warmer than the air outside, thanks to a massive hearth that took up most of the opposite wall.

Silhouetted against the hearth's flames, the drow who begrudgingly allowed them to enter stood in the middle of the room on an intricately patterned circular rug.

"Against my counsel, His Eminence has agreed to grace you with an audience. He will receive you in the throne room on the top floor." The rug he was standing on began to slowly ascend.

Katherine stepped toward it uncertainly. "Should we..."

He sneered at her. "You may take the stairs."

The rug ascended faster up the empty central column of the tower. Katherine had half a mind to turn into a bat and knock his smug ass off of it, but they were probably in over their heads as it was.

Katherine led Jay and Butterbean up three flights of stairs, resisting the temptation to peek out and see what was happening on the second and third floors of the keep. The air was surprisingly fresh and sweet for a dark staircase in an ancient tower. If she didn't know any better, she might have thought she was walking through a rose garden.

The only light came in through holes in the outer wall that looked barely big enough for Katherine to put her head through. With the heavy rain, that didn't allow for a whole lot of light to navigate the stairs with.

But if the stairwell was dim and grim, it was nothing compared to the darkness that welcomed them from the entryway to the fourth floor.

"This is the fourth floor, right?" Katherine whispered to Jay.

"It better be. There are no more stairs."

Katherine peeked into the near complete darkness. "Hello?"

"Open the curtains," said a more jovial voice than Katherine was expecting. "We have guests who require light."

A crack of brightness appeared to Katherine's left, shedding light on the monstrosities who were pulling the curtains open. From the waist up, they looked like any other drow. Not that all drow looked the same to her, of course, but these two differed much more conspicuously than any drow she'd ever seen in that their bodies below the waist were more like giant spiders. They met her gawking with hateful scowls.

"Sorry," she said, trying not to let on just how fucked she realized they were. "Hi. Are one of you the High Drow?"

"Enter, dear friends," said the jovial voice from deeper within the room. "I always welcome a visit from the Knights of Jordan. Come in and tell me how I might be of service to you this fine evening."

He seemed nice. Even if it was just a display of political ass-kissing from someone who was desperately trying to hold on to what little power he had left, she felt like she could make a lot more headway with this guy than she would have been able to with the pouty little shit who'd greeted them at the front door.

And although she knew she would eventually have to confess to not being a Knight of Jordan, she could at least use her false position to establish herself as someone to take seriously when she made her first impression.

She took a deep breath, then stepped into the throne room, trying to project an air of confidence and slight superiority.

"Good evening, she said to the smiling drow seated upon the largest chair on the other side of the room. It wasn't what Katherine would have thought of as a throne, but it was nice enough to look out of place in her Gulfport apartment. He was younger than she expected, perhaps in his late thirties or early forties, and still had a boyish handsomeness to his features and a twinkle in his violet eyes.

A drow sat on either side of him in lesser chairs. One she recognized immediately as the pouty little shit. The other was a female drow. She was making a point to look away, as if she couldn't be bothered to acknowledge a lowly Knight of Jordan.

"My name is Katherine," she continued, addressing the High Drow. "This is my friend Jay and my Animal Companion –"

"YOU!" bellowed the female drow to the High Drow's right, whipping her head around to glare at Katherine. She had two long scars, which looked new, running down the left side of her face, but Katherine recognized her as Lady Vivia.

*Shit.*

# Critical Failures VIII

She was suddenly a lot less concerned with the spider people monsters by the window.

"Oh, hey!" Katherine said as if she was running into someone she used to work with. "I certainly didn't expect to see you here."

*Shit.*

She regretted it as soon as she said it. That's just not what you say to a person you left to be mauled by angry wolves.

"I suppose you wouldn't!"

"I didn't mean it like that. I just meant that it's funny, us running into each other again like this, you know?"

"Are you acquainted with this woman, cousin?" asked the High Drow.

"This is that crazy mongrel I told you of," said Lady Vivia. "The one who ate Mittens, and who tried to disguise herself as a drow by painting her face black."

*Shit.*

"Wow," said Jay. "So I guess your little proposition on the beach last night wasn't entirely hypothetical."

Katherine felt like she was about to implode from the pressure on all sides. The only one who wasn't openly hostile to her right now was the High Drow. She faced him when she spoke.

"I've made my share of mistakes and regrettable decisions."

"How fascinating," he said. "But then you redeemed yourself by joining the Knights of Jordan." The sarcasm in his voice was as thick as cake icing.

"As a matter of fact, I have not. We borrowed these clothes from..." Katherine turned back to Jay, who was predictably staring back at her with disappointment in his eyes. Disappointment turned to panic when he came to the same realization that she'd just come to. It must have been at least twenty minutes since he'd last changed the air in the Bag of

Holding. One more corpse to haul around. On the bright side, at least it seemed to knock him off his high horse for the time being.

"You are not Knights of Jordan?" asked the High Drow.

"No."

"Forgive me, Harzos," said the pouty little shit on his left. "They claimed to be Knights of Jordan. They were wearing the –"

The High Drow silenced him with a raised palm, but kept his violet-eyed gaze fixed on Katherine. "I grow more curious with every new surprise. Tell me, then. To what do I owe the pleasure of this visit?"

"I've come to ask you for a favor," said Katherine. She could have opened with what she could do for him, but she felt like he was the kind of guy who would appreciate her being upfront about what she wanted in a deal rather than pretending she was here for his benefit.

"Ha!" said Lady Vivia. "You have some gall, mongrel. How dare you enter my cousin's audience chamber under false pretenses and demand –"

With a slight raise of his palm, he shut the bitch up just like he'd done to the pouty little shit.

"Forgive my dear cousin's rudeness," he said. "As I am sure you are aware, she has suffered some recent hardships. What is the favor you seek of me?"

"I have some dead friends I need resurrected. I spoke to the clerics at the Temple of Oxlos, and they said you were the man to talk to for the materials and permission they need."

"Quite right," said Harzos. "Would these friends of yours happen to be drow?"

"No." Katherine knew by now that it would only be counterproductive to bring up the fact that Tanner was half-drow.

"What you ask is hardly a pittance. The components required for such a divine act are expensive and difficult to come by. And the very thought of those backward fools channeling the power of their feeble-minded god in such close proximity to my keep makes my skin crawl."

"I understand that –"

Harzos slammed his fist down on the arm of his chair. "You understand nothing!" He pointed at the observation balcony behind her. "Have you not seen my island? We are overrun with zealots! Our very existence depends on keeping them appeased until they find the trinkets they seek, if such trinkets even exist. And you presume to come in here wearing clothes you stole from them? If what my cousin says of you is true, I suppose I can assume that the previous owners of those tunics met with an untimely demise."

"They attacked us," said Jay, for what little it was worth. "We were acting in self defense."

Harzos glared at him as though he couldn't comprehend the words coming out of his mouth. "Have you any idea what repercussions we will suffer if the Knights of Jordan discover that I am harboring a couple of mongrels responsible for murdering two of their number? Those crazed imbeciles are likely to eat us alive!" He narrowed his eyes at Katherine. "So please tell me, Miss Katherine, why I should not have my driders spin you, your friend, and your dog, in web cocoons and deliver you to the Knights of Jordan for judgment?"

Katherine guessed the driders were the spider monsters working the curtains. It made sense. An amalgamation of *drow* and *spider*. But that was neither here nor there. Harzos had dropped the friendly act, so it was time for her to lay down her cards. She kind of wished Jay hadn't spoken up about them acting in self defense. The perception of them being a couple of violent psychopaths might actually do them some good right now. Then again, Lady Vivia could probably vouch for her in that regard.

"You know we wouldn't have come here if we didn't think we had something worth offering in return."

"My morbid curiosity of what preposterous offer you would make is the only reason you remain standing before me."

Katherine took a deep breath, mustering all the confidence she could before speaking. "Jordan Knight."

"The bard?" Harzos rolled his eyes. "The last thing we need is for these idiots' idol to bring droves more of his followers here."

"What?" said Katherine. "I'm not talking about booking him for a fucking show. I mean to take him out of the picture. Without a leader, there's no cult."

Harzos smiled sadly, as if he had actually believed they might be able to help, but she'd just pulled the rug out from under him.

"And what makes you think that you two mongrels can get close enough to Jordan Knight to assassinate him?"

"We know him," said Katherine. "We knew him before he became Jordan Knight. We know his desires and weaknesses, and that will allow us to set the perfect trap. But we can't do it alone, which is why we need you to bring back the rest of our team. And I didn't say we were going to assassinate him. I said we were going to take him out of the picture. What we do with him after that isn't any of your concern."

"I have heard enough," said Harzos. "Seize them."

"What?" Katherine suddenly felt like the situation had slipped away from her a while back in the conversation. She took a step closer to Harzos. "But you don't – What the fuck?" Her entire back, from her head to her ass, was engulfed in something warm and sticky, like someone had just thrown a bucket of warm glue on her. Before she had a chance to see what it was, she was jerked backward onto her ass.

# Critical Failures VIII

"Shit!" said Jay, turning around and lowering his spear toward one of the driders.

The drider squirted more of that sticky white substance out of its abdomen, covering his face and torso. He looked like the inside of a fifteen-year-old boy's shorts.

Butterbean barked as he lunged at the drider who'd attacked Katherine, but he had another load ready to squirt, engulfing Butterbean almost entirely in spider spunk. These guys must have been holding it in for months.

"So... fucking... gross!" said Katherine, trying unsuccessfully to fight her way out of the crystallizing strands of white goop.

"Let me kill her, Harzos," said Lady Vivia. "Please!"

Harzos shook his head. "She claims to have personal knowledge of Jordan Knight. His Knights will want to interrogate her, and it would be unwise of us to deny them that."

"Then at least let me kill her wolf. It is only fair after what she did to poor Mittens."

"Very well. The wolf is of no use to them. Make it quick."

"NO!" shouted Katherine as Lady Vivia rose from her chair and smiled wickedly at her.

"I shall use Alessandro's dagger," said Lady Vivia, walking toward the stairwell. "It is what he would have wanted." She winked at Katherine. "Do not go anywhere. I would not want you to miss this."

"You're making a big mistake!" Katherine said to Harzos. "We're the only chance you have of ever getting your island back!"

Harzos sighed. "I promise you, if I believed for a moment that you could rid my island of these loathsome fools, I would have your friends resurrected in a heartbeat. Sadly, you have given me nothing but empty words and a diplomatic nightmare. To think that I would risk so much on the ludicrous claims of two mongrels is beyond my –"

"Uncle!" cried a younger drow, gasping for breath as he ran out of the stairwell.

"Not now, Fezzil. I am in a foul mood and have no patience for your antics."

"Something is happening at the south harbor. A ship has docked there."

"Wonderful," said Harzos. "Another boatload of cretins to terrorize the islanders."

Fezzil stepped out through the open curtains, onto the balcony. "I do not think so. From what I have heard, they are causing great disruption among the Knights of Jordan."

Harzos hurried out to join him. "Cedric! Fetch my spyglass!"

The pouty little shit stood up from his chair, then rummaged through a chest behind Harzos's throne.

"What's happening?" asked Jay, who had finally managed to scrape enough drider goop off of his mouth to speak.

Katherine wasn't sure how to answer that, but there was no point in not going all in on claiming responsibility for it.

"I believe you owe me some resurrections," she said to Harzos. "And perhaps an apology."

"Quiet your blathering, mongrel. What does this have to do with you?"

"If that ship in the harbor is named *Seastalker*, then it has everything to do with me."

Harzos snatched the primitive looking telescope out of Cedric's hands, then twisted it into focus as he peered out at the harbor. After a moment of staring, he lowered it with a sigh.

"Vivia is going to murder me."

# CHAPTER 38

"There is another ship in the distance," said Akane.

Julian would have been glad to take her word for it, but he had to open his eyes to identify Katherine's ship, if indeed that was the ship they were flying toward. Even worse, he wasn't familiar enough with the ship to identify it from a distance, which meant that Akane had to fly down low enough for him to see if he recognized anything or anyone on it. Flying at a steady altitude was bad enough, but the ascending and descending parts were what really turned Julian's stomach.

It wasn't only bad for Julian's nerves either. Every ship they flew down to check out wasted precious time.

"If this is not your friend's ship, shall we stop to ask if they have seen it again?"

"No," said Julian. "If this isn't it, just keep flying." The last two ships they'd boarded were full of Jordan Knight's nutcase followers, who Julian vaguely remembered Randy mentioning at the Whore's Head Inn. They didn't look much like seasoned sailors, and Julian suspected that the ships they'd encountered had been commandeered. They weren't exactly forthcoming with information either, returning every question Julian asked with a demand that he and Akane submit to a search. Julian, with nothing to hide, had been happy to submit in return for information, but Akane was proud, stubborn, and hungry.

"Are you sure?" asked Akane. "The sea is vast, and finding your friend will be all the more difficult with so little information to go on."

Julian lifted his head to face the direction she was speaking from but didn't open his eyes. "Don't give me that. The only reason you want to go down there is to provoke them into starting a fight so you can eat them."

"Flying such a great distance requires a lot of energy."

"Between the last two ships, you've killed and eaten three men already. The way you talked about colored dragons..." *Yikes. That was a problematic term.* "What was that you called them?"

"*Chromatic* dragons."

"Right. The way you talked about them, I took you to be a Good dragon." Julian hoped that wasn't received as condescending as it sounded when he said it.

"I *am* good," said Akane. "That is why I provoked them. Killing in self-defense is justified."

Under the circumstances, that seemed like a moral very dark grey area to Julian, but he was not in any position to argue.

"How could you be hungry again so soon? You've flown a lot farther than this on far less food already."

"I can fly for miles and miles at a steady altitude. But all of this descending and ascending is taxing on my wings."

"We can stop at the next island we come to and get something to eat there."

They had leveled off again, and Julian could feel salty mist on his face. Figuring they must now be gliding right on top of the water, he opened his eyes. And for the first time, he was actually enjoying the ride.

They were moving fast, and falling off would probably hurt like a bastard, but it wouldn't be fatal. At least, not from the impact of hitting the water. It was exhilarating, like a

# Critical Failures VIII

roller coaster after cresting that first big hill. He could have ridden like this all day without a care in the world.

Unfortunately, Julian could tell from here that the ship they were fast approaching wasn't Katherine's. This was a much bigger vessel. The fun part of the ride was over.

"That's not them!" he shouted over the wind. "Pull up!" Willing himself to keep his eyes open for as long as he could stand it, Julian saw the ship's crew fire off a few arrows as Akane headed skyward again. They didn't even come close to hitting her, and the lightning she breathed in return was likewise a few yards short of connecting with the ship. Julian was glad nobody got hurt in the encounter, but he had to admit feeling a tinge of satisfaction as he watched them hit the deck in terror.

They repeated the process with two more ships. Akane was getting crankier now, and Julian was afraid he wouldn't be able to keep her from provoking another attack if she didn't eat and rest soon.

"There is an island!" she said about half an hour after the last ship they'd encountered. The excitement in her voice made Julian feel the slightest bit guilty about not letting her eat any more sailors. She was clearly exhausted and hungry, and she was showing real consideration for Julian's feelings. Honestly, if she'd decided to ignore his protests and gobble up every sailor on every ship they'd encountered, what was he going to do about it?

Julian was excited too. Not only did he long to plant his feet on solid ground again, but he also had to pee. Cracking one eye open, he spotted a speck of land on the horizon. He was starting to get a little more comfortable with the height they were flying at by now, but the wind and rain still stung his eyes, keeping him from holding them open for very long.

Now that his bladder knew it would soon be relieved, it started to get impatient. As Julian opened his eyes periodically to check on their progress, the tiny speck of land grew a little bit larger until he could make out what appeared to be a man-made structure erected atop its highest point. A small black tower.

"It looks like that place is inhabited," he shouted to Akane. "We'd better fly in low in case they're not accustomed to being visited by dragons."

"I fail to see how that is my problem," Akane responded a little testily.

"And it shouldn't be, but we're here to carry out a specific mission. If you want your gold, then – SHIT!"

Akane dived toward the sea like a plane that just lost all its engines at once. Julian shut his eyes and held on tightly to her neck until they were once again cruising just above the surface of the water.

When he opened his eyes again, he spotted a group of five people in matching white tunics running along the beach. Each was armed with a long spear. A brief glance up and down the beach failed to reveal what they were in such a hurry to get to... or away from.

He hadn't made anything of it at the time, but now Julian recalled that a significant portion of the sailors on the last two ships they'd encountered were similarly dressed. Whatever this strange movement was, it was quickly getting organized. That didn't bode well.

The people running along the beach, however, looked anything but organized. Julian and Akane were only about a hundred yards away by the time one of them took notice of the dragon flying toward them.

She stopped running and shouted something at the others. As they huddled together to discuss their best course of action, Julian was amused to see hands jutting out pointing down the beach in both directions when there was clearly nothing in either direction that would change their situation in the time it took for Akane to reach them.

Even more amusing was the course of action they ultimately agreed upon, which was to crouch down in the shadow of a large rocky overhang jutting out over the beach. Julian wasn't sure how, even if he and Akane both rolled natural ones for Perception, they could have failed to see this sad attempt at hiding.

"Shall I take my human form when we reach the island?" asked Akane.

"No," said Julian. "They already see you're a dragon, and they look pretty scared. It's about time some of these nutcases are properly intimidated. Let's see if we can shake them down for information. Look menacing, but don't eat anyone."

"What if they attack me? Shall I roll over so that their spears may more easily pierce my belly?"

"You're bigger than they are," said Julian. "You can take those spears away as easily as I could take a knife from a baby. But I don't think it'll come to that. These people don't exactly look like they're itching for a brawl."

Julian prepared himself for Diplomacy. They were obviously scared, and he was riding in on a dragon, so it made sense to lean into dominance and intimidation. He'd loosen up once he was satisfied that they'd given him all the information that they –

*I'm riding a fucking dragon.*

With all the stress and anxiety and fear he'd been going through recently, it only now occurred to him how cool that was. If only his fourteen-year-old self could see him now, it might have almost been worth having to move to Mississippi.

"Let me do the talking," he told Akane. "And, if it's not out of line for me to ask, would you mind acting subservient to me. I mean, only for this one encounter."

"For the sake of expediting this mission, I shall play your silly game. But I have my limits, elf. You would be unwise to push me beyond them."

"I'm not going to ask you to do anything weird. But since I'll be the one asking the questions, it would be useful if they were at least as afraid of me as they are of you."

As soon as Akane touched down on the beach, Julian slid off of her back, trying not to show his relief at feeling the sand under his feet.

The frightened people continued cowering in the shadows, as if still hoping that maybe Julian hadn't seen them. The two women were both human. One of the men was human as well, the other two were half-elves.

"Master Julian," said Ravenus, crawling up out of the back of his serape. "Do you mind if I help myself to that rotting carcass?"

Julian looked to his right, a little bit annoyed that Ravenus had said his real name out loud. Not far away, a mutilated giant squid sat festering on the beach. It looked like someone had cut all its legs off.

"Fine," he whispered. "But don't overdo it."

"Very good, sir! I shall be the very definition of moderation."

Julian turned back to the people hiding poorly under the rock. "Who are you?" he demanded. When none of them answered, he took a step toward them. "Foolish weaklings! Do you truly believe you can hide from Julian Dragontamer?"

He heard a small snort from behind, immediately followed by a quick zap and a loud pop. When he looked back, he saw a scorched crab the size of a football smoking in front of Akane.

"Apologies, *master*," said Akane before picking up the crab and popping it into her mouth.

Julian ignored the obvious sarcasm in her tone as he addressed the frightened strangers. "If you do not step out of that shadow at once and identify yourselves, my dragon shall feast on more than crab."

Akane coughed. "A thousand pardons, *master*. A bit of shell got caught in my throat."

The human man stood up, fending off the rest of the group who were trying to pull him back down.

"We beg your forgiveness," he said, letting his spear fall onto the sand as soon as he had pulled himself away from his still-cowering companions. "We are frightened and confused. For weeks, our minds have been under a powerful influence."

"You're drunk?"

"No," said the man. "But that may help settle our nerves. Might you perchance have a drop of stonepiss to spare?"

The expressions on the rest of the group's faces turned briefly from fearful to hopeful.

"Sorry," said Julian. "I kind of wish I did. What's got you all so shaken up, anyway?" He seriously hoped he wasn't opening them up to some sort of side quest, but information had been scarce, and he couldn't afford to ignore any news about anything out of the ordinary going on.

"It is as though we have just awakened from some terrible dream," said the man. "And now we are many miles from our homes, stranded on this island which has descended into revolt. Imagine our fear when, after we barely managed to flee the chaos at the south harbor, we see a dragon and rider flying toward us. Our only wish it to return safely to our homes and families."

A lot of questions were popping up in Julian's head. What had happened to these people? How had they unwittingly traveled so far from their homes? What caused them to snap back to lucidity? But one question was in more immediate need of an answer than all the others.

"What's going on at the harbor?"

"A new bard has arrived. He has awakened our minds, freeing us of our compulsion to do the bidding of Jordan Knight."

"I'm sorry. Did you say a *bard*?" Julian tried not to get his hopes up.

"One of the finest I have ever heard. He sings of a sinner in search of redemption. Truly inspiring."

While Julian could totally picture Neil Diamond writing a song like that, he couldn't think of any particular songs from Chaz's playlist that fit that description. Oh well. It was worth a shot. At least someone was doing something about this Jordan Knight nonsense. This person might come in handy to weaken Mordred's defenses.

"Did you happen to catch this bard's name?" asked Julian.

All the fear flowed out of the man's face as he stared out at the rain like he was thinking of his first true love.

"Razzmachaz."

"Are you fucking kidding me?" Julian grinned back at Akane. "That's Chaz! He's here on the island!" Julian never thought he'd be so excited to see Chaz. But if he had escaped, maybe the rest of his friends had as well. He couldn't wait to reunite with them.

"Excellent," said Akane, though her enthusiasm didn't really sell it. "One less person I can eat."

In his excitement, Julian had forgotten how hungry Akane was. He considered suggesting that she eat the rotting squid carcass that Ravenus was pecking at. It was no less gross than eating animated human corpses, after all. But it kind of felt like telling a poor person to go look for food in a dumpster.

"We'll get you something to eat when we catch up with Chaz. In the meantime, it's probably best if you take your human form."

As Akane's body shrank and changed, Julian remembered that her human form didn't come with any clothes. Walking around town in the company of an insanely attractive naked woman wouldn't be any more conducive to keeping a low profile than walking around in the company of a big-ass lightning-spewing dragon.

"I do not believe I have introduced myself," said the man Julian had been talking to. He was making an effort to keep his gaze up level with Akane's eyes. "My name is Greyson."

Julian rolled his eyes. "The pleasure's all ours. I'm going to need your clothes."

"What?" Greyson jerked his gaze away from Akane to stare quizzically at Julian. "My clothes?"

"That's right. She can't go walking into town like that."

"But what about me? This tunic is all I have to wear."

"One of your friends over there can tear theirs in half, and you can cover what needs to be covered until you find something else. We don't have time to waste. Come on."

Greyson leaned close enough to Julian to speak in a whisper. "Man to man, this is not the most opportune time for me to undress. It has been a long time since I have beheld any sight so... *arousing*."

"I don't give a shit," Julian whispered back. "Go strip down in the water if you have to. Your clothes are already soaked through, anyway. Just keep in mind that she's still a hungry dragon, and I'm Julian Dragontamer. I've been merciful so far, but my patience has its limits."

"About that. Since you are taking something of mine, does it not seem fair that you would return the favor by allowing me to satisfy my urges with your dragon? I promise it would take no more than a minute."

"Akane!" shouted Julian, startling Greyson, who had been expecting another whispered response. "If this man does not remove his clothing in the next five seconds, you have my permission to eat him."

Greyson ran toward the water, frantically untying the rope that held his tunic around the waist.

Satisfied that they were both on the same page now, Julian jogged to the ancient stone wall that separated the beach from the rest of the island to relieve himself.

It was one of the most relieving pees Julian had ever taken, his greatest concern eased by the knowledge that Chaz was alive and now more than capable of pleasing a crowd. Akane hadn't come out and said it, but Julian had a strong suspicion that she'd be able to find a way to justify eating him if he wasn't able to make good on his promise. His bladder was nearly drained when he heard screams coming from the water.

When he turned around, he saw Greyson struggling in the water, naked but for the purple tentacles dragging him farther out to sea. On the bright side, at least his tunic was safely on the beach.

"Akane!" shouted Julian. "Help him!"

Akane shot him a warning glare as if to say that she was getting very close to her threshold of how many of his orders she was willing to carry out. Thankfully, he hadn't quite reached that threshold yet. Kicking up explosions of sand with each step, she charged into the water, grabbed one of the creature's tentacles, then stomped back onto the beach, dragging it behind her.

The massive squid, at least as big as the one whose remains Ravenus was still feasting on, darkened the surrounding water with black ink before letting go of Greyson to focus all of its effort toward a futile attempt at self preservation.

With the exception of the one it was being dragged by, it groped at the sand with all of its tentacles, trying desperately to pull itself back into the water. Akane answered its resistance with a swift punch in the face, cracking its beak and knocking it out cold.

# Critical Failures VIII

Julian looked for Greyson and found him still in the water, covered in jet black ink from his head to just above his waist where his body disappeared under the water.

"Greyson?" Julian called out to him. "Are you okay?"

"Never better!" He smiled like he was trying to shrug off pain.

"Do you need some help?"

"I am fine!" he snapped back. "I will be finished in... I mean, I will be out of the water in a minute."

It only now occurred to Julian what he was doing as he stared lustfully at Akane.

"Really?" Julian went over and picked up his tunic. "If you get attacked by another squid, we're not coming in after you again."

"Then what was the point of asking me to go in the first time?" asked Akane. "If I had waited another minute, he would have drowned, and I could have eaten him."

Julian wanted to convey his frustration to Akane and Greyson, but he kept his glare fixed on the open sea instead, lest he become distracted by the latter's masturbating or the former's boobs. "You really don't see any ethical issue with letting a man drown so you can eat him?"

"I did not tell him to go out there. That is on you. But now he foolishly chooses to continue tempting the fates while I starve. What if a shark swims up and eats him? That would do none of us any good."

"What are you complaining about?" Julian gestured to the unconscious squid sprawled out on the sand in front of her. "You've got the freshest seafood in the world right there at your feet."

Akane grimaced down at the squid. "Ew."

"What do you mean, *ew*? I saw you eat rotting orc corpses. What's so gross about eating a squid?"

"I do not care for seafood. It is so slimy."

"Have you ever tried it before?"

"I tasted a bit of eel once," said Akane. "I did not care for it."

Julian thought about his encounter with one of the black cock eels and had to admit that "tasty" wouldn't be among the top ten words he'd use to describe what they looked like.

"Squid doesn't taste anything like eel. If you blast it with enough lightning, that should cook away most of the slime."

Akane frowned warily at the squid. "I will try it if you try a piece first."

Julian laughed, hardly able to believe he was having this conversation. "I would love nothing more than to eat a chunk of this squid."

"Very well. Stand back."

Julian took a couple of large steps back while Akane turned into a dragon again.

"NO!" cried Greyson.

Julian turned to look at him. "Greyson! What's wrong?"

"Can you tell her to change back into a human? Just for, like, twenty more seconds?"

"Shut up and get out of the –"

BZZZZZZTTTTTTTTT!

Lightning lit up the grim rainy evening as Akane pumped a gazillion volts of electricity through the now certainly dead squid. Its amorphous tubular head went rigid as the flesh cooked. Its eyes burst open, leaving puddles of ocular fluid in the sand. By the time she was done, the ends of its tentacles were all a crispy golden brown.

Julian held up a tentacle. "May I borrow your claw?"

Akane raised a finger and allowed Julian to saw off the end of a tentacle.

His stomach grumbling, Julian took a huge bite of the chewy flesh. He hadn't realized until now just how hungry he was. Whether it was that hunger alone, or some culinary effect of cooking with lightning, this squid instantly jumped to the top of his list of favorite foods.

"You have got to try this," he said to Akane through a mouthful of tentacle.

Akane held up the rest of that tentacle, then sliced it off where it met the head. After a moment of hesitation, she closed her eyes and put it in her mouth.

She chewed for a moment before her eyes shot wide open. "That was amazing!" She picked up the squid with both hands and tore the top of its head off with her teeth.

Julian took another bite, happy to have brought such joy to a new friend.

"Pardon us," said a voice from behind him.

Startled, Julian turned around to find the rest of Greyson's beach companions nervously approaching him. They had left their spears back by the rocks.

"Oh, hello."

"Master Dragontamer," said one of the women timidly.

The sound of someone else calling him that made him feel a little douchey.

"Yes?"

"We have not eaten in more than a day, and we wondered if you would be kind enough to..." Her nervous gaze drifted up to Akane.

"Of course!" said Julian. "There's plenty enough for..." He turned back to Akane just in time to see the last bits of tentacle slide into her mouth. She'd devoured the entire thing already. "Oh." He had only scratched the surface of his own hunger, but he couldn't stand the thought of letting these poor people starve after all they'd just been through. "You can have the rest of mine."

Perhaps his example might even teach Akane something about the benefits of helping others in need.

The woman accepted it with tears in her eyes. "Thank you. May the gods bless you." With that, she bolted down the beach, ditching her companions.

"Jillynn!" the other woman shouted at her. "Come back here, you greedy bitch!" She and her two male companions chased after her.

Julian sighed. Akane almost certainly hadn't learned anything about the benefits of helping others in need.

"Yes!" said Greyson, still going at it in the water. "Oh, yes! There it is!"

Julian was relieved that Akane was in her dragon form so that he had something else to look at. Akane, however, had her attention fixed on Greyson.

"What is he doing?"

"He's masturbating," said Julian. "I don't know if that's a thing that dragons do."

"I have never heard of it, but he seems to be enjoying himself. How do you do it?"

"I'm not super comfortable going into explicit details, and I'm not sure if it would even work the same way for you as it does for humans."

"Yes!" Greyson continued. "Oh merciful gods, yes! Just like that. Just... like... NO!"

Julian turned to him and found himself relieved to see that Greyson was wrapped in the arms of another giant squid. He felt a little guilty for not sending Akane out after him again, but he had given him more than ample warning, not to mention more time than any man should reasonably need to

Akane's left wing slapped the top of Julian's head, knocking him flat on the sand. When he shook off the surprise, he spotted her flying toward Greyson.

"Are you okay, sir?" asked Ravenus, flapping down to land next to him.

# Critical Failures VIII

"I'm fine. I just wasn't prepared for that." He smiled in Akane's direction. "Look, Ravenus. I think she's finally getting the hang of what being good is really all about."

Akane grabbed the squid with her rear claws and flew higher into the air.

"Help!" cried Greyson, still wrapped in the squid's tentacles. "Not so high! What if it –"

The squid shut him up with a gush of black ink, then let go of him. Coated entirely from head to toe, he plummeted blindly toward the shallow water, then barely made a splash upon impact.

Julian ran over to see if he was still alive.

"Where are you going?" asked Akane as she flapped down on the beach. "I got us another squid."

Much to Julian's surprise and relief, Greyson was pushing himself up out of the Greyson-shaped crater he'd left in the seabed.

"Are you okay?" asked Julian.

Greyson looked up wearily at him. The water rinsed most of the sand from his ink-coated body, but enough remained trapped in his hair and beard to make them look grizzled and grey. "I think I may have broken my member."

"If that's all you broke, you can count yourself lucky. Can you walk?"

"I... believe so." He winced as he got to his feet, and Julian turned away before he could confirm or deny Greyson's broken member.

Julian removed his serape and tossed it in Greyson's direction. "Wrap this around your waist. If you'd like to lead us to the harbor, I'll ask Chaz to heal your junk."

Greyson's blue eyes shined with confusion through the inky darkness of his face. "Chaz?"

"RazzmaChaz," said Julian. "He's a friend of mine." He chuckled to himself. "Come to think of it, I'm actually his manager."

*BZZZZZZTTTTTTTTTT!*

Julian looked back to find Akane cooking the second giant squid. "Come on. We'd better claim a leg before she eats the whole thing again."

# CHAPTER 39

"They wrote back," said Tim, hobbling into their room with an annoyed look on his face and a rolled up scrap of dirty fabric in his hand.

Cooper swallowed the big chunk of fried chicken he'd been chewing and chased it down with a generous gulp of stonepiss. Whoever Tim's inside man was had outdone himself.

"What does it say?" asked Cooper.

Tim scoffed. "Just show up."

"That's it?"

Tim let the fabric unravel to show Cooper the message. Being illiterate, all he could make out was meaningless scribble written in blood.

"That's not helpful."

"Yeah, that's it," said Tim. "Just show up. What the fuck are we supposed to do with this information?"

Cooper shrugged. "Maybe we shouldn't do anything."

"You really want to trust our fates to those two hillbilly fucktards?"

"No. I mean, maybe we shouldn't do anything at all. Like, we shouldn't try to escape."

"What the fuck are you talking about? We're prisoners, forced to fight to the death for the entertainment of assholes."

"True," said Cooper. "But have you tried this chicken? This is even better than that shit you used to serve at the Chicken Hut, no offense."

"I can't say I'm not taking just a little bit of offense at that. Who else on the coast served four flavors of chicken wings?"

"I'm just saying. This is almost Popeye's quality."

"You may want nothing more out of life than chicken and stonepiss, and it might be a good idea for you to stay here for a time, so I know you're safe and staying out of trouble." He grabbed himself a bottle of stonepiss from the fresh crate his inside man had delivered during the night. "But as for me, I've got shit to take care of. Wheels to set in motion. Palms to grease, seeds to plant. All that shit." He uncorked his bottle and took a long swig. "Those assholes at the Whore's Head are going to be lining up to suck my balls when I get a hold of Mordred and his dice."

Cooper snorted. "From what I can tell, the only palm you've greased is your own, jacking off to fantasies about winning the respect of people who don't give a shit about you. Why do you give a shit what they think about you?"

"I don't expect you to understand." Tim picked up the special backpack he'd made to hold his costume. "It was crazy to even entertain the idea that Randy and Denise could mastermind a prison break. So once again, the responsibility to do everything falls on my shoulders."

Cooper licked chicken grease off his fingers. "Where are you going with your costume?"

"After reading this bullshit, the Plan B I'd put on the back burner just got moved back up to the front burner. There are some people I need to talk to in order to make sure everything runs smoothly on the big day, and I find people take me more seriously when I'm dressed the part."

"Who's taking you more seriously in that? It makes you look like a fucking rodeo clown."

"Never mind who. The less you know about it, the less likely you are to fuck it up. All you need to do is stay here, eat chicken, and drink stonepiss. Leave the thinking and planning up to me."

# Critical Failures VIII

With that, Tim grabbed a fresh bottle of stonepiss and limped out into the hallway.

Cooper could understand Tim wanting to keep sensitive information close to the chest, but that wasn't what he was doing. By his own admission, he was currently on his way to talk to other people about his *brilliant* escape plan. Who could he trust more than Cooper? It wasn't like he was swimming with friends around here. Their fellow gladiators were outwardly friendly out of obligation, but Cooper had noticed that most of them tended to avoid Tim as much as they could without it being too obvious.

Tim was smart, but he was also arrogant and a terrible judge of character. He saw himself as being way more important to other people than he actually was, which constantly set him up for disappointment and left him unprepared for betrayals.

Cooper hadn't gotten too close with anyone since Yavin died, but he'd managed to get a general feel for just about everyone through weeks of casual observation. One thing that seemed true across the board was that they had all resigned themselves to the fact that they were going to be here for the rest of their lives, and Cooper couldn't think of a single one of them who wouldn't give up whatever dirt they had on Tim about a proposed escape plan to keep themselves from getting picked for the next Full Moon Brawl.

Well... maybe one, but Cooper didn't know who it was. Tim's inside man, whoever that was, clearly had connections that went beyond the walls of the arena. The man who had access to booze and fried chicken was the only one who could possibly be able to offer Tim a way to escape.

But that raised two questions. First, who was he? And second, what was Tim offering in exchange for his help?

The only possible answers Cooper could think of to the first question were Zimbra and Rocco. They were the only ones from outside the dungeons who ever had contact with the gladiators.

As for the second question, the only answer Cooper could come up with was butt sex. That might explain Tim's obsession with perfecting his costume. Maybe that was fulfilling some weird fetish of Rocco's. It might also explain why Tim was still walking funny. Maybe there was more to that than just his foot injury.

Cooper frowned at the chicken leg in his hands. As good as it had tasted a mere moment ago, he wasn't sure he'd be able to continue enjoying it knowing that it came at such a cost to Tim's poor little halfling ass.

No. It would be far worse to let the chicken go to waste, lest Tim let himself be cornholed by orc dick in vain.

In honor of the sacrifice Tim was making for them, Cooper finished his chicken leg and bottle of stonepiss, then carefully slid their contraband food and drink under his bed.

Sitting alone with his grim thoughts, he reasoned that Tim's sacrifice would be better honored by having a bit more to drink.

Over the course of the next bottle of stonepiss, Cooper started to question the conclusions he had come to. Would Tim take an orc dick in the ass to save them? The more he thought about it, the less likely it seemed. He thought of his own half-orc dick. Was a full orc's dick twice as big? Could Tim's ass take that much dick? Cooper gulped down half the bottle to shake free thoughts of his dick in Tim's ass.

The fried chicken and stonepiss were enough to make Cooper consider abandoning their plans to escape. Tim talked a big game about his heroic ambitions, but he'd seemed pretty content to do nothing but drink himself into a stupor when he was free. Were those heroic ambitions really enough motivation for him to make such a sacrifice?

Now that the stonepiss had cleared Cooper's head a bit, the answer was obvious. No fucking way.

The only thing Tim ever cared about was Tim. He even said his motivations for trying to get everyone back to the real world

## Critical Failures VIII

were so that everyone would line up to suck his balls. In Tim's mind, everyone owed him. He didn't owe shit to anyone, and he wasn't about to take an orc dick in the ass for them.

So what, then, was he up to?

Cooper finished off the stonepiss bottle, then set off to find out. Not having a clue as to where Tim had gone, he decided to check the communal bathroom first since he needed to take a piss, anyway.

It had been some time since he'd had a significant amount to drink, and he quickly found that he was a lot drunker than he'd expected to be. He needed to keep one hand on the wall to make sure he was walking in a straight line.

He wasn't sure how long it took him to find the bathroom, but he was sure that it had taken a lot longer than it should have. Strangely enough, though, he found that he didn't need to go as urgently as he had when he'd left his room.

When he got to the piss trough, he discovered that the front of his loincloth was soaked with piss. One mystery solved. He wrung it out over the trough. That pretty much amounted to the same as pissing the conventional way, only with an extra step. All's well that ends well.

"Cooper," said a stern voice from behind him.

Cooper shook a few more drops of piss from the front of his loincloth, then turned around to find Rocco standing in the entrance to the bathroom.

"Hey."

"You seem disoriented. Are you unwell?"

Alcohol was strictly forbidden in the gladiator dungeons, and Rocco was a hardass about keeping the prisoners in line. Cooper needed to think up an excuse for looking as drunk as he was.

"I was just whacking off. I squirted about a quart. It got me a little lightheaded."

"In the piss trough?" asked Rocco.

"There's a series of cracks in the wall that kind of looks like a tit." That much was true, an observation Cooper had made while wringing the piss out of his loincloth. It wasn't actually enough of a likeness to inspire him to jerk off in the piss trough, but it was a detail he thought might help sell the story.

Rocco barely glanced at the crack Cooper pointed to. "I am looking for your friend, the halfling."

"Tim?" Cooper felt a familiar tug in the pit of his stomach. The booze had gotten to him. It was a matter of seconds before he threw up, and that wasn't something he'd be able to explain away with a wank. He had to get rid of Rocco as soon as possible. "He's, uh... not in here."

"He is not in your room, either. Nor is he in the dining hall."

If Cooper had known where Tim was, he would have said so. He appreciated how this list of places where Tim wasn't could help him in his own search for Tim, and he would have loved to press Rocco a little about why he was looking for Tim, but what he wanted more than anything right now was for Rocco to get the fuck out of the bathroom. What was it going to take?

"Maybe he escaped," suggested Cooper, hoping that he wasn't giving away their intentions but desperate to end this conversation. The elevator from his gut was about to reach the top floor.

"Ha," said Rocco, which was as close to mirth as Cooper had ever seen from him. "Impossible. Nobody and nothing comes or goes from the dungeons without my knowledge."

The chicken and stonepiss in Cooper's stomach disagreed, both with Rocco's assessment of dungeon security and with Cooper's stomach.

Cooper let out a long belch. It tasted like bile. He was about to blow.

Rocco took a step back and scowled with disgust. "You may deliver a message to him for me, since it concerns the both of you."

# Critical Failures VIII

"Gladly," said Cooper, his palms starting to sweat. "What is it?" His time was up. The next thing that came out of his mouth was going to be a torrent of puke.

"You and he have been selected to participate in this month's Full Moon Brawl."

Cooper dropped to his knees and puked his guts out into the piss trough. The first wave was accompanied by an equally forceful gush from his other end, as was the second. The third was a dry heave, and he managed to not shit himself anymore than he already had.

"I see you are upset by this," said Rocco.

"Huh?" Cooper wiped vomit off his mouth with his forearm. "Oh, yeah. That sucks."

"Your fears may be unwarranted. I have seen much improvement in your fighting technique. There are few in North Pen who I would wager on to best you in combat. Your friend, however, I have less faith in. His foolish prancing about may win him a few laughs from the crowd, but it will do little to protect him from the swords of men who mean to save their own necks. I, for one, will not mourn his departure."

Cooper had gotten lucky with the timing of his puke, but he was still kneeling in a puddle of his own shit. He'd gotten everything he could hope to get from Rocco, and still wished very much that he would leave.

"Thanks for the talk. I feel a lot better about the whole thing now."

"You have five days of training left. I recommend you stay vigilant. In the meantime, clean up your shit."

Cooper took a moment to catch his breath after Rocco left, then stood up and grabbed the long-handled brush from where it was leaning against the wall.

The bathroom floor was slightly tilted toward a hole in the corner about as big around as Cooper's neck. As far as he knew, this hole was the only way in and out of the gladiator dungeons besides the main gate. He really hoped Tim wasn't smuggling chicken in through this way.

The floor was cleaned once a week with lye and water, and the most recent cleaning had been the day before. While the brush was effective at plowing most of the shit into the hole, it left behind a telltale smear that would remain until after the Full Moon Brawl had come and gone. Whether he escaped or died in battle, he would be remembered here as the asshole who shat on the bathroom floor and then fucked off.

By the time he had brushed away the worst of it, he had to pee again. That gave him an idea. If he pissed on the smear, he might be able to scrub it to the point where it wasn't so visible. If that didn't do it, he could go back to his room, drink more stonepiss, and do it again.

Feeling good about his plan, he lifted the front of his loincloth and let it flow. He had a nice hard stream going, and it was lightening the floor where it hit like a power washer. All was going well until Tim walked in.

"Jesus, Cooper!" he cried, shielding his eyes with his arm. "What the fuck are you doing?"

"Defending my honor."

"There's a fucking trough right next to you!"

"If I don't piss on the floor, everyone's going to..." Cooper's brain was still swimming in too much booze to articulate exactly why he was pissing on the floor. Now that he tried to explain it aloud, he wasn't quite sure he remembered the reason. "Where the hell have you been? Rocco was just in here looking for you."

"Rocco? What the fuck did he want?"

"He told me to tell you that you and I have both been selected for the Full Moon Brawl."

Tim nodded. "Excellent news. I thought they might only send you."

# Critical Failures VIII

That was an interesting concern for him to have, considering the feelings Rocco had just expressed toward Tim.

"Why's that?" asked Cooper.

"Because I'm too valuable as an entertainer. I wasn't sure they'd want to risk losing me in a bloodbath."

"That circus act we put on only works when I'm throwing you around."

"But my acrobatics would be harder to replace. Any of the fucking brutes in here could toss me around, and most of them probably wouldn't shit themselves while doing it." Tim took a deep breath. "I'm just explaining it from their point of view. Obviously, *I* don't think you're replaceable."

Cooper went back to brushing his urine-diluted shit toward the hole in the corner. "Did you take care of the shit you needed to take care of?"

"Sure did. Everything's all set. Get prepared to say goodbye to this shithole."

That sounded good to Cooper. His arms were getting tired from scrubbing, and his head was feeling clear enough for another bottle of stonepiss. He waved to the hole in the corner of the floor.

"Goodbye, shithole."

# CHAPTER 40

*I*f there was one upside to being held against his will, it was the sleep. Monsters sneaking up in the middle of the night weren't Dave's responsibility, nor was making sure the prisoner didn't escape. That burden was all on Stacy and Alroth. Shorty, who had made it clear on their very first night that guard duty wasn't part of the deal he'd signed up for, was the only one who got anywhere close to as much sleep as Dave did.

That's not to say that Dave didn't have a lot on his mind, and he'd lain awake at night in the past over lesser matters. But there was something satisfying about getting twice as much sleep as his captors, so he Willed himself to get as much sleep as he could. He enjoyed watching them wake up groggy and tired even more than he enjoyed how refreshed he felt. They were bringing this upon themselves, after all.

Last night, however, had been an exception to the rule. Dave had slept, but it was anything but restful. He woke up frequently from dreams he couldn't remember, then lay awake consumed by regret that he'd healed Stacy.

The perfect chance to escape had been handed right to him, and he'd blown it. Alroth and his stupid healing potion had forced him to make a quick decision, and he'd made the wrong one.

Intervening seemed like the right move at the time. As long as she would be healed anyway, he might as well cozy up to her by doing it himself. Make her think all was forgiven.

# Critical Failures VIII

But as he thought about it later in the evening, Dave guessed that Alroth's potion was probably a Cure Light Wounds, which would have restored between two and nine Hit Points. That might have put her back on her feet, but she would have been fucked if they'd encountered another ettin, and Alroth wouldn't still be holding that potion over his head.

Fear had gotten the better of him. Not only had it cost him a great opportunity, but he'd also risked letting on to Stacy that he'd been holding out on her.

No. It was pointless to think like that. He might have been able to get away with saying he'd used one spell on himself after tripping on a root and skinning his knee or something, but there's no way she would have bought that he'd used up his entire allotment of spells for the day. His choices had amounted to healing her and waiting for a more opportune time to make his move or trying to finish her off right then and there. Even if Shorty had stood on the sidelines, Dave wouldn't have been able to take on Alroth, Lucia, and a crippled Stacy at the same time.

Giving into that temptation would have been the easy move, but not the right one. He'd done right to heal her. For now he just had to play nice or bide his time. Stacy had nearly gotten herself killed facing off against one ettin. She'd definitely get slaughtered when she went up against a group of them. Even if she didn't, there was no way she was going to raise the money she needed in time to get Dave "cured". All he had to do was run out the clock.

Stacy sat up with a stretch and an obnoxiously long yawn. "What time is it?"

"It is late in the morning," said Alroth. "But since we are near the ettins and should not have to travel far to find them, I thought it was better that you got some extra rest."

"That was sweet of you. Thanks." She rubbed the sleep out of her eyes, then turned to Dave. "Good morning."

"Good morning," Dave replied as cheerily as he could fake.

"Did you say your prayers or whatever?"

Who the hell did she think she was? His mother? With every word that came out of her whore mouth, it became clearer that she only cared about him for his ability to heal. Well, that and maybe his dick. She'd never admit it, of course, but he'd felt something that second time he healed her the evening before. The way she tensed up and pretended to try to pull away. She was craving the D. Maybe next time she needed healing, he'd do it with his dick.

But first, he needed to pray.

He closed his eyes and allowed the sounds of the forest to clear his mind of all distractions.

"Gurlog!" shouted a sound of the forest. It sounded like a giant water buffalo had been granted the power of speech.

"Zugburt!" called out a similar voice from the same direction.

Dave opened his eyes. "Who is that?"

"I'm guessing Dick Head," said Stacy, crouching behind a tree as she peered into the forest. "His real name must have been Zugburt."

"What are you talking about? Who is that shouting?"

"Oh. It sounds like another ettin. It must be looking for this one." She looked down at the dead ettin on the ground below them.

"Just one?" said Shorty. "If we all work together this time, we should be able to take one with ease."

Stacy pulled her hood over her head. "I'll get into position by the body to pelt it with rocks when it gets close enough."

Alroth picked up his bow and turned to Dave. "Can you handle a bow?"

"Sure," said Dave.

"Good." He handed Dave the bow and his quiver of arrows. "You stay here and assault it with arrows." He unsheathed a dagger and longsword. "I shall confront it directly, keeping it distracted from Stacy."

"What shall I do?" asked Shorty.

"There is a Potion of Healing in my bag. Administer it two whoever needs it should one of us be struck." Alroth smiled. "If the gods continue to smile upon us, sending these beasts one at a time, I may yet clear this wood of ettins for good."

"Gurlog!" the first voice called out again, this time a little closer. "Where are you?"

Stacy scurried quickly but quietly down the hill, barely visible but for the leaves she kicked up in her wake.

Dave prepared an arrow and waited. Another single ettin probably wouldn't stand much of a chance against an actual coordinated attack by Stacy, Alroth, and Lucia. Dave would stay back and intentionally miss his target while he monitored the fight. If it looked like Stacy and Alroth were headed toward a decisive victory, Dave would put a couple of arrows into the ettin so that he could appear to be on their side. If the ettin should get the upper hand, Dave would continue missing until Stacy, Alroth, and Lucia were dead. If he was really lucky, they would all beat each other within an inch of their lives, and Dave could pick off each of those inches one by one.

"Mercy of the gods," Alroth whispered when the second ettin finally stomped into view.

This one was even bigger than the first, and female. Her tits looked like a couple of Halloween pumpkins in mid-January. The hair on both her heads was matted and filthy like she bred lice professionally.

"Gurlog?" the left head said when she discovered the corpse. She ran over and prodded it with her club. "Zugburt! Wake up!" said the right head. "Chief kill unicorn. Come before meat gone."

"NO!" screamed Alroth, jumping to his feet, his eyes burning with rage. He charged down the hill brandishing both weapons. Lucia followed him.

Dave had pegged Alroth as a pretty chill guy up till now. He was surprised to see him completely lose his shit over a horned horse. He'd probably have a stroke if he spent fifteen minutes with Julian.

The ettin prodded her dead friend harder. "Gurlog, Zugburt. Wake up! Angry man and leopard come this – OW!"

Stacy appeared behind the ettin as one of her rocks bounced off the head who had been speaking.

As the ettin bent over and grabbed her dead friend's club, Dave decided it was about time he looked like he was helping. He nocked an arrow, pulled back the bowstring, and released. It was a perfect shot, missing the ettin entirely, but not by so much as to look like anything but a poor die roll.

Alroth ducked a swing from one of the two tree trunks the ettin was now wielding, then screamed as he savagely attacked her, driving both blades into her left leg while Lucia tore into her right with teeth and claws.

Stacy used the distraction to disappear again, but Dave spotted her blurred form when she splashed through a puddle. She was repositioning herself for another shot. That reminded him that he should probably take another one as well.

He sent an arrow harmlessly between the ettin's heads as she swatted Alroth off her leg with the handle of one of her clubs. Alroth flew a good ten feet through the air before crashing to a heap on the ground.

"I suppose I should bring this to him," said Shorty, holding up a vial of dark green liquid.

"Yes," said Dave. "Hurry!" The sooner that potion was consumed, the sooner Dave would hold all the cards regarding who got healed and who didn't.

# Critical Failures VIII

While Shorty was making his way down to Alroth, Stacy reappeared behind the ettin and hurled another rock.

The ettin screamed in pain and frustration as she dropped one of her clubs and grabbed Lucia, who was still clinging onto her leg. She tore the leopard away, then threw it at Stacy, catching both Stacy and Lucia by surprise.

Stacy just managed to push Lucia off of her in time to spot the ettin's club swinging down at her and roll out of the way.

Dave remembered how hurt Stacy had been after just one hit and reasoned that this fight could go either way. Still, he couldn't risk a third whiff with his arrows. Even if he got as close as he had with the last two, three misses in a row would be suspicious.

*Stick to the plan, Dave. Don't get impatient. We're still moving the pieces into place.*

Nocking a third arrow, he took aim at one of those huge leathery tits and released. It sailed about three feet over her heads.

"Come on, Dave!" said Stacy. "How hard is it to hit someone the size of a house?"

The ettin slammed her club hard at Stacy again. "We not fat!"

Stacy jumped back to avoid the blow. "I didn't mean it like that."

Lucia leaped onto the ettin's back, raking large gashes into her skin as she tried unsuccessfully to hold on.

Having drunk the Potion of Healing, Alroth was now back on his feet. He screamed an inarticulate battle cry as he rushed at the ettin, giving Stacy another chance to disappear.

Now that they'd gotten their rhythm down, the situation was starting to look pretty grim for the ettin. A lucky swing might still give Stacy or Alroth something to remember her by, but the writing was on the wall, penned in ettin blood.

Dave fired another arrow, surprising himself by actually hitting the ugly bitch. She staggered backward, dropping her club to grab at the fletching poking out of her left throat as blood spilled out of that head's mouth.

Stacy struck her between the eyes of her other head while Alroth drove his sword deep into the back of her knee.

The ettin dropped to her knees, then fell forward over her friend's body. The battle was over.

Dave waddled down the hill to feign concern for the others. "Is everyone okay?"

Stacy nodded. "These creeps are tough. I didn't think she was ever going to go down. That was a nice shot you made at the end. For a second there, I thought you were missing on purpose."

Dave faked a laugh. "That's crazy. What would be the point of that?"

"I'm just messing with you, Dave. Everybody misses sometimes."

Was she just messing with him? Or was she letting him know that she was onto him? He couldn't read anything in her face as she cut the ettin's pouch free.

Stacy was a rogue. Masking her emotions was part of the package. Dave didn't have the Charisma for that. She could probably read his face like a book. He made a mental note to not try that again. No more pussyfooting around with intentional misses. Next time he fucked them over, he was going to fuck them hard.

"This one feels heavier than the last one," said Stacy, weighing the looted leather pouch in her hand. Just like she had with the last one, she dumped all of its contents on the ground for everyone to see.

There were some miscellaneous odds and ends. Some shiny black rocks, a withered frog corpse, a steel dagger hilt.

# Critical Failures VIII

But there were also quite a few more coins than the male ettin had on him.

"Hot damn," she said. "That's a much better haul. That's got to be at least thirty gold pieces."

"We're still a long way from a thousand," said Dave.

"Don't worry. What this tells us is that there's no way to predict how much money each of them is carrying. If these two are on the low end, we might have the money we need after just a few more kills. And I'm still not giving up on the idea that they might have some communal treasure in the group."

"These weren't exactly easy fights we had with single ettins," said Dave. "Have you given any more thought as to how we'll take on a big group of them?"

"That's what we brought Shorty for. He's going to be our inside man. Right now, we're just thinning the herd while the opportunities present themselves. If we had more time, we could probably take down the whole tribe this way."

Dave shook his head and laughed.

Stacy narrowed her eyes at him. "Something on your mind, Dave?"

He'd committed to playing the part of a loyal ally until the time was right, but he just couldn't resist bringing up her hypocrisy. Maybe that was for the best, though. Acting too friendly would arouse suspicion. He wasn't playing the part of Stacy's new best friend, after all. His role was that of someone who was resigned to his fate and trying to make the best of it.

"I just think it's kind of funny how you think I'm the one that needs to have some evil force driven out of me when you're over there casually contemplating genocide."

"Don't even try to go down that road. These freaks are invaders, not to mention slavers."

Dave shrugged. "I haven't seen any slaves, and I also haven't seen a deed that says Alroth owns this forest."

"I do not claim ownership of the Cedar Wilds," said Alroth, once again a picture of chill now that his murder frenzy was over. "I am merely its protector."

Dave kept his attention fixed on Stacy. "All I've seen is you murder two people in cold blood. Four if you count each head separately."

Stacy pointed to the female ettin. "That's not my arrow sticking out of her neck."

"I was acting in self-defense once the fight was already underway. You were the aggressor, attacking entirely unprovoked."

"Are you going to honestly tell me you don't think they would have attacked me or tried to enslave me if they saw me first?"

Dave shrugged. "Who knows what they would have done if you hadn't greeted them with rocks to the head?"

"I'm a rogue. Sneak Attacks are my most effective weapons. But in order to use them, the target can't know that I'm there. So I don't have the luxury of being able to formally introduce myself to a giant and wait for them to swing a tree at me before I defend myself." Stacy took a step closer to Dave and jabbed her finger at him. "Don't think I can't see exactly what you're doing here."

*Did she know? Was she laying her cards down? Was the jig up?*

"And what's that?" asked Dave, trying not to look or sound as nervous as he felt.

"It's obvious. You're cherry picking and misrepresenting my actions to make your behavior look less horrible in comparison."

Dave let out a small sigh of relief. "Yes. I suppose I was doing a bit of that."

"Well, it's not going to work," said Stacy. "So you can knock it off."

"Okay."

## Critical Failures VIII

Still fired up for more arguing, Stacy took a moment to process Dave's unexpected surrender.

"Good," she finally said. "Go say your prayers."

That sounded just fine to Dave. He was looking forward to a full hour of not being bothered by any of these assholes.

Retreating back to the top of the hill, he found himself a comfortable spot to sit down against a cedar trunk. He closed his eyes, cleared his mind, and let the gods' magic flow into him.

He'd never been one to take prayer seriously as a means to solve real world problems. But this time was different. The gods provided him with just the solution he needed. He wouldn't have to run out the clock after all.

# CHAPTER 41

"One step at a time," said Tony the Elf, his back against Chaz's as the crowd grew denser with spears and white tunics. "Don't make any sudden moves. We'll get back on the ship and figure it out from there."

They had reasoned that they could snap more people out of Mordred's influence if Chaz were to get off the ship and sing his song in a more accessible location, allowing more people to get close enough to hear it.

That worked for a short time. But once the so-called Knights of Jordan got wind that someone had arrived to disrupt their master's plan, they started swarming in. At first, that was even better. The first wave snapped out of their trances just as quickly as the Hollinites they'd sailed here with. But while the Hollinites aboard *Seastalker* had had a bit of time to come to terms with the situation and realize the need to protect the only person who could awaken the rest of those affected, the people he was freeing now were coming out of their trances in the middle of a violent uprising. They were understandably confused and scared, and most of them tried to flee the bedlam rather than join the resistance.

To make matters worse, the Knights of Jordan had caught on to what was happening, and now most of them were chanting, "Oh, oh, oh, oh, oh!" to drown out Chaz's song.

The crew he'd sailed in with, in addition to a few of the Knights who hadn't immediately fled when they came to their

# Critical Failures VIII

senses, pushed back toward the dock, allowing Chaz to inch his way to the relative safety of the ship.

Being stabbed to death by an angry mob would almost be a blessing at this point. He'd sung the same song thirteen times in a row. He was getting sick of it, but didn't dare try something that hadn't been tested for this particular function. And so he kept strumming and singing.

*Oh, but ain't there a cleric to come heal me?*
*Ain't there a cleric for my HP, baby?*

And the surrounding crowd chanted back even louder.

*Oh, oh, oh, oh, oh!*

"They're boarding the ship!" shouted Captain Logan, who had stayed behind to prevent just that sort of thing from happening. It wasn't the end of the world. They hadn't gone too far from the ship, and it would be easier to subdue the Knights on the ship after they boarded it and raised the –

"They're raising the gang-plank!"

Shit.

Now they were fucked.

Resigned to his fate, Chaz decided not to continue his performance after this song. If he was close enough to the water, he'd try to jump in and... Well, that was as far as he'd thought that plan through. Otherwise, he'd surrender himself to the mercy of the Knights of Jordan. They were a lot more pushy than they were stabby as they closed in on him, like maybe his song had partially awakened them. They weren't ready to completely let go of the toxic hold Jordan Knight had taken of their minds which led them to this place in their lives, but neither were they willing to bet the house that they'd been right to follow him by running their friends and neighbors through with spears. It wouldn't be enough to save Chaz, because the cult would regain full control of their minds once they had Chaz in their custody. But maybe they'd go easy on him?

He didn't really believe that. As he sang the last verse of the song, he knew that he was singing away the final sands in his life's hourglass.

*Ain't there a cleric? It hurts when I pee, yeah.*
*A little divine magic from you to me, ooo ooo* – "Oh, shit."

It was all he could think to say when he spotted a stunningly beautiful woman punching, kicking, and elbowing her way through the crowd to get to him.

She was dressed in the same white tunic as the rest of the Knights of Jordan, but Chaz was sure he would have remembered her if she had gotten close enough to be freed by his song.

The Knight's chanting turned into grunts and cries of pain as she bulldozed her way through the crowd.

"Oh!"

"Oooh!"

"Ow!"

"Ah!"

"Ugh!"

"Hangin' tough?" said Chaz, at a loss for anything else to say now that she was standing in front of him, especially now that the fighting had been put on hold while everyone wondered who the hell was this babe kicking everyone's ass.

"Are you Chaz?" she asked.

Chaz took a deep breath as his heart beat faster. So this is what it's like to be a rock star.

*Be cool.*

"Why, yes. As a matter of fact, I am. Do you want, like, an autograph or something?"

# Critical Failures VIII

"My acquaintance would like to speak with you." She stepped aside to reveal a familiar face at the back of the parted crowd.

"Julian?" said Chaz.

Julian nodded. "Hey." It wasn't as warm a greeting as Chaz would have liked, but Julian clearly had his mind on other things, such as the Knights of Jordan, the sphere of fire he held in his raised hand, and the half naked guy with jet black skin standing next to him with what appeared to be Julian's serape wrapped around his waist.

"Welcome to..." It occurred to Chaz that he had no idea what this island was called. "...wherever the fuck we are."

"My name is Julian Dragontamer," Julian announced to the crowd.

"Seriously?" That sounded kind of lame to Chaz. It would probably be better for Julian to stick to being a manager and let Chaz keep the spotlight. Chaz detected a hint of annoyance in the hot badass woman's face. Even she thought it was lame. "Are you married to that name, or –"

"SILENCE!" demanded Julian, clearly having forgotten the dynamic of their professional relationship. "If any of you so much as wiggles an eyelash, I will cast this fireball down here at my very feet." He pointed to a random Knight of Jordan. "You there. Tell me what is the cause of all this commotion."

The Knight nervously pointed his spear toward Chaz. "This charlatan seeks to poison our minds."

"Bullshit!" said Chaz. "If anything, I'm trying to –"

"Quiet, bard!" Julian stared at him severely. "I will hear the Knights' grievance." He turned back to the Knight he was questioning.. "How do you believe he seeks to poison your minds?" Chaz couldn't believe Julian was actually listening to this guy. Had the Knights of Jordan gotten to him?

"Through his wicked song," the Knight answered. "He weaves some kind of dark sorcery into the music to make us forget our master's orders."

"Jordan Knight has poisoned us!" shouted a voice from the other side of the mob. "Razzmachaz has set us free!"

Julian closed his eyes and waved a hand in Chaz's direction. "I sense no such magical aura coming from the bard. How is it that your faith is so easily shaken by the strumming and wailing of this kitschy buffoon?"

"Dude," said Chaz. "What the fuck?"

"My faith in Jordan Knight is as strong as Thabor's Hammer, but I fear for those of my brethren who are weaker of mind."

Julian scanned the crowd. "Knights of Jordan. Who among you has faith less strong than Thabor's Hammer? Make yourselves known." When not a single Knight raised their hand or stepped forward, Julian raised his eyebrows at the Knight he'd been speaking to. "If your faith is as strong as you claim –"

"It is!" insisted the Knight.

"Then it should be no concern of yours if the bard plays his song."

The Knight shrugged. "Fine. Let him play. I do not care."

"Excellent." Julian looked at Chaz. "Play your song, bard."

Chaz sighed and began strumming his lute.

*There's a black man –*

"His name is Greyson," Julian snapped at him with an annoyed glare. "And that's squid ink. Just sing the goddamn song already."

Chaz glared right back at him as he kept singing, hoping that Julian felt foolish for his interruption, but secretly relieved to know what the deal was with the mostly naked black guy.

By the time he got to the end of the first verse, the Knights immediately surrounding him were starting to freak out and drop their spears, and the ones beyond them started up their chanting again. Julian's gambit had only delayed the inevitable. He would have stopped playing if it wasn't such a pleasure to watch this improbably strong and attractive ass-kicking machine do her stuff.

But then he heard something else begin to penetrate the Knights' chanting.

*Oh, but ain't there a cleric to come heal me?*
*Ain't there a cleric for my HP, baby?*

It was only a few voices at first, but others quickly joined in. Looking out at the crowd, Chaz saw that Julian had extinguished the ball of fire in his hand and was now going from person to person, encouraging them to sing along.

When the recovered Knights caught on, it spread like wildfire, completely drowning out the chants, until everyone was singing along to the best of their limited talent and knowledge of the lyrics.

When the song was done, Julian ran up with a big goofy grin and grabbed Chaz by the shoulders. Whatever that Julian Dragontamer bullshit had been about, he'd completely abandoned it.

"This is it!" he said. "This is how we're going to get Mordred. He thinks he's impossible to touch because of his legions of followers, but we can rally these people to go take back their homeland."

"Do you think that would work?" asked Chaz, scanning the crowd of recovered Knights who were hugging each other and reveling in their newfound freedom.

"I think it just did."

Finding a kink in Mordred's armor was nice, but it quickly took a back seat to another potential consequence that suddenly occurred to him.

He grabbed Julian's shoulders. "Think of the publicity this will bring in. Razzmachaz saves the fucking world! Oh my god, my balls are sore just thinking about all the sperm they'll be pumping out."

"Your balls?" asked the woman who had arrived with Julian.

Chaz became acutely aware that he was embracing a dude while talking about his balls in front of her. He let go of Julian.

"Hi," he said, offering her his hand. "My name's Razzmachaz. Perhaps you've heard of me?"

She glanced curiously down at his hand but didn't shake it. "You have balls that produce sperm?"

"Indeed, I do. If you'd like to join me on my boat, I'll be happy to show them to you."

Julian grabbed him by the arm. "Can I talk to you in private?" Without waiting for an answer, he dragged Chaz into a tavern near the docks. "You don't want to mess around with that girl."

It did seem odd that she appeared to be genuinely confused at the concept of balls. "Why? What, is she retarded or something?"

"Or something."

"I always say, love knows no IQ."

"Would you shut up for a second?" said Julian. "We need to talk business."

While it was totally on brand for Julian to be a stick in the mud, Chaz was surprised that his foremost concern at the moment was their career. "You mean, like, show business?"

"Yes. We need to do some shows as quickly as possible. I've got a little debt to pay off."

## Critical Failures VIII

"To who?"

"Akane. The woman I arrived with."

Chaz looked over his shoulder toward the tavern entrance, then back at Julian. "She's a hooker?"

"Good evening," said the barkeep, having disengaged with the customers at the other end of the bar to come take their orders. "What can I –" His eyes widened as his gaze met Chaz's. "Say, are you not the bard who just freed our town from the Knights of Jordan?"

Chaz flashed him a wide smile. "It was nothing, really. I only did what any responsible citizen would do, given that they were blessed with as much charm, talent, and dashing good looks."

"I would like to buy you and your friend here a drink." Rather than ask what they wanted, he produced a dingy bottle and two semi-clean glasses from under the bar and started pouring.

"That's very generous of you," said Julian. "My name's Julian. I'm Razzmachaz's manager."

"Manager?" said the barkeep, giving Julian a distrustful look as he took a swig from the bottle he'd just poured their drinks from.

"I work behind the scenes for him. Booking performances, negotiating fees, that sort of thing."

"I know what a manager is, son. But I thought you said you were some kind of dragon tender or something."

"Dragon*tamer*," Julian corrected him. "I have my fingers in a number of different pies. I wonder if you might be interested in having Razzmachaz play here tonight. For a modest fee, he could have this place packed wall to wall with paying customers."

Chaz downed his drink. He wasn't sure what it was, but it went down strong and smooth. He happily accepted a second pour and watched with interest as Julian finally seemed to be taking his job more seriously. Even if his main motivation was to put a shameful memory behind him as quickly as possible, it would still give him some much needed hands-on managerial experience. The question was, what exactly did Julian feel so guilty about?

Was it that he'd fucked a retarded chick? That didn't seem so bad to Chaz, especially if he was paying her enough that he had to arrange a show to cover it. Besides, that girl was definitely on the low end of the spectrum. And she kicked ass even harder than... Oh, so that was it. He and Stacy must have gotten pretty serious, and he was losing his shit because he'd cheated on her. That's just adorable.

"How modest a fee are you proposing?" asked the barkeep.

"Two hundred gold pieces," Julian responded.

Chaz choked on his drink.

*Jesus, Julian! That's probably, like, a year's worth of money to these people.*

The barkeep laughed. "I am sorry, friend. I am not equipped to pay so high a price. For weeks, the Knights of Jordan have kept our harbors free of thirsty sailors. The economy of the entire island has borne the burden of their presence. You might fare better on the mainland. The Knights would have had a much harder time trying to occupy a big city like Pargos."

"How far away is Pargos?" asked Julian.

"Not far. Mayhap half a day's journey by sea."

"Then that's where we've got to go next." Julian sucked down his drink, then winced. "Thank you again."

Chaz barely had time to pour his second drink down his throat before Julian had him by the arm again.

"What's the hurry, man?" asked Chaz. "I think I deserve to enjoy a drink or two after what I just did."

"We need to get back on the ship."

# Critical Failures VIII

"Hey, slow the hell down. Katherine's on this island somewhere. We can't leave without her." He brought his voice down to a whisper. "Also, tell me you didn't offer that girl two hundred gold pieces. I mean, like, at least half of that was supposed to be my cut, right?"

Julian sighed. "I offered her a lot more than that. I was aiming low because I didn't think this place could realistically support a thousand gold pieces. Hopefully, we'll find a venue that can afford us in Pargos."

"A thousand fucking gold pieces?" Chaz was having a hard time keeping his words to a whisper. "Are you out of your mind?"

"I saved your ass, didn't I?"

"I don't see how that applies to this conversation." Chaz opened the door so that he could yell at Julian properly outside. "That's like swiping an old lady's credit card and using it to remodel your kitchen because you pushed her out of the way of a speeding bus. You can't show up and sing a song with me, then expect me to pay a thousand gold pieces for a retarded hooker."

"She's not a retarded hooker!"

"Hey, guys," said Katherine as she walked toward them with that Jay guy, her half-drow friend, and several formerly deceased members of the Whore's Head gang. She smiled at Julian. "I didn't expect to see you here."

"Katherine!" said Julian, wrapping his arms around her in an embrace that probably would have gotten Chaz stabbed if he'd tried it. "Funny, we were just talking about you."

She pushed Julian away and scowled at Chaz. "Did you call me a retarded hooker?"

"What? No!" Chaz frantically scanned the crowd until he found the woman Julian called Akane. "I was talking about her."

"She's a hooker?" Katherine looked genuinely impressed. "She's got to demand more than you bums can afford."

"That's what I was just saying to Julian."

"She's not a hooker," Julian insisted. "Her name is Akane. She gave me a lift here. That is the extent of our relationship."

"Who's the drow standing next to her?" asked Jay.

Julian chuckled. "That's Greyson. He's human. He just got hosed down with squid ink."

Katherine laughed obnoxiously at Jay. "Wow! That's just... Wow."

"Jesus, Katherine," said Chaz. "Give the guy a break. He's new here."

"I'm just saying, the guy doesn't even look like a drow."

"And I'm just saying, you're being a dick about it."

"We can argue about this on the ship," said Julian. "Right now, we need to go to Pargos."

Katherine shrugged. "Awesome. Where's my ship?"

"What are you talking about?" said Chaz. "It's the only goddamn ship in the – Oh shit."

*Seastalker* was no longer docked where they'd left it. Looking out to sea, he spotted it about a quarter of a mile away heading north.

"Logan!" Katherine's eyes burned with anger as she peered out at the fleeing ship. "That son of a bitch just doesn't know when to quit." She sighed. "I'll be right back."

"Wait," said Chaz. His heart skipped a beat when Katherine turned her glare on him. "I think you should just let him go."

"Why the fuck would I do that? I've taken that ship from him twice already."

"And both of those times you had the element of surprise on your side. The first time you had him over a barrel because he and his crew had nowhere else to go. The second time you had a cargo hold full of freed slaves at your back. This time you've only got yourself, and he'll be expecting you. Logan's taking a calculated risk, and the numbers are on his side."

"Besides," said Julian. "Were you planning on pulling your hole-in-the-hull stunt again?"

Katherine frowned. "Yeah, so?"

"We don't have time to hang around while you bail out the ship. We have to find a different way to Pargos as soon as possible."

Chaz didn't feel quite the same sense of urgency about paying off Julian's hooker bill, but he welcomed the solidarity.

"Where is Pargos?" asked Katherine.

"The barkeep said it's about half a day's journey by sea."

"Well, I sure as shit can't fly that far, and we're on an island with no boats. The only way out of here is me taking my ship back."

"We could ask the drow," said Jay.

Katherine laughed for a moment, then stopped. "Oh, you're serious."

"They are not exactly popular among the locals," said Tanner, Katherine's recently re-resurrected half-drow friend. "I would be surprised to learn that they did not have a plan for evacuating themselves in case of a sudden uprising."

"We just duped those guys out of a lot of expensive shit to bring people back to life who they would have much preferred to remain dead," said Katherine. "Did you see Lady Vivia's face when Harzos told her she couldn't kill Butterbean and that he was going to do everything I asked and let me go? I honestly thought she was going to have a stroke."

Jay laughed. "Yeah, that was some intense shit."

"I think we've spent all the goodwill we're going to get from the drow."

"But we're not looking for goodwill. We're making them an offer."

"What the hell else do we have to offer them? We've solved their big problem, and I don't think any of us have any money."

"We've solved *a* big problem," said Jay. "They've still got an island full of extra mouths to feed and a wrecked economy. They're not going to start seeing any new ships in their harbors until the rest of the surrounding area is free to sail without being molested by Knights of Jordan. Chaz here has proven that we can deliver. It would be in the drows' best interest to set us loose in a neighboring city."

"I like it," said Chaz. "Let's not forget that we've got Charisma on our side. I can wow them with a song. Julian can use his Diplomacy. If there are any dudes there, Julian's new friend can, um…" The only thing he knew she was good for was kicking ass and high-end sexual favors. The former wasn't going to win anyone over, and they couldn't afford to hire her for the latter. Being retarded, she probably wasn't very useful for Diplomacy.

"Be present?" suggested Tony the Elf.

"Sure. A little eye candy never hurts." Chaz could see in Katherine's tight-lipped scowl that something about what he was saying was pissing her off. He'd noticed that before when he'd seen her interact with Stacy. She must feel insecure about not being the hottest girl in the group. "And, of course, you could also be, like, *diet* eye candy."

"Shut up, Chaz," said Katherine. "Fine. Let's do this. Just don't blame me if it all goes to shit." She and Jay started leading the rest up the island's muddy dirt roads.

"Come on, Akane," said Julian as they passed her and the guy covered in squid ink. "It was a pleasure to meet you, Greyson. Thanks for everything."

"Where are we going?" asked Akane. "Greyson was just teaching me about masturbation."

# Critical Failures VIII

Ravenus looked up from a dead rat he'd been pecking at. "I remember learning about that from Chaz. Is that when a female stores acorns in her –"

"Ravenus!" said Julian.

"Speaking of masturbation," said Greyson. "My member is still quite sore."

"Shit. Sorry about that. Chaz, do you have any healing spells handy?"

Chaz hadn't used a healing spell since saving Cooper's life from those goblins. He'd all but forgotten he could cast them.

"Sure," he said. "Let me see if I remember how that goes." Thinking back on the incantation he'd used, he wished he's spent some time reworking the lyrics. He kicked off his left shoe and lifted his foot toward Greyson. "Would you mind holding my foot?"

Greyson frowned down at the foot in front of him. "I suppose not, but may I ask why?"

"I need to be touching you in order for the spell to work, and I need both hands to play my lute."

"Oh. That sounds very reasonable." Greyson grabbed hold of Chaz's foot with both hands and held it firmly.

Chaz strummed his lute and sang the incantation.

*Cure Moderate Wounds. Hear my moderate tunes. Cure Moderate Wounds.*

"That was inspiring," said Julian. "Truly, you are a legend among bards."

"It's a work in progress." Chaz turned to Greyson. "How's your junk?"

"Much better now, thank you. Would that I had more semen in me, I think I might have soiled this colorful garment."

Chaz pulled his foot free from Greyson's caressing hold. "Thanks."

"And thank you for not soiling my serape," said Julian. "I'm actually going to need that back. Katherine, do you have any extra clothes in your bag?"

Katherine turned around, looking even more annoyed than usual. "Weren't you the one in such a hurry to get to Pargos? I could have had my fucking ship retaken and bailed out by now."

She pulled a pair of not-quite-jeans out of her bag, which Julian swapped Greyson for his serape. Twenty minutes later, they were standing in front of a small black tower.

"Everyone keep quiet and let me do the talking," said Julian.

"Are you sure?" asked Katherine. "I mean, I'm the one they're used to dealing with. They might be more comfortable negotiating with me."

Jay laughed. "They were about to make you watch them murder your pet wolf."

"Animal Companion."

"Whatever. My point is, they hate you."

"They hate everybody who isn't a drow.. But I'm the only one who's managed to successfully –"

"You again!" shouted a drow from the window above. "How dare you return here!"

"Hi, Cedric," said Katherine. "I need to speak to Harzos one more time."

"Absolutely not! We have fulfilled our end of the deal. Go away at once or I shall have you all flayed!"

"Don't be such a dick. We just want to talk. I think he'll like our proposal."

Cedric scowled down at her. "This is your last warning, cat eater. You would be wise to disperse by the time I get down there." He backed away from the window.

# Critical Failures VIII

"Maybe we should leave," said Fritz. "I just came back to life. I'd rather not be flayed."

"He's not going to do shit," said Jay. "I got a strong vibe that he was trying to get between Lady Vivia's legs. If he had the authority to kill Katherine without Harzos's say so, he wouldn't bother to warn us. He'd be all over that shit."

Julian stared up at the empty window. "A little pointer for using Diplomacy. 'Don't be such a dick' rarely diffuses a confrontation."

"I could try a song," suggested Chaz.

"That actually sounds like a good idea. We'll hit them *Say Anything* style. If that song was powerful enough to bring the Knights of Jordan to their senses, it might be powerful enough to sway a single drow from hostility to annoyance."

Chaz sighed. "Does it have to be *that* song? I'm getting kind of sick of it."

"Yes. Go with what we know works."

"Fine." Chaz begrudgingly started strumming his lute.

*There's a black man with a –*

"Shit," said Julian. "I forgot about that. Maybe we should go with a different song after all. *Sweet Caroline*'s always a solid –"

"What the fuck?" cried Chaz as he felt a warm stream of liquid hit the front of his shirt. He jumped back and looked up to confirm that he had, in fact, just been pissed on. He couldn't see Cedric, but the yellow stream was still flowing down from the window. "What the hell is wrong with you?"

Cedric laughed as his pee stream stopped, then poked his head out the window again. "I warned you, did I not?"

"You said we'd be flayed, not sprayed!"

"We deeply apologize for disturbing the mighty drow who rule this island," said Julian. "But you must believe that we would not dare to do so if we didn't have something to offer the High Drow that we truly believe would please him enough to spare our lives."

If Julian shoved his nose any farther up Cedric's ass, Cedric would be able to pick it with his tongue. Chaz turned back to Akane, curious to see her reaction to the guy she apparently knew as Julian Dragontamer practically sucking drow dick for the opportunity to grovel in front of a –

Where the hell did she go?

"You may make your proposition to me," said Cedric. "I shall relay it to my brother."

"Forgive me, noble drow," Julian continued laying it on thick. But to his credit, it seemed to be getting him further than Katherine's approach. "But what we would ask in return, though a pittance for those as powerful as you, may not be something the High Drow would like me to bellow from the street."

Since Julian was engaged in conversation, Chaz inched close enough to whisper to Katherine.

"Back off," she whispered before he got the chance. "You smell like piss."

"What happened to that girl who arrived with Julian?"

"The retarded hooker?"

"Yeah."

Katherine glanced over her shoulder at the rest of their group. "I don't know. Maybe she got distracted by a butterfly. Who cares?"

"She couldn't have gone far. I'm going to see if she wandered around to the other side of the tower."

"This isn't the time to go chasing tail, Chaz. And trust me, if she's a pro, you're not going to get anything out of her with a serenade."

"I'm not chasing tail," responded Chaz quasi-honestly. "If things go south with the drow, we'll want her on our side."

## Critical Failures VIII

"What's she going to do? Suck their dicks?"

"I know she doesn't look it, but this chick kicks ass in a fight."

"Would it kill you two to keep it down while I'm talking?" asked Julian. He wasn't quite whispering, but he was using an inside voice.

Katherine looked up at the empty window above. "What happened to Cedric?"

"He went to ask the High Drow if he'd be willing to grant us an audience."

"Nice work."

"What were you two bickering about?"

"Chaz wants to boink your new girlfriend."

"That is *not* what I said," said Chaz.

Julian squinted at Katherine. "New girlfriend? You mean Akan– Shit! Where the hell is Akane?"

Chaz shrugged. "I was just wondering the same thing. I was going to go look for her around the other side of the tower."

Julian nodded. "I have to stay here in case Cedric comes back. Don't be long."

"Buddy system," said Katherine. "Every time one of you idiots wanders off alone, you wind up getting whisked away to the other side of the world. Take Tony the Elf with you."

"Why him?" asked Chaz.

"Why me?" asked Tony the Elf. "Why can't Tanner go with him?"

"Tanner's been dead all day. I need someone who can look after Chaz. He's afraid this eighty-five pound girl is going to kick his ass."

"Again, not what I said." Chaz turned his back on her and started walking. "Whoever wants to come with me is welcome to do so. Whoever wants to stay here is even more welcome to do so."

"Slow down, Dancing Queen," Tony the Elf called after him after he'd rounded the corner.

Chaz neither slowed down or looked back. "What's that supposed to mean?"

"Nothing. It was just a reference to your ABBA costume."

That stopped Chaz dead in his tracks. He whirled around to give Tony the Elf a warning glare, but Tony the Elf just averted his eyes and tried not to laugh.

"This isn't *ABBA*, asshole. I modeled this costume after –"

"I don't care. Shut up."

Chaz's instinctive reaction was to say, "Fuck you", but he could see that Tony the Elf was distracted by something as he peered out at the expansive rose garden behind the keep.

"What is it?" asked Chaz, hoping that Tony the Elf's attention was focused on something other than how pretty the roses were. He had to admit, however, that they were indeed very pretty. Red, yellow, purple, and apricot petals glistened with raindrops, adding some cheer to an otherwise very bleak setting. He grabbed a fistful of petals off one and rubbed them on his shirt to mask the smell of drow piss.

"I hear something," whispered Tony the Elf. "It's coming from over there." He pointed down a narrow flagstone path running through a sea of wild rose bushes.

"What is it?"

Tony the Elf put a finger over his lips and drew a machete from one of the two sheaths on his back, then started creeping down the path. Chaz wasn't sure if he was supposed to follow or not, but there wasn't a whole lot else left to explore on this side of the keep. If Akane was anywhere nearby, the odds were good that she was involved with whatever it was Tony the Elf heard in the rose garden.

They hadn't crept long before Chaz could also hear something out of the ordinary. Some kind of grunting and smacking noise, like an exceptionally gluttonous pig or a chunker at Golden Corral on cheat day.

Tony the Elf stopped dead in his tracks near a trellis poking out above the roses. "Oh my –" He turned around quickly and threw up in the bushes on the other side of the path.

Chaz's curiosity was stronger than his sense of self-preservation, but not by much. Prepared to turn and bolt at a nanosecond's notice, he stepped forward to find out what had so disturbed Tony the Elf.

"Akane?" he said after suppressing the wave of nausea that he had braced himself for. She was naked and crouched down over a young, dead drow, holding its half-eaten arm in both of her hands. One of its legs had already been devoured all the way down to the bone. Her face looked like that of a child who'd been caught with her hand in the candy jar, except that it was heavily smeared with fresh blood. "What the fuck?"

"I am sorry," she said. "I was hungry."

"This isn't the fucking Donner party! Julian could probably negotiate a loaf of bread or something into the deal."

"You are not going to tell Julian about this, are you? It makes him terribly upset."

"Julian's... seen you do this before?"

Akane hung her head. "A few times."

No wonder he was in such a hurry to clear his debt with her. This bitch was hardcore.

"I... I have to get out of here," said Tony the Elf. He began staggering back toward the keep.

"Hold that thought," Chaz said to Akane, then chased after Tony the Elf. "What are you doing?"

"What does it look like I'm doing?" Tony the Elf panted heavily. "I'm going back to join the others."

Chaz glanced back to make sure they were far away enough from where they'd left Akane to safely whisper. "You know we can't tell them what we saw here, right?"

"Why the hell not? We have to!"

"And we will. When the time is right. There's something off about this girl."

"You think?"

"No, I mean she's stronger than she has any business being. There must be a reason Julian hasn't told us about this, and I'm guessing it's for our own protection. I've seen her fight, and I don't think she'd break a sweat killing us all at the same time if she wanted to."

"So what is she?" asked Tony the Elf. "A vampire or something?"

"I don't think so. Vampires suck blood. She's actually eating that dude's flesh."

"Oh, God." Tony the Elf doubled over like he wanted to puke again, but he didn't have anything left to give.

Chaz patted him on the back. "Just take it easy, dude. Whatever she is, Julian seems to think she'll leave us alone as soon as she gets her money. So let's just focus on getting to Pargos so I can do a show, then hopefully we can put this all behind us."

He took Tony the Elf's machete, meeting no resistance, and slid it back into its sheath. Then they both tried to look casual as they walked back toward Akane. The act fell apart as soon as Akane stepped out onto the path.

"SHIT!" cried Chaz, feeling like his heart had leaped about a foot out of his chest. "I mean, Akane. Hello."

Akane smiled at him. She was dressed again, and her face was no longer smeared with blood. If Chaz hadn't witnessed it with his own eyes, he never would have suspected she'd just been eating a dude. "Hello to you." Her unsettlingly nonchalant gaze pivoted to Tony the Elf. "And to you."

# Critical Failures VIII

Tony the Elf raised his hand in a weak wave. "Hey."

"If you're, um... finished," said Chaz, "we should probably go back and join the others."

"Are you going to tell Julian what you saw?"

Chaz forced a laugh. "What? I don't even know what you're... Oh, *that*? Of course not!"

Tony the Elf just kept his mouth shut, which was probably for the best after Chaz's less-than-stellar performance.

"Good," she said. "It would displease me if anything should get in the way of your ability to perform."

Chaz just gawked back dumbfounded at her, unsure of how he was supposed to respond to such a bald-faced threat so emotionlessly delivered. This chick was a straight up sociopath.

"Because he is your manager," she added in response to his continued silence. "At least, that is what he told me. Am I mistaken?"

"Huh?" Chaz forced himself to snap out of it. "No! Not at all. He's totally my manager, and absolutely vital to my ability to perform." He was trying to convince himself that it was a misunderstanding, that she hadn't meant that as a threat.

When she took the lead back to the keep, walking between Chaz and Tony the Elf, he peeked quickly through the rose bushes to see what was left of the drow body. She hadn't made so much as the slightest effort to hide it. Almost all of the flesh and muscle tissue was gone, leaving behind a horrifying mess of bones, blood, and viscera.

Chaz decided that the safest option was to go ahead and assume that what she'd said had been a threat after all.

# CHAPTER 42

"The more I interact with these ettins, the better I feel about our chances of getting rid of them," said Stacy while Alroth meticulously cleaned ettin blood from his weapons. "I figure there are two ways we can go about it. We can take out their leader and let them duke it out in a battle for who takes over."

Alroth raised his eyebrows in interest. "How do you propose we get to their leader without alerting the rest of the ettins to our presence?"

"I haven't worked that part out yet, but we'll figure it out if that's the plan we decide to go with."

"What is the alternative?"

Stacy shrugged. "We set their slaves free. They're pretty much bringing an opposing army with them wherever they go. If we give the slaves a means to stand up to their oppressors, I'm sure they'd –"

"Flee as quickly as possible?" suggested Alroth.

"I was going to say *fight*."

Alroth nodded. "I suspected as much. You have an optimistic nature. Myself, I would prefer not to gamble my life on the courage of orcs and goblins." He turned to Shorty. "I mean no offense."

"None taken," said Shorty. "If I was in their place, I would not stay and fight. What good is being freed if you immediately get squashed by a club afterward?"

# Critical Failures VIII

"You wouldn't be just a little hungry for revenge?" asked Stacy.

"I expect they are hungry for more than that," said Alroth. "That is something else to consider. These slaves are likely weak and malnourished. Plus, we have no weapons with which to arm them."

"And there is the matter of coin," added Shorty, squatting on the female ettin's back and sawing into her flesh with Alroth's dagger.

"I don't really think they'll expect us to..." Stacy could no longer pretend to ignore Shorty's mutilation. "I'm sorry, but what are you doing?"

"Looking for a kidney. They must be higher than human kidneys, more like an orc's." Shorty pulled the dagger out of the wound, then stabbed it higher in the ettin's back, just below the ribs.

"If I asked why you were looking for her kidneys, would I regret it?" Unless he was harvesting it to sell on the ettin black market, the only other possibility Stacy could think of was –

"I want to eat it."

Stacy turned to Alroth. "Are you okay with this?"

Alroth shrugged. "We humans tend to frown on eating the flesh of creatures that look similar to ourselves. Goblins have no such reservations. Is it better to let the corpses fester when they could fill a hungry friend's belly?"

"What are you talking about?" asked Shorty, plunging his arms up to his elbows into the new gash he'd just cut. "These freaks look nothing like me." After a little bit of struggling, he pulled out a bloody purple kidney as big as his own cartoonishly big head.

Stacy looked away, agreeing to disagree. "Okay, fine. This is gross. Talk about something else. What were you saying about coin?"

"Supposing they would stay and fight," said Shorty through a mouthful of raw ettin kidney. "And supposing we collectively defeat the ettins, that bunch of slaves would have as much claim to any treasure we recovered as we would. Mayhap more if it was what the ettins took from them at the time of their capture."

"Shit," said Stacy. "I didn't think about that." She didn't know if she had it in her to steal money from slaves. This would require some heavy rationalizing. "But let's look at the facts. I only agreed to come out here because of the money, right?"

Shorty shrugged. "How should I know?"

"You'll have to take my word on it. Now, there are probably thousands of slaves around the world. Is anyone who doesn't spend every waking moment of their life trying to free those slaves a bad person?"

Alroth and Shorty exchanged a quick glance, but neither answered her.

"Of course not. Everybody's got their own stuff going on in their lives. They can't be expected to drop everything to go fight all the world's injustices. What I'm getting at is that we aren't ethically bound to risk our lives to set these people free. Doing so for money might not be the most noble endeavor to undertake, but I think it's fair to say that it still counts as a good act. As long as we can all agree that we're not in this strictly for altruistic purposes, which is okay, it stands to reason that our options come down to either aborting the mission and letting them remain slaves, or leaving them free and poor. I don't know about you, but I think I know what option will help me sleep better at night."

Shorty grinned, his pointed teeth red with ettin blood. "That was very impressive, but you need not justify your decisions to me. My caution is more a practical matter than an ethical one. I, for one, would not turn my back on a hungry goblin, much less one I had just stolen money from."

"You make a good point, but your disgusting theatrics undermine it."

"Oh? And how is that?"

"Any goblins that survive the fight will have as much ettin as they can eat lying right there in front of them. If they still want to come at me, I'll put them down without batting an eye. But it shouldn't come to that if you do your job correctly."

"And what is my job, exactly?"

"You get them primed and ready to fight. Let them know that the cavalry is on its way. Maybe embellish our strengths and numbers if you have to. I'll sneak into the ettin camp at night while most of them are sleeping and set you all free. But before I do that, it's important for you to convince them that the odds are heavily in our favor if and only if we all strike at once. And most of all, make sure they understand that I'm not the bitch they want to fuck with."

"This could actually work," said Alroth. "But I have an idea that could really turn the tide in our favor."

"There you go! See what we can do when we put our heads together?" Stacy was ecstatic to finally hear some good news. "What have you got?"

"We shall do just as you said, except for the part about you freeing them."

Stacy's optimism fell a couple of notches. "But isn't that, like, the most crucial step?"

"If our goal was to free the slaves, then yes. But my goal is to rid this wood of the ettins, and you said yourself that your goal is coin."

"That's my *primary* goal, sure," said Stacy. "But freeing the slaves was a nice secondary goal. What use are they going to be if they're all chained together?"

"Much more use than they would be fleeing through the forest. Especially if we arm them."

"Arm them with what?"

"What else?" said Alroth. He picked up a bloodied rock. Stacy recognized it as one of the rocks she'd thrown at the male ettin. "These have proven to be surprisingly effective against ettins."

"That's not so much the rocks as it is the Sneak Attack damage I get for being a rogue. I know that probably doesn't make much sense to you, but a bunch of goblins and orcs throwing rocks isn't going to be very effective if they can't move out of the way when the ettins start swinging their clubs."

"They'll be more effective fighting with rocks than they would be running away. Shorty may be able to inspire them to work together if forced to fight, but I have little confidence that he will be able to inspire them to fight if they have the option to run. Also, you will have a much easier time running away with the ettins' treasure if the survivors are busy passing around manacle keys."

If that's what Stacy sounded like when she was rationalizing a few minutes ago, she didn't like it at all.

"What do you think, Shorty?" she asked. "If we go with this plan, you'd be chained up with all the other slaves."

"I would never have agreed to any of this if I could not pick a lock. I shall hide an ettin finger bone in my butthole. As soon as the fighting starts, I will set myself free and make a break for it."

"You'd leave all your fellow goblins to get massacred by ettins?"

Shorty shrugged. "Hopefully not *all* of them."

"How noble of you."

"The only way to avoid spilling innocent blood is for us to walk away," said Shorty. "The four of us cannot defeat the ettins in time for you to get the dwarf to the temple before the coming full moon. Alroth is correct in that, given the choice, every single orc and goblin will flee rather than fight. I do not wish to be smashed with a tree trunk. The only conceivable plan proposed so far is Alroth's. And if what you said before was true about you not being willing to interfere if there was no reward, this is the only hope for any of those slaves to be freed."

Stacy sat on the freshly felled cedar trunk. "That's a heavy burden to bear, having to decide for someone else whether or not to risk their life for their freedom. What would you choose?"

"I cannot choose for anyone else," said Shorty. "I can only choose what best serves me. That said, having spent some time in involuntary servitude myself, I would risk death for a reasonable chance at freedom every time."

"Sounds like I walked in on some heavy shit," said Dave, returning from his prayers with Alroth's bow and quiver in hand. "What did I miss?"

Stacy sighed. It was time to make a decision.

"We've just worked out how we're going to take down the ettins."

"Oh yeah? Does it involve Shorty biting all their fingers off?"

Stacy turned back to find Shorty nibbling the flesh off one of the female ettin's severed fingers, then quickly turned back to Dave.

"No. Just that one."

"It sounds like you guys really thought this through, but I was thinking we might hang back and see if we can pick off one or two more stragglers. Thin the herd a bit more before going after the whole group."

"We don't have time for that. It's a long hike back to Cardinia, and we don't even know if this will be a big enough score to cover the temple bill. I'd like to have at least a little wiggle room in case we need to make a couple extra bucks to make up the difference."

Dave frowned at the ettin corpses. "So what is this big plan of yours?"

"Short answer, we're going to let Shorty get taken prisoner by the ettins. But first we need to find them. I'll fill you in on the details while we walk."

"Walk where? We don't even know where they are."

"The two we've encountered so far both came from that way." Stacy stared out at the broken branches and flattened undergrowth the ettins had left in their wake. "I don't think Alroth and Lucia should have too much trouble tracking the group down."

"It should be exceedingly easy," said Alroth. "Ettins are about as stealthy as a dire badger on fire."

"But wouldn't it be better if we forced them to come to us?" Dave asked, almost pleading. "Home field advantage and all that?"

What was going on in that hairy head of his?

"Home field advantage doesn't factor into it," said Stacy. "We're not trying to fight them yet. We're just trying to get Shorty captured, which will be a lot less complicated if he doesn't have to explain two dead ettins."

"Or we could use the two dead ettins to our advantage. Imagine this scene from their point of view. Two of their comrades dead at our feet. We've barely got a scratch on us. Maybe we're badasses. Maybe we've got reinforcements hiding in the woods, bows nocked and aimed right at their faces. We make our demands, and they have no choice but to lay down their clubs and obey."

"I don't know, Dave. That sounds like a pretty tough bluff to sell. Even if they believed us, which I don't really see happening, they'd probably be more pissed than scared of us for killing their friends."

"Come on, Stacy. If anyone can sell the bluff, it's you."

"That's kind of you to say. But I really don't think that I can."

"At least take a second to think about it." Dave was getting desperate, which made Stacy feel uneasy. Why was he so hellbent on this objectively stupid idea?

"I have taken a second to think about it. That's all it took to see how catastrophically bad that idea is. It depends on selling an implausible story to a bunch of angry giants who aren't likely to give us a chance to tell it. It also depends on me forfeiting my Sneak Attack, which is the biggest combat advantage I have. But most importantly, it depends on us waiting around for them to show up, which may never happen. And time is currently a luxury we're in very short supply of."

"But –"

"But you know all this," Stacy continued. "So my question to you is why are you trying so hard to sell us on this idea? What tricks do you have up your sleeves? What are you biding your time for?"

"I'm not *biding my time*," said Dave. "I just don't think it's wise to rush headlong into a dangerous situation without considering all of our –"

The sharp crack of a branch in the distance shut Dave up. It came from the same direction the ettins had come from. Stacy, Dave, Alroth, and Shorty stood still as statues to listen.

"Gurlog!" shouted a male ettin voice.

"Lugburt!" shouted another.

"Lagra!" shouted a third. "Mugmug!"

Stacy looked at the dead female ettin. "I guess those were Lagra and Mugmug. They really did have tits like an old man's jowls."

"At least two ettins approach," Alroth said to Shorty. "Are you ready?"

Shorty nodded.

"Ready for what?" said Dave.

"Ready to put the wheels in motion," said Stacy. "You stay here, Shorty. Make like you just stumbled upon the bodies and decided to have a bite to eat. When they see you, grovel and beg for mercy. If they take you prisoner, great. If they try anything else, we'll be hiding close by."

Dave grabbed Stacy's wrist, which very nearly got him a fist-shaped indentation in his face. "What are you doing?" he said. "This is the perfect opportunity to thin the herd some more. We can take two ettins if we organize just a little better."

"Let go of my arm, Dave."

Dave let go and stepped back. "Sorry."

"Alroth said *at least* two," said Stacy. "The two we've already fought individually were closer calls than I'm comfortable with. We might be able to take two at a time, but I think this is a better opportunity for Shorty to do his job. Capturing a slave will probably score them points with the chieftain. But if they opt to attack instead, we still have a chance at taking them down and thinning the herd."

"But you don't –"

"Mugmug! Lugburt!" The voices were getting closer.

"The discussion is over," Stacy whispered firmly at Dave. "Now shut up and find a place to hide." She pulled up the hood on her Cloak of Elvenkind and crouched behind the ettin corpses.

Dave waddled behind a boulder, squatted down, and sulked.

Alroth and Lucia took positions behind the fallen cedar.

Stacy gave Shorty an encouraging nod as he stood out in the open. She admired his courage and hoped that a little of it might rub off on Dave. She couldn't wait until she got the rat curse out of him. It would take a while before she'd be able to trust him again, but she was really looking forward to starting down that road.

"Lagra! Gurlog! Mugmu–" Two male ettins stopped dead in their tracks when they spotted their two dead companions and Shorty standing next to them.

"Please!" begged Shorty, dropping to his knees. "I had no part in this, I swear by the gods! Please do not –"

THWACK!

"YAAAAAUUUUGGGGHHHHH!" cried the ettin who suddenly had the back end of an arrow sticking out of his chest.

"It is trap!" shouted his other head. "Goblin is bait!" He lifted his huge club and slammed it furiously down at Shorty.

Stacy didn't have a line of sight to see if Shorty had been hit or not, so she did the only thing she could do.

Her anger got the better of her, and she hurled her rock wide to the left of the head she was targeting. But now that she was visible, she figured she might as well give Dave a piece of her mind.

"What the fuck, Dave?"

Instead of answering or firing another arrow, Dave turned into a rat and scurried away.

Alroth screamed a whirlwind of barely comprehensible profanities as he and Lucia charged out of hiding to attack the ettin Dave had struck with an arrow. He must have had some tragic backstory involving ettins, because he really seemed to hate the shit out of them.

While Alroth drove his sword up into its hamstring, Lucia stifled one of its cries of pain by launching herself from Lagra and Mugmug's body onto its left face.

Unfortunately, it was the right head who was controlling the arm with the club. He ignored the leopard on his other half's face and took a swing at Stacy. She jumped out of the way and dived between Lagra and Mugmug's heads where she found Shorty hiding. He appeared to be unharmed.

"What happened?" he asked. "Why did you attack?"

"That was Dave," said Stacy. "I don't know if he was just being stubborn or deliberately being an asshole, but he fucked us."

"Perhaps a bit of both?" suggested Shorty.

The biggest problem with facing more than one enemy at a time, especially when those enemies have more than one head, is that the odds of all of them taking their eyes off Stacy long enough to set herself up for a Sneak Attack are significantly reduced. This could very well be her last chance to hide before the fates decided who would come out of this battle alive.

Stacy pulled her hood up. "I'm going to need you to make a distraction so I can –"

The uninjured ettin pulled one of the dead female ettin's heads up by the hair, exposing Stacy and Shorty. Shorty darted out and drove a dagger straight down into his foot.

That was just the distraction Stacy had been looking for. She was down to her last two rocks, so she was careful to make this one count. When the ettin leaned over to grab Shorty, Stacy let one fly. It cracked in half as it struck the bald top of its right head.

Painful as that must have been, it didn't stop the ettin from grabbing Shorty and throwing him at a tree. Fortunately, his aim seemed to be impaired from the crack on the head he'd just suffered, and he missed the tree. Still, it was a hard throw. Stacy gave Shorty about fifty-fifty odds of surviving the landing.

Shorty had let go of the dagger, which was still hilt deep in the ettin's foot. If Stacy kept her attacks focused on that foot, she might be able to buy herself a little more maneuverability.

She pounced onto the ettin's injured foot, drove her own dagger in beside Shorty's, then pulled both hilts toward her like she was trying to keep an airplane from crashing into the side of a mountain.

Both the ettin's heads howled in agony, which Stacy savored until something big and hard smashed into her back.

For a few seconds, Stacy didn't know if she was awake or asleep, alive or dead. All of her senses melded into one another, a blur of darkness, numbness, and muffled screams.

Her hearing was the first sense to reorient itself. The ettin's screams became sharp and crisp, as did Alroth's continued barrage of profanity farther away.

Alroth was still alive. Hell, Stacy was still alive. That was good.

Her vision came back to find the other ettin standing over her, lifting his club to smash her a second time. The head glaring down at her was pissed, but not half as much as his other one. Lucia's claw and tooth marks spilled blood down his entire left side, though there was no sign of Lucia. His left hand had a firm grip around Alroth's torso, but Alroth was still swearing up a storm as he repeatedly stabbed the arm that held him.

Relieved that she could still move, she rolled out of the way just as the club came down. That one would have done her in for sure. She didn't know how many Hit Points she had left in her, but she must have been in the single digits because she felt like she was in the negative triple digits.

The ettin she'd attacked was on the ground, cradling his injured foot. The blades of both daggers were sticking out of the bottom, and the foot looked unnaturally flattened. It must have taken the brunt of the impact when the club had hit her.

They could still win this if Stacy was smart about it. Both ettins were hurt pretty bad, but one of them was effectively crippled. If she steered clear of that one, she could use her Sneak Attack against the other one until it died and released Alroth. The other one should be easy enough to dispatch from a distance.

The standing ettin decided it had enough of being stabbed in the arm. Dropping to one knee, it opened the hand holding Alroth and smashed him down hard into the rocky earth.

Stacy used the distraction to don her hood again while the ettin gripped his club with both hands.

"Come on, Alroth," she whispered. But Alroth only stirred a bit as the ettin raised his club to finish him off. She needed a distraction.

With the last of her rocks in hand, she cocked her arm back to hurl it at the ettin. If this didn't kill it, she had no idea what they were going to do.

But the distraction she needed didn't come from her rock.

Something moved in her periphery, and she turned to find Dave, once again in his dwarf form, slapping his palm on the left ass cheek of the dead female ettin.

"Oh, Dave," she whispered to herself. It was one thing to fondle a corpse if he thought nobody was looking. He was going through some stuff, and people got up to weird shit behind closed doors. But *that* corpse? And under these circumstances? That was a depth of depravity she just couldn't comprehend.

Unfortunately, the distraction had worked on Stacy more than it had on the ettin. While she was wondering what the hell Dave was doing, the ettin brought his club down hard on Alroth. It sounded like a combination of snapping twigs and exploding meat. He was gone.

Stacy was down to a single rock, probably just as many Hit Points, and her only ally was fondling a corpse. She almost

## Critical Failures VIII

felt bad wasting her last rock to distract the ettin from clobbering Dave when he seemed to be going out of his way to call attention to himself. But saving him was what she'd come out here for in the first place. Besides, he was the only one around who would be able to heal her –

"What the hell is he doing?" she whispered as the dead female ettin began to push herself up off the other one. "Is he *healing* the ettins?"

Was that why he wanted them to stick around here? What possible reason could he have for doing that? Stacy could understand him wanting to betray her. He hadn't exactly been coy with his contempt for her, or his desire not to have his curse removed. But how could he possibly think that he would be able to cozy up to a gang of ettins? Even if he brought a couple of them back from the brink of death, he didn't have the Charisma to rely on them not killing him anyway, or at least taking him as a slave.

Dave laughed giddily, like he'd just cracked the neighbor's wi-fi password. Apparently, he had a lot more faith in his ability to woo them than she did.

"Mugmug?" said one of the ettin heads with daggers in his foot. "Alive?"

One of the female ettin heads, presumably Mugmug, stared vacantly back at him.

"Mugmug!" shouted Dave. "Kill him!"

"Nnnnnnnnggggggghhhh," said Mugmug, getting the attention of her partner head. Both of them lumbered toward the lame ettin.

"Mugmug?" he repeated a little nervously.

Mugmug only groaned in response before dropping to her knees on top of him, then pounding her fists repeatedly into his faces. She punched with all the passion of someone hammering nails into a piece of wood in the hopes of getting a C in shop class.

Stacy was impressed. Dave must have picked up on some desire in that poor ettin girl that the men in her tribe weren't fulfilling. She felt bad for her. How undesirable does one have to be before she'll betray her own people for the first dwarf to come along and grab her ass? She supposed the answer was right there in front of her, beating the shit out of her former friend.

"I raise thee!" shouted Dave, his palm firmly against the other fallen ettin's right arm.

*I raise thee?* That wasn't the incantation Dave usually used for healing spells. That didn't even make –

Stacy turned back to Mugmug, still punching the now unconscious ettin's faces to pulp. She still had the gaping wounds in her back from where Shorty had pulled out one of her kidneys. Dave hadn't brought her back from the brink of death. He'd brought her back from actual death!

The standing ettin, having gotten over his shock at seeing Mugmug and Lagra lose their shit on the other ettin, stomped angrily toward Dave. That took him out of Stacy's Sneak Attack range, so she hurried after him to rescue Dave from his own idiocy.

Dave didn't need rescuing though, at least not yet. Gurlog and Lugburt got up and stood in the attacking ettin's way.

Dave grinned up at him. "Kill him."

Having just seen what had gone down between Mugmug and his friend, the attacking ettin only hesitated for as long as it took to look into Gurlog and Lugburt's dead eyes before swinging his club at them.

Stacy winced at the sound of crunching ribs, but Lugburt didn't even flinch as the massive club left a dent in his side. He grabbed the arm that had swung the club and pulled the ettin closer for Gurlog to punch.

# Critical Failures VIII

The fight didn't last long. Alroth and Lucia had already taken a lot out of the ettin. A few more punches was all it took for Gurlog and Lugburt to finish him off.

By then, Mugmug and Lagra were standing over the other dead ettin with vacant expressions on their faces like substitute teachers waiting for the bell to ring.

"Stacy?" Dave called out. "Where are you? We did it!"

Stacy remained still, her last rock in her hand, wondering what she should do.

"Stacy?" he shouted again, his gaze almost meeting hers when he scanned past her.

Why hadn't he told her he intended to raise the dead ettins as zombies or whatever? The only explanation for him being so stubborn about staying there was that he wanted to test out some new spell he'd discovered that allowed him to raise the dead. Could there be any reason then, other than the very obvious, why he would choose to keep that from her?

Dave sighed. "Have it your way." He grinned up at Mugmug and Lagra, then at Gurlog and Lugburt. "New friends. Find the human girl and kill her."

That certainly cleared up any doubt in Stacy's mind.

Poor, stupid Dave. How far did he have to push her before she finally wrote him off as a lost cause? Maybe they'd finally gotten to that point. There wasn't much she could do for him now. She was battered all to hell. There was no way she could take on two ettin zombies and Dave at the same time.

She watched the zombies trudge around looking in random directions, not even coming close to spotting her. They wouldn't be difficult to outsmart, and Dave would need to sleep eventually. She would follow him, then distract the zombies somehow while she abducted him. Fighting Dave for Dave's sake was getting harder and harder to justify to herself with every new act of assholery. The anguish he would feel when the curse was removed was something she would savor until she was finally able to forgive him someday. From now on, she would continue fighting Dave for that.

"That cloak won't hide you for long," said Dave. "The stench of your cunt will give you away."

Stacy refrained from gasping.

*The stench of my cunt? You can be evil without having to be so... gross.*

Dave morphed into his hybrid dwarf-rat form and started sniffing the air.

Stacy didn't think her groin had a particularly strong smell, but she didn't know how sensitive Dave's rat nose was. Holding her rock at the ready, she backed away slowly.

One direction neither Dave nor his *new friends* were looking was up, so Stacy carefully backed her way among the lowest branches of a nearby cedar. Keeping her hands and feet as close to the trunk as she could to minimize the movement of the branches, she started climbing.

Below her, Dave was sniffing around the battle scene while his zombies wandered aimlessly. His nose seemed locked onto something, which would have been frightening if it wasn't leading him away from her. Instead, it led him to Alroth's crushed remains.

Dave rifled through Alroth's clothes until he found what he was looking for. When he stood up again, he was holding a fistful of pickled pig dicks. Alroth must have kept them as snacks for Lucia. Dave must have acquired a taste for them in the past few days, because he was chowing down on them like Slim Jims.

Since she was already in a tree, Stacy decided to make the most out of her time while she waited for Dave to call off his search. She climbed higher to get a better view of her surroundings. About halfway up, she heard voices in the distance. She couldn't make out what they were saying, but they sounded loud, angry, and plentiful.

# Critical Failures VIII

"Forget her!" Dave said to his zombies. He was a dwarf again. "The others are coming. We have to go." He pointed to Mugmug and Lagra. "You. Pick me up!" When she grabbed him under his outstretched arms and lifted him up to her chest, he looked around. "Good luck, Stacy. I'll come back someday to animate your corpse. Then we'll really have some fun."

Stacy trembled at the implications, trying to think of anything he might have meant other than that he intended to fuck her dead body. She made a mental note to try dying either in an active volcano or a wood chipper.

Her trembling, she soon discovered, was only partially due to being grossed out by Dave. The tree trunk she was hugging was also shaking. The ettins were getting closer, and it sounded like there were at least half a dozen of them.

The tree trunk shook more violently the closer they got. The thick boughs of the surrounding trees didn't allow for much of a view anyway, so she started climbing down. First, she'd see whether or not Shorty was still alive, then she'd follow Dave at a discreet distance.

But just when she was about to hop down from the lowest branch, she found that she'd underestimated how near the approaching ettins were. The ones who were bickering noisily with each other were still quite a ways back, but less chatty ettins were walking ahead of them, two of them heading her way.

"Shit," she whispered, then scampered back up the tree as quickly as she could. It was one thing to be able to hide from Dave and a couple of zombies, but Stacy dared not push her luck trying to stay hidden from so many approaching eyes.

Each ettin carried a club in one hand, and a handful of chains in the other. Each chain ended with an iron ring locked tightly around a goblin's neck. The goblins walked ahead like dogs on leashes. They pulled eagerly, sniffing and panting until one of them spotted the two dead ettins on the ground.

"There!" cried the goblin, pointing at the bodies.

"There! There!" yipped the other two excitedly to the ettin holding their leashes.

The ettin heads frowned at their fallen companions, then the one on the left turned back toward the others that followed.

"Over here!" he bellowed. "We find them!"

"Look," said the head controlling the leash arm as he pointed at Alroth's body. "They fight with human."

The other head frowned over one of the ettin corpses' heads. "Tiny human no punch like that. They killed by ettins."

"Grubgar will not be happy."

"Over here!" the other ettin on the scene called out. "We find goblin. Bring chains!"

Stacy sighed with relief. She didn't envy what Shorty was likely to go through for the rest of the day, but at least he was alive.

They were too far away for Stacy to see what kind of shape Shorty was in, but she could make out the chained goblins laughing and jeering as they prodded him with their feet. She was beginning to have doubts about their original plan. These goblins might be too far gone to turn against their masters, too indoctrinated into their roles as slaves. She'd kill Shorty before she let him turn into one of them.

The rest of the ettins started arriving on the scene, some with chained goblins, others with chained orcs. They chatted nervously, speculating on what had happened to their two fallen companions. The general consensus seemed to be that Gurlog, Lugburt, Lagra, and Mugmug had murdered these two and then run away together. They pretty much ignored Alroth's body, the claw marks all over one of the ettin's face and upper body, or any other evidence that didn't line up with the conclusions the first ones came up with.

Eight ettins, about twenty goblins, and at least a dozen orcs all became still and silent as something else approached from behind them. When they stood aside, Stacy saw an ettin being carried on a palanquin by eight strong orcs. They had to be strong, because the ettin they were carrying was obscenely overweight. At least twice as big as any of the others, his tits were bigger than Lagra and Mugmug's. Wearing a relatively clean blue linen toga, he was the only one of them dressed in anything more than a filthy loincloth. But what really set him apart from the rest of the ettins, at least in Stacy's eyes, was that one of his heads appeared to be dead. Its skin was grey, hanging loosely on its face. Eyeless sockets stared blankly at nothing in particular as its mouth hung open, making it look like it was permanently surprised.

When they came upon the bodies, the fat ettin prodded the front most orc in the back of the head with his club, prompting them to stop and lower the palanquin. His club was as big as any of the others, but it was the only one Stacy had seen that had any actual craftsmanship put into. Rather than a mere tree trunk stripped of branches, this club had been shaped, sanded, polished, and fitted with steel studs on one end and a leather grip on the other.

When he started to rise, another ettin stepped forward to assist him.

"Easy, Grubgar. Let me hel–"

CRACK!

The assisting ettin caught some of those steel studs in the side of his head. He stumbled backwards, then the other head apologized.

A young female ettin put her left hand on her hip. "You no have to do that, Father. Bobor only want help." Her other head looked terrified as it raised the hand it controlled to try to cover the first head's mouth, but she slapped it away.

"I am Grubgar!" bellowed Grubgar. "I need no help!"

"Only one month pass since Goran die. You not yet have full control of body."

Grubgar used his club as a cane to support himself as he pivoted toward his daughter, his left leg dragging behind. When he was balanced, he lifted his club to point it at her.

"Speak not my brother's name, or you share his fate."

The eyes of both her heads went wide for a second, then she lowered the head that had been speaking.

"Yes, Father. Forgive me."

Grubgar planted his club on the ground again and turned back toward the dead ettins. "Morrick. What happen here?"

The ettin he'd clubbed in the face rubbed a swelling lump on the side of his injured head. "Mugmug, Lagra, Lugburt, and Gurlog sneak away to make sex. When they are discovered, they kill Habar, Tumbum, Cramil, and Dung, then run away together."

"They think me weak," said Grubgar. He tried to make a fist with his left hand, but only managed to curl his fingers up a little. "Mugmug MINE!" He lifted his club and swung it furiously at the trunk of the tree Stacy was hiding in.

"Oh!" she cried as she was thrown from the trunk, but she managed to catch herself on the branch below. Had they heard that? Stacy held her breath while the ettins all looked up in silence.

"Someone hiding in tree," said Morrick, pointing almost directly at Stacy. "Sound like human."

*Shit.*

"You want I send goblins up?" asked another ettin.

Grubgar laughed. "Yes. They want eat. Let them hunt food."

# Critical Failures VIII

"Go!" the ettin said as he let go of his goblins' chains. "Find human! Kill!"

Their chains rattled behind them as the goblins excitedly ran for the base of the tree. Stacy had a decision to make.

She knew she wouldn't be able to kill everyone. A lucky hit by one of these goblins might be enough to bring her Hit Points down below zero.

Hiding would only be a viable option for so long. The only choice left was to surrender and hope she could make herself seem more valuable as a slave than as goblin food. But that was a case she'd have to make to Grubgar. The goblins climbing up to eat her now were doing so on his orders and not likely to be swayed by reason.

They were quick little freaks, scampering up the branches like big-headed spider monkeys, occasionally getting yanked back down when their chains got snagged.

Stacy felt a little bad about having to defend herself with lethal force, but she planned on stashing her Cloak of Elvenkind in this tree when she eventually surrendered, and she couldn't risk these goblins reporting a missing cloak to their ettin masters. She eased her guilt by reminding herself that they were, in fact, climbing this tree to murder and eat her.

The goblins hadn't spotted her. Their eyes were all focused way up the tree trunk, no doubt assuming that their prey would want to get as far away from them as they could to put off the inevitable as long as possible. But Stacy was perched on a branch about a third of the way up the tree, far enough away from the trunk to let the goblins pass.

When the last of them had passed, Stacy waited until the very end of its chain went by, then grabbed it and gave it a hard yank.

"Gah!" said the goblin as it was ripped from the branch it was holding onto. It bounced off a couple more branches on its way down before falling past Stacy. She gripped the end of the chain, jerking it upward just as the slack ran out. Satisfied by the audible crack of its neck, she let go of the chain and braced herself for the other two goblins.

They jumped down at her simultaneously. One of them landed on a branch that wasn't quite strong enough to support its weight falling from a height. It snapped off, sending the surprised goblin down another ten feet to a stronger branch.

The other goblin looked equally surprised when Stacy caught him by the iron ring around his neck. He clearly wasn't expecting her to be as strong as she was. She slammed his head back against the tree trunk, impaling it on the freshly broken piece of branch jutting out.

The last goblin climbed up toward her, his eyes full of rage and hunger, but not even a hint of fear or trepidation. The poor little guy had no doubt seen far scarier things than her, and probably experienced far scarier things than the quick death she could offer.

Stacy waited for him to pounce, then let herself drop. She caught herself on the branch with one hand and the goblin's chain in the other. Jerking the chain down as hard as she could, she forced the goblin's face down onto the branch. He fell off, disoriented but still very much alive. With about eighteen inches of chain between her hand and the goblin's neck, she flailed him against the tree trunk until he stopped screaming.

When she was satisfied that he was dead, she swung the chain around a few times before launching him out of the tree toward the ettins. There was still a chance she could get out of this. They didn't know who she was. Hell, they couldn't be certain of even *what* she was from what little information they had to go on. If she could play up that mystery, destroying all the little minions they decided to throw at her,

# Critical Failures VIII

they might eventually take the hint that she wasn't something they wanted to fuck with and go on their merry –

CRACK!

The tree shook violently as Grubgar struck the base again with his club. Instead of causing him to flee in terror, killing three of his goblin slaves had only pissed him off even more. In hindsight, Stacy supposed that was the reaction she should have expected.

CRACK!

She held on tight, barely keeping from being shaken out of the tree with each successive hit. It wouldn't remain standing for very much longer. Soon she would be on the ground surrounded by angry ettins, subservient orcs, and hungry goblins. Faced with no choice but surrender, she took off her cloak. She stuffed that, along with her bag, into a hollow five feet down the trunk.

The next crack was followed by a loud snap, then a series of creaks and crashes as Stacy rode down, shifting her balance from a branch to the trunk as the latter went from vertical to horizontal. In other circumstances, such as her having more Hit Points than an elderly mosquito, it might have been fun.

When the tree finally crashed to the ground, Stacy was surprised at how dense the foliage was now that so many branches had snapped off upon hitting the ground and mingled with those on the side facing up. If she hadn't stowed her Cloak of Elvenkind, she might have had a decent chance at hiding. But that was neither here nor there, as she was currently standing like a jackass in plain view of all the ettins, goblins, and orcs.

"Hi," she said, holding onto a tree branch with her right hand and giving Grubgar a friendly wave with her left.

Grubgar looked down at his own left hand, as limp and useless as the decaying head that used to control it, then glowered at her.

"Kill it."

"Wait! Stop!" she said to the several ettins who stepped forward to smash her with clubs. Much to her surprise, they actually stopped. That wasn't going to last long if she didn't get a conversation going with Grubgar, so she blurted out the first thing that came to mind. "You don't want to kill me."

"Yes," said Grubgar. "I do."

"For what? Goblin food? Look at me. I wouldn't last a day."

"Is one less day I have to feed goblins."

"I just killed three of your goblins."

Grubgar furrowed his brow, like he was confused as to how that argument was supposed to help her case. "Yes. And now I kill you." He nodded to the other ettins, and they took another step toward her before she could continue.

"No, you don't understand," said Stacy. "That's three fewer mouths for you to feed in exchange for my one, and I don't eat much." She knew time wasn't on her side, so she hurried through the rest of her pitch. "I'd make a great slave. I'm a lot stronger than I look, and..." Trying to think of what other qualities an ettin might value in a slave, she went through her ability scores. "And I'm charming, and wise." Just saying those two aloud kind of disproved the charming claim. "I'm also smart, and –"

"Too smart," said Grubgar. "Orc is good slave. Goblin is good slave. Nice and stupid. No tricks. No mind games." He lifted a finger to his head. "Human brain always plotting, always scheming. Better to use for goblin food. No more talk. Bobar, kill human."

The ettin who Grubgar had just clubbed across the face stepped forward, drooling blood as he grimaced down at Stacy and raised his club.

"Stop!" cried Stacy, scrambling to think of something else to say, some last second trick to vindicate Grubgar's distrust of humans, but Bobor didn't stop. Finally, she thought of something. "I know where Mugmug went!"

"Bobor!" said Grubgar. "Wait!" Using his club as a cane again, he stepped slowly toward Stacy, dragging his left foot behind him. "Where is Mugmug?"

Stacy put her hands on her hips and peered up at him defiantly. "I'm not telling you."

Grubgar raised his club. "You tell me, or I kill you!"

"What difference does that make? You were just about to kill me, anyway."

"If make no difference, why you no tell me?"

"If I agree to tell you, will you let me live?"

Grubgar's expression looked like he was trying to wrap his mind around the square root of negative one.

"No," he finally said.

Stacy sighed. "You're supposed to say *yes*."

"Why I say yes?"

"Because that's how deals work. I give you something you want, and you give me something I want."

"But I no care what you want."

This was so frustrating. Stacy felt like she was getting close, but Grubgar was somehow too stupid to fall for her trick.

"Excuse me," said Shorty, the only goblin not yet wearing an iron collar. "I think I may be able to help clear up some of the confusion."

Grubgar lowered his club and nodded at Shorty.

Shorty began speaking in a language Stacy couldn't understand. It was thick with grunts, growls, and snarls. When he stopped, Grubgar responded in the same language, only louder and angrier. They went back and forth for what felt like far too long to explain the concept of a simple negotiation. But as far as Stacy could make out from Shorty's hand gestures, that was exactly what he was doing. Grubgar's gestures, which mainly consisted of pounding his own chest and slamming his club on the ground, suggested that he was still having a hard time comprehending why he shouldn't just get his way without any reciprocity.

The discussion finally stopped when Grubgar's rage suddenly subsided. He gave Stacy what she assumed was supposed to be a friendly smile. His brown teeth, swollen gums, and obvious lack of practice with that particular expression were unsettling to say the least.

"You tell me where find Mugmug. I let you go. Yes?"

"No," said Stacy.

Grubgar's smile faltered like a house of cards during the first tremors of an earthquake. "No?"

"How do I know you aren't going to flatten me as soon as I tell you what you want to know?"

"NO!" shouted Grubgar, bonking himself in the head with his club. "Get out my head!"

When it became clear that he wasn't hitting himself hard enough to do any real damage, Stacy interrupted him.

"I wasn't reading your mind. You're a terrible liar. Your intentions were obvious."

Grubgar shouted at Shorty in their shared language, like it was his fault Stacy didn't fall for his hastily thought up ruse.

"He is confused," Shorty said to Stacy when Grubgar finished. "He wants to know what is stopping him from killing you if you refuse to tell him where Mugmug is."

Stacy addressed Grubgar directly. "I can't tell you, because you've already proven yourself untrustworthy. But I can lead you there."

Grubgar sulked on it for a moment. "How I know you speak truth? Maybe you not know where Mugmug."

"I was hiding right here the whole time," said Stacy, trying to recall the exact phrasing the ettins had used when first assessing what had happened here. "I saw and heard

# Critical Failures VIII

everything. Mugmug, Lagra, Gurlog, and Lugburt came here to make sex. They were discovered by these two." Stacy gestured toward the two dead ettins. "They had a fight. Mugmug and the others killed these two, then ran off together."

"This exactly conclusion I made when first arrive," said the ettin whose assessment Stacy had just ripped off. "She speak truth."

And now to add a pinch of urgency.

"They knew you would never accept their love, so they went to gather forces in –" Stacy put her hand over her mouth, then smiled up at Grubgar. "Oops. I almost gave away the secret."

Grubgar frowned thoughtfully. "Gather forces. Lugburt and Gurlog mean to overthrow me." He pointed his club at Stacy. "No time to lose. You lead way."

An ettin approached with chains and collars for her and Shorty. She briefly entertained the idea of refusing to wear a collar, but ultimately decided not to push her luck. For her plan to work, whatever that turned out to be, Grubgar needed to feel like he was the one calling the shots.

The collar fit tight around her neck, giving her the sensation that she was being lightly strangled. A hard enough jerk from the other end of the chain might crush her windpipe.

Stacy wouldn't be able to survive like this for long, and not just because of the collar. Grubgar didn't strike her as a very patient or even-tempered individual. He would only wait but so long until he either figured out that Stacy was bullshitting him or decided that Mugmug's leathery tits weren't worth all of this effort. Either way, she was on borrowed time.

"Which way?" asked Grubgar once Stacy and Shorty were secured on their leashes.

Her time would definitely be up if they actually found Mugmug in the state she was in, and probably Dave's as well. Stacy wanted to be angry with Dave for fucking them all over, but she knew in her heart that it wasn't his fault. It was the curse. The whole reason she'd come all the way out here was to rid him of it, and she'd let him down. She'd let down Alroth too. There was still a chance for her to save herself and Shorty, so she pointed in the direction almost directly opposite of the way Dave had gone with his zombies.

"It's this way," she said.

*Sorry, Dave.*

# CHAPTER 43

$\mathcal{T}$oday was the big day, and Randy was a lot calmer than he'd expected to be considering how much was at stake for him and his friends.

He'd briefed Basil the night before about what to expect and gave him strict instructions not to kill anyone who wasn't attacking him.

Captain Longfellow was currently in the cafeteria putting his crew's mind at ease. Ever since Rocco had announced that they'd all been "randomly" selected to participate in the Full Moon Brawl, they had made a show of being excited to kick South Pen's ass, but Randy could tell that many of them were hiding their fear.

It wasn't so much a fear of death, as they had always fought fearlessly at sea under their captain's command. But those fights often promised treasure for those who survived it. Here in the gladiator arena, the only reward a survivor could hope for was to prolong their life of slavery until the next pointless fight to the death. But today they would have something real to fight for, a chance at regaining their freedom. Randy had little doubt that they would use that freedom to return to a life of murder and theft at sea, but that was on them. He couldn't live everyone's lives for them.

Even Denise seemed cheerier than usual despite their exceptionally low odds of success.

"I ain't got no more!" she said to Fatty. "Look at these titties. They look like a pair of limp ogre dicks. You done sucked me drier than a desert whore's cooter."

"Mama," Fatty responded. That was still the only word it knew.

"Well, I'm sorry. But you're just gonna have to wait until we get out there and start killing folks. Then you can eat as much as you like."

"We ain't aiming to kill nobody," Randy reminded her. "The whole point of this is so we can all work together to get out of here."

"That's a nice theory, Randy. But ain't nobody told that to the folks in South Pen. I reckon I'll have to drop a couple of motherfuckers by the time they catch on that we ain't tryin' to kill them."

"Randy, Denise," said Olumba, one of the most seasoned orcish warriors in North Pen, standing in their doorway, his body covered in splattered blood. "It is time. You have a receptive audience. I warmed them up for you. I stabbed a tiger so hard that I lost my sword inside her chest."

Denise pinched Fatty's cheek. "See there. Fresh meat on the field already waiting for you."

Olumba squatted down and reached out to pinch Fatty's other cheek, but jerked his hand back when Fatty snapped at him with a pincer.

He stood up. "Not only that, but now you know there is a hidden weapon near the center of the pit if you need it."

"Thank you for that," said Randy.

"May the gods guide your blades to spill the entrails of our enemies. Now I must go and summon the others." Olumba slammed his fist against his chest. "For the honor of North Pen!" With that, he went off in search of Captain Longfellow and crew.

## Critical Failures VIII

Randy shook his head. "I don't understand what drives folks to act so tribal. Olumba ain't never said more than two words to me before. But now that we're supposed to go out and murder people we ain't got no qualms with, he acts like he's my kin."

"Tell me about it," said Denise. "You'd think this was the fuckin' Rose Bowl." She got to her feet and took Fatty by the hand. "Whatever happens out there, you stick close to me, hear?"

Together, the three of them walked toward the arena gate. Thanks to Denise's slow pace, Longfellow and his crew caught up with them about halfway there.

The captain must have given his men a good pep talk. Randy sensed a lot of nervous excitement coming from them, but not so much fear now. They knew they might very well die, but at least they weren't putting their lives on the line for nothing. Those who survived this day would be free men again.

Olumba had been right about the audience being riled up. There wasn't even any fighting going on right now, but their roars and cheers grew louder and louder as Randy and the others got closer to the gate tunnel.

When they arrived at the gate tunnel, Randy was surprised at how little light was coming in from outside. He was so used to seeing the pattern of bright squares on the tunnel floor where the bright desert sunlight shined through the gate's bars. Of course, he usually trained in the morning or early afternoon, and currently it must have been pretty well into the evening. It was difficult to tell what time of day it was living underground.

As they moved closer to the gate, the roar of the eager crowd ringing even louder in his ears, Randy confirmed his suspicions about the time of day when he saw the first sliver of lavender sky over the high outer arena wall.

Rocco was waiting for them on the other side of the gate.

"You are late," he said. "The crowd grows impatient. I feared you may not show."

"We came as soon as we got the summons," said Randy. "Denise ain't so fast on account of she's got such short legs. I can't help but think you get a lot of folks being less punctual than you'd like, though, considering they're headin' for a fight to the death. Y'all might consider sending escorts or something."

Rocco peered through the bars past Randy and the others, then pulled a lever on the wall. The portcullis on the other end of the tunnel slammed down, trapping them inside.

"The governor delights in cowards who make him wait. He has already released two of his prized carrion crawlers as a penalty for your tardiness."

"What the fuck's a carrion crawler?" asked Denise.

Rocco stood aside and pointed toward the middle of the arena, where two huge green worm-like monsters, each of them at least nine feet long, feasted on a large tiger carcass.

Denise sighed. "Well, shit. There goes the surprise weapon Olumba left for us."

"A variety of weapons lay scattered about the arena grounds," said Rocco. "It would behoove you to move quickly and find one that best suits your talents."

A series of explosions that sounded like rumbling thunder drowned out the noise of the crowd as giant braziers burst into flames around the perimeter of the fighting pit. Each was suspended from large steel poles mounted in the stands. The light they gave off more than made up for the quickly diminishing sunlight.

When the echoes of the last brazier exploding into flames died down, the crowd hushed to a dull murmur, as if they were waiting for something.

# Critical Failures VIII

"Our distinguished governor, Gur Lakha," boomed a voice that sounded like it was coming from everywhere at once. Randy recognized it as Zimbra, but he couldn't see him. "Citizens of Olan Meb and honored visitors. It pleases me to announce the final and grandest performance of the day. We have with us tonight some of the most vile beasts known to orc kind. We have *dwarves*."

The crowd jeered excitedly.

Denise squatted down and took one of Fatty's pincers in her hands. "Don't you listen to them, hear? That's just ignorance talkin'. You ain't got nothin' to be ashamed of for being a dwarf."

Randy was trying to figure out the most sensitive way to ask Denise what she was talking about when Zimbra's booming voice interrupted his train of thought.

"We have *halflings!*"

A bit of jeering came from the crowd in response, but most of them were laughing now.

"We have *humans!*"

All laughter stopped at that announcement, and the jeering was off the charts. Orcs in the audience started hurling rocks down into the fighting pit.

"They really don't like us," Randy observed aloud.

"Aye," said Captain Longfellow. "It be known far and wide that the orcs of Meb'Garshur hate we humans above all other races."

"Not all other," Rocco corrected him. "There is one we hate with an even greater passion."

Not that he favored any one form of racism over another, but Randy really hoped he wasn't going to say Jews.

"But lowest of them all," said Zimbra when the shower of rocks subsided. "We have *orcs* who have betrayed their own kind!"

The roar that followed threatened to shake the whole stadium to rubble. Something else rained down from the audience, but they didn't bounce or thud against the ground like rocks. Instead, they landed softly and burst into dark splatters. More than a few splattered close enough to get a good whiff of what was inside them.

"Are they throwing bags of poo?" asked Randy.

"It is a custom of the arena," Rocco explained. "So that traitors may walk in the shit of those whom they've betrayed."

"What about the rest of us?" asked Denise. "We got to walk around in that shit too!"

Rocco laughed. "That is the least of your concerns."

"It takes some nerve to look down on other races when they been carrying around bags of their own shit all day. When those motherfuckers all come down with pink eye, I ain't gonna feel one bit sorry for them."

Zimbra, wherever he was speaking from, waited for the jeers and rain of shit bags to die down before continuing.

"Tonight, we will witness these vilest of vile creatures tear each other to pieces!"

The audience stood up and began beating their chests, chanting some phrase that Randy couldn't understand. It must have been orcish, which begged the question...

"Hey, Rocco," said Randy. "Why ain't Zimbra speaking y'all's orc language?"

"It keeps things simple," Rocco explained. "So there is no need for him to explain the rules once to them, then again to you."

"Ain't we just supposed to go in there and kill everyone?"

Rocco nodded. "Like I said. Simple."

"The fight shall go on until one of two events occurs," said Zimbra. "It shall end either when one group slaughters the other down to the last sniveling maggot!"

# Critical Failures VIII

To Randy's understanding, that was the only way the fight was supposed to end. He waited eagerly for the crowd to finish cheering, hoping that the alternative conclusion to the fight might offer them some sort of peaceful resolution.

"Or," Zimbra continued, "in the event that our esteemed governor decides that he is unsatisfied with the amount of blood that has been shed, until the last man from the remaining team stands!"

Randy's heart sank as the crowd cheered even louder.

Zimbra waited for the cheers to die down. Shouting turned into shushing because veteran attendees knew that he wouldn't continue until he had their undivided attention. Eventually, the shushing turned into a dull murmur of nearly complete silence. Until Zimbra shattered it.

"Let the Full Moon Brawl commence!"

The crowd erupted into a cheer so loud that Randy couldn't even hear the whine of the gate opening right in front of him.

"Everybody stay close together!" Randy shouted as loud as he could, but he might as well have been shouting in space for all the good it did. Longfellow and his men charged out past him and immediately dispersed, trying to get their hands on the weapons that had been scattered haphazardly on the orc shit-covered fighting pit floor. Even Denise waddled away from him in search of a weapon.

Randy was the last of them to step out into the pit. Not because he was afraid, but because he knew that whether they lived or died wasn't going to come down to what weapon he picked up off the ground. The most important weapon in his arsenal was communication, followed closely by a celestial basilisk. As Rocco retreated into the tunnel and closed the gate, Randy started jogging for the other side, hoping to spot Tim and Cooper before any blood was shed. The two carrion crawlers had noticed by now that they would not be able to continue eating their meal in peace, so they disengaged from the tiger corpse and reared up to defend themselves from all the gladiators that suddenly surrounded them.

They were even more disgusting than Randy had previously thought. Each of them had eight bulbous-tipped tentacles protruding from their faces like if Medusa had a goatee. Randy opted to give them plenty of room, jogging wide around them rather than trying to dart straight across the pit.

Unfortunately, neither Tim nor Cooper was the first member of South Pen that he encountered. Even more unfortunately, the man he encountered appeared to take his gladiatorial career very seriously. He was in peak physical shape and had already armed himself with a long-handled trident.

Randy displayed his unarmed hands, palms forward. "Listen, man. I don't wanna hurt you. If you give me just a –"

"YAAAAAH!" cried the man, lunging forward as he thrust the triple-pointed end of his weapon at Randy.

Randy pivoted to the side, grabbed the trident handle just under the fork, and yanked hard. Using its wielder's own inertia against him, Randy threw him off balance and spun around to elbow him in the head, stunning and disarming him just as Rocco had taught him during his training.

Of course, Randy failed to follow through with the next step of that particular lesson, which was to skewer him with his own weapon while he was down.

"I asked you not to do that," said Randy. "I'm gonna hold on to this."

He picked up his pace and finally spotted Tim and Cooper. He'd been searching for Cooper, figuring he'd be easier to pick out of a crowd, but Tim was the first one he spotted. Dressed in some sort of brightly colored patchwork clown outfit, complete with matching boots and backpack, he stood

# Critical Failures VIII

out like a screaming thumb among the rest of his fellow South Pen companions.

He also stood apart because, while the rest of the group he was in seemed to be gathered together with weapons, trying to form a defensive unit against their North Pen opponents, Tim seemed more concerned with picking a fight with someone up in the audience.

Tim pointed angrily and shouted something up into the stands that Randy couldn't hear over the crowd's rowdy cheering.

The orc he was pointing at laughed in response, took a long swig from a silver pitcher, then pointed the mouth of the pitcher down at Tim. A gush of water shot out from it, hitting Tim in the crotch and knocking him down on his ass. That got a raucous laugh from the crowd, as well as some giggles from his penmates.

"Look sharp!" one of them shouted when he spotted Randy approaching. The rest of them turned to face Randy, brandishing their weapons and looking like they were ready to pounce.

"Wait!" cried Tim, staggering past them toward Randy, soaking wet from the crotch down.

"Hi," said Randy, unsure of what else to say.

"What the fuck are you staring at?" Tim pointed to his crotch. "This is just water."

"Are you drunk?"

"Fuck your mother."

"I'll take that as a yes."

"Don't worry about me," said Tim. "You said you had some sort of big plan to get us out of here. So what is it?"

"I'm gonna set it in motion just as soon as you and Cooper let the others know that we got something planned and not to attack any of –"

"I'M REALLY ANGRY!" shouted Cooper from behind the armed South Pen gladiators. His eyes turned red as his body grew about fifty percent larger. He shoved his penmates aside like stalks of wheat, then charged straight at Randy like a pissed off freight train.

Randy didn't know what this sudden aggression was about, but he stood his ground, trying to read Cooper's moves so that he could jump out of the way in time. There wasn't much to read. Just pure rage running directly his way. It was easy to step out of the way and let Cooper barrel right past him.

As it turned out, the attack had been even easier to dodge than Randy expected because it wasn't meant for him. When he turned around to defend himself against a second attack, Randy found Cooper engaged in fist-to-face combat with one of the carrion crawlers that had been approaching him from behind.

Cooper drove a fist deep into the creature's pulpy flesh, messing it up pretty bad. But it counterattacked with all eight of its tentacles, most of them suckering onto Cooper's chest, back and shoulders, all massive and unprotected targets, causing Cooper to freeze like a statue and fall flat onto his back.

Tim pulled a flask out from an inner pocket of his clothes and took a swig from it. "I totally didn't see that coming."

The carrion crawler turned its eye stalks toward Randy.

"You stay back!" said Randy, jabbing at it with his trident. But the beast reared back out of his way, snarling and hissing from its toothy maw.

"Suck my ladynuts!" cried Denise. For a moment, Randy couldn't see her. Then the carrion crawler fell forward under the weight of Denise riding on its head. She was holding onto one of its tentacles that it had attacked Cooper with, gripping it tightly below the sucker pod on the end.

# Critical Failures VIII

It whipped its other seven tentacles back at her, but had neither the accuracy nor the reach to land a hit. Denise, on the other hand, chopped two of the tentacles clean off with the small hatchet she'd acquired somewhere on the pit floor.

Randy used the distraction to make a more earnest attack.

"SMITE!" he shouted as he plunged his trident into the creature's rubbery flesh. He felt a surge of holy energy pass from his hands into the trident, then the carrion crawler's head exploded like someone had stuffed a Thanksgiving turkey with a live grenade.

What remained of the creature slumped to the ground. Denise, covered in dripping bits of carrion crawler flesh and still clutching the severed tentacle in her hand, fell forward into the puddle of gore that used to be the beast's head.

The audience roared with approval at the spectacle.

"Denise!" said Randy. "Are you okay?"

Denise sat up and spat out a chunk of carrion crawler. "Yeah, no thanks to you."

Randy turned his attention to Cooper, still on his back and frozen in rage. "What happened to him?"

"He's paralyzed," said Tim. "Hopefully it will wear off before long."

One of the South Pen fighters behind Tim got struck in the head with a bag of shit. It dropped him to his knees and splattered all over the ground in front of him.

The crowd nearby laughed and shouted.

"Stop standing around!"

"We came to see a fight!"

"Go South Pen! Kill North Pen!"

The South Pen gladiators stepped forward, nervously brandishing their weapons.

"Stand aside, halfling," said one of them. "We must kill these two while we have them alone."

"Back the fuck up, Bub," said Tim. He took another swig from his flask in flagrant violation of the gladiator dungeon rules. "Randy's going to bust us all out of here, so nobody's killing anybody until he does his thing." He turned to Randy. "I'm three fucking feet tall and unarmed. I've done as much as I can to stop these nice men from stabbing you to death. If they need more convincing, then maybe you should get to doing whatever the fuck it is you're planning to do."

Randy nodded, then scanned the stands for the least crowded section so he could summon Basil without crushing anyone.

"Hurry the fuck up, Randy!" said Denise as Fatty nibbled bits of viscera from her beard.

Finding a relatively uncrowded spot near the top of the stands on the North Pen side of the arena, Randy pointed and shouted his Special Mount's name.

"BASIL!"

As predicted, the crowd erupted with panicked screams as the massive glowing reptile spontaneously winked into existence among them. They shoved and trampled over one another, shielding their eyes as they desperately tried to flee.

"Everyone please stay calm!" Zimbra's voice echoed down from all over the arena. Randy finally spotted him near the governor when he caught sight of the governor's personal bodyguards struggling through the stampeding crowd toward Basil.

"There is no need to panic," Zimbra continued. "We have the situation under control." He was speaking into some sort of round device at the end of a stick. If Randy didn't know better, he would have guessed it was a microphone. It certainly seemed to function like one, but where was the sound coming from?

He looked up and found his answer suspended below the nearest brazier. A cobblestone with an animated mouth

# Critical Failures VIII

shouted Zimbra's increasingly agitated voice. Looking around the rest of the arena, he found similar stones hanging from each of the braziers.

"Please!" he shouted, barely audible over the screaming crowd. "We are doing everything we can to…" He sighed as he watched orcs in Basil's section spill over into the fighting pit. "Would you just calm the fuck down?"

Tim gulped down what was left in his flask. "I gotta say, Randy. I'm impressed. I honestly didn't think you had it in you. What happens now?"

Randy shrugged. "I ain't exactly sure. We was plannin' on having Cooper toss you up over the wall, and having you secure a rope for the rest of us to climb up. Then maybe we'd take the governor hostage or something. I ain't exactly sure. But with Cooper paralyzed, I don't know if anyone else could throw you that high."

"Everyone's mobbed at the top of the wall anyway," said Tim. "I wouldn't be able to secure a fucking rope in all that."

"That's just as well," said Denise. "We ain't got a rope."

A loud crashing noise drew everyone's attention back to the North Pen side of the arena. There was a giant gaping hole in the stands where Basil had been summoned. He must have fallen through.

"Basil!" cried Randy, though he sensed through their Empathic Link that Basil had survived the crash mostly unharmed.

Tim laughed and shook his head. "Forget what I said about being impressed. This is more or less exactly what I expected from you." His eye started twitching, then he clutched his stomach as he doubled over in pain. "Fuck!"

"Tim?" said Randy. "What is it? What's wrong?"

"Full… moon," he croaked like he was trying not to shit his pants and about to lose the battle. "Must… resist."

"Is there anything I can do?"

Tim stood straight again and wiped sweat from his brow. "No, thanks. I'm good. But sadly, that means it's time for me to say goodbye." He frowned down at Cooper, still paralyzed on the ground. "Sorry, buddy. I really wanted to take you with me."

"Where are you going?" asked Randy.

Tim smiled at him. "Good luck." With that, he clicked the heels of his boots together and disappeared.

"Where the fuck did he go?" asked Denise.

Randy had no idea, but he also had no time to ponder on it. Fortunately, the South Pen group who had clung together with Cooper and Tim was impressed enough with the chaos Randy had created to continue holding off their attack.

Unfortunately, the members of South Pen who'd decided to run out on their own now had no way of knowing that the chaos had been Randy's doing and was the first stage of an escape plan. They looked to be more seasoned fighters on the whole. This was clearly not their first time fighting in the arena, and probably not the first Full Moon Brawl for a lot of them.

As such, they were only briefly distracted by the screaming crowd, quick to seek out the most vulnerable targets of Captain Longfellow's crew. Those were the ones currently engaged with the second carrion crawler.

Several men from both pens lay paralyzed on the ground. The monster was in bad shape but lasting beyond its expiration date, mostly because all the attacks from the surrounding men that should have been aimed at it were instead being directed at each other.

Randy started running that way to finish off the monster and try to reason with the South Penners when a series of loud bursts made him stop in his tracks and whirl around.

*POW! POW! POW! POW! POW! POW!*

# Critical Failures VIII

By the time it was finished, the arena had gone so silent that Randy could hear the clicks that followed as Tim continued pulling the trigger.

"What in the Seven Hells is that?" Zimbra wondered aloud over the loudspeaker stones.

Tim's brightly colored clothes made him easy to spot in the stands as the bullet-riddled orc next to him fell forward into the fighting pit. Randy wouldn't have recognized the orc if Tim hadn't poured water from a silver pitcher onto his dead body. It was the same orc Tim had been shouting at when Randy first spotted him in the arena.

"Fuck you," Tim said in the tense silence, then disappeared again, along with the silver pitcher and a revolver about the size of his forearm.

The next sound to break the silence was the agonized scream of the second carrion crawler shortly before its enormous body collapsed lifelessly to the ground.

Captain Longfellow pulled himself out from where he was burrowed headfirst up to his waist in the creature's backside. His entire upper body was slathered in blood and... other fluids.

"Did me ears deceive me, or be we under attack by cannon fire?"

"Captain!" said Randy. "Did you get swallowed?"

"I've no time for such flirtations. I went straight in the backside, where I find both man and beast to be most vulnerable. Smooth going in." He lifted both hands straight above his head, tucking the blades of the two daggers he carried close to his wrists. "Rough coming out." He tilted both blades outward so that his hands looked like the tip of a barbed hook, then brought both hands slowly down like he was tearing through monster colon. "That be not the first anus I've destroyed."

The relative calmness of the crowd, thanks to all the distractions, ramped quickly back up into chaos again when another section of the stands collapsed, doubling the size of the hole Basil had made when he fell through, and swallowing at least two dozen orcs who had been standing there.

"It is attacking the support columns," Zimbra whispered, perhaps forgetting that he was still speaking into his magic broadcasting stick. "We have to get out of here."

That drove the crowd into full panic mode as everyone made a break for the nearest exit at once. Those nearest Basil's path of destruction found themselves taking a shortcut as another section of stands collapsed beneath them.

Randy glared at one of the South Pen gladiators who was staring dumbfoundedly at the bedlam taking place in the audience. "Stop fighting each other. We're gettin' out of here."

The gladiator nodded and lowered his axe.

A ferocious roar from behind Randy caused the air around him to tremble. Randy turned around to find that Cooper's paralysis had come to an unexpected end.

"What the fuck is that?" asked Denise. "I thought he was s'posed to be a rat."

That had also been Randy's understanding, but Cooper was no rat. Instead, he was the biggest, meanest-looking grizzly bear Randy had ever seen, even on TV. Randy didn't know if his Barbarian Rage was still in effect, or if it was a symptom of suddenly turning into a bear, but he looked madder than hell.

Cooper's rage-filled gaze stopped on the nearest living thing he spotted. Fatty was only a few yards away, blissfully devouring the remains of the first carrion crawler.

Denise ran at her child faster than Randy believed her capable of and wrapped her fat arms around him just as Cooper took a wild swipe with one of his massive paws,

## Critical Failures VIII

swatting them through the air like he was serving a volleyball.

A foot or two higher, and Denise and Fatty would have been free of the fighting pit. Instead, Denise slammed against the top of the wall and fell to the ground, both of which looked incredibly painful. Fortunately, Fatty had been spared the worst of it.

Another section of the stands caved in, and some audience members were now jumping voluntarily into the fighting pit. It must have seemed safer than getting crushed by falling rubble despite being full of armed prisoners and an enraged bear.

Others chose to climb their way out of danger on the steel poles that supported the flaming braziers. Not built to support the weight of seven orcs in addition to a brazier, the first of them ripped free from its housing in the masonry and crashed down into the fighting pit with a fiery explosion.

"Thar it be!" shouted Captain Longfellow. "Our way out!"

It would require a Dexterity check for balance, but the fallen pole did indeed form a bridge from the pit to the crumbling remains of the outer arena.

As Longfellow's crew ran over to throw sand on the flaming brazier, Cooper, snarling and drooling, ran at a group of orcs from the audience huddled together near the wall. Randy had no doubt he would tear them to pieces if he didn't interfere.

As much as he hated the idea of attacking someone he considered his friend, he couldn't let Cooper murder a bunch of innocent orcs. He raised his trident, then hurled it like a javelin, burying its three points deep into Cooper's hairy bear ass.

Cooper reared up on his hind legs and let out a furious howl. Randy had gotten his attention.

"Take it easy, Cooper," said Randy. "I know you're in there somewhere, and I know you don't want to kill those people."

Randy was more right than he knew. From the look in Cooper's eyes, it was clear that he no longer gave a shit about the orcs huddled by the wall, and that he very much wanted to kill Randy instead.

Unarmed and completely outmatched for a hand-to-hand brawl, Randy was surprised at how calm he was with almost certain death staring him in the face. He still had plans for the future, goals that he'd like to accomplish and places he'd like to visit. But he was perfectly content to abandon all of it if dying here in this shit-splattered pit meant giving everyone else a chance to escape. When he started running from Cooper, it wasn't out of fear, but because he knew that a chase would keep Cooper distracted longer than a fight would. Heck, it might even buy enough time for his friends to pull off some miracle rescue.

"Women and children first!" shouted Denise, shoving some of Longfellow's crew out of her way so she and Fatty could walk up the brazier pole. She only made it a few steps before falling off and landing hard on the ground.

Randy looked back to find Cooper was quickly gaining on him and hoped that a few people might make it to safety before he was mauled to death.

He was running along the perimeter of the pit, and just ahead of him he saw another section of stands cave in. Basil was still wreaking havoc, which was good since it meant that he was still alive and hadn't stopped to eat anyone. Be that as it may, Basil's path of destruction was probably causing a bunch of innocent people to get hurt. Randy's friends had as good a chance to escape as they were going to get, so he couldn't see any justification to let Basil keep destroying the place.

## Critical Failures VIII

"Go on back!" he shouted, sending Basil back to the Celestial Plane. It was for the best. He wasn't sure what would happen to Basil if Randy died while he was around. Maybe they'd reunite in Heaven.

Unable to outrun Cooper, Randy turned around to face him, hoping that if he couldn't subdue Cooper, he could at least dodge a few of his attacks and stay alive long enough for a few more people to escape.

Blinded by his violent bear rage, Cooper didn't even seem to notice that Randy had stopped running until he plowed right over him. Randy let himself fall backward to absorb the impact. He knew he didn't have the Strength to throw a 700 pound grizzly bear, but he drove a foot up into Cooper's nuts as he trampled over him.

Instead of rolling into a massive ball of fur and cradling his balls in his giant paws, Randy's kick only seemed to enrage him further. As Randy struggled back up to his feet, Cooper lunged at him, swiping both of his front paws. Randy wasn't even close to being able to jump out of Cooper's way, and quickly found himself in a tight furry embrace that reeked of sweat and pee. The smell, along with his compressed lungs, made breathing next to impossible.

Wrapped in Cooper's enormous forearms, the only way Randy could think to stave off death a little longer was to keep Cooper's mouth from biting his head off. Fortunately, he'd had the presence of mind to raise his hands to avoid having them pinned by his sides. He grabbed Cooper's throat with both hands and pushed his thumbs as hard as he could into Cooper's windpipe.

Much to his surprise, this actually stifled Cooper's furious roar a little. Randy couldn't believe he was really strangling a grizzly. If he could keep this up, and it came down to a contest of which of them could last the longest without passing out, this might actually be a fight Randy had a chance at winning.

Cooper, however, wasn't in the right frame of mind to play the waiting game. He released his hold on Randy so he could take a proper swipe at him. Greedily sucking in as much air as his lungs would take in, Randy was once again unable to avoid the attack.

Four black claws raked across Randy's chest, slicing it like thick cuts of deli meat. He could feel the claws scrape against his ribs and sternum, and he heard a loud crack that he first assumed was the snapping of his own bones.

But the sound hadn't come from inside him. It came from above. One of the wooden beams in the framework that supported the towers overlooking the arena entrance had snapped. The whole structure was wobbling like it was on the brink of collapse. The aftershocks of Basil's demolition hadn't finished quite yet.

CRACK!

With the snap of another beam, the shadow of the brick towers fell over Randy and Cooper, making it very clear where the actual bricks were about to fall.

Cooper wasn't in the least bit concerned about the building that was about to land on them. He was still single-minded in his pursuit to tear Randy to pieces. Rearing up on his hind legs, Cooper put his front paws together to bring them down on Randy.

Fortunately, Randy was able to find the Strength in him – and perhaps the Dexterity – to roll out of the way of Cooper's attack. Unfortunately, all the Strength and Dexterity in the world wouldn't be enough to let him roll out of the way of the falling towers. The best he could hope to do was to use his body to shield a friend's.

Cooper had reared up again to attack him. But instead of rolling out of the way this time, Randy lunged at Cooper shoulder first, hoping that if he could knock him back, he

## Critical Failures VIII

might absorb enough of the falling masonry so that Cooper might survive.

It wasn't even close. Cooper might as well have been a brick wall for all Randy was able to budge him. He wrapped his arms around Randy again and started to squeeze the air out of his lungs when the towers came down on both of them.

It sounded like a bomb going off and felt like getting punched by a hundred angry drunks at the same time. But if Randy was honest, it wasn't as bad as he'd expected. The fact that he was still thinking about it must mean he'd survived it. That is, unless he was in one of those afterlives where folks didn't immediately realize they was dead.

But if that was the case, Randy couldn't see much point in it. He was still sore all over. He couldn't see or hear nothing on account of he was buried in bricks and mortar dust. He could still feel Cooper's arms wrapped around him, though they were no longer squeezing him. Now that he thought about it, his plan might have had exactly the opposite effect he'd been going for. Had Cooper just inadvertently saved Randy's life?

Then Randy heard a voice coming from beyond the rubble. It was soft at first, almost soothing. He couldn't make out what it was saying, but as it grew louder, Randy was sure it was a woman's voice. Maybe this was what it was like for an unborn child to hear its mother's voice from inside the womb. Maybe Randy was dead after all, about to be born again into the next phase of his existence. Maybe the Virgin Mother Herself was coming to guide him along that path.

"Women and children first! Women and children first!"

Or maybe it was Denise.

Randy tried to take a deep breath to call out to her but found that even shallow breaths were a chore. Between all the squeezing and dust inhalation, his lungs were shot. But he only truly appreciated how badly he was hurt when Denise stomped over the rubble he was buried under. Jagged chunks of broken brick pushed deep into his head and right upper arm.

But that was only the beginning. The debris of the fallen towers must have provided an easier means of climbing out of the pit. Shortly after Denise trampled over him, a whole stampede of folks unknowingly pounded bricks into Randy and Cooper.

And good for them. Randy felt bad about not being able to save Cooper, but he was happy to know that he'd saved a whole lot more people than he'd expected to.

"Lord," he whispered. "Thank you... for allowing me... to be here today. I know I ain't always... lived up to... your expectations. But I appreciate... you lettin' me play the part... I done today. Please look after... Denise and Fatty... and Captain Longfellow... and all his crew. And see them safely... to freedom. I'll die grateful... to have been part of your plan... to save them."

With that, Randy closed his eyes and let himself slip into unconsciousness.

\*

*DING-DONG*

Randy awakened to a familiar smell.

*Grandma? Weed?*

His grandmother had spent sixty years living in that house before she passed away, and her old person smell still permeated every nook and cranny of it even three years later. The stink of weed was his own contribution.

When he opened his eyes, he was surprised to see all the members of Lynyrd Skynyrd glaring back menacingly at him, as if challenging him to explain just what the hell he thought he was doing there. He was about to apologize when he realized he was just looking at a poster on his wall.

*His* wall! He was in his own bed in his own house back in Gulfport, Mississippi! The past few months must have just been some crazy dream. Either that, or the secret to coming back to the real world was that you had to die in the game world.

No, that was ridiculous. He'd clearly just been dreaming. But damn if it wasn't the most vivid dream he'd ever woken from. He could recall everything he'd experienced, everything he'd learned, everything he hadn't realized he already knew how to do. If the situation should arise, Randy was strangely confident that he'd be able to competently engage in a sword battle on horseback.

*DING-DONG*

The doorbell. That was what had woken him up. Whoever was at the door had rung it at least twice now. Randy got out of bed to go see who it was.

He didn't get many visitors. The only one who came around with any regularity was Denise. Randy shook his head to clear the dream out. *Dennis.* The only one who came around with any regularity was *Dennis.* He shuddered, recalling what had happened to Dennis in his dream, and what a mess he turned out to be.

"Jesus," he whispered to himself before opening the door. "JESUS!"

"Hi, Randy!" said the Pillsburg Doughchild, standing as tall as Randy on his front porch. "May I come in?"

"But... but... You can't be real."

The pudgy bread monster shook his head and sighed. "It's Thomas all over again." He spread his arms wide and thrust his round white belly toward Randy. "Go ahead. Give me a poke."

His hand trembling with fear and awe, Randy did as he was commanded. He jabbed his index finger into the Doughchild's belly.

"Hee hee!" squealed the Doughchild as he retracted his belly and covered it with both fingerless hands.

Whatever this creature in his doorway was, it was real. Randy couldn't deny the soft doughy resistance of his belly anymore than he could deny his own eyes and ears.

"Jesus?" he said. "Is that really you?"

"Sure is! Now, are you going to invite me in or turn me away?"

Randy stood aside and opened the door wider. "Please come in!" He frowned as he surveyed the state of his living room, with clothes hanging off every piece of furniture and a half-eaten bowl of cereal on the coffee table. "Sorry about the mess. I wasn't expectin' company."

"Not expecting?" said Jesus, waddling through the living room and into the kitchen. "But it was you who called on me."

Randy followed him into the kitchen and found him fiddling with the oven knobs. "Called on you? I don't remember –"

"You prayed to me while the others were trampling you to death." Jesus pulled a baking tray out from a cupboard and placed it on the counter. Then he tore a chunk of flesh from his own belly, rolled it into a perfect sphere between his palms, and pushed it down into a plump cylinder on the tray, which he then put in the oven. He turned around to give Randy an encouraging smile. "Nothing says lovin' like laying down your life for your friends."

It must not have been a dream after all. All that stuff had really happened to him. And now...

"So... I'm dead now? Is this Heaven?" Randy glanced around his dirty kitchen. He didn't want to be rude to Jesus, but he was a little disappointed.

*DING!*

# Critical Failures VIII

The tray hadn't been in the oven more than ten seconds when Jesus pulled it out again, revealing a perfectly golden loaf of bread. The odors of weed and Randy's grandma were completely flushed out by the warm buttery scent of freshly baked goodness.

"Don't worry, Randy. You're not dead."

"But you just said –"

"Laying down your life for a friend is your choice," said Jesus, placing the baking tray on the kitchen table in front of Randy. "Whether or not you actually die is mine." He gestured to the loaf on the table. "Please, eat."

Randy felt weird about eating in front of Jesus without offering him anything in return, but he felt even weirder about offering the Son of God a bowl of stale Cap'n Crunch or a chunk of his own baked flesh.

"Thank you," he said, tearing away a piece of the loaf. It came off like cotton candy and melted similarly in his mouth. It tasted better than any bread he'd ever tasted. "This is really good."

"Your work is not yet finished, Randy," said Jesus. He reached into a gaping wound in his side, pulled out a wooden chalice, then filled it with blood from the nail wound in his right hand. "Your friends still need you." He set the cup down in front of Randy.

"Are they here?" asked Randy, picking up the cup with both hands and placing it to his lips as he stared up into Jesus's circular blue eyes. Jesus stared patiently back at him until Randy gulped down every last drop of wine.

"They are on a boat. They are waiting for you, and you must go to them. But first, one more poke." Jesus spread his arms again, exposing his broad round belly to Randy.

Jesus's blood was potent stuff, and Randy was starting to feel a bit woozy. His vision blurred and his mind fogged back into that quasi-dream state where he couldn't tell what was real from what wasn't.

"You want me to poke you again?" he asked Jesus. "Like, with my finger?"

"Stretch forth thine hand."

"Okay," said Randy. "If you say so." He staggered toward Jesus, his hand stretched out in front of him, barely able to stay on his feet. As his fingers plunged deep into Jesus's soft doughy belly, Randy fell into darkness to the sound of an echoing giggle.

"Hee hee!"

\*

"Goddammit, Randy! Stop poking me! That fuckin' tickles!"

Randy woke again, this time to smells even worse than the combination of weed and his dead grandmother. The sudden olfactory onslaught of fish and body odor was a jarring contrast to the scent of freshly baked Jesus.

Fortunately, opening his eyes to find Denise and Captain Longfellow staring down at him was an easier transition between realities than his Skynyrd poster.

"What happened?" asked Randy. "How did I get here?" He sat up, surprised to find himself not in the least amount of pain. "Did y'all heal me?"

"All we done is rescue you."

Captain Longfellow cleared his throat.

Denise shot him an annoyed scowl. "Maybe I ain't dug him out of the rubble, but I held his legs when we carried him to the ship, didn't I?"

"Mama," said Fatty.

"Fine," Denise said to Randy. "I held your legs *by proxy* of my ungrateful spawn. I can't say nothin' as to how you healed

## Critical Failures VIII

up so fast, though. You looked like you'd spent the night in a goddamn rock tumbler when we dragged you onto the ship."

Randy stood up and scanned the deck, then looked back to find nothing but endless sea behind them. "What about Cooper?"

Captain Longfellow frowned. "'Twas hard enough to drag your heavy arse on board. Not all of us combined could have hoped to escape with our lives while hauling a dead bear."

"Are you sure he's dead?"

The captain shrugged. "Who can say? I did not expect ye to survive, but here ye stand before me with nary a scratch on yer body. But even if yer friend remain among the living, there be no place on this ship that would contain such a beast. He would have ripped a breach in our hull wider than yer mum's gaping butthole."

Randy nodded. They'd made the right call. There was nothing more he could do for Cooper.

"So, where are we going?"

"I've a score to settle with Captain Logan. Our first port of call be Nazere."

# CHAPTER 44

"Where the fuck am I?" asked Cooper, waking up feeling like he'd gotten blackout drunk in a stone golem orgy the night before. Every square inch of his skin was throbbing with pain, and he soon discovered that a lot of that had to do with the fact that he'd been sleeping under a pile of rubble.

He pushed his arms up and outward like he was trying to swim to the surface of broken bricks, scooping away enough debris to make breathing a little easier and let a bit of the dawn's light in. After a few more swipes of his arms, he was able to sit up and get a look at his surroundings. The arena was almost unrecognizable, like a bomb had gone off inside it. The only people around were scattered corpses in the fighting pit, but none of them looked like gladiators.

Spotting one of the dead carrion crawlers jogged his last memory of the evening before. At least, he hoped only one night had passed. The carrion crawler had attacked him with its face tentacles, rendering him completely paralyzed and helpless. He'd fully expected to die shortly after that, but it appeared as though the gods had decided to spare his life at the last second by chucking a meteor down at the arena.

But where was Tim? Where were Randy and Denise? Cooper was happy to see that they weren't among the dead bodies, but would they really have just ditched him here, leaving him for dead?

He started to remember more from the previous day, then the days leading up to it. Maybe he deserved to be ditched by

## Critical Failures VIII

his friends and left for dead. He'd been in a pretty fucked up frame of mind these past couple of weeks, full of hate, and fear, and violent urges. What the hell was wrong with him? He'd even...

"Oh, shit!" he said aloud, ignoring the pain surging all through his body as he got to his feet. "Nabi!"

Grabbing two large chunks of brick to feed anyone who decided to fuck with him on the way, he climbed out of the fighting pit, out of the arena, and headed out of Olan Meb and into the desert to find his friend.

*The End*

# About the Author

Robert Bevan took his first steps in comedy with The Hitchhiker's Guide to the Galaxy, and his first steps in fantasy with Dungeons & Dragons. Over the years, these two loves mingled, festered, and congealed into the ever expanding Caverns & Creatures series of comedy/fantasy novels and short stories.

Robert is a writer, blogger, and a player on the Authors & Dragons podcast. He lives in Atlanta, Georgia, with his wife, two kids, and his dog, Speck.

# Don't stop now!
# The adventure continues!

Discover the entire Caverns & Creatures collection at
www.caverns-and-creatures.com/books/

And please visit me on Facebook at
www.facebook.com/robertbevanbooks

Printed in Great Britain
by Amazon